OHIO
DOMINICAN
UNIVERSITY™

SINCE 1911

Listening
at the Gate

Also by Betsy James

Long Night Dance

Dark Heart

Listening
at the Gate

Written and illustrated by

Betsy James

Atheneum Books for Young Readers
New York   London   Toronto   Sydney

Atheneum Books for Young Readers
An imprint of Simon & Schuster Children's Publishing Division
1230 Avenue of the Americas
New York, New York 10020
Book design by Debra Sfetsios
The text for this book is set in Zapf Calligraphic BT.
The illustrations for this book are rendered in
pen and ink on scratchboard.
Manufactured in the United States of America
First Edition
2 4 6 8 10 9 7 5 3 1
Library of Congress Cataloging-in-Publication Data
James, Betsy.
Listening at the gate/Betsy James;
illustrations by the author.—1st ed.
p. cm.—(The seeker chronicles)
Sequel to: Dark heart.
Summary: After seventeen-year-old Kat leaves the
Creek home of her mother's sister, she returns to Downshore
and becomes embroiled in upheaval there and
in the land of the Rigi, as well as in Nall's
quest to go to the Gate.
ISBN-13: 978-0-689-85068-4
ISBN-10: 0-689-85068-9
[1. Fantasy.] I. Title. II. Series.
PZ7.J15357Lis 2006
[Fic]—dc22 2005002113

For all my midwives,
some of whom
are men

At the gate of the great deep,
Souls are finding bodies,
Hearts are finding words.
Nothing turns to every shining thing, and rises
Like a flight of birds.

Origin Chant. The Rigi.

Beginning

1

Aash, aash,
Huss, huss,
Shuu, shuu,
Aah.

Lullaby from Selí. The Rigi.

A SUMMER NIGHT, black and starry. The wind blew from the west, urging the waves onto the shore, chasing veils of sand stinging and scouring up the beach. The short grass bowed to the east in the darkness, whistled, and bowed again.

Underground, though, all was still. In the great warren-house of Selí, in a low, driftwood-beamed room that was her own, an old woman sat on a reed mat, spinning by candlelight.

A little naked boy lay against her, as near as he could get but for the spindle, watching her hands work.

Odor of beeswax, whirr of the spindle, rattle of the whorl in the clay cup. A cricket creaked. Away down the corridors of the warrenhouse the voices of the clan were indistinct. The surf said *suff, suff* on the beach below.

As though to herself, the woman sang,

> Thou art a man upon the land,
> Thou art a beast upon the deep,
> Thine the fin that hides the hand,
> Thine the dream that riddles sleep . . .

The boy stirred at his great-grandmother's thigh and whispered, "Ama."

"Bij." That was not his real name, just a little name he had.

"Ama, I hear the Gate."

She frowned. "It is the wind you hear, my mouse. You cannot hear the Gate from here. It is far away, and out in the great sea."

"I hear it."

"What does it sound like?"

He listened, his head raised from her thigh. "Like Tinga."

The gray cat sleeping by the fire pit heard her name and opened her eyes.

"Shaking," he said. He sat up and shook himself to show her how it was. But he could not purr as fast as Tinga, and he said crossly, "No."

"*Shu-shu-shu.*" His *ama* pushed the brown curls from his face and looked at the eyes raised to her, gray as rain—her granddaughter's eyes, which she had gotten from a father nobody knew, a spirit, maybe, or the sea wind, or rain itself. "The Gate is not for you, mouseling," she said. "Leave it to the Reirig."

"Why?"

"It is his now."

"Was it mine before?"

"Maybe. But now it is his, and if you meddle with it, he and the elders will take away your skin and your name, and they will kill you."

His round face showed only interest. Killing was common, but not the other part. "Take away my skin?"

"Yes. The skin of your seal, the one that your father hunted for you when you were born." She pointed to it, folded on the goods pole: a dark, smooth pelt. "They would burn it, and burn your name, and lay you in the caves. You would not *be* anymore," she said.

He gazed at her. "I would still be your *nani*."

"And I your ama." She caught him to her old breasts. "When I am dead, I shall be my seal again and play in the sea; and someday, my nani, when you are old with many children and you die, you shall be your seal again, and we shall play together. Will that be good?"

His nodding head bumped her collarbone.

"So you must not meddle with the Gate or the Reirig," she said, "for to lose your skin is to lose your seal. You would not be one of the Rigi anymore, only a man, no better than a Black Boot. And then where would your ghost live, eh? In the east with the sun and the seal-killers?" She tried to make him look at her, to be sure he heard.

He stood on her thighs with dirty brown feet, looking not at her but westward, where the sea itself shook, the whole world trembled at once. "What is the Gate?"

"*Tcha!*" She lifted him down, turned him round, and spanked his bare bottom. When she was done, he straightened his back and said again, "What is the Gate?"

"You are a demon child!"

He said nothing. His chin stuck out.

"You have seen the Gate. It is two stones in the sea." She took up her spindle again, but the gray stare defeated her, and at last she put the thread aside, muttering, "Better from me than from your mad mother!" Taking him on her lap, she said, "The Gate is where the world is beginning to be."

He frowned. His great-grandmother amended it to, "Where the world is coming from. Where do you think *you* came from?"

"Mother found me in an oyster shell."

"And you are my pearl! But that is not how you came. This is how. Your mother dreamed you. In her heart she could feel you longing to come. You were at the Gate, but a little on the other side, just beginning to be. Your mother could make a body for only half of you, so she lay with your father, and he made your other half. Then you came through the Gate into your mother's belly, and you grew there, and came out yelling, and here you are."

The boy stared at himself. "Which half of me did Mother make?"

"Your halves are all spiraled together, like water in a tide race or your father's tattoos."

"Where was I before Mother dreamed me? Before I longed to come?"

"You are too young to wonder that!"

He gazed.

She dropped her eyes. "I told you. You were swimming in

the sea just beyond the Gate, to the west, with everything
that is not yet."

"If I was not yet, how did I swim?"

"What seal priest's ghost is speaking through this baby's
mouth?" The old woman looked at the roof beams as though
some spirit hovered there, but there were only the shadows
cast by the wavering candlelight, the boy's shadow made big
by it.

"I am not a baby," he said. "I am a man, and I will go to
the Gate."

"No."

"I will go."

She tried to snatch him up and spank him again, but he
dodged her, nimble as a minnow. "I will go west to the Gate
and east to the sun," he said. "I will go everywhere in the
world, and then I will come home to you."

"Nobody comes home from those places," she said with
wet eyes.

"I will," he said.

2

I have a gold swan
That swims a gold lake
Within a gold cage
Safe out of the rain,
Locked with a gold lock
That never was opened
Except by the key
On my father's watch chain.

Girls' Hand Slap. Upslope.

WINTER IN A DARK HOUSE, night at the window. Everything tidied and scrubbed, even the hearth. A meager heap of coals glowed there, and on the table one candle.

On a high black chair a little girl sat, heavy shoes dangling. Her skin was starry with freckles, her lashes were red-gold, but she wore black and her hair was hidden by a black kerchief.

Standing, his back to her, a tall man stared at his black boots and turned his broad-brimmed hat in his hands. Outside, the wind howled. A draft fanned ash across the hearth, and the gray cat that lay there tucked in its paws.

The girl squirmed a little. "Father."

He jumped. His face was furious, miserable. "What?"

"Is Mother in the fire?"

He glared at the coals, at her. "What do you mean?"

"Olashya says she isn't in the good place," the child said in a whisper, lisping a little; she had lost her first baby teeth. "Because she was bad."

"Why should you listen to trashy women's gossip?" He slammed the table with the flat of his hand; it made the candle hop. "Your mother's in the dirt, and that's over!"

She flinched.

"Katyesha. You'll go to your uncle Jerash until you've learned to keep house. Your brother, too, until he gets his sums and can join the League. I'll hear of no trouble from either of you. Is that clear?"

A tiny nod.

"Where is your brother?"

A boy a few years older sidled out of the shadows to stand by the chair.

The man put his hat on backward. Clenched his teeth, took it off, and put it on right. "Mind your sister till your uncle fetches you both."

The children leaned toward each other. The boy said, "Where are you going? Please. Sir."

"Nowhere! I don't know. To—to the warehouses, to see that the last delivery of sealskins is in order. Stay with your sister."

Striding in his black boots, he plucked a cloak from a peg, opened the inner door onto a rush of cold, slammed it behind him. The latch fell with a snick. The outside door opened and slammed in its turn.

The children drew breaths, moved a little.

The girl said, "Dai."

The boy scuffled with one shoe.

"Dai, it will hurt her. To be in the fire."

"She's not in any fire! That old fat Olashya with brains like—like a dog turd! Mother's not in the fire, and she's not in Olashya's prissy old good place, either. Who wants to be there?"

"Where is she?"

"East. She told me once. She said, 'When I die, do you know where my soul will go? East to my own sunny mountains, to walk there forever. I shall be a bear.'"

The wind roared. The girl's cold hand stole to her brother's, and she said, "Something's growling!"

"Wind."

"No."

"The sea at the cliffs, then. Don't be a ninny, Kat." But he let her lean against him.

Her eyes went to the dark window. "What's out there?"

"Nothing. The sea . . . and things."

"What things?"

"Nothing! Don't you believe—"

"They grab you and pull you under, Olashya said. She said—"

"Stupid baby song!" Mincing, mimicking, he chanted,

Out of the dark place, out of the deep,
The Rigi drag you from your sleep.
Their hands are fur, their claws are bone,
Their mouths are slime, their hearts are stone—

"*Don't!*" She covered her ears.

"Pff! If one of those Rigi things tried to get you, I'd punch it in the eye. I'd punch it on its old *nose.*" He punched the air. "Anyway, she's lying. There aren't any Rigi."

"Does anybody not lie?"

He shrugged.

"Mother's in the east," she said. "Those Rigi things are in the west—"

"I told you they're not."

"—and we're here in the middle, and everybody's gone, even Father."

"*I'm* not gone. Small Gray isn't." He lifted the cat from the hearth and put it on her lap. It fidgeted, settled, and began to purr, kneading her thigh. "And I'm glad Father's gone."

She bent her head, stroking the cat. Under her hands its purr grew to shaking, so vast and deep that it must have traveled from the world's end, and she began to cry.

Growing

1

East, light.
West, night.
North, freezing.
South, easing.
Up, free.
Down, sea—
   deep, dark, beating heart,
   steady breath from birth to death.
Here in the middle,
Me.

Seven Directions Hand Slap. Downshore
   (from an old Rig chant).

I AM A WOMAN who sang a man out of the sea, and who was eaten by a bear.

My name is Kat. I grew up in the small League settlement of Upslope, high on the windy cliffs above the western sea. My father, Ab Drem, was a Leagueman: one of the wealthy traders who ply their pack trains and paidmen across the west country, trafficking wholesale in cinnamon and brandy and gold.

But my father was not wealthy, for he had ruined his reputation. In youth and folly he had got a baby on a native woman, a fire-haired Hill girl from the village of Creek in the eastern mountains. Had he paid her for his pleasure and left, the League would have winked at it; but when she was big with his child, he set her up on his mule and brought her home with him.

He lived in Rett then, the mill town where there are many Leaguemen, dressed in gray or black in spite of the sun. Rett has many gossips, and Father gave them plenty to gossip about, for that bastard child was born with a face like a bear's, and lived only a day.

That was the end of my father's love for my mother, and— a worse thing, to him—of his standing in the League. To atone for his sin, he married her; she fell silent, she covered her bright hair and laid her Hill clothes—a wedding dress never worn—in a chest rarely opened. In time she bore my father two more children: my brother, Dai, and me.

Did she sing, I wonder, before we two were born? To the League, singing and dancing are sinful. Sometimes, with Dai on one knee and me on the other, she sang soft lullabies—but never when Father was home.

When I was five and Dai nine, we moved north, to Upslope on the windy coast. Father's two brothers lived there and might find Father better work with Upslope's chief Leagueman, Ab Harlan.

When Father told us we were to go, I was sitting on my mother's lap. She caught me to her and said, "Upslope? Above the village of Downshore, where they dance the Long Night?"

Father told her to shut her mouth, she was not to interest herself in native wickedness. Nor did she, for we had not been in Upslope a month when my mother fell ill and died.

She was a native; she could not be buried with the League, among the tombstones that stood in rows straight as ledger entries inside the Rulesward wall. Instead they laid her in the kale yard of my father's house, which stood alone and lonely almost at the sea cliff's edge, on a winter day when the wind blew the dirt right off the shovel.

Dai and I were sent down the road to our aunt and uncle Jerash, to learn to be human beings, which was to say members of the League. That is, Dai would be a member; I was a girl, and so must learn to be a wife.

But Dai hated trade. He hated the League. He was clumsy and sweet and cautious, and he loved animals. He could cure a calf of the staggers or mend the split hoof of an ox.

The son of a Leagueman a cowherd? said the gossips. *Shame! But then, what would you expect? His mother was a native, you know. And his sister—*

This talk fell heavily on me because I looked like my mother: freckled, with red hair that coiled like a nest of snakes. My auntie Jerash could not in propriety shave me bald, but she kept my hair clipped close as a lamb's fleece. Once I was out of mourning, she made sure that, besides my gray linen skirts and bodice and cloak, I covered my hair with a gray kerchief, always.

Auntie Jerash had six daughters, all mean as geese. I shared their big box bed. They pinched, they slapped, they stole the coverlets and pillows and made me lie against the gap where the door of the bed did not quite close and the drafts came in. I pinched back, but secretly, because I was slight and small and because my aunt always took their part. I was grateful that I had not been sent to my aunt and uncle

Seroy, whose children, all boys, called me "native pig" and twisted my arm behind my back.

From my auntie Jerash I learned to cook, to scrub, to sew, but not to read or write—League girls are not taught, it makes them troublesome. I learned to shop for necessaries at the native market in merry, untidy Downshore—for indeed Upslope and Downshore were neighbors, as my mother had said.

The latter was a native harbor town that sprawled around a central plaza. It was riddled with alleys overhung by two or three higgledy-piggledy stories of gray stone; outlying houses straggled across the narrow plain below the cliffs. I was not to speak to anybody in Downshore but the fishmongers, nor touch anything.

As for Dai, he was sent to the accounting hall to learn his sums, and I saw little of him. But sometimes on Rulesday I could sidle near enough to lean on him unnoticed, and he would lean back.

When I was ten, I was judged skilled enough to be sent back to Ab Drem, my father, to be his housekeeper. Dai came too, for he had failed at his sums—and in the League's estimation. This did not trouble him; he traded work for a little heifer calf, he built a cowshed, and except for meals, he lived in the shed with the cow.

Father was often gone. He preferred to be gone. Our house stood far from the rest, near cliffs that fell in steep steps almost to the water, and though the weather was seldom cold enough for snow, the winter surf burst so high that white spume spattered the windows. I lay alone in the black box bed that had been my mother's, listening to the wind sob in the chimney, the sea crash on the rocks far below. I curled tight and tried not to think of Mother's bones chill in the garden, or of fat old Olashya's chant about the Rigi.

But when I was twelve, I learned another song about the Rigi.

It was in Downshore that I heard it. I had gone to market with my aunt and cousins. I had just started my monthly bleeding. My aunt, with disgust (for her own daughters all started late), had instructed me on what to do, but not why or what it meant; my girl-cousins said it was my native nastiness leaking out. In the middle of the Downshore plaza I was struck by such bad cramps that I could hardly stand. My aunt scolded me in a furious undertone. She left me to sit miserably on a bench, trying not to touch anything.

Among the busy stalls with their striped awnings half-naked native stevedores ogled and joked, fishwives cried their wares, bare-bottomed children in colored shirts laughed and sang. Roadsoul mountebanks rollicked in dirty silks, and lazy dogs slept in the shade.

The sun shone warm on my drab clothes. Like a hand lifted away, the pain ceased, and for a moment the world was holy with relief.

I heard a drum, and a man's voice singing.

> I am a man upon the land,
> I am a beast upon the deep,
> I am the fin that hides the hand,
> I am the dream that riddles sleep.
>
> I am the wind that breaks the door,
> I am the pulse that fans the pain,

I am the wave that grinds the shore,
I am the rock that turns the rain.

I am the flesh that loves the flame,
I am the fur that loves the wave,
I am the cloak, I am the name,
I am the bright blood and the grave.

I am the skin that sleeks the bone,
I am the sun on the black sea,
I am the heart that heals the stone.
Come to me! Come to me!

I never saw the singer. Yet in that song I saw everything: a mystery glimpsed in a lightning flash, then lost. But for an instant I had seen it.

A plump old woman sat next to me on the bench. I laid my hand on her arm and said, "What is he singing?"

"The Rigi's song, for the dance at Long Night."

The Rigi were not monsters, she said. They were people: a tribe that lived west-away at the world's end, on islands in the sea. "They are seals," she said.

"Truly seals?"

"They're people like you and me, dearie, but when they dance, they're seals."

I knew what seals looked like from the carcasses and hides my father bought. In my mind I saw a creature like a man, but with a cat's face; its skin split, and it slid forth wet and human, coming toward me.

I did not know what the song meant, but I carried it home with me. I never sang it aloud. I sang it in my heart. While I scrubbed the hearth, stirred the porridge, milked the cow, I sang it. Carrying water from the cistern, mending socks, wringing laundry, I sang it.

Near our house there was a path down the sea cliff. Maybe goats had made it. To go there was forbidden, for Leaguemen are terrified of the sea. But because our house stood apart and Father was so often gone, there was no one to see me steal down that path, singing inwardly, to the little cove that lay below.

There I watched the waves. They hurled among the rocks and sea-stacks, white and rioting as far as I could see; or they rose as long, slow darkenings, each one pinching into a green shadow that crisped and curled along its length, then fell with a thump. Retreating, they left little rivers and fan patterns on the sand. Their hoarse hush echoed from rock and cliff. I smelled salt and iodine and the tide-line odor of creatures spawning and dying. But I never touched the water.

Like any sinner, I needed to justify my sin, so I gathered bundles of driftwood for Ab Drem's thrifty fire and carried them up the goat path on my back—heavy bundles, to punish myself. As I carried them, I sang the Rigi's song, but not aloud. At home sometimes I even let my lips move, singing with no sound, and Father thought I was at prayer.

Come to me! Come to me!

On a night near midwinter—I was fifteen by then—Father was on the road with his paidmen, and Dai was at the pub. I lay alone as always, behind the locked door of my box bed, listening to the sobbing wind. I thought I would die with longing—but for what, I did not know. The wind beat in the chimney like a drum. In that close darkness I sat up, and for the first time in my life I sang the Rigi's song out loud.

Come to me!

I opened the doors of the box bed, and climbed out. It was long past midnight. I dressed and went out into the night, to stand on the cliff above the sea. The wind was cold but not icy; it blew my kerchief off, blew my short curls straight. I shouted my name to the dark west: "Kat! I'm Kat!"

Singing, I crept down the cliff path to the sea.

On the beach the wind was less. Soft waves burst among the starlit driftwood, the seaweed and scoured tree trunks. I found a stick to poke things with and wandered the damp sand in the fading starlight. The little cove was all my own.

There was a dead seal at the tide line. I went close to look, singing the Rigi's song that was wide and limber, now that it was free and not all crushed up in my heart.

It was not a seal, but a man.

A young man shining with water, naked as water. He lay on his face. His back jumped with breathing.

I did not move. Could not think or run. Then I saw how the surf had battered him on the rocks; his arm was broken, his foot was smashed, he bled from thigh and shoulder as if he had been scoured. I crept close. I could see the shape of his face, his mouth open against the sand. Then, in the first dawn light, he looked up at me. His eyes were gray as rain. In the Plain tongue that all peoples can speak, he said, "You sang that?"

As if I had called him.

He was a Rig—one of the Rigi. But he was an outcast: His people had "killed" him, his own father had cut off his braid and torn the earrings from his ears, had burned the sealskin that he, like every Rig, had been given at birth. The Rigi had bound him and laid him with their dead. But he had broken his bonds and come swimming, swimming east across the water from the world's end.

To me.

He was lean and broad-shouldered, not much taller than I was myself, and he shook with cold as a cat shakes with purring. I did not know what to do.

I pulled my gray sweater over my head. Held it out. He shook too much to put it on himself; I had to touch him. He was clean and cold, like an apple. He was too spent to rise. He closed his eyes and fell back onto the sand. But I grappled him onto my back like a load of driftwood and carried him up the cliff to Father's house.

That was a mistake. Father came home.

He found the naked, bleeding man sprawled on his white hearth. He might as well have found a viper there, or a demon. "Get it out!" he cried, trembling with rage. "I will have no more natives in my house!" He thought Dai had brought the man up from the sea. Why should he imagine that of me, his little daughter?

Dai carried the Rig out to the cowshed. He wrapped him in an old blanket and laid him in the straw against the flank of his good cow, Moss. But the man would not warm, and he would not wake, and I could not win away from Father's task-making to see to him.

I knew he would die. And he could not die, I would not have it. I had called him.

At last, come evening, it was time to milk the cow. I wrested myself from Father's fussing and ran to the shed.

The Rig was cold, he was slipping away like a wave. I snugged my knee against him. He opened his eyes.

"What is your name?" I said. Names are magic; maybe I thought if I knew his name, I could hold him.

In a whisper, he said, "They burned my name with my sealskin. But maybe a new one will come."

Well, that was no use. In the League it is your father who names you. Yet I held his hand tight and said, "You're like a long wave, it comes up onto the shore for a moment, and then sighs back. Don't, don't go back!"

In the dusty lantern light he smiled. "Nall is my new name," he said. "In the Rigi's tongue *nall* means 'long wave.'"

It seemed I had named him. "Nall, Nall," I said. But his eyes had closed.

When Father slept and it was dark enough to hide us on the cattle paths, Dai and I carried Nall to Downshore.

There was a healer there, Mailin the herb woman. Her house was on the beach, you could hear the surf there like a great voice. She spread a striped pallet on her hearth for him.

But he did not warm. He did not wake. I could feel him sinking back into darkness, like the wave he was named for.

I said to Mailin. "Heal him!"

She shook her head. That task was not hers, she said, but mine.

"Mine?"

"He has come," she said. "What does he need, now, to stay?"

I had no answer, only grief. But maybe grief was the answer; I held Nall and wept until I had no tears left, and when I raised my face at last, his eyes were open, looking at me. Warm, worn out, he moved his face on my wrist.

"What is your name?" he said.

That night on Mailin's hearth, with all my clothes on, I fell asleep under the weight of his arm.

In the morning I had to go home to my duties before Father

woke. But the world was changed. I had called him, I had named him; Mailin said he had called me too. He was mine.

Father, of course, knew nothing about this. So it was not difficult for me, two days later, to go to Downshore as if to market. I ran straight to Mailin's house instead. There—battered, waking, hungry as an otter—was Nall.

I sat with him on Mailin's veranda. I loved him so much that I could hardly look at him. I asked why his people had cast him out.

"I sang," he said. "I listened and sang."

"What did you listen to?"

"I just listened. I am a listener. I hear new words for old songs."

He could have told me he listened to the dreams in my heart, they spoke so loud; he could have told me anything. He said that when he had listened, he had heard new words for the Rigi's song, different from the words I knew. He had sung them out loud. To his father and the other Rigi that singing was a profanation and a sin, so they killed him.

I began to think that his father must be much like my own, and I loved him even more.

But, unknown to me, something else had happened: Father had sold me, like a pig at the fair. To redeem his position in the League, he had struck a bargain with Ab Harlan, the chief Leagueman of Upslope, and had given me to be the bride of his youngest son.

With his face lit by joy and pride he had never shown for me before, he summoned me to him. "You are to be married!" he said.

I was a Leagueman's daughter. To say no to my father was unthinkable.

I said no.

I knew who I loved. I stood on the hearth I had scrubbed so many times and said, *"No!"* to Ab Drem, my father. I told him the man I loved was the dirty native he had ordered off that very hearth.

Father hit me across the mouth.

But I had carried a man out of the sea on my back. When my father raised his hand to hit me again, I caught his wrists and held them—and I was stronger than he.

My strength shocked us both. He wrenched his wrists out of my grip, and did not try to stop me as I left him in the ruin of his hopes, snatched my mother's wedding clothes from the chest, and ran away.

But I did not know how to be that strong, or how to be a woman—only how to be a man's pig for sale. So I ran to Downshore, to Nall, and offered him the only thing I had: myself. I wanted to be safe, owned by Nall as I had been owned by my father.

Nall would not have me. He did not want a slave.

I did not know what to do then, who to be. Alone, I ran to the beach, thinking to drown myself from self-pity and spite.

But I did not do that. Instead, as I paddled and splashed at the edge of the great sea, the thought rose in me that if I did not find out who *I* was first, I would lose myself in Nall like a water drop in the ocean, and never be anything but servant.

I did not go back to him. I put on my mother's wedding clothes and went to the Downshore festival grounds. It was midwinter solstice, Long Night, the great dance which all the tribes attend. I searched in the crowds until I found Hillwomen, and among them, by pure chance, was my mother's sister, Bian. I arranged to go with the women at the festival's end, far away to the mountains where my mother had been born. That way, I thought, I would find out who in the world I might be, besides my father's daughter.

I knew I would come back. Once my departure was sure, I went to Nall.

We sat together on the beach, huddled beneath an old blanket. I held his fist hard against my chest. I told him where I was going and why. He said—

But that story comes later. That is the real story. For now only this: If you call what you long for out of the sea, your life will change. I left Nall and my father and my brother and went away from everything I knew, nine days' rough journey east to my mother's mountains.

It was there, in the red-tiled Hill village of Creek, that I was eaten by the bear: something quickly told, but hard to understand.

To find out who in the world I might be. How was I to do that?

To anyone in Creek the answer was obvious: I must be eaten by a bear.

Not eaten actually, the way a bear eats raspberries or a honeycomb, but ritually, in a ceremony. Every girl in Creek had to be eaten, in order to become a woman.

The ceremony is like this. First the girl must fast for three days, drinking only water from the holy spring. While she fasts, the hunters go high into the mountains. They catch a bear, harness it, bring it to the Bear House, and tether it to a stake.

Then, in front of the whole village, the girl goes to her bear. She sings holy chants to it, and it grows mild, they say; she kisses it, she strokes it with her hand. She offers it the spirit of her girlhood, and the bear eats it, they say; her girlhood is gone. There is great singing and shouts and eddies of blue smoke; the bear is let go, and from then on the girl is a woman, they say. She wears long skirts, and can marry.

But I failed the ceremony. When they brought me before the red bear in harness, I panicked, thinking, I don't want to be eaten!

"I won't!" I cried, and thrust the bear away. In front of the whole village it knocked me down and mauled me with its claws.

I was ruined.

I was already a Leagueman's child, and Creek folk hated the League. They were suspicious of all foreigners; you may be sure I said nothing to anybody about a seal man! And after the bear attacked me, Creek thought I was cursed outright. When I walked down the street, people crossed to the other side. When I went to the Clay Court, where the unmarried girls learned to make pottery, no one would sit near me. Only my aunt Bian and her daughter, my cousin Jekka, stood up for me.

But of what use was their loyalty? The claws of the bear had left four long, purple, puckered scars across my breasts. No man could want me now—not even the man I had left on Mailin's hearth.

Yet one man did.

His name was Raím. He lived outside the village—and outside the village rules: a red, handsome, furious young man who had been a hunter and a dancer once. His eyes were blue as stone, and they saw what a stone sees, for Raím was blind.

He could not see my scars, and like me, he was shunned as unlucky. He was uncanny, all right, for even blind he was the best weaver in Creek. He was arrogant and bitter and proud, he cursed like a stevedore, he had a blue serpent tattooed around his hips, and the only being he loved—not that he would admit to loving anything!—was a little tabby cat.

My aunt Bian disapproved of him. The only way to see him was to let loose somebody's goat and then pretend to hunt for it in his direction; it was amazing how often those goats got out.

We argued and fought. Little by little, Raím let me see the grubby stone hut he lived in. He let me see his Great Loom, which women are not supposed to look upon. He let me see his heart, and it was as scarred as my breasts.

I did not mean to forget Nall. I did not mean, one day in springtime, to look into Raím's freckled, angry face the way you look at the night sky full of stars, so deep you could fall into it. I did not mean to kiss him.

But I did. And having opened that door, I did not know how to shut it, or what to do with the passions, his and mine, that came pouring out.

I loved Nall; wasn't that so? How, then, could my mouth rush to Raím's, like a creek to another creek? My father had called me a slut; I saw that he was right. I was depraved, out of control.

And if I could not control myself, then I must find something or somebody to control me; I did not care what or who, as long as the terror stopped. I ran to my aunt Bian and begged again for the bear ceremony, thinking to lock myself away safe in Creek's tiny, lawful world the way I had used to lock myself into my black box bed.

Bian was overjoyed. The hunters went out that very day; a bear was caught, brought, and penned at the Bear House. For three days I fasted, drinking the holy springwater and gabbling the chants.

But I did not go to the bear. Not to that one.

My mind did not decide this. My body did. Or maybe my heart decided—or my soul, which would not be penned in Creek's narrow little vision of the world.

At almost dawn on the day of the ceremony, as the bear waited for me in harness, I rose and left the fasting house. No one was there to stop me; no girl had left before. As the sky grew light, my feet, like a sleepwalker's, carried me up the mountain by the animal trails.

Dawn birds called, deer ran, the dew rained down like tears. The mountain was as big as the sea, it was the sea's equal, earth so alive that it trembled with itself—and it was mine, as the sea was Nall's. Up and up I ran through the thickets until they were too dense for running, then I crawled, then I squirmed on my belly like a snake. The thorns were like knives but they did not stop me, I did not stop until the way opened a little, like a door, and I lay at the edge of an aspen meadow. There, standing against the trees' new green, I found what waited for me.

Bearlike, but not a bear; not a wolf; not a cat; a creature dark as shadow, warm as blood, lovely, terrible, shining in the morning.

It was nameless, with no being but Being. It was myself.

I stroked its sooty fur; I looked into the living eyes that met mine. "Oh you, beautiful!" I said. I leaned into the mouth that opened for me, that grew wider, deeper as I leaned into it. "Yes," I said, and the white teeth came down.

So.

I woke on the hillside by the holy spring. My cousin Jekka found me there and ran to fetch the women of Creek. Frightened, weeping, they raised me up. I had been gone three days.

"A bear came to you!" they said. "It ate you after all!"

For, to them, it was a bear. It had to be a bear. If it was not a bear, then their narrow, certain world had gone vast and unknowable, out of their control; it *had* to be a bear.

But it was not a bear. Whatever I had been for those three days—when, transformed into the being that had eaten me, I ran wild and alive upon the mountain—it did not fit inside the little word "bear."

In that timeless time I had heard the hawk cry, had snuffled the wet night meadows, tasted blood, watched the red sunrise. The world had spread out beneath my flying paws like spiderwebs on dewy grass, a loom of countless threads in a wordless order, and I was part of it.

Then, as I had given myself to that being, it gave itself back to me. Once more just Kat, I woke, naked and shivering, by the spring where my cousin found me.

The sisterhood of Creek brought me home. They gave me long skirts and deference; they said I was a woman. Even Raím had changed—his heart was not healed, but he no longer hid its wounds. He still loved me.

But I did not know who or what I loved now. I was puzzled, unfinished, restless as water on a griddle.

I had wanted to know who I was. Now I had a strange knowledge but no words to describe it. What was I to do? What I knew did not fit within Creek's theology—and certainly not in the League's; it did not fit anywhere in the world I could think of.

I had no one to talk to about it. And what could I say? How do you talk, or even think, about something that has no name?

So I named it. What had eaten me—the Being in whose being I had run upon the mountain—I began to call "the Bear," with a big letter. I was just learning to read and write, and my spelling was terrible, but I knew that important things got a big letter.

I longed for my brother Dai. He would think I was crazy, but that would not matter; his love for me was as steadfast as morning. Creek felt too small. In the weeks after my time as the Bear-with-a-big-letter, spring turned to summer. I used any excuse to get out of my aunt's house and climb the mountain—listening, wondering, watching snakes and squirrels, hearing the bees in the sweet grass hum till the meadow shook like a purring cat.

I wanted to be *in* the world again, as I had been in it when I was the Bear. I wanted to sing it or speak it, but all I had were words, clumsy and common, not the right ones. The world hummed; I listened and listened.

Cautiously, with the edge of my mind, I thought about that other listener, Nall. I wondered whether I had dreamed him. He felt long ago and far away, part of the time before my breasts were scarred by that first, very ordinary bear. A voice in me began to speak, saying, What now? What next?

And it is here that the story really begins.

Listening at the Gate

1

Before the green sea
struck the black rocks,
I was.
Before the blue earth
rang like a bell,
I was.
I breathed before breath.
I am beneath and above
and through you,
the sound of a soundless gong.
I was, I will be,
I am nothing at all.
Nothing. At all.
I am nothing,
and the shore on which I break
is all.

Old Chant. The Rigi.

ON THE DAY AFTER my seventeenth birthday I was on the mountain, digging wild celery root for my aunt Bian. It was near midsummer, but the peaks were still white; the aspen meadow was cool with spray from the snow-water creek that hurried to get down off the mountain, west and away.

The meadow soil was black and damp, and the roots smelled like the cellar of the world. I was digging with both hands when a bear came down the mountain, along the far side of the creek.

I stopped digging and sat quietly. I was not afraid; I had been eaten by the Bear, so this one was my sister. She was black and had two cubs, both brown, that rolled and pounced and fell in the creek and scrambled out. She was digging roots the same as I was. She grunted; her loose coat shone as she moved, and the meadow grass shimmered.

She raised her nose from her digging and saw me.

The meadow went still. *Something will happen. Something.* It was the hush before an earthquake, or the pause of a bell at the top of its swing, the clapper not yet fallen.

Then the wind blew, the grass dipped. She dropped her head and snorted, and her children came rollicking. Without haste they ambled away down the creek.

I watched them move out of sight, the pungent root in my hand. Not thinking, but with something shaping itself in my heart like thought.

They disappeared beyond a willow bank. Then, from somewhere beyond that bank, a woman's voice rose up.

> I am a man upon the land,
> I am a beast upon the deep,
> I am the fin that hides the hand,
> I am the dream that riddles sleep.

I was on my feet, leaping toward the voice, scattering the roots in my lap. At the brink of the creek I saw nothing, but the voice rang like a bell.

> I am the wind that breaks the door,
> I am the pulse that fans the pain . . .

I jumped from rock to rock, slipping and sprawling, plunging into a deep pool to claw and spit, for I could not swim well yet, only in the millpond. But when I had floundered abreast of the willows on the far bank, I did not see a singing bear, or a seal, or a Rig. I saw a Roadsoul girl no older than myself, kneeling on a stone and scrubbing a green shirt.

I knew she was a Roadsoul by her tattered silks. She was alone; no encampment, no painted carts, no horses or campfires or lounging, laughing men. Only a pile of laundry and her little fat son, maybe a year old, naked on the grassy bank with both hands crammed in his mouth.

When she heard me sputtering, she did not cease to scrub or sing, but fixed me with that look Roadsouls have, as if the rest of us are here for their amusement.

> I am the skin that sleeks the bone,
> I am the sun on the black sea.
> I am the heart that heals the stone.
> *Come to me! Come to me!*

I had come, heart and eyes wide open. Mouth open too: I gaped at her. If a bear were to turn into a woman, I did not think it would choose to be a Roadsoul. Roadsouls are disreputable, and for two cubs, shouldn't there be two boys? Forgetting all courtesy, I shouted over the water's noise, "How do you know that song?"

Now, with a Roadsoul one does well to be polite. She narrowed her eyes and grinned, showing teeth inlaid with gold stars. Then she harked about and said, "Do I smell a bear fart?"

She did not mean those real bears which must have passed close. It was me she wrinkled her nose at. In that part of the world everybody knows a Creek girl must be eaten by a bear, and she could see that my long skirts were new.

"A wet fart," she added.

"It's horse droppings you smell," I said. Roadsouls burn those in their campfires. Scowling, I straightened my sopping clothes.

Then *she* stared. Though my aunt Bian had sewn a special blouse for me, water had dragged down the cloth. The girl could see the four scars, purple across my breasts.

I let her look. I told myself I was not ashamed. Her own breasts were unmarked, big with milk. Her eyes moved between mine and the scars. She said, "Did the one that marked you eat you?"

"No."

"What ate you, then?" She asked this without scorn. She was my own age, she was not from Creek, she had sung that song.

"In Creek they have to call it a bear," I said. "They can call it that if they want to."

She spat into the eddies. "And they have to wrap you up safe in those long skirts?"

Then I really wanted to know what she knew—and why. I asked again where she had learned the song.

"All water sings that song," she said.

If it did, I had never heard it. But I did not say so.

"It belongs to the First Ones. The Rigi." She looked at me to see whether this hayseed knew who the Rigi were.

I made my face be humble.

She said, "The Rigi came out of the sea, at the beginning of the world. They were seals, but they took off their skins and were people. Sometimes they come among us."

"Do they?" My blush began. I said, "*Why* do they come among us?" Stammering: "Do you know any Rigi? Were they men? Why were you singing their song?"

She made the slightest shrug. "I shall not tell you."

I wrung my hands. "Oh, please—only tell me, where did you learn that song?"

"Everybody knows it."

"Not in Creek!"

Her face said what she thought of Creek. "That song is for Long Night."

I shivered. She saw it. I said, "Did you ever dance Long Night in Downshore, by the sea? Roadsouls go there, I've seen them. Were you there last year? Did you see them dancing?" For he would have been dancing. Surely she would have seen him.

"The year is near turned to Least Night. Why should I speak of Long Night?"

"But—but—"

Her little son took his hands out of his mouth and mimicked me. "*Buh! Buh!*"

She bent to her scrubbing. Now and then she stole a glance at me. I could only fume and listen to the mountain water that—she said—had been singing the Rigi's song all along, tumbling from every high place, west and down across the folded continent, past every gate and weir until it spilled into the sea.

Maybe that mystery showed in my face. She laid aside the shirt and said, "Give me your palm, Eaten Girl. I shall scry your fortune."

"I have no money to pay you."

"Give me your palm."

I held it out, frightened. Fortune-tellers can see who your lover will be.

My hand was strong, with earth under the nails. Hers was slender and took mine as if it had taken many. She gazed into my palm. As she gazed, her touch grew light, lighter, until my hand only lay on hers.

I thought this meant she scorned it, and I tried to pull away. But she caught it again and held it as you might hold a bird. She looked up at me—looked and looked.

I grew uneasy. "What do you see there?"

"Nothing."

"You mean—I am to die?"

"I did not say I saw a death. I saw nothing." But her eyes narrowed again, her voice was singsong. "This hand shall be full and have nothing. This hand shall be heavy with gold and empty. This hand shall embrace the sea—" Her voice went ordinary, mocking. "But nobody can do that! You just get wet."

Indeed, my palm was still wet from the creek. To my surprise she kissed it, picked up her baby from the bank, and held him out to me, saying, "Thus is your fate. I shall tell you no more. Now give my child a gift, Eaten Girl."

He was sunburned and dirty; he kicked and crowed and laughed so that all in a moment I laughed too. Offering up my palms, I said, "But I have nothing!"

"Give him a song."

I could not think of any songs but the one she had sung. "My father was a Leagueman," I said. "We weren't allowed to sing."

She threw me a sharp look, jigging the child. "Give him a song," she said again.

"The only songs I know are baby games."

"He's a baby."

I thought of the League children's chants and taunts, of

which I had most often been the target, and could not find one kindly enough to give to a little boy with a tuft of brown fuzz like a bear cub. Then I said, "Wait, I know one. It's not League, it's Creek. My mother was from Creek. She sang it to my brother and me." I put it into the Plain tongue, and thinking of the family of bears I had seen, I sang it to the baby.

> Bear in the black rock,
> Bear's two children.
> My red cub, O!
> My brown cub, O!
>
> Warm in the black rock,
> Bear's two children.
> My red cub, O!
> My brown cub, O!

"*O ba!*" cried the child, and wet in the creek. We laughed, and that made the baby laugh. She washed him in the rushing water—he squealed—and let me hold him, squirming and warm. Then she kissed me and said, "Blessings on you, and on your brother, and on your parents and all your ancestors!"

That seemed a big blessing for such a little song. Also, Father's half of my ancestors would despise to be blessed by a Roadsoul. I gave the baby back, feeling that a person with such rude ancestors did not deserve him.

Maybe she saw that sadness in my face, for she said, "Ask me one question, and I will answer it."

I could have asked again about those Rigi who come among us, or why she had sung their song, or what, truly, she had seen in my hand. Instead I pulled down the neck of my blouse and said, "Would a man—if he hadn't seen me since I was an ignorant little girl, before I got these scars—would he still—?"

She swung the baby to the bank, bent again to the pile of silks, and said, "The answer is: Go find out!" Then, when I did not move, "The child has his song, and you have yours. Go."

I went. Wading again across the creek that rushed down and down, jostling and sprawling in its haste to reach the sea, I looked back and saw for the first time the tracks of the bear and her children pressed into the mud at the bank, passing or stopping between the Roadsoul and her child.

2

Button, button,
Tell me true,
Who'll she marry?
Who'll she woo?
Fisher, tinker,
Slacker, stinker,
Shoreman dog,
Hillman hog,
Leagueman, pig man,
Bald-with-a-wig man,
Beggar with a tin can,
Thief!

Button-counting Song. Upslope.

I GATHERED UP THE ROOTS I had dug, thinking of the man I had called to me with the Rigi's song. I remembered the smell of him, like a young cat come from hunting with night in his fur. I walked down the mountain and straight home, to tell my aunt Bian and get it over with.

I knew she would not want me to go. She had made the nine-day journey to Downshore twice, chosen by the Circle to be among the women who carried Creek's pottery to sell at the great market that attends Long Night. It was on her second trip that she had found me there, dressed in my mother's wedding clothes, searching among the festival crowds for her people.

But Bian did not want to go to Downshore again. Her grandmothers and great-grandmothers were Hillwomen, she thought Creek was the world's navel, and she hoped never again to leave it. So when I came to her where she hoed among the young melon plants and said, "I will go back to Downshore for Least Night," she was not happy.

"You're a bear of the Circle now," she said. The hoe blade chopped the young weeds with strokes that grew sharper as she spoke. "That is an honor dearly bought. Why should you go away now, into the big crazy world where there's nothing but fighting and paidmen, and nobody knows the signs and rites? Back to your father, who hit you on the mouth?"

Her voice had risen. My cousin Jekka, picking the last peas, straightened and looked at us with eyes bright as a fox's.

"I won't go to Father," I said, lowering my voice. "I'll go to my brother, Dai, and to Mailin the healer."

"It's to that lad you'll go," said Bian.

I blushed hot.

"Let's speak the truth," she said. "One look from that lad carries more weight than duty or custom, more honor than being eaten by the bear—"

"It wasn't a bear! I don't mind calling it that; I have to call it something. But it had no name. It wasn't some little, harnessed bear in the Bear House—"

"I won't hear it!" Hoeing again, she spoke between whacks. "You made the proper fast. We said the proper prayers. If, instead of to the Bear House, you chose to go up the mountain alone; and if, as I believe, Ouma the Bear Mother herself found you and ate you, and in three days brought you back to us; still"—she thumped the hoe handle into the dirt and leaned on it—"still I say it was a bear that ate you, and you are a woman of Creek."

"I'm a woman of more than Creek."

I had not meant to say that. It sprang out of my mouth. But it was true. There were things I loved about Creek—making pottery with the other women, picking peas—but it was not my home. No place was. Home is where you belong, and the only times I had belonged anywhere were moments with Dai, his warm shoulder warding off the world's demons.

And when I had run on the mountain as the Bear; then I had truly been at home, part of the living world itself.

"You are so young," said Bian. "You think you know yourself."

I thought, I know myself better than *you* do!

She had straightened her back to scold but now turned half away. Since the time of the Bear she had been a little afraid of me. Jekka tried to look busy among the peas.

Her face soft with grief, Bian said, "My sister, Lisei, ran off with your father—a Leagueman!—and died reviled and lonely in a foreign place. By a miracle, her daughter has been given back to me. The Leaguemen killed Lisei with their cruel ways—don't tell me they didn't! Should I want her child, my heart's light, to go back among her mother's killers, for the sake of some lad's bright eye?"

I felt naked and guilty and angry. But I knew I would go. If she forbade it, I would go anyway, in peddler's cart or Roadsoul wagon or on foot if I had to. I would not be stopped, any more than the creek would be stopped on its road to the sea.

She saw it in my face. The sorrow in her own grew deeper, then resigned.

"So be it," she said. "You'll go. Then go blessed, dear daughter, and may Ouma, who ate you, care for you."

I burst into tears, feeling like a snake for the pain I was bringing her. We embraced and stood in the melon patch weeping on each other's necks until Jekka bounced over, asking, "What's the matter?" As if she had not heard every word.

"Tell me about your lad, then," said Jekka. "You little sneak! Tell."

"No."

I winced as she tugged the hairbrush through my curls. Each night we sat on the edge of the bed we shared and brushed each other's hair. Mine was always worst. In Creek it had grown to a fiery mop, tangled like fleece.

"You pick up brambles like a dog," she said. "Tell me about your lad, or I'll torture you. I'll find a sparrow's nest in here, there's everything else. Besides"—she put her arms around me, brush and all—"if you're going away, you *have* to tell me. Because you won't be here to tease anymore."

I did not know what to say or do. Loving was easy for Jekka, but I could not seem to get the hang of it. It was like jokes—I always got them a half beat behind everybody else and laughed into their silence.

I turned and hugged her—awkwardly, for I had had little practice. She wiped her eyes, attacked my hair again, and said, businesslike, "Your lad."

"He's not a lad."

"He's a fish?"

I flinched, not from the brush. "He's a *man*. And I don't know for sure if he's—what you said. Mine."

Jekka leaned close and whispered. "No cabbage worms?"

I grabbed my pillow and smacked her with it. She grabbed hers, and in the hot summer dusk we fought all over the bed till hers leaked feathers that stuck to our faces and we flopped down panting. She said, "Thank me, Cousin. What if you still thought that's how it is?"

For it was she who had explained to me where babies come from. When I first came to Creek, fifteen years old, I still thought they came from cabbage worms, the fat green kind you pull off and step on. My League aunts wore gray linen so voluminous that you could not tell when they were pregnant and claimed they found their babies under cabbages in the garden.

I had hunted for babies there. I wanted one. Babies laughed, and you could hold them. But it seemed you needed a husband to find one, which made no sense, as my uncles would have nothing to do with gardening.

Jekka—she was a year older than I—had found this so funny that she had rolled in the grass kicking. Her own explanation was so appalling that for weeks I could not look at the men of Creek. I wondered why my cousins in Upslope had not told me—Siskya, for instance, who had taunted me cruelly about my mother—in order to watch me squirm. Then I realized Siskya had not been told either and had been sent to her marriage bed dreaming of cabbage worms.

"Thanks," I said now, spitting out feathers.

Jekka sat up, her braid all fuzzy from being whacked. "So—you and your lad weren't lovers?"

I wished she were not so frank, I wished I would not blush or feel my heart wrench where it beat. "I just barely met him."

"Yet you'll go back to him? Cousin, you're crazy! What's his name?"

I blushed worse and said in my smallest voice, "Nall."

"Nall."

It frightened me to hear that name from Jekka's mouth. It made everything real as bread.

"Tell me about him," she said. "In a week, two weeks, you'll be gone."

Her voice was falsely stern and full of tears. I said in a rush, "All right. But don't tell Bian."

"That *would* be crazy." Jekka hooked her little finger with mine and promised silence for life—unlikely, since she chattered like the jay she was named for. I began the story as I have told it. But without thinking I slipped from the Hill tongue into the Kitchen Hessdish I had spoken as a child.

Jekka said, "What?"

"I'll speak Plain," I said. The Plain tongue is what all peoples speak, though with different accents, and what they write in. Careful not to slip back into Hessdish, I told Jekka about my father's cold, thrifty house; my cruel cousins; the harsh, correct men in black boots and hats—among them my father and two uncles—who sat in my aunt's parlor smoking pipes, watching one anothers' eyes, speaking in half sentences that bought and sold anything and everything in the west country, including girls.

I told her how Father had sold me to Ab Harlan, the chief Leagueman, to be the bride of his son. Jekka hugged her knees. "Oh, Kat, it's like a wicked ballad! You never said you were to marry. Was his son handsome?"

"*Homely.* Like a fumbling white grub, with pimples. His name was Queelic."

Jekka squealed, I knew she would. In the Hill tongue *cuilic* means "midden," the place you throw kitchen scraps and chicken droppings. "But you were only fifteen," she said.

"If you're a League girl, they marry you off young. You have to be untouched—'an unmarked lily,'" I said, quoting my auntie Jerash. "They won't tell you where babies come from, but you'd better know how to make cream dill sauce."

"Oh well, I like your cream dill sauce. So your father tried to sell you. What would he have gotten for you?"

"His reputation back." That was all. Except he could work for Ab Harlan the rest of his life, and there would be money in that. "But it didn't turn out that way."

I told her about the night beach, about seeing the big-shouldered wet shape of the drowned seal half raise itself and show me the face of a man. "Jekka," I said, "you won't believe this. But there's a tribe of people out there, on islands in the sea. They're called the Rigi, and—"

"Rigi!" Jekka grabbed my shoulders. "Kat, are you telling me your lover is a *Rigi*?"

I shushed her, afraid Bian would hear. "A *Rig*. That's how they say it. And he wasn't my lover. I'm not even sure if he still—"

"There are songs about the Rigi! They're seals. Then they take off their skins and they're people. They're *magic*."

"Don't be stupid! Bian calls us daughters of the bear; do we turn into bears? Do we go about in bearskins?"

"We wear bearskins for the ceremonies."

"But we don't *turn into* bears. It's the same with Nall and seal-skins," I said. "Probably." Except he had no sealskin anymore.

"But, Kat, a Rigi—or a Rig, you said—cast up by the sea, like a man in a song. How could you stand to leave him?"

"Because I couldn't— Because back then I wasn't—"

How to explain to Jekka what I had only begun to understand myself? Slowly, I said, "You know how it is—when you don't know anything, but maybe you *know* you don't know anything?"

"When you first came to Creek, you certainly didn't know anything," Jekka said generously. "But, Cousin, such a story! Does Mother know?"

"Only that there was a—a lad I liked, in Downshore."

"Glory!" She was delighted to know something her mother did not. "But still. To leave him!"

"I had to. I just *went*. Before I could change my mind."

It had felt like tearing myself in two. Winter daybreak, dressed in my mother's wedding clothes so I would look like a Hillwoman in the home-going holiday press, I had stood on Mailin's hearth and wept. On the striped pallet at my feet Nall slept hard, one arm flung out, and it was the end of everything because he would not wake and say good-bye to me.

Then I had done something important. Jekka would have done it without thinking, but to me it had felt like jumping off a cliff. I knelt down beside him and whispered, "Nall!"

He did not stir. His eyelids jumped with dreams. I slid my hand under the blankets, against his thigh. He grunted like a puppy, opened his eyes, and looked up as if I were the dream he was in.

"I'm going," I said. My tears fell straight down.

He looked straight up. "You will come back to me," he said. It was not a promise or a command, but what he knew would be. As if he had said, *The sun will rise.*

"I will come back to you," I said. Unless I died, I would come back.

He smiled. His lips were chapped from salt water; they tucked back at the corners. He had a broken canine tooth.

"Kat," he said. He raised his good hand and fumbled it into my curls, he pulled me down and kissed me. That was how I knew the wild smell of him, my mouth against his.

I did not tell Jekka any of this. All I said was, "I told him I'd come back."

"Well, of course you must!"

I was grateful to her. But I did not want to be asked anything else. Let Jekka pry all she would, the real thing was how I felt: like a root groping in darkness for water it knows is there, that it must have. Nall was that water.

Jekka saw my face and shut up. But she could never be silent for long. She fidgeted and said, "Have you had news of him, all this time?"

I shook my head. News from the world outside Creek was scanty. Bian had had a letter or two from Mailin and had read them to me because I could not read them for myself yet. All they said were things like, *Dai lives in Downshore now* and *Dai's cow had a calf.* At least, that was all Bian had reported; suddenly I was suspicious.

"So you'll just go to him and see what happens," said Jekka. "You're crazy. You're brave. Cousin, how do you do it? You're little and red and cross, yet the men are all over you, like bees on a fruit loaf."

"They are not," I said, red and cross.

"Says who? I know one Creek lad who wishes you'd let him hook his sash loom to your hearth."

"I don't have a hearth, Jekka. If you mean Raím, I'll always care for him. But it would be fight, fight, fight—you know what he's like! He *tries*, but he's in a rage half the time. And before he was blinded, he had a girl in every market town."

Jekka shrugged. "He's a man. You think your Rig won't be like that?"

I did not answer. She did not know Nall.

"Anyway," she said, "are you so perfect yourself?"

"I'm not *that* bad!"

"Better you than me, then. I'm rotten when I'm crossed. But I do see that you must leave Raím and go back to Nall."

I nodded, not happily. I did not look forward to telling an angry, grieving man that I would come to visit him no more, even for talk. I would go back to Nall; but there were the scars on my breasts to remind me that I was not the naive child who had pledged to return. I was no longer an unmarked lily.

"Mother will be growling like Ouma herself for weeks, I hope you know," said Jekka. "Oh, Cousin, I will miss you, miss you! If the roads are safe, I'll come visit. I'll make Mother take me to Downshore for Long Night. Will I meet him then? Nall."

"I don't know." The room was hot, but I shivered. The whole world shivered, one deep tremor, then nothing. "I don't know what will happen."

"Watch out for cabbage worms," said Jekka.

I shoved my feet under the sheets and against her thigh until she fell off the bed onto the floor. That was another thing she had taught me: that when you love someone, you must jokingly mistreat them, just a little. It makes it easier when you leave them, or they die.

Raím worked alone in his stone bothy outside the village. Even with the door open it was so dark in there that I barely saw how his hands paused at the weft, his head bent for a moment.

"Go back to him, then," he said.

"You knew I'd go. Sooner or later."

He would not answer. We had been over it a hundred times, and it never got easier. He was too much like me—"freckles like a trout and a temper like a tomcat," as Bian said.

Maybe because he had been a hunter, it was hard for him to want something except the way a hunter does, who kills what he wants and then gobbles it up.

He tapped the weft with a wooden comb. Because he would not speak, I did not say anything either. I could see the bold pattern on his loom better than his hands, and watched it grow a little. His designs were as strong and startling as a lightning strike. Once, galled by Creek's rigid traditions, he had cried out, "There must be a place where all patterns came from, before the world was made!"

"Rotten piece of shit!" he shouted now. The wooden batten comb had broken in his hand. "Devil's rotten son of—" He threw it on the floor, and I could think, See how you are? You're not a listener, you're a *curser*! If you weren't so impossible, maybe I could stay in Creek and love you!

That made it easier. A little. I stood in the square of sun from the door and wept—silently, because I did not want him to hear me—catching each tear on the end of my tongue.

He heard, though. His voice softened a little. "If you're going to go, then go. There's a gift for you on the shelf by the door. In that bowl you made."

I looked in the bowl. To make it I had gathered red clay, wedged it, rolled it, coiled and pinched it up from base to rim like a sleeping snake. I had scraped it and polished it into a bowl the size of Raím's cupped hands, empty and light as an eggshell, and had fired it in the Clay Court, where only women can go, and brought it to him.

It was not what he wanted, but it was what I could give him. Now it held a rolled-up sash.

I unrolled it. It was woven of cotton spun fine as silk, patterned with the footprints of the deer mouse, brown on cream.

"Thank you," I said. My voice quavered.

"Put it on."

It fit perfectly. His hands knew the measure of my waist.

"Now go," he said.

Still weeping, I stood in the doorway. He began to sing to himself, as if I were no longer there.

> Stag in the forest lies,
> No one will bury him.
> Only the gray wolf
> Will own him, sing over him.

I took up the bowl I had made. I sat down in the dust against the doorjamb and picked up a twig of charcoal from the dirt floor, and on the smooth red pottery I began to write.

He heard me there. He had ears like the wolf in the song and could hear the scratch of the twig. He pretended not to hear.

I wrote his song on the bowl, spelling the words as well as I could, beginning along the outside rim and spiraling them down and around like a snake. Beautiful and strange, silent as a snake coiled in the sun, yet singing at the same time. A snake that had swallowed a song.

He would never see it. Nor would anyone. In a day his hands would rub it away.

I set it back on the stone shelf with a little clink. His hands and his singing did not pause, and I did not say good-bye. As I went out, his little cat ran in with its tail straight up, so I did not leave him entirely alone.

That was the first song I ever wrote down. Not the Rigi's song, but Raím's, on an empty bowl that I left in Creek.

3

She went away,
Following the loud water.
As far as it could stumble,
My heart followed after.
She said she would come back
Up that long track to me,
But the creek runs onward, downward,
Till it meets the sea.

Song for Someone Leaving. Creek.

ON THE MORNING I LEFT CREEK, there were five oxcarts going, full of carters and sellers and families with children. The road was not much troubled by bandits, though the Leaguemen said it was and hired paidmen who were worse than bandits to guard their pack trains. Usually it was safe to travel village to village, if you knew people to stay with. Bian knew the Low Track; that was the way we had come from Downshore in midwinter, following the river valleys below the snows. But she knew people on the High Track, too—friends and friends of friends.

"She goes to Marga's house. Marga's," she told the carter for the fifth time, talking right through her tears, stopping sometimes to hold me where I stood.

I was ashamed because I was not bleeding tears the way she was. She and Jekka and Raím would stay here, in the red-tiled town with its rosebushes, watching the mountain and feeling the emptiness of my leaving; but I would see the mountain grow small, as I passed through door after door into new worlds.

From the beginning I had not been what Bian had hoped for. Or what my father had hoped for, or my League aunts, or Raím, either. What, then, if I were not what Nall—

A great wail burst out of me, so that everybody stared and Bian gathered me to her breast. For a minute I had a mother and could scream the way a baby does and be comforted by arms.

Then I could not breathe, mashed up against her bosom. She peeled me off, wiped my eyes and nose with her hand as if I were little, and said, "You'll be fine. You'll be safe. You'll be with friends all the way. I don't need to tell you—" *to mind your manners,* she almost said. Then she remembered that I had been eaten, though not by the right thing, and was as much a woman as herself. She looked away.

I kissed her and said, "I love you," and climbed up over the hub of the wheel into the cart along with the other passengers. Jekka, her face as blubbered as mine, handed up my bundle. My little cousin Mamik cried because everybody else was, and my uncle Emmot blinked a lot and puffed fast on his pipe. The cart jerked; we fell over in a heap, and when we got up, we were moving, everyone trotting alongside down the red road at an ox's pace, crying, "Good-bye! May fate will that we see you in the winter! Be happy—oh, be happy!"

I wore the deer mouse sash, but Raím did not come. I had not thought he would. The mountain, big as the world, began to grow smaller behind me, to dwindle and disappear.

The cart jolted so much that once we were around a bend in the creek and hidden by the broad-trunked river poplars, I got down and walked. The wooden wheels creaked, and the carter sang.

> Your mother calls me a dirty trucker
> Who can't read or write or think.
> Tell her not to foul the water
> That someday she'll have to drink.

He had tied bells to the ox yoke, and as the oxen's shoulders dipped, the bells rang. The ox bells jangled, the axles squealed, and the carter's voice wove itself into that music until his ugly song was sweet.

Near noon we came to Ten Orchards, but because it was not market day, there were no booths with their shady awnings, the streets were empty and dusty, and all the little shops were closed up against the heat. We kept straight on, following the creek westward into narrow canyons. Because I had traveled only on the Low Track, everything past Ten Orchards was new.

Soon our creek lost itself and its name into a little brisk river, and our cart track joined a highway that wound between cliffs and tablelands, following the water. We began to see other travelers: Roadsouls first, in green or purple wagons full of children dressed in stolen silks. Then, in the late afternoon, we met a train of Leaguemen heading east.

I had not seen Leaguemen in more than a year, for Creek had banished them from the village. Every few months a couple of them would bring their mules and paidmen to Ten Orchards, lay out their wares by the fountain, and sell to the little shopkeepers—wholesale only, brandy and molasses, mirrors and beads and milled goods like the silks that would someday end up on the backs of Roadsouls. I had taken care not to go to Ten Orchards when the Leaguemen were there. I was afraid one would know me and take me back to my father.

Now, seeing the mules in the distance like a line of ants, I climbed into the cart and looked for a scarf to hide my hair. Then I realized that since at my father's house I had always been made to crop and cover it, who would know me with it long? I let the wind blow my curls across my face and peered through them at the mules and men, like a creature peeping from a thicket.

The paidmen rode first. They were called "road guards" and rode on ponies, armed—men of all colors and sizes, nicked and nocked by the swords of who knows what distant wars. Some had eyes or fingers missing. Their gear was patched and outlandish, gathered from foreign tribes, half of it no doubt rifled from corpses. They sang as they rode, loud grunting songs hardly recognizable as the Plain tongue. Seeing these men, you wondered what kept them from seizing the mule train and turning bandit themselves.

I knew the answer to that. It was money. Within the paidmen's ranks, bribes and counterbribes, double-edged blackmail, payoffs, threats, and sudden disappearances—no one called them murders—were the rule; any trouble ended, often as not, in an unmarked grave by the roadside. I had heard this myself, as I played with my doll in a corner while my father and uncles talked in low voices over their games of War.

It was money that kept the paidmen under control, and that money belonged to the Leaguemen. Several rode with each train, on mules, for mules are steadier than ponies. Most Leaguemen were tall, and pale in spite of their travels. Even in the heat they wore dark tweeds and twills, as if they were cold, for they trace their line to a cold country, north, where farmers starved and only a trader with a sack of gold could thrive. They worshipped Light. This always seemed strange to me, as so much of their time was spent worrying about darkness. The natives—which is to say everybody but Leaguemen—called them Black Boots. I remembered my father coming home, weary and bitter as always, beating the dust of the road from his tall black boots with the brim of his broad hat.

That made me think, What if this train has come from Upslope and one of these Leaguemen is my father?

I jumped off the cart and darted behind it. But I soon saw by the style of their hat crowns that they were from the South Road. They were indifferent to me; I was a native and a woman.

But our caravan was not indifferent to them. As soon as they passed, two women trudging by my cart began to cluck their tongues and say, "Black Boots! The country is overrun!" and "I wouldn't have them in my house!" as if they were a plague of spiders.

The first woman, who earlier had given me four apricots, asked me, "Did you ever hear of a Black Boot who had a heart in his body?"

I was ashamed and said nothing. I was half Black Boot.

She hardly noticed my silence—she was a talking woman—and went on to say how dreadful they were, that proper as they seemed, at night they turned into demons and sucked blood from the necks of goats.

My shame turned to astonishment. She said that away west, where the sun set, there was a Black Boot devil king laying waste to the countryside because he had been robbed by the king of the sea, that he had swallowed the Long Night fire and could breathe smoke, and a lot more such truck; but I was so entertained by the thought of my father sucking at goats' necks that I hardly heard her.

I thought how I would tell that story to Dai. Maybe I would tell Nall, and he would laugh; I remembered how he laughed with his whole body, the way a puppy barks. Thinking about him, my cheeks got hot. I did not notice that the conversation had switched to garden pests until one of the women turned to me suddenly and said, "How do *you* deal with cabbage worms?"

With a gasp I said, "I—I never have yet!"

She looked surprised. "And they're such a common nuisance!"

"Decoction of stenchweed and red pepper," said the other. "With a little tobacco juice. Sprayed lightly on the cabbage."

The first woman shook her head. "Would it were so easy to get rid of the Black Boots!"

※　※　※

That night I stayed at Marga's house in Weedrun as Bian had ordered, sleeping crosswise on a big bed with five children laid in a row like kippers, though kippers do not kick. The ceiling was smoky black, but the sky through the open window was white with stars.

I was careful always to hide my scars. I did not want to explain them, and so went apart from the others to wash; no one questioned this. In the morning Marga brought me back to the carter as he harnessed the oxen, with directions to Beshko's in Little Water.

"You'll be fine," she said, like Bian. "Just keep your eyes open." She scowled and gave me a little pat. "They're all mad down there."

"In Little Water?"

"No, where you're going—those Shorefolk. Too many Black Boots; one of them's gone mad, we hear," and she repeated the story of the devil king. "Anyway, it's too damp there by the water. How do they dry their laundry? Give me a sunny hillside." She hugged me and went off, trailing her children like ducklings.

We trudged and trundled, thirty people and five carts, down each twisting canyon and out again onto each narrow plain. Every morning we set out singing. I had told the Roadsoul girl that I did not know any songs, yet now it seemed I heard a song at every turn. And at every turn the same story about the Black Boot king, or some version of it.

Not far beyond Marga's I walked and bantered awhile alongside a Weedrun boy my own age. He was merry; he let me string his bow so I could feel the satisfying *thuck* when the bowstring slipped into the nock. But when I told him I was going to Downshore, he looked fierce and said, "I hear it's not so good in that place."

"Not so good as what?"

"As it was."

As it was when? I remembered Mailin's house, smelling of biscuits, a basket of kittens on the hearth. How could anything be better than that? I thought of Nall on that hearth, pulling me down to a kiss. My heart gave a soft lurch. I said, "What's the matter with it?"

"Black Boots, they say."

"The Black Boots live in Upslope, not Downshore."

"I heard there's a plague of them in Downshore, like rats. And a big king rat." Whipping imaginary arrows from his quiver, he shot the empty air—*thip! thip!* "Let those Shorefolk eat rats! If the Black Boots stepped outside the market in Weedrun, we'd skewer them. We'd throw them to the snakes." He pushed down his sash a little to show me the serpent tattooed around his hips, like a Creek man's, but a different pattern. "There's my sign, darling. Show me yours."

He wanted to see the breast tattoos all Creek girls wear—all but me—so he could know what clan I was and whether it would be right to keep on courting me.

"No," I said.

"Are you married, then?"

"No."

He looked confused and edged away, though he turned back once and made a kissy-mouth.

I pulled up the neck of my blouse. We traveled westward and downward, following the river.

I spent one night in Lilygate at the home of Erissilie, a

wise, wiry woman who lived in a house with painted lintels.

"Who will you go to in Downshore?" she asked me next morning, as we walked back to the carts.

"To Mailin. A healer."

"Is she a relative?"

"A friend."

"You'll want friends there. Downshore has troubles."

It was one thing to hear this from a spotty-faced Weedrun boy, but when I heard it from this quick woman, my heart chilled. "Has something happened?"

"Only the usual." She made a scornful face. "Black Boots! If they stay within bounds, they're a blessing of sorts; but when they multiply, they're like leeches on a body. Downshore is the body."

I fell silent. I did not want her to know I was a League-man's child.

"Tariffs and taxes and fees," she said. "And those strutting road guards! I didn't travel to the Long Night dance this year, for I couldn't bear to deal with them. There'll be few dancers this Least Night."

At least she was not going on about demon kings. And nothing she complained of was new. In my father's house, as I cooked and sewed and cleaned, I had overheard conversations and thought nothing of them: such-and-such native beaten for striking a paidman at the tariff booth; so-and-so of Downshore evicted from his fields for failure to pay a debt. I had paid little attention. They were just natives. My task was to darn my father's socks. Now it occurred to me that the people being beaten and evicted would be Mailin and Dai. And Nall.

"On the coast the Leaguemen are everywhere, like roaches," said Erissilie. "Any house may have a few, but it's bad housekeeping that makes them swarm."

I smiled and thanked her and climbed into the cart. But that evening, when we came to Stonehallow, my eyes were sharpened. It was a market town like Ten Orchards, with many little shops, and everywhere I saw signs of the Leaguemen: windows dressed with mirrors and silk ribbons, all overpriced; casks of foreign rum; milled and printed linen. Yet who would not yearn for those things, in a little town where otherwise a girl's showiest kerchief would be dyed with berry juice? But nobody seemed unhappy, and the rum sold briskly.

In Stonehallow I stayed at Hamarry's house. Hamarry was old, she smelled fusty and had a pet ferret even fustier. Her knuckles were red with arthritis, but she could knit like lightning, shouting at the reluctant children who had been sent to clean her house. I cleaned too, because the children were no good at it.

She said nothing about the Black Boots. "That's it, that's it!" she said, her needles clicking like crickets. "Erissilie-Marga-Beshko's sister-friend, Bian-from-Creek, she's your aunt? I heard she married some hunter, well, they all marry hunters, so did I, ha! You're just as foolish I expect, young girls are, some lad catches your eye and there's your whole life gone, snap, a lap full of babies and grandbabies and it's all over, you're an old woman knitting at the hearth and that's it, that's it!"

I could not wait to get out of there. She shrank my whole life to the size of a poppy seed, and ate it. And the ferret stank; I could still smell him on my blouse the next day though I washed my clothes, hung them to dry, and slept naked under a ferrety quilt.

I walked on with the carts. I spent a night in Marsh, where there was no marsh, and a night in Towers, where there were spires of black stone riddled with holes like gassy cheese, with flocks of birds living in them. Everywhere it was Black Boots this and Leaguemen that—I got sick of it. We came to the coastal hills. We began to see hardy northern olive trees, and voices had a round, soft sound like Downshore's, like Nall's.

The weather grew warmer. For traveling Bian had sewn me a new undershift, rabbit brown, with a pocket for valuables (but I had none); as the heat increased, I wished I could skin off skirt and blouse and walk in nothing but my shift and the deer mouse sash.

By now I hated to tell anyone I was going to Downshore. But it was not possible to lie, so I had to listen to the Black Boots' every sin—how they had raised the road tolls, sold shoddy linen, and watered the rum for sale at Long Night. I could not see how weaker rum would make for a worse night.

Sooner or later the story always came out, patched and strange, that the lord of the Leaguemen had been defiled by a sea monster, or that a water demon had snatched away his daughter—such wild reports that at last I thought, *Someone has heard that awful chant of fat old Olashya's and has made a tall tale of it.*

This consoled me, but it reminded me how much I did not want to see any of my Upslope relatives. I was so lonely with traveling that it was not Nall I yearned for, but Dai, to make the crazy world right.

At last I came to Loyeme's house in Fenno Pass. Before I knew it, I had an apron on, a ladle in my hand, and a two-year-old drooling on my leg. We were getting supper, and there was no time, in that busy kitchen, to make up lies about the Black Boots.

4

The things the heart tosses forth
Are polished like brook stones,
Semiprecious like amber.
No king would war over them—
They don't have that glitter—
But a child would carry them pocketed
From full to slender moon,
And guard them in a wooden box forever.

Year Altar Song. By Nondany, Downshore.

LOYEME HAD A SECOND GUEST, a man going home to Downshore.

When I heard this, I was all terror and hope. Maybe he knew Nall? For all Downshore had heard about him, the man who came out of the sea.

But Nondany, as the other traveler was called, had been gone from Downshore even longer than I. It was only after some trouble that I got even that much out of him, because he was on the floor knee-to-knee with Meg, Loyeme's little daughter, playing hand slaps.

"*I* know one," the girl said.

> The miller had a goose, goose, goose,
> And the goose got loose, loose, loose . . .

And they were off, slapping hands and thighs and elbows, so funny! He knew dozens of them and was quicker than she was. He was a tiny man with a round body and spindly legs, not old like Hamarry, but not young. "Here's one for you, Meg," he said. "It's from the mill town of Rett."

I listened. I had been born in Rett.

> Night and day, bright or black,
> Shuttle and heddle go *klik-klek-klak* . . .

It went on for many verses. I liked the goose song better, but Meg loved this one because it had a part where you cuff your partner's ears. She would have played it all night, but her mother herded her off wailing.

Nondany got up off the floor, dusted his knees—he wore a Downshoreman's short pants—and bumbled across the room to his luggage. Opening a battered case, he took from it a box, and from the box a quill, ink in a corked bottle, and a sheaf of fine, thin paper. I saw the page, dense with writing and with designs and diagrams like tattoos. Murmuring, his nose an inch from the sheet, he wrote among what he had already written and up into the margin. Nodded. Wiped pen, corked bottle, folded paper, and put it all away.

I thought he must be a holy man of some sort, making

religious notations. I would have asked Loyeme, but she was putting the children to bed, so I said right out, "Sir, what are you writing?"

He squinted at me, wiping his inky hands on his tunic. "That shuttle song from Rett. I've known it for years, I don't know why I never wrote it down before."

It was a hand slap. Why should anybody write it down? I said cautiously, "I was born in Rett."

"Were you! Kat is your name, am I right? Did you sing that song?"

As if I had been allowed to sing anything! "No. We left when I was five."

"The perfect age, five," said Nondany. "Teeming with songs. But *what* you sang would depend on which sector of Rett you lived in, of course. If your playmates were Mill children, or the children of Roadsouls or artisans from Welling—the hand slaps are quite different for each group. Leaguemen have the fewest, as you can imagine." I blushed, thinking he had guessed my parentage, but all he said was, "It has been terribly difficult to learn League children's games. A tragedy, really."

He talked half to himself, as extremely nearsighted people sometimes do—as though the rest of the world were not quite real. His face was wistful.

I said, "I know one."

"A hand slap from Rett?"

"From the Leaguemen."

"By life! You do? What is it? Will you teach me?" He was back on the floor, cross-legged and slapping his thighs, looking like a child on his birthday.

Feeling foolish, I sat down too. It was a plain slap, no ears or elbows, but my hands remembered it. His hands matched mine magically. I thought I might have forgotten the words, but as I slapped, my mouth remembered them.

> Asked your father for a penny.
> *Go away! I haven't any!*
> Asked your father for your hand.
> *Give me gold and give me land!*
> Gave your father seven acres.
> *Kiss her! Keep her! Tie her! Take her!*

As I spoke that last line I was tiny again, taking for granted that fathers sell their daughters. My eyes stung with tears.

At my quaver Nondany cocked his head, peering at the blur my face must have been to him. He put his small, firm hand on my knee. "These songs are what we sing while we are making our souls. Do you wonder that I love them?"

"I'm a Leagueman's child," I said, for the first time on this journey. "But only half."

"What's the other half?"

"Creek."

"And the other half?"

I stared at him.

"And the half besides that? And besides that?" His face was merry. He patted invitingly at the air between us. I put up my hands and he sang, slapping them.

> One for the hurdy-gurdy,
> Two for the show,
> Three for the fiddle-player,
> Four for the—*No, no!*
> Over to the shimmy-dancer!

Over to the queen!
In comes Kat with a tambourine!
The milk's in the cow
And the honey's in the hive,
In she goes,
Out she goes,
Five, five, five,
And a six, and a seven,
And Kat stole the leaven
And the bread won't rise!
Speak no lies
And an eight, and a nine,
And you can't have mine,
And a ten!
Hen!
Shout it all over again!
Dance, old lady!

It was a fancy one! Elbow slaps and ear cuffs and nose tweaks, he did it over till I had it, then faster and faster, we laughed so hard that little Meg in her nightshift ran out crying, "Why didn't you invite *me*?"

So we had to teach it to her, until she was mollified and would go back to bed. Then Nondany turned to me and said, "Properly, that's a skipping rhyme, from Downshore. But it's played as a hand slap when the weather's too wet for skipping."

"What did you mean, all my halves? I only have two halves."

"Is that so? Lucky you. Most of us have more than *ten! Hen! Shout it all over again!*" he sang, tweaking my nose at the right place. "I think I have an infinite number. So many that I have to take notes, or I lose track of them. Sing me that Leaguemen's slap again, Half-and-Half, so I've got it right."

He got out his ink bottle. I recited the words, and this time they did not bother me. He wove them into his overwritten page like a house spider repairing its web.

"I wrote a song on a bowl once," I said.

"And why did you do that?" he asked, wiping his hands on his tunic.

"I was trying to keep it."

"Did it work?"

"It wasn't the same as the song was, singing." It had been its own thing, though. I tried to put that feeling into words, but I could not think of any except, "The clay spiraled up, and the words spiraled down."

"What was in the bowl?"

"Nothing."

He peered at me, stroking his chin. But all he said was, "Would you sing me the song you wrote on the bowl?"

I did. He wrote it down. I said, "Are you writing down all the songs in the world?"

"Only my share of them. Whatever the sea casts up to me. I'm a beachcomber, you might say."

I wanted to tell him the sea had cast up a man to me, and that man was a singer. But I did not dare. Anyway, Nall's songs had felt magical and important, but Nondany, it seemed, liked nursery rhymes.

"Teach me another Leaguemen's chant," he said greedily, rubbing his hands.

Of course then I could not think of any, only the common sayings that my auntie Jerash would rap out, like,

Love dreams, but money buys land or *Children's tears mean
nothing*. To my surprise he liked these just as well and
wrote them down too. I looked over his shoulder and I saw
that his drawings were indeed tattoo designs from this
town or that, even a whole line of Roadsouls' hand tattoos,
and some embroidery patterns and face paintings, and
two sketches of painted lintels like Erissilie's in Lilygate.
It seemed he was interested in everything. Yet he never
asked how I came to be half-and-half, a Leagueman's child
dressed like a Hillwoman.

When he had put up his ink again, he opened the battered case he had sat on. From a nest made of his spare clothing he took a lute sort of instrument that had a round belly
like his own.

He settled it on his knee like a baby. It looked old; it had
wooden strakes like a boat and wave shapes inlaid between
the frets. He leaned his ear toward it and, softly, plucked
two strings.

Bee-hum and wind and sorrow, made music. It hung in
the air. I had never heard a sound like that.

"Oh, sir," I said, "what is it?"

"My *dindarion*. You like it?" Quiet as moths at a window, his
fingers moved on the strings and a little melody came wandering, as if it had found its way into the room from the night
outside.

I swear the fire burned more quietly while he played. He
put his hand on the strings to hush them, then held out the
dindarion to me.

I leaned back, as if it were holy, or dangerous. "I can't
play," I said.

"Oh, I know. But feel it."

I took it in my hands. It was light as a blown egg.

"It is older than I am by far," he said. "Can you guess what it's made of?"

I felt ignorant. "Wood?"

"A bit of wood, yes. But look in the sounding hole and tell me what you see."

I looked. "Nothing," I said, stupider still.

He nodded. "That is the most important feature of a dindarion. And of a bowl." He took the instrument from me and laid it back in its nest. "No songs tonight; we'd have Meg out of her bed again."

The truth was that he wanted more League hand slaps. But after that sweet melody everything I could remember seemed so awful that I pretended I had forgotten them all. Then, when the stars peeked through the window, I thought of a circle game I had played with my cousins. Even the boys played it.

> Along came a king on a big white horse,
> He asked for the eldest, it was "Yes, of course."
> Along came a prince in a great gold carriage,
> He asked for the youngest, it was love and marriage.
> Along came a beggar boy, ragged and brown,
> And asked for the middle one.
> They kicked him up and down,
> They said, "You shan't have our daughter,
> Nor any food or water,
> Not a snip, not a speck,
> But a swift hard kick
> And a stretched neck!
> *Hang him!*"

Then, in a whisper:

> *But the beggar boy had the moon for his white mare,*
> *And he bore her away weeping.*

Those last lines had always made me shiver and yearn, with a kind of foreboding; yet it was only a nursery rhyme.

Nondany was ecstatic. "You're going to Downshore too, are you not?" he asked when he had written it down. "I'll look you up. By life, surely you know more Leaguemen's rhymes!"

"I'll be staying with Mailin, the healer. Do you know her?"

He beamed like the sun. "Of course! How right! I'm in and out of Mailin's house all the time. My dear Mailin!"

We sat in satisfying silence. The fire snapped in the grate. Around us Loyeme's family made tinkering sounds and soft talk as they came in from their chores.

Nondany said, "There's a Rig at Mailin's house."

All the blood in my body went to my heart. Then to my face. I said, "A Rig?"

"A seal man, from the westernmost isles. I was in Welling-in-the-Mountains when I heard the rumor, and I thought, I'll go downriver to Rett, then work my way through the Hill towns, gleaning my bits and pieces, and so back to Downshore."

He leaned back. "Think of it! There hasn't been a Rig come ashore in years. They used to come in their boats to the great festivals, Long Night and Least Night—and why not, when those celebrations were theirs in the first place? The Rigi founded Downshore, if we are to believe the songs."

He spoke happily, like a storyteller who has found a new audience. And he had; I listened as though my very skin had ears.

"There are plenty of Rig relatives in Downshore still," he said. "There's even a Seal clan; Mailin is a Seal. The clans and moieties are mostly those of the shore tribes now—I'm a Badger myself—but in the beginning, they say, Downshore was all Rig, and the Rigi traveled between Downshore and the islands as if the great sea were a highway. Rig men wed mainland girls and vice versa; until the Exile, they did. You know about the Exile?"

I made no answer. He took this as an invitation to tell the story. "Some four generations ago it was. Maybe less. Downshore had begun to kill seals and sell the skins to the Leaguemen. There was bad blood over that, you can imagine! To the Rigi those seals are their ancestors and relatives, and those skins the most sacred link between human and seal. Yet here were the Downshore sealers, selling them to the League to make hearth rugs and ladies' coats! Such an uproar in the clans and fighting in the council! And the sealers hearing only the clink of coin.

"Then one Long Night a gang of League lads, drunk, killed a Rig and stole his skin—his ceremonial sealskin, that is, embroidered in silver and jet. To the Rigi that was like stealing his soul. Without his skin, when he died, how could he return to his ancestors and be once more a seal?

"So that was that. The Rigi got into their boats; they were off through the surf and west-away. Of the full-bloods, only a few who had married stayed in Downshore. Since that hour the Rigi haven't come to the mainland, and the main-landers haven't gone to them. In fact, if tales be true, the Rigi have put a bit of magic round themselves—a barrier of sorts. Magic," said Nondany, like a man contemplating a good dinner. "As if anybody knows what magic is. But how I do natter on. You'll know all this already." He squinted at me. "Or, given your parentage, possibly you don't?"

"I know a little," I said. "But the Rig, he's at Mailin's? Still? He's alive? You heard that?"

Nearsighted or not, Nondany gave me a sharp look. "A rumor. Reliable source, but a rumor. I don't know why people won't learn to write, it keeps the message exact."

"What did— How did the rumor go?"

"That a Downshore girl had sung a Rig out of the sea. The girl ran away, but the Rig stayed, at a healer's house. That was all. The healer in Downshore is Mailin." He looked out the window at the stars. "They say that when a Rig comes ashore, you can count on either luck or storms. That is called an understatement. Downshore has been spoiling for a storm for some years now; by all reports the weather is thickening as we speak. Mailin's house would be a safe place for him. I've never met a Rig. Maybe he knows some hand slaps."

"But he's alive!"

"I gather you've heard about him?"

"Gossip," I said with a gasp.

Nondany peered. Opened his mouth, shut it, sighed. "How old are you?"

"Seventeen."

"I wish I were seventeen, and at Mailin's house, and a Rig there. However, I am not. So I'll come to Mailin's house anyway. I look forward to knowing you better, Half-and-Half." He stood up and stretched his little toad body. "Good night. We'll talk in the morning. You are delightful."

I went to bed on a pallet on the floor of Meg's room, but I did not sleep. Nall was at Mailin's house, and I was the girl who had called him, and news of the two of us had reached as far as Welling-in-the-Mountains.

5

It is not a flower,
but something in me
parts its mouth to morning,
shuts its heart to heat.
And something deeper,
noon or dewfall,
opens,
inexorable
as a rose.

Gardener's Year Altar Poem. Downshore.

OF COURSE THE NEXT DAY I wanted to travel with Nondany and
made sure our bundles were put in the same cart. Mine held
little more than a few clothes and a lidded crock I had made
myself and filled with wild honey for Nall.

There were three goats in the cart that would have loved to
put their noses in the honey. "No you don't, my dears," said
Nondany, checking their tethers. He tilted a board to make a

goat-proof corner in the cart and put my bundle behind his knapsack and the case with the dindarion in it, then climbed out over the wheel. Like me, he preferred walking to being jolted all day, and his legs, though scrawny, were strong.

He was the nicest man I had ever met, and the oddest. He could not see beyond the end of his arm, but his blindness was not darkness, like Raím's. To him the larger world was only moving color; yet little, close things—children and their songs, the finger games they played, the toys and tokens of people small and big—these he saw and loved so clearly that they were, for him, the same as the big world.

He got a pebble in his shoe as we walked in the chill mountain morning and had to stop and take it out. It was the size of a bean, but he held it up to his eye and said, "Here's a pretty one!"

He gave it to me to look at. It was red, with a band of crystal round it. He took it back and put it in his pocket. "For my Year Altar. To remind me that sometimes, at least, what lames me is beautiful."

"What's a Year Altar?"

"How does it happen that you know Mailin, but not what a Year Altar is?"

I had said little about myself. I did not want him to guess I was the runaway girl of the rumor. Maybe I was afraid he would laugh and say, "You, little Half-and-Half? *You* called a Rig out of the sea?"

I looked away, saying, "I went to the Long Night dance, year before last." Plenty of Hillwomen go to the Long Night dance.

He squinted at me. But he did that all the time, trying to bring the world into focus. "Then you understand about the Year Fire?"

"You throw things into it. Things you're done with." I had thrown my cumbersome old name, Katyesha Marashya N'Ab Drem, into that fire.

"That's it. And a Year Altar is made of things, or tokens of things, that will be thrown into the fire when Long Night comes. Watch for those altars in Downshore, Half-and-Half; you'll find them at the threshold of each dwelling. With a candle at least, maybe a toy boat, a doll, a pebble—whatever. Odd and pretty things. You'll like them."

"We had an altar like that in Creek. But it wasn't holy, just a place to put things we liked: flowers, and my cousin's baby teeth when they fell out, and a hummingbird's nest. We never burned them. Just, every so often my aunt would say, 'This clutter's been here long enough!' and she'd clean it away. Then we'd start collecting all over again."

"It's the same principle," said Nondany. "Pulling things into a pattern of sorts. A little temporary weaving of the countless threads."

I stared. How could he know about what I had felt when I was the Bear—that the world was a loom of countless threads in wordless order? But all I saw was a little dusty man, trudging and smiling.

I said carefully, "Threads of what?"

"'Threads of what,' she asks. My dear, if I could answer that, I could tell you what the universe is made of. I'd know whether we're formed from the Light and the Dark in a death struggle, as the Leaguemen think; or knit from the breath of the Great Snake, which is what they believe down south in Enillara; or hawked up by a cat, as I was recently informed by a six-year-old in Bream. Roadsouls call the world's beginning the Big Fart—but who'd believe a Roadsoul?"

The man could have been bawling like a calf for all the sense
he made. Yet, listening, I felt the way I had when I had run on
the mountain: that the world was not narrow, as Bian or my
father saw it, but teeming, multiple, intertwining. Yet I could
not grasp an understanding that would stay, only fleeting bits.

"I'm bewildering you," said Nondany.

"Yes. No. Yes," I said. "I like it."

"I don't mean there are actual threads. I am saying that
this world, which I don't understand, reminds me of a loom,
which I do."

"What *are* you?" I said. "A weaver?"

"In a way. I collect and organize, as a weaver does. I collect
songs—among other things. I locate them." He waved his
hands vaguely. "I *recognize* them."

At that he fell smack over a stone. I helped him up, thinking he would not recognize a king's crown unless he banged
his head on it.

He dusted his elbows. We trotted to catch up with the cart,
where, in its case in the goat-proof pen, the dindarion hummed
faintly with every jolt. "And what are *you*, Half-and-Half?"

"Seventeen," I said.

"True—until you're eighteen. I should say rather: What is
your calling?"

Nall was my calling. But Nondany had meant my work, so
I said, "I don't know."

"A chickenhearted answer."

"Well, I *don't* know! I can paint pots. I can scrub floors. I
can make cream dill sauce."

"What do you like to do?"

"Paint pots. Scrub floors. Make cream dill sauce."

"Well enough," he said, laughing. "Curiosity is my virtue

and my curse. If you like whatever you do, you'll have a happy life."

After a moment I said, "I liked that bowl I made. The one I told you about."

"I could see your pleasure."

"It wasn't just the bowl, though. I mean, it was a bowl, but—" It was a bowl the way what had devoured me was the Bear, the way the shivery song about the beggar boy was a children's game: because there was no other name for it. But it was not the truth.

"Why do I have to *be* anything in particular?" I said, stamping in the dust. "When I die, I'll be thrown in the fire, same as that Year Altar clutter!"

Nondany clutched his head, gingery and balding, and danced about as if he were trying to pull it off. "By life! My brain is too crowded—I should throw it into the Year Fire! Half-and-Half, what can I put on the Year Altar to stand for my brain?"

"Your papers," I said, laughing again. "You write everything down; doesn't that empty out your brain? Throw your papers in the fire!"

He gave me a look I could not read. "Someday they'll burn. This earth is old, and nothing lasts forever, not even children and their songs. But that time is not yet, I hope."

On the low branch of an ash tree I saw an empty wasps' nest, round and weightless as paper. I fetched it down and gave it to him, to stand for his brain.

"Perfect! Perfect!" he said. "Onto my altar it goes!"

I did not tell him I thought he kept those songs not on paper or even in his brain, but in his heart. I told him about Dai instead. To speak of Dai made me feel the way I had when I milked his cow, Moss, in the winter darkness: quiet, patient, safe.

"He's learning to be a healer of animals," I said. "Mailin and her man, Pao, are teaching him."

"Is he waiting for you at Mailin's?" Nondany balanced the wasps' nest on three fingers as he walked beside the cart.

"He doesn't know I'm coming. Nobody does. It's a surprise."

"Surprises are good. But if things get too surprising, Half-and-Half, you're welcome at my sister's house. Her name is Lilliena. Ask for her at the Downshore market."

I nodded. I would not admit even to myself that I was grateful. We walked on without speaking, Nondany whistling softly through his teeth. I was thinking about Nall's mouth with its broken tooth, and what it looked like smiling, when I caught a snatch of that whistling. It was the Rigi's song.

Instantly I was blushing and hot. Nondany slid a glance at me, grinning like a kid. He kept whistling, kept walking, his brain in his hand.

The road spent all day winding up, winding down, winding up again through ragged hills. Outside of Golden, my last overnight, we were overtaken by another pack train, headed for Downshore this time, the mules unladen and traveling fast.

This time I knew one of the Leaguemen, Ab Lesh, a broad, hard man who hit his wife. I had minded his children some-times. He had rarely been home, and when he was, he had surely never noticed the nursemaid; but now, when he passed on his big mule, I thought he looked at me and looked again. But he went back to picking at his nails with a pocketknife.

I thought of his little daughter rocking her doll, whispering in her soft voice the lullaby her mother had whispered to her.

> Father's gone. He'll come home.
> If he sees you crying, you'll be sorry.
> If you snivel, you little lout,
> He'll give you something to cry about.

When the train had passed our caravan, the words "Black Boots" ran from mouth to mouth, along with many stories that I tried not to listen to, about how Least Night was spoiled, and what person of sensibility could tolerate it, and so on. I noticed, though, that even the most resentful wore shop-bought ribbons.

I taught the lullaby to Nondany. I was ashamed of it, but he loved it and said he would write it down that night. He was to stay in a different house, and in the field where the caravan camped he hugged me, promised to see me in the morning, and went off with his case and knapsack, whistling.

I sought the house of Milis, so weary and anxious that I could hardly drag my feet. Its portico was a grape arbor, where a little girl sat singing to a grubby cloth doll. Her lullaby was so much kinder than mine that, tired as I was, I fell into despair about my parentage, feeling that my very blood was spoiled.

Milis was harried and worried. Her oldest boy had a cough, a weasel had taken her yellow hen, and, right before I got there, the uncle of a second cousin had appeared with a cartload of caged, indignant turkeys, expecting to be fed and housed on his way to the Least Night market, like me.

"I'll sleep in the barn," I said, near tears. "Please don't be troubled! I'll be gone before breakfast."

"The barn! Don't think of it. Let that old man sleep out there. I never could bear him—he's owed Arthes a month's work for fifteen years, and now he's too old to do it. He'll carry you to Downshore, if you can stand the smell of him. Let him square the debt that way. If his cargo were yellow hens, one would be mine!"

The old man's name was Jake. He had red eyes, a week's beard, and not many teeth, and he mumbled his corn bread. When Milis told him I would be his passenger, he glared. I thought, I'll spend the day walking with Nondany, thank you.

But out of courtesy to Milis, I agreed to put my bundle in Jake's cart. What did I care? Tomorrow night I would be in Downshore.

I washed the dinner dishes for Milis, feeling frightened and strange. I would not think about Nall. I thought about Dai instead, his bearded face with its doubting, patient look.

Milis snapped around like a sheepdog, herding her family into a bunch and keeping them there. The boy was dosed for his cough, the girl put to bed with her doll, the husband scolded for muddy feet though there had not been a drop of rain all week. The dog itself slunk out to sleep in the barn with Jake. Milis herded me with the rest, putting me to bed with the little girl as if I were a bigger doll.

"You just be careful down there," she said. "I've had a word with Jake; he knows there's a new toll on the road, but he won't believe how much. He'll learn soon enough."

"There was a toll when Bian and I left Downshore. After Long Night, two years ago."

"That's when this all began. Those Black Boots, they'll lay on taxes and pop debtors into jail however they like, who's to stop them? They've got the money. But not like it's been this last while—this last week, even. Road guards, indeed! Murderers, more like. Who'll argue with a knife? They're careful who they pick on, but it's a fist tightening, a cruel fist. That man!"

As she spoke, Milis flashed about the room, dusting here, tucking there, as if she could fix the world by tidying it. Her daughter watched her from under the coverlet, big-eyed.

"That man!" she said again. I thought she meant Jake until she added, "He knows the people must get to the shore and dance Least Night and sing the songs, or what will happen to the sun? We must dance for it. He's twisting the screws tighter and tighter. What will happen to us?"

"Who's twisting the screws?"

"That madman in Upslope, Ab Harlot."

A creeping cold went through me. They pronounced it differently in Golden, but it could only be Ab Harlan, the Leagueman to whom my father had sold me.

"A Rig came out of the sea," said Milis. "He stole the bride of Ab Harlot's son and carried her off to be his queen under the waves—that's what they say—and Ab Harlot's gone mad with rage. It's Downshore he's punishing, worse every day. I wouldn't go there, daughter. You have your reasons, I'm sure, but if I were you, I'd turn right round and go back the way I came."

Here Milis seemed to see me for the first time. She pushed back her hair and said, "Well, *I'm* in a fit! I need a rug to beat. Go well, daughter. But mind what I say."

She left, quick as a hummingbird. Her little girl, for comfort, held up her dolly and whispered, "Sing to my baby."

"Your song is nicest," I said, when I could speak.

She sang in her little froggy voice.

> I love the sun, I love you.
> I love the moon, I love you.
> I love the dew on the green thorn.
> At the moment you were born,
> Sun and moon and thorn were born—
> Born to laugh and born to mourn.
> O love, o grief! I love you.

I thought, I must remember that for Nondany.

That was all I could think. My mind did not want the rest of it, that I had become the queen of a hundred stories, stolen from a devil king and carried away under the sea by a Rig, or by a sea monster or a water demon—by Nall, whatever he was. When in fact I had been in Creek, making pottery and tending goats.

"I know somebody who will like your song," I told the child.

"Me," she said, and yawned, shutting her eyes.

I patted her to sleep and turned on my side. At first I could not sleep, thinking of the morrow. Then I slept, and dreamed.

I dreamed a fire. In it a child lay crying and burning, lifting up its arms to me. I snatched it out. Fire burst from its back. But it crowed, it patted my face with cool baby hands, and I saw that what flickered at its nape were not flames, but wings.

6

A woman's *no* means *yes*.
Woman and rug are the better for a drubbing.
Pain is the surest teacher.

Sayings. Upslope.

I WOKE SHIVERING and clambered into damp clothes, tying the deer mouse sash. The air was cold and dewy and smelled of pines. I could feel how high up I was, among the coastal mountains, so that the day must be spent going down and down and down.

But first it was spent catching Jake's turkeys. Four of

them—there were twenty-eight in all—had gotten out in the
night. One was gone forever, for whatever had eaten it had
left only the feathery pelt, with feet still attached. The other
three had to be searched for. Stinking Jake cursed in his Hill
dialect, Milis bewailed and compared the death of her hen,
neighbors sympathized.

Meanwhile the caravan began to leave, and Nondany
with it. "See you on the road, Half-and-Half!" he said, laughing, and recited a rude rhyme about jailbreak. It was only
when their plume of dust had grown puny with distance that
we found two more turkeys staring stupidly at each other in
a corncrib. We grabbed them, stuffed them into their mended
cage, and carried them on toward their fate at the market,
leaving the last one to the foxes.

Sweaty and harried, I thanked Milis and slung my bundle
under the cart seat. Jake beat the mules' bony haunches with
a switch, but they plodded slow as beetles. Each time we
drew near enough to see the other carts beneath their plume
of dust, the mules slowed to a creep, flapped their ears, and
jerked at their traces, right and left.

"Demon spawn!" cried Jake. "Can't you go but in circles?"
For they had spent their days walking a mill wheel round
and did not know how to walk a straight line.

I was beside myself, stuck with this stinking uncle while
the caravan, with Nondany and his merry talk, dwindled
ahead of us. I would have run ahead and walked with them
anyhow, but the way began to go steeply down, and there
were places where I had to swing on the wooden brake to
keep the cart from overtaking the mules.

Being small and light, I had to hang off the brake lever
like a monkey off a mountebank's arm. The turkeys

crooned hopelessly. Jake's curses began to sound like a chant, almost religious.

> Ho, *Dop!*
> You reeking wart-mouth witch!
> Ho, *Ben!*
> You flap of rotten meat!
> You walleyed, pig-faced tripes!
> You flyblown carrion!
> Get up! *Get* up! *Move,*
> You fox-bait, lick-shit, scum-dog, louse-hung mules!
> *Dop!*
> *Ben!*

We had to go carefully, and on the flat stretches we were still behind. We nearly caught up at noonday, in a canyon by a waterfall, but the rest had already watered their stock and were ready to set out on the last long descent to the coast.

I spoke with Nondany for a moment. "Don't fret," he said. "You're right behind us. There'll be plenty of time for talk at Mailin's house."

"Don't tell them I'm coming!"

He put his finger to his lips and was off, waving, as we watered Dop and Ben.

Then a turkey got out. We chased it here and there among the rocks, both Jake and the turkey cursing. I all but killed it, tackling it, and did not care.

"Young girls have no respect for creatures," said Jake, jailing it again.

"We ought to keep up with the others."

"Young girls haven't a fly's patience."

We hurried to catch up, hurried to slow down for the hill. The turkeys gabbled *Fire! Murder! Fire!* and if I had had a hatchet, I would have chopped their heads off then and there. The sun sloped west. We were still in the dim canyon, far behind the rest, when, at a narrow turning, I felt the sea.

The air changed. It had been dry, the Hill air I had grown used to. All in a moment the breeze went moist and soft, like a hand laid against me. I smelled salt and iodine, fish and weed, the coast and all that dwells there—its countless lives.

I could see only the canyon walls, jerking as we jolted over the ruts. Then we rounded a great boulder and the air brightened, as if we had been in a box and it had opened.

Far below lay the narrow plain and bleak outbuildings of Upslope, widely scattered, though clumped a little closer around the Rulesward and Ab Harlan's estate. A mile or so west of the settlement the land dropped in broken, half-grassy cliffs to the strip of green seacoast and Downshore's untidy sprawl, where hearth smoke rose. Beyond Downshore, still and shining, lay the sea.

I forgot to hang on the brake and stood up, shading my eyes.

The cart lurched forward; its weight pushed the mules faster and faster, like prisoners hustled by a guard.

"*Ho,* Ben! *Ho,* Dop! *Ho!*"

Stones flew, the cart walloped and banged, the turkeys shrieked and despaired. Jake hauled at the reins, and I hung on the lever till white smoke curled from the brake block. We careened around two steep corners and into a straightaway, long and rutted, missed a cliff's edge by inches, and jangled to a halt in a briar bank.

The mules hunkered, twitching and blowing, dust settling on their ears.

In a whisper I said, "I'm sorry, sir."

Jake got down, stalked to the back of the cart, and checked each wheel, each cage. The turkeys sobbed *boo-hoo, boo-hoo,* wagging their wattles. A wisp of dust far below was the caravan, leaving us behind.

"I'm sorry. I saw the sea and forgot about the brake."

"Young girls will dream," said Jake, climbing back onto the cart. Grinding my teeth, I ducked under the seat to check my bundle. The honey crock was unbroken. I stood up and retied the deer mouse sash.

"Young girls will primp and preen," said Jake. "Get up, mules."

I went back to my post at the brake. I did not forget it again, though I stared at the sea with new eyes, Hill eyes, thinking, The ocean is a prairie. You could travel on it, far and away to the end of the world.

We rattled down switchback after switchback, the distant water glinting and changing until we reached the plain and it hid itself beyond the cliffs. I crept up to sit beside Jake, sweaty and trembling, with blistered hands. I had forgotten how ashamed of myself I was supposed to be and said, "We're nearly to Downshore!"

"Young girls will jump first, look second."

I did not care what he thought, the withered old crank! "Well, *I'll* be glad to get there."

As if our bucketing ride had jarred him into speech, he said, "I got to live. Means I got to sell them turkeys. Means I got to deal with the devil, but I ain't in a hurry to do it."

"The devil?"

"Hurling. Him and his deputy."

"Hurling?"

"Young girls think they're wise."

"Please, sir—"

"That Leagueman felly, Ab Hurling. The one looks like a maggot."

Would I never hear the last of him? "Ab Harlan never goes to Downshore."

"And where must we pass through to get to Downshore, little miss? And who owns the road guards?"

I said nothing.

"Give me a chance to beat one of them vermin, it'd be worth anything they could do to me," said Jake, under his breath.

I looked at that old stinking man and shivered worse and differently than I yet had at Ab Harlan's name. "What *have* they done?" I said. "Harlan and his deputy—who's his deputy?" For surely I would know who it was, as I had known Ab Lesh.

"Better you don't know too much. If they ask you anything, play stupid."

"If *who* asks me anything?"

"Anybody."

I did not think Jake was as ignorant as Milis had supposed. But weariness and fear made me angry. What, was I to turn around and walk back to Golden?

The sun was near setting. We drove right into it, shading our eyes. The highway, crossing the north edge of Upslope, was empty except for one cart, not of our caravan; a distant herd of cattle; and, wearing nothing but a pink shirt too short for him, a small boy who flapped a stem of grass at a nanny and her kid. A Downshore child; an Upslope boy would never herd goats.

"You'd think there'd be more people about," I said. "With Least Night so near."

"Who wants to meddle with Ab Hurling? And there's the curfew: All travelers to be off the road by dusk."

"What happens if we're not?"

Jake pointed with his chin.

Seen now from the level, Upslope's scattered stone houses lay a quarter mile south of the highway, each with its kitchen garden. I could pick out the homes of my uncles, Ab Jerash and Ab Seroy, and that of my father—my own—far away south, a speck at the edge of the cliffs. In the middle of the settlement stood Ab Harlan's walled estate, a little city of mansion and warehouses, the accounting hall, the Rulesward. In front of its high, spiked gates sprawled something new: an army camp—dozens of dirty canvas tents, their cookfires smoking. I saw the glint of pikes.

"Got to have his road guards," said Jake.

"So many?"

"Guess he can afford 'em. Mostly they're bought from other places. But sometimes the press gangs'll take Downshoremen that's debtors, or that ain't paid their breath tax."

"*Press* gangs? *Breath* tax?"

"Regular little emperor they got here," said Jake. "It don't concern me. Nor you, neither, long's we're past the checkpoint by dusk. Because if we ain't, it's fines or jail."

"*Checkpoint?*"

We were coming up on an ugly wooden building with several wings, raw and new. The wagon ahead of us had stopped for an exchange that sounded angry. Something was handed across, and the wagon creaked on. The little goatherd had stopped to watch.

"Checkpoint," I said again. A road toll meant somebody to take it. If we had stayed with the caravan, there would have been a crowd, diversion, places to hide; alone with Jake, I would never pass unnoticed.

I put my hands to my hair. Should I cover it? Who might know me? What could they do?

"Wait," I said. I pulled my bundle from under the seat. "Stop. I'll get down here, this is a good place. I'll go to Downshore by the cattle paths."

He stared. "What're you sneaking about for? You in trouble?"

"No, no! The cattle paths are quicker." I stood up, gripping my bundle. The wind shifted, bringing the smell of sea, of water, weed, and bone.

The goatherd gaped. So did the fat little clerk in a white shirt who waved us forward.

The cart jerked. I sat down with a bump, my bundle in my lap.

The clerk bustled over. "Your papers," he said.

"Papers?" said Jake.

"That's right." The clerk was nobody I knew. He spoke the Plain tongue with a South Road accent.

Two paidmen armed with truncheons and dirks and short, black fighting bows lounged on benches in the low sun. They perked up and strolled over, looking for fun.

"Papers," said the clerk.

Wariness came down over Jake's face like the membrane over a reptile's eye. His voice went dull and stupid. "Un never needed no papers."

"It's a new rule. It does not apply to caravans. Drivers of

solitary carts transporting merchandise across the Upslope borders must show papers."

It would not apply to caravans, I thought, because the carters were big men and too many to bully.

The clerk's eyes had strayed to my bare ankles. In Upslope women's ankles were hidden under gray hems and black wool stockings. I tucked my dusty feet back out of sight.

He recovered himself. "Your papers. And the girl's."

"Them ain't merchandise," said Jake. "Them's turkeys. And that's my granddaughter; she was proper got, and I don't need no papers to prove it."

I stared at Jake. He glared stonily ahead.

"It's the law," said the clerk. "As of this afternoon. Show your papers. Your other options are: to turn back; to purchase said papers; or to pay a fine."

"A fine!" said Jake. His alarm was real. "I can't pay no fine. I got nothing in this world till I sell them turkeys!"

The clerk read from a folded parchment. "'All single carts crossing the borders of Upslope shall be registered. Merchandise shall be inspected, and upon it a tariff shall be paid—'"

"Tariff!"

"'—or a fine shall be levied, equal in worth to one fourth part of said merchandise—'"

"*One fourth!*"

"'—in cash or kind, payable at the guardhouse.'" The clerk folded the paper with a flourish. The mules startled and the cart jerked forward, nearly throwing me from the seat. The paidmen sniggered.

"This way," said the clerk. The guards laid hold of the

harness and led the mules plodding to the near wing of the guardhouse, where the clerk disappeared into an office and came back with a portable writing desk. He sat on a bench and laid it on his knees, opened it, got out quill, ink bottle, paper. I thought of Nondany writing down the songs of children. He would be arriving at his sister's house now, embraced and welcomed.

The clerk rolled up his cuffs, adjusted the gold ring on his forefinger. He tried another keek at my ankles. When it was unsuccessful, he scowled up at Jake and said, "Name?"

"There's never been no tariff! Not to cart turkeys to Least Night!"

"There is now. Name?"

"Jake."

"Jake what? Second name."

"The name's Jake. First, second, and nothing else. Jake what raises turkeys."

"We'll register you as Jake Turkey," said the clerk. He would ask me next. What name could I give? He raised the paper, blew on the ink. "Your granddaughter will be a Turkey as well."

I opened my mouth. "I'm—"

"Excuse me, dear. Your grandfather's name will suffice. Mister Turkey, ask the girl to stand."

Jake gaped. I did not move.

"Assessment," said the clerk. "For the tariff. Buyers and sellers both. All merchandise."

"Merchandise," said Jake.

"Come now. A pretty girl like that? At festival time? She's income. Stand up, dear, and turn around—let's have a look at you."

He leaned forward. Heat rushed to my face and arms, not from shame. I leaned forward too.

"I'll see your papers first," I said.

The paidmen roared; they slapped each other's backs as the clerk cried, "I am a customs officer! This is a border crossing! Humor is not appropriate!"

He snatched at the mules' harness and tugged them into a shambling walk. "We'll see what the deputy says about this!"

The cart jarred in the ruts, the guards ran alongside laughing, the turkeys gobbled like a host of fiends. From a safe distance the goat boy gawked.

Under the pandemonium Jake muttered to me, "You're my granddaughter. Don't forget it. They don't like women here."

I could only nod, pulling my tangled curls across my face. The cart brought up at the far wing of the building, and a gangly young man put his head out the door, open-mouthed. He had a beak nose, ash blond hair, and a bad complexion, and he wore the sober clothing of an Upslope Leagueman: white shirt, tweed jacket and trousers, high black boots. He settled his broad hat on his head, looked stern, and said, "Yes?"

He had grown. It took me two looks to know him.

But he barely glanced at me. Puzzled, then officious, he said, "State your business."

"I'll talk to the boss, sonny," said the clerk.

"He's not to be disturbed."

"Go get him. We have a violation." The clerk returned to stand beside the cart.

The boy shuffled his feet in their big boots, then took off his hat and turned it in his hands. Clutching it to his chest, he disappeared indoors. I heard his timid rap and call. "Sir?"

Jake leaned toward me. Without moving his lips he murmured, "Away with you and run."

Sweating as if in fever, I gripped my bundle. My legs tightened to jump. Yet I whispered, "No. I've already brought trouble on you."

"My life is my own. Get gone!"

"What could they do—"

"Ye stupid chit. To a *woman*?"

The boy called again. "Ab Seroy?"

No answer. Rap and call were repeated, answered at last by a muffled shout. "What the hell do you want?"

"We have a violation, sir."

"Damn it to hell!"

"Hey!" said the clerk. "Stop her!" as Jake gave me a hard shove and I half fell, half jumped down over the far wheel, and ran.

The paidmen leaped after me. But Jake slashed the reins down across the clerk's round face. "*Hup!*" he cried, and for once the mules obeyed. The cart slammed forward, knocking one man to the ground. The other leaped backward, stumbling; he recovered, dodged round the back of the cart, and in three jumps was on me like a greyhound on a rabbit, pinning my arms.

I did not struggle. He dragged me back, snatched up my bundle, and hurled it on the steps. The second guard had scrambled to his feet and caught up with the cart, had hauled Jake off the seat, and was beating him with a truncheon. The goatherd scampered off, whipping the nanny with the stem of grass.

Ab Seroy came out in his shirtsleeves, a lean man scowling with sleep, the boy at his heels.

"This had better be good," he said.

"I'm wounded!" The clerk dabbed at his cheek with a handkerchief. "The girl submitted a false identity! She attempted to effect an escape!"

"Well, well," said Ab Seroy, buttoning one pearl cuff link. "Who are you, sweetheart? And what are you running away from?"

His hand began on the second cuff. Stopped.

"Good evening, Uncle," I said.

He flushed. He gripped me under the chin, as one grips a dog's jaw to make it stand straight for show.

"I know who she is," he said. "And I know who she's running from." He turned my face to the boy. "You ought to recognize her. You almost married her."

"She's grown to be a pretty wench," said Ab Seroy. "Makes the blood race."

Queelic blushed and stared, picking at his chin. Ab Seroy jerked me around to face himself. "Come to dance on your father's grave?"

Through his hold on my jaw I said, "Is Father dead?"

"If he is, you killed him." Ab Seroy dropped his hand. I could feel bruises starting. He took my elbow. "Come along, girlie. You're home, and you want a welcome."

He half dragged, half lifted me across the yard. The paidman hauled Jake to his feet; the old man held his bleeding mouth. From my abandoned bundle a tongue of honey oozed.

Ab Seroy yanked me up the broad steps of the guard-house, through double doors into a wide hall dark with evening. Even in the dusk its walls gleamed with new white-wash, its oak floorboards with scouring. I had scrubbed many floors in Upslope, and remembered the smell of the bleach. There was another odor under it, of garbage or decay; it made my nose wrinkle.

One of the guards lit a candelabrum, eight candles on a wrought-iron stand. The other shoved Jake against my elbow. In the Hill tongue I asked the old man, "Why did you do that for me?"

Ab Seroy slapped me. "Shut up!"

As if to himself, Jake said in the Plain tongue, "Travelers got to stick together. There's vermin on the roads these days."

The clerk pressed his hankie to his cheek. "No conversation!" he said.

"I's remarking, like. On the state of the roads."

"That's what we're here for! Your tariffs at work! You have attacked an Upslope official who keeps your roadways safe from criminals!"

"I was sweating about that goat boy," said Jake.

"Shut up," Ab Seroy said again. He gave a low-voiced order to a paidman, who left running. The remaining guard lit a second candelabrum.

The hall could have held a hundred men. It had two sets of wide double doors, standing open now to let out the heat of the day; perhaps paidmen were marched in review—in one set of doors and out the other, past whoever might sit at the broad, empty desk in the middle of the room. In the hall's south wall were smaller doors with barred windows, above them a clerestory that let in the last daylight. Dozens of straight wooden chairs lined the walls; otherwise the polished floor was bare.

My mind was still on its way to Downshore. It ran to the end of its tether, stopped with a jerk, came back, and ran again. Ab Seroy threw his hat on a chair. Queelic stared and bit his nails until his fingers bled.

Jake and I were shoved to stand in front of the desk. Behind it the clerk bustled, straightening its few papers, flicking away imaginary dust. He did not pull up a chair and sit down. Someone else was waited for.

Boots rang on the steps. My younger uncle entered—Ab Jerash was his proper title. It was in his house that I had lived after my mother died, and of my two League uncles he had been most nearly kind. Now he looked wary and angry.

"Niece," he said.

Ab Seroy took his elbow, scowling. He fell silent and went to stand beside Queelic, frowning at his bitten nails. Queelic put his hands behind his back.

One by one up the broad steps and through the double doors came those Leaguemen of Upslope, heads of households, who were not away on the roads. I knew most of them. Cruel Ab Lesh was there, the road dust still on him; Ab Hiun, young and jut-jawed; Ab Spelmar, who secretly drank; a dozen others. I had seen them in the Rulesward, I had cooked for them, pulled weeds in their gardens, washed their children, traded milk for raspberries at their kitchen doors. They looked at me and looked away. Their hands were in their pockets, jingling small change.

At this sound I began to be truly there, and truly afraid. I was small again, Katyesha Marashya N'Ab Drem, listening to the beginning of my father's rage.

But Father was not there.

The clerestories were soft with evening light. Through them, to the east, I saw something invisible from the road: a short gibbet. From it a bundle dangled, turning a little. A crow picked at it. At first I thought nothing because I could think nothing. Then I thought, So that's what smells.

There was a stir at the back of the crowd as it parted for Ab Harlan, chief Leagueman of Upslope, Queelic's father, and owner of the desk.

Perhaps he had once been gangly like Queelic. Now he was fat, and moved as though he did not often walk. The details of his plain, new-washed garments were exquisite, down to his gold cuff links and the ring with one diamond. He carried a gold-headed cane. That, and his polished boots, rapped the hollow floor.

"Well, look who's here," he said.

The League made way for him. They took their hands out of their pockets.

Ab Harlan leaned close. His clean face shone. He tipped his head this way and that and did not so much look as whiff at me, drinking my odor here and there.

I shrank away.

He smiled.

"I thought you'd come," he said. "I wasn't wrong to expect you. You've grown up, and prettily too. But I don't like how you're doing your hair." Shortening his grip on the cane, he used the tip of it to lift a curl from my cheek.

I stood straight, though I shook.

Quick as a snake, he raised the stick. I cowered, my arms

over my face.

He laughed, lowering the stick. "So you know what you deserve. And you'll get it, wench, with plenty of people watching. A good beating has set many a wandering woman right."

His face did not change, nor the pleasantness of his voice. "Not that we want you back in Upslope. Would we want a dirtied cloth? Unless . . ." He turned to the other men. His eyes twinkled. "Unless one of you has use for damaged goods?"

They looked uneasy. Ab Jerash said, "Harlan. She's my niece."

"A spell of Detention for her, then? Shall we kiss her? Since she's one of us."

Ab Jerash bit his lip.

"She's your niece, Jerash, but"—Ab Harlan pointed the cane at Jake—"*that's* her mother's father. Lice breed lice." To a paidman he said, "Take the old man outside and send him on his way."

"I ain't going!" said Jake. "Where's my turkeys?"

"Government property!" said the clerk. "Tariffs and fines! The mules, too!"

"I ain't got no living without my mules!"

"Just my point," said Ab Harlan. As the paidman bundled Jake, scuffling, out the door, he added, "We all know what market towns are like, especially at festival time. A man sells his turkeys, drinks the profit, fights, and gets a drubbing. Indeed, he might die in a brothel, or run off. Who's to know?"

The Leaguemen looked at one another. From the courtyard came the sound of blows, regular and slow.

Ab Harlan brought his face close to mine. His voice was mild. "You shamed me," he said. "You shamed my son. You disgraced your father and your race. You will pay me in full. With interest." Smiling, he said, "Queelic, come here."

"No, Father!"

"Come here."

Queelic sidled from the crowd as though his boots dragged the rest of him.

"Here she is," said Ab Harlan. "Your wife-to-be. See what you missed? Don't you long to touch her, even now?"

"Stop it, Father!"

Ab Jerash said, "Harlan."

"Such a sweet wench? In such a pretty bodice?" Ab Harlan gripped his son's wrist and dragged his hand to my neck. "Be a man, damn you! Aren't you a man?"

He forced the hand downward. My blouse tore. Queelic jerked his hand away, screaming in a high voice, "She's horrible! She has scars all over her!" He wiped his hand on his thigh, again, again.

I stood before them all, my breasts marked by the claws of the bear.

Ab Harlan drew back. His eyes bulged. Behind him muttering voices said, "They said she slept with a native, a devil. There's its mark!"

"You," whispered Ab Harlan. "Witch. Dirt of darkness. Filth that crawled on this coast before we civilized it. Beast men—hair and flesh in the dark."

He caught himself. His voice went shrill. "Lock her up!" He sweat, he shook. "*Animal!* I shall purge myself of you!"

He left, with a clatter of boots.

It was a paidman who seized me—the Leaguemen would not touch me—and tied my hands at my back with a prickling horsehair rope. In a buzz of argument I was pushed to the nearest cell. I caught a glimpse of my uncles: Ab Seroy avid, Ab Jerash shocked and stern. The cell had a high, barred window, a tin chamber pot without a lid. The paidman gave me a shove and slammed the door.

I lay where I fell, my cheek on the bare floor. Then I sat up.

Boots shuffled outside the door. Maybe they were looking at me through the little grate; I did not look at them. After a while the voices died down. Boots were leaving, loud on the steps.

Daylight was almost gone. Outside, I heard shouts and thumps. A ladder was carried past the high window; I saw its shadow. More shouts.

After another long while I stood up. Even on tiptoe I could not see out.

I pushed the chamber pot to the window, turned it over with my foot, and stood on it. I looked as far west as I could, but I could not see the sea. I looked east, and there, just at the limit of my vision, I saw the gibbet.

From it, turning slightly in the evening breeze, hung the body of Jake the turkey man. No fear that anyone might recognize his battered face.

7

One a-down,
Two a-down,
Three a-down,
   Pulled under—
Four a-down,
Five a-down,
Six a-down,
   Torn asunder—
Seven a-down,
Eight a-down,
Nine a-down,
   Drowned—
They found her braid and bracelet,
But her heart they never found.

Count for Playing Jacks. Upslope.

THE SUMMER NIGHT was hot and black. From outside the guardhouse came the sounds of day ending: tramping feet, an argument, a road guard beginning a song.

      Bring me a drink, brothers!
      Bring me a pretty broad,

Or an ugly broad, no matter,
A jade for the prod—

He was hushed in mid-verse. A late drover braved the curfew with his lowing cattle. In Downshore at this moment Dai would be stroking the nose of his cow. I wondered whether he had paid his tariff.

Quick steps. Ab Jerash's voice low and hurried. "Niece."

I turned where I stood. Saw his eye, his cheekbone, dusky at the grate. In our lives he had rarely addressed me. I had more rarely spoken.

"Niece, what have you done?"

"I—"

"This is not good. It will not be good. Where have you been?"

"With—with Mother's people."

"And the man? The demon. The one you . . . went off with."

"He—"

"You were quiet. A quiet child. Katyesha! To go with a demon's get! Not even some—some beggar boy with the moon for his white mare, but an animal. A beast."

The beggar boy. Even my uncle remembered that game.

"No matter. It's done, now we've to deal with it. Harlan will have the pus out of the pimple. And you've ruined your father." The dim eye closed as if in pain. "God of Light! Harlan will—"

Outside, a little clatter; my uncle's cheek disappeared from the grate. I heard boots, his voice and Ab Seroy's in low quarrel. I stood in the dark thinking nothing, trying to make myself invisible, to not be.

Their voices faded. Day sounds ceased.

My legs began to shake. I sat down against the wall and drew up my feet. Sometimes I sat straight, to ease the strain on my bound arms. Sometimes I put my head on my knees. Every few minutes the boots of a guard passed the door of my cell, the candlelight blinked with the shadow of a body. But the boots never paused, as if their owner was afraid to look through the barred window at the witch. Crickets sang. The night went on and on, and I could not think, I could not breathe.

All my childhood, winter and summer, I had slept in a black box bed with the doors latched. It had been smothery like this. I had never been clear whether the box was to protect me from the demons that roamed the night or to protect my father from me: my dreams, my red hair, my nasty woman's body that yearned and bled. Now I was back in that bed, and it was alive with Ab Harlan's terror, his avid disgust. Again and again his hand forced Queelic's onto my breasts. I could not get away from it by writhing, or shaking, or clenching my body into a ball. A rat rustled under the floor.

Yet in that same closed bed I had sung the Rigi's song.

The song had been too big for the bed, it had burst it open. The bear bore her children in darkness, then brought them out into the spring sun. Jake had said, *My life is my own.*

I stood up. I began to kick the tin chamber pot around the cell.

The guard came at once and put a frightened face to the bars.

"I'm thirsty," I said. "Bring me water, please."

"You'll get none, witch," he said, and went away.

I kicked the pot, singing a stamp dance from the Hills.

Trout! Newt! Otter!
Sound of rushing water!

The guard came back. "Stop, or I'll use force!"

"Bring me water, or my demons will blister your mouth till your lips peel back from your teeth!"

He disappeared like a chipmunk down a hole. I went to the door of the cell and stood on tiptoe to look into the hall. In the nodding light of the candelabra both its doors stood wide. At the western one three paidmen milled, clutching their truncheons. The first guard had gone looking for someone; already boots were clumping down the corridor.

Queelic's frightened face appeared at the grate, the guard behind him. I stepped close; he scrambled back away from the barred window and said, "You have to be quiet."

"No, I don't. I'm thirsty. He won't bring me water."

To the guard Queelic said, "Get her some water, then."

"Get it yourself," said the guard, and walked out into the night.

Queelic looked around for the others. Two of the paidmen had discovered they too had business outside, where the lowing of cattle announced another drover ripe for a fine. The third crossed his arms and turned his back. Queelic wilted, biting his thumb. His wretched face grew still with thought.

He moved out of sight. Splash of a dipper in a pail. He returned with a tin cup and held it to the bars.

"Take it."

"My hands are tied."

He looked nonplussed.

"Hold it there and I'll drink," I said.

With his fingertips barely touching the handle he jittered

the cup at the bars and tipped it just far enough for me to put my lips to it.

The water was stale and warm. He watched me drink, watched his hand holding the cup.

"Thank you," I said.

A slight nod. He set the cup on the floor and wiped his hand on his breeches. "Don't bother the guards."

I laughed.

"He'll kill you," he said. We both knew who he meant.

"Queelic—"

"You have to be quiet. It'll be worse if you don't."

"Trout! Newt! Otter!"

The last guard had deserted the hall to join in a shouted argument outside. Cows bellowed. Queelic clutched his big hat.

"Sound of rushing water!" I sang.

He ran to the west door and shouted, "Quiet out there!"

Nobody paid attention, certainly not the cows. A paidman was yelling, "You people try to sneak past in the dark. You think I chose to be stationed on this stinking coast? Show me your papers and pay in full—tariff on forty-seven cows *and* a fine. You're out after bloody curfew and you know it."

"Forty cows," said a cheerful voice.

I knew that voice.

"Forty-seven. You think I'm blind, you dirty Shoreman? Bring them past the post there. One, two, three . . ."

On tiptoe I strained to see beyond the doors. Someone had lit a torch, and by its light I saw cattle mobbing right up to the steps; Queelic; the three paidmen; and a bald, broad-shouldered man in a farmer's sandals and short pants.

It was not Dai.

Then he turned his face, seeming to look straight at me across the dark. It *was* Dai, but his wild hair and beard were shaved clean off, as they had never been since he could shave. His face was as smooth as a boy's.

"Forty," he said, grinning, rocking on his heels. "Count the legs, divide by four. Old joke. Ha."

I drew breath to yell. Saw the paidmen's shining dirks, Dai's empty hands, and shut my mouth.

Something scuffled at the other set of doors, the east one. The goat boy we had seen on the road poked his head in and looked around. He withdrew, and was replaced by the nose of a cow.

At the west door the guard had shoved his face close to Dai's, saying, "Don't give me your bullshit."

The cow trotted into the wide hall. It was followed by a second cow, then a third. A brisk, silent dog nipped at their heels.

These were not placid milkers, but the hairy little beef cattle that are quick as goats, with bad dispositions. Their horns were long and sharp. There were seven in the hall now, more coming fast; they began to jostle and bellow, they trundled against the big desk, crushed a chair. One candelabrum pitched over with a crash and snuffed out.

"Hey!" It was Queelic at the west door, running.

"*Moo-uh!*" bawled the cows, now fifteen.

"What?" cried Queelic. Wet manure hit the floorboards. The second candelabrum fell over, and the hall went black.

Dai shouted, "Yo-o *hup*! Brother!"

Thump, screech in the cell behind me. I spun round. Shadows moved at floor level, opening.

"Kat," said a low voice, breathless with laughter, "come down into the dark."

🖐 🖐 🖐

"Nall!"

He was an invisible heat that tugged at me, groping for the rope that bound my hands. He smelled like night.

Cold metal at my wrist. The rope fell away. He was back down the blacker gap left by the shoved-up plank, dragging me after him. The tramp of cattle was loud. There were shouts and a cry.

It stank down there, of slop water and refuse pushed out of sight. I crawled on my elbows. His heel was hard and cool, slipping away.

New air fanned my cheek, and the darkness changed. I saw the line of his shoulder; he grabbed my arms and with the sound of tearing cloth yanked me out into yelling black dark, the smell of cattle, thunder and roar. He was a hissing shadow that looked left, right, grabbed my hand, and jerked me into a crouching run, straight west across the plain.

Shouts followed us, then the clang of metal. I pulled my hand away to run. My blouse shone white and I pulled it off, pulled off the flapping torn skirt and ran in my dark shift. A horse crashed past, ridden by whooping phantoms. Under the bare sky and waning moon I ran through brush and grass, away from the deserted main road and south along the cliffs, following a shape that loped with a lurching gait like an ape's.

Ran and ran. There was no place to stop, there were fires where there should be none, and the smoke of torches. Ran stooping, so as not to break the skyline.

We came to my father's house, passed it. No light shone there. A notch in the cliff marked my old path to the sea.

At the cliff's edge the shadow I followed crept among the snapping pine boughs and crouched, panting; it heard night noises inaudible to me, jerked its head to listen, then lunged down the path. I followed. Below me the sea trembled like molten lead, surf hissed among rocks and sea-stacks. Waves had all but consumed the little beach where I had sung so long ago.

At the bottom the path spilled onto the rind of sand. Nall—if it was Nall, I could hardly tell if it had a man's shape—grabbed about in the sea wrack. From among the drifted logs, he dragged a dead seal—I was dreaming—no, it was a tiny boat. He ran it into the water, snatched me round the waist, and thrust me into it. I sat down in wet, clutching anything, and was thrown into the sea.

Pulled under, water at my breast. I could neither cry nor call, only hold on as the waves came, higher than my head.

They did not touch me. The balance of the boat changed, settled. On either side of my thighs warm human legs braced with each stroke of a two-bladed paddle that flicked at the edges of my sight.

As each wave came I cowered, we cut through it, the spray wet me and ran away down the oiled skin deck. We leaped like a deer running, we jumped and dove and did not sink. Through a wilderness of rocks fallen from the cliffs above, we rode the moving sea.

Behind me the oarsman grunted as he drove the blades into the waves. I could not see him, did not dare turn. We pulled beyond the shallower surf, and our leaps became glides; the stars did not jerk in crazy zigzags anymore, but swooped and swung. The panting behind me became a half-shouted song.

> *Eh, he,* hau!
> *Eh, he,* hau!

Eh, he, hásjele sásjele!
Eh, he, hau!

I tried to turn and see the singer. The boat wobbled.
"Sit still!"
I sat still. The paddle flickered. The sea was dotted with great rocks, like houses on a plain but not houses; there was nothing of earth.

Everything I had been too afraid to feel rushed up as panic. Clinging to the boat, I shouted straight forward at the sea. "Is there land? Where is there land?"

"Eh," said the voice behind me. The paddle's rhythm changed. Another dozen strokes and the boat slipped into the lee of a rock as big as a tiny island, where spring storms had built a narrow sandspit. There, as if something had grabbed us, the plunging stopped. The paddle clattered on the hull. A starry shadow splashed round and straddled the prow.

This time he looked down, and I looked up. Short and strong, naked except for breechclout and knife, his face still in shadow. I put up my hands, maybe to ward him off. He took them, and as if I were a fish on a line, he lifted me out and set me on wet but solid earth.

I staggered. He caught my waist. Waves burst white and soft. I had no breath, I was afraid to look anywhere.

He said, "This is a safe place."

Then I could look at him. Last time it had been he who needed a safe place and I who brought him to it.

He was smiling. He said, "Is your name still Kat?"
I nodded.

"Mine is still Nall." He smiled broadly. He had a broken canine tooth.

I said, "Oh—it *is* you!"

He laughed clear down to his feet. Nobody else could laugh like that. I raised my open palm, wet with sea, and he kissed it.

8

Smell of the nape
of your neck, of your hair,
rise and fall
of your side with the tide
of your breath,
warmth of you all up the front
of the warmth of me—
see,
see,
see in the dark,
see in the dark without eyes.

Winter Dreaming Croon. The Rigi.

"YOU CAME BACK," he said. "I knew you would. You have
grown up, grown beautiful."

"You don't know that, it's dark, you can't see me—"

"Oh, I see you."

It was his hand he was seeing with, gentle as an eye. But I
felt Queelic's hand, I heard Queelic scream *She's horrible!* as
he wiped and wiped to get me off himself.

Nall's hand found the scars. Went still. I tried to push it away.

It would not be pushed. "What made these?"

I was ashamed as dirt. "A bear."

He drew a hissing breath, moved his hand along the puckered lines.

"*Don't!*" But if I pulled away, I would fall into the sea. "I'm sorry— It's— In the place where I was, every girl has to be eaten by a bear—"

"Eaten," he said. "Some holy thing?"

"Yes! A ceremony. But it went wrong, it didn't happen the way it was supposed to—"

"Eaten, yet not eaten. As I was killed, yet not killed."

"Yes." I felt relief like rescue and, still, such shame. "But I'm so sorry—"

"To be scarred? Kat. Look." He made me look with my hand as he had, guiding it to the marks of rope on his wrists, the lines on back and thigh left by the rocks the surf had tumbled him through. He drew me down to feel his right foot; it was covered with a skein of ridges like a tangled net.

"It never healed right," he said. "I am lame."

Then I understood his lurching run.

He said, "Every holy passage leaves a scar."

The world got huge, and clean, and me clean in it. I put my hands on his feet and said, stammering, "Don't you dare let them scorn you! You're a *seal*. On land you're *supposed* to lollop along."

He laughed; he laughed till he sat down backward, pulling me with him. He kissed my scars. Around us the ocean burst and roared.

"Oh," I said, "wherever did you *come* from?"

"From the Gate!"

I heard the big letter. "What Gate?"

"My ama would smack you for asking," he said, and laughed more. He put his arms around me and drew me up to stand leaning against the warmth of him.

I did not believe any of this, not even the sea itself. I began to laugh too, or maybe cry. "Ama? What's an ama?"

"A great-grandmother. Mine. Smaller even than you, with white hair and a hard hand. And the Gate is the truth of the world, you Leagueman's child!"

"Tell me the truth of the world," I said. If anybody knew it, he would. Anything he said would be truth.

He put his lips to my ear, I could hear him smiling. "Are you listening?"

I was.

"The Gate is two stones in the sea. It lies west of the last island of all, at the world's edge. Two stones in the sea—and everything that is, is born from it: seals, and cows, and Leaguemen, and songs. The whole world. You." He touched his mouth to mine. "And me. From the Gate I came. I wanted to. My mother and father made my body, and my ama smacked me and told me not to meddle, and I meddled; and the Reirig with his elders killed me, and you called me, and I came, and you kissed me, and now you have come back to me, and I shall kiss you, kiss you."

This he did. I could hardly stand, crazy with him, shaking.

"And now you have been reborn from a bear—"

"Eaten! Eaten and given back—"

"Spit back out, I think. It was your red hair. That bear's mouth burned! It spat you—"

"Ptah!"

"Bear Spit. Is that what your name is now?"

I hit him with my soft fist. But he was stronger, he could trap both my hands in one of his and tickle until I squealed and then sobbed in earnest, because Ab Harlan was a nightmare and Nall was real.

He held me. Then he wiped my eyes with his knuckles, kissed me again, and said, "Let's go, Bear Spit. Dai is waiting."

"Dai—oh—Dai—"

"He was up behind Eb the brewer, on the horse that passed us. Didn't you hear him laugh? The bull was chasing that blond boy." Nall laughed too and wiped his own eyes. "You've come home to the hornets' house!"

Sometimes he spoke fast and slangy, like a Downshoreman, sometimes quaintly, like a Rig. His hands smelled of tar, he was as full of life as a nut is of meat, and when I touched him I thought my heart would stop. "Get into the *manat*, Bear Spit," he said.

"Manat?"

He turned to the little boat and slapped the hull. "Greased sealskin, from seals washed up dead on the beach—when there were still seals. Whalebone frame."

The round-bellied manat reminded me of Nondany's dindarion. "You made it?"

"I work at the shipyard. We build big, timid boats that hate to leave the shore, but for myself I built this." He lifted the manat into shin-deep water, pulled out the double-bladed paddle, and slid into the rear hatch as if he were pulling on trousers. "When I'm alone, I use two water skins to balance my weight. But with you in front it will trim just right."

He had built it knowing I would come back. I said, "Is there a paddle for me?"

He jumped out again and kissed me. "Take off your shoes."

I shed my wet sandals, waded into the sea, and stowed them in the stern. The little boat dipped and nodded. He steadied it against his thigh and showed me where to set my hands on the coaming of the front hatch.

I put one foot into the hull. It slid out from under me, dumping me on one knee in the baby waves.

He caught it as if it were a runaway pig. "Stay low. Keep your weight on your hands."

I tried again. The manat rocked wildly as though it had no weight, and I did not dare step onto my foot.

Again he steadied the hull. "There is only one thing to know. The manat is *you*. A little skin and bone to keep the sea out—but you are its weight, its balance. You and I."

The boat bobbed, light as a cup. I took hold of the coaming again and thought myself in. The inside of the hull kissed one bare heel, then the other, and I sat down sweetly like a coot on the water.

"I knew it!" He tossed his paddle into the air, caught it, and gave it to me still warm from his hands. He began to push the manat away from the sandspit.

"Wait—aren't you coming?" I tried to jump up. The manat rolled over like a barrel.

He fished me out, spitting, and caught the escaping boat with the other hand. "I was coming. Now you can learn how to shake the water out."

I shivered, soaking wet, thinking how I had put out my hand to catch myself and felt it go through water as if through nothing. "If we tip over, we'll drown."

"We might."

Between us we dumped the water out of the manat, repacked it, and set it again on the sea. Paddle in hand, I held the coaming and hopped into the front hatch.

"Bear Spit," said Nall, and I knew it was praise. The boat's balance shifted as he entered it, steadying around our two bodies. At the corner of my eye I caught the flick of his paddle.

"You can use the blade to stop yourself from rolling over," said his voice behind me. "Shall I teach you? Or shall I be boatman for us both?"

"I want to be my own boatman. Boatwoman."

He showed me how to paddle myself back upright with my wooden fin. I could not do it, but it gave the water substance, something to push against. I thought of where I had been not long before, standing by a little creek that hurried to this sea.

"Home," said Nall. "Mailin's."

We pushed away from the sandy refuge. As my arms began to understand the stroke, I looked past the surfy skerries to the whole ocean, broad and black. The prow wavered like a compass needle around some point in the west, as though I had a destination, still formless, out there.

"Nall." So strange to speak his name, after so long thinking it. "I want to go back."

"Back?"

"And trade places with you. I'm not afraid. I just don't like being in front."

We paddled back to the sandspit and changed seats. With his shoulders as foreground the horizon felt more stable.

I laid my cold legs along his thighs. Away across the breakers stood the cliff we had scrambled down and the deserted beach—*my* beach. Lights bobbed there.

"Nall, look! Torches!"

"Yes."

"But nobody goes there, ever. Leaguemen don't go near the sea."

"Money does." He turned the manat's nose to the north. "Those will be paidmen."

I am quick to learn work. Soon I could match him stroke for stroke. But when we were well out on the water, I looked back and saw the torchlight still prying along my little beach. I began to shake, so that my paddle clattered on his.

He glanced over his shoulder and began softly to sing the Rigi's song. Listening, I grew quieter and caught the paddling rhythm again. When he had sung it once through, I said, "Sing the new words. The ones they killed you for."

"Sing it with me."

> I am the ash that snuffs the fire,
> I am the knot that halts the loom,
> I am the tangle of desire,
> I am the love that clouds the womb.
>
> I am the sigh that stills the scream,
> I am the word that frees the dumb,
> I am the light that ends the dream.
> I am the child. I come, I come.

Something lived between the words of the song—I could not name it. I thought of the child I had dreamed, its wings of fire.

Not for the first time I wondered how he had come to hear

those words and why to someone—his father?—they had seemed so wicked that he must be killed. *The Reirig with his elders killed me,* he had said. I knew his father was an elder of some sort, but the word "Reirig" was new.

And Nall sat here before me. *Nall.* I could speak to him.

I said, "Are there paidmen among the Rigi?"

"There are men who kill for pay."

"Your father and the elders, did they kill you for pay?"

He paddled awhile in silence. "Yes. But not for money."

I thought of pay that is not money—that is reputation, for example, what my father had wanted in exchange for me. "What was the elders' pay?"

"The favor of the Reirig, the One Seal Priest. His favor means food—food and women—and food means strength. Someday the Reirig will weaken, and someone will kill him and be the new Seal Priest. Some strong man. Someday." Nall gave a short laugh. "He's not weak now."

"Did your father want to be the new Seal Priest?"

"No one knows what my father wants."

I had begun to believe Nall was real, but I could not make the Rigi's land be real—a nation with priests and fathers, children and hunger. Maybe little girls there played hand slaps. For the first time I wondered whether all of Nall's scars were new, and how he had broken that tooth.

I did not want the Rigi's land to be real. I wanted only Nall.

We rounded the cliffy point called Horn Loft. From this vantage the lights of Upslope were hidden. Away to the north I could see sparse campfires on the festival fields, many fewer than there had been at Long Night. Closer in, Downshore's two and three stories of tiled roof angles caught the starlight like an untidy crystal. The quays laid dark arms on the water. Where the prow of the manat pointed to the beach south of the harbor, torches jerked and fluttered like disembodied spirits.

I was afraid again. "What are those?"

"They're waiting for us."

"Paidmen!"

"No. Friends."

"So many?"

"Nobody has trouble alone."

I thought of Jake the turkey man. In faint starlight, then fluttering torchlight, we slipped toward the beach. Shadowy bodies met us, splashing waist-deep into the waves, tugging at the manat.

"Got her. He's got her," said soft voices. Men's faces looked up, tense and wary, palms slapped the hull.

Nall slid out into the water. I was afraid the manat would roll, afraid of the dark bodies and hard eyes. The hull hissed on sand and went stable. My paddle was wrested from me, someone seized me under the arms and lifted me into the air, and I wept onto Dai's neck like a found child.

"Ho, Sister." He patted my back, carrying me to shore. "Hey, now. You got here. All's well. Don't drown me, eh?"

He set me down, but I would not let go of him. With my face still buried I heard a whisper, a syllable spoken and spoken till it sounded like crickets: *"Kat. Kat. Kat."*

I peered under his arm. In this, the dead middle of the night, a crowd stood staring. Torchy shadows became fishwives in mended skirts, mustached brewers and lean fishermen, shopkeepers and farmers with lined faces. Roadsouls in rags, festival travelers, grandmothers, young girls, babies carried blinking out of bed.

I had seen Downshore crowds, but those had been merrymakers of market or carnival. These people were quiet. Nall lifted the manat higher on the sand. In the torchlight all eyes moved from me to him, then back to me. Faces were veiled, watchful. Even the children, tottering with sleep, were watchful.

I pushed my face back into Dai's shirt.

I heard Mailin say, "Neighbors!" Turning, I saw her among them, silver-haired and strong. "This much is set right. Go back to bed. Who knows what tomorrow will ask of us?"

A little ripple went round the gathered bodies. No one moved. They held their children tighter and gazed at me, at Nall. Someone said, "He'll close the roads now, Mailin. No one to move to or from the town."

"Pay 'em off," said another voice. A riffle of bitter laughter. "Call the council?" More laughter.

Mailin said, "Yes. The council, tomorrow. We still own our hearts and voices. Have we better than that?"

The people looked angry and shamefaced. Again they turned to me, with eyes that said, *Do something.*

"Go home," said Mailin. "Tonight is for rest and readiness."

No one moved. Nall set the manat on the sand between me and the crowd and straddled it. They edged back from him a little. He said, "Go now."

There was a little stir, looks of distress and doubt. Then, with a shush of feet in sand, the people shouldered their children and left. Like that. The beach was empty, pitted with footprints, and the torches were bobbing back along the tide line toward town and the Least Night camp.

I stared at Nall as if he had told the rain to stop raining and it had. He was stowing the paddles in the manat. Dai handed me to Mailin and joined Nall; from her strong arms I watched the two men embrace.

"Lali Kat, did you plan this homecoming?"

"Oh, Mailin!" No one had called me *lali,* which in Downshore means "sister," since the day I left for Creek. Between one breath and another I was destroyed with weariness and rescue, weeping and shivering, stumbling in the slipping sand. Someone took my other elbow: Nondany, his hair gingery silver in the starlight.

"Oh, you *said* you'd see me at Mailin's!"

"Half-and-Half! By life, this was all my fault. I should never have left you to fall so far behind. I'd guessed you were my rumor. But I never dreamed it had gotten so bad. The Leaguemen—"

I would not hear about Leaguemen. "You broke your word!" I said. "You told Mailin I was coming!"

"He did," said Mailin. "Thank goodness."

"It wasn't how you think. I simply— There *is* a Rig at Mailin's house." Nondany looked back at Nall like a henwife assessing a good layer. "I came straight over. When I got here, the news was all over: Piki the goat boy had seen the guards seize a red-haired girl. So I spoiled your surprise; but I think it has been sufficiently surprising."

"Quite," said Mailin.

I told Nondany, "I learned a song for you. The paidmen sang it."

"Then life is back to normal," said Mailin. "We're bringing our songs to Nondany, like children with their frogs and buttercups."

Indeed, Downshore looked just as I remembered it, like a childhood dream. Mailin's house stood on its pilings above the beach, the high doorway casting a stripe of firelight down the steps and out across the sand. The steps still made their hollow boom; the black-and-white cow was still tethered, lowing, beneath them. On the broad veranda the otter's little black shape stood poised against the orange light.

Mailin's man Pao limped out. He scooped up the otter, and flung it over his shoulder like a fur piece. "Welcome!" he said, folding me in his huge hug. The otter trampled over to my shoulders and back to his, the parrot screeched like a gate hinge, the kitchen smelled of bread and garlic.

"Nothing's changed," I said. "There's even a boxful of kittens on the hearth!"

Also on the hearth was a pretty woman, very pregnant, tugging at her braid.

"This is Robin," said Mailin.

Dai ran up the steps, took Robin's hand, and said, "Sister, like you to meet my wife."

"*Wife!*" I gawked at her belly. Truly, Bian had not read me everything in those letters.

Robin burst out laughing. "Two more months," she said.

"Dai!"

He blushed and said, "You've been gone awhile."

Robin dropped his hand and took mine. "We live below the south brow, near the Upslope boundary. It's good pasture. Dai bought the land, and Nall helped him build the house and cowshed."

Dai slipped his arm around what was left of her waist and told me the really important news. "Moss calved. This spring. A pretty white heifer."

"I'm glad," I said, for wife and child and calf. The world lurched and shifted like the manat. I could not get used to

Dai. Was it his shaved head or his new fatherhood that made his face look older, even hard?

In the bright kitchen his glance sharpened on me. "Sister! *They did that?* Oh, the bastards!"

He seized my shoulder. The torn shift still covered my breasts, but I had turned my head, making the claw marks ride higher. Everybody stared, even Nondany, and Mailin said, "Lali Kat!"

I put my hands to my neck. "No, no! Those are old— they're Hill scars—"

I looked for Nall, because the scars had not shocked him, and saw him stepping in over the threshold. In the common firelight he was a sunburned stranger, nobody I knew.

"Just Hill scars," said Mailin, with a relief I did not understand. "I smell a story. But tell it later—already it's less night than morning. Lali Kat, how long since you ate anything?"

"I don't remember."

"So I thought." She began to ladle bowls full of fish stew.

"Mailin thinks all evils can be set right with soup," said Pao. He dragged up benches and crates. "But she's wrong. It takes biscuits." With his bare hands he began to pitch biscuits off the griddle and into a basket.

Mailin kissed Pao. Dai kissed Robin and pulled her onto his lap. Abandoned and jealous, I looked away.

A warm hand took my wrist. Nall's; as I looked at him, I knew his face again. He drew me to the hearth where he had kissed me from the striped pallet and pulled me down to sit between his knees.

I blushed all over, even my feet. Dai curled his tongue and whistled; Pao pinched Mailin, who fanned herself with a soup bowl; Nondany grinned like a maniac; and the parrot yelled, "Hot biscuits!"

I leaned against Nall's chest. The life I had lived until that instant burned up and was gone, as if I had thrown it in the Year Fire.

With two spoons we ate from one bowl. The fire jigged in the grate. The only sounds were those that people make with soup, kittens make with a cat, and waves make on a beach near morning. In that round hour the world grew perfect, like a sun hanging just below the horizon.

9

Where do the winds go? What does the rain know?
Where is the egg when the bird has flown?
Where does the moon sleep? What makes the sea deep?
Where is the soul when the breast is bone?

What makes the mouth sing? What loves listening?
Where is the tune when the song is done?
Where is our joined heart, when at last our hands part
And we have returned to be sea, to be sun?

The Question Song. Downshore.

NONDANY SAT APART with Mailin and Pao, and they fell into talk of their own, hushed and grave. He held the dindarion on his lap but did not strum it, only now and then laid his hand on the strings, then lifted it to make a deep hum.

I still leaned against Nall. I could not see his face, but his hand liked teasing—it nipped my chin or wrestled with my hand, fingers and thumb. I wanted Jekka there so I could say, *See? I told you!*

Dai and Robin nudged and kissed over their soupspoons. I said, "Robin, did you make Dai shave?"

"Not *me*. He looks awful. Like some paidman."

"Shaved tonight," said Dai, scratching. "Best disguise. Last time they saw me hairless up there, I was in the cradle." He set down his soup bowl and said, "So, Sister. Welcome home."

Nall's hand stopped wrestling. The world moved forward out of its suspended ease.

"Seems Father's folks welcomed you first." Dai's mouth had that new, tight look. "*Was* that our grandfather? The goat boy said it was."

"No. He was just—he let me ride with him. When they asked, he said I was his granddaughter. To protect me."

Robin said, "Probably he had a granddaughter."

"They beat him," I said. "Then they hanged him."

"Yes," said Dai.

"How—"

"How are things in merry old Upslope?"

The brother I had left two years ago had been sweet and anxious, as incapable of bitterness as a baby. Seeing his face now, I stammered, "There always was a guardhouse."

"With two paidmen standing guard. Six at festivals."

"There was a jail."

"No Leagueman ever saw the inside of it. And there was a gibbet."

"There was not!"

"There was. Hidden in Ab Harlan's compound then. But

nobody we knew was hanged on it, or ever would be. Sister, forgive me, but—you were a girl."

Just a girl. I had scrubbed floors, gone to market, gone to the Rulesward, gone to bed; I had grown cabbages and milked the cow; I had been privy to the network of secrets and acid gossip by which my aunts maintained themselves against their husbands; and I had heard half sentences as I served my uncles tea. But while I lived in Upslope, I had never thought to connect my father's big world of roads to my small, domestic one.

"Was there a tariff?" I asked now.

"Not on what *we* bought. Sister, there's more to being a Downshoreman than dancing on Long Night."

"I might at least have wondered!"

Mailin, Pao, and Nondany had stopped their talk and were listening to us. Mailin said, "I don't think you were helped to wonder."

"Not by our aunts," said Dai. "Revenge and recipes, that's their life. Nor by our uncles, who think a woman's job is to make the bed and then lie in it."

Robin said, "You're so hard on them!"

"They're my family."

"I'm your family."

"But it *is* worse now," I said. "There's gossip everywhere. Nondany, you heard it. Even the old man said how bad it was, before he—before they—"

"—kissed him," said Dai. "That's Harlan's word. 'I'll kiss you,' he says. He has different ways to do it. Doesn't he kiss sweet?" He turned back the cuff of his short trousers. On the inside of his thigh was the scar of a deep burn, as if a poker had been laid along the muscle's length.

"*Dai!*"

He covered the scar. "Just a kiss. More promised next time."

I went hot and sick, hearing Ab Harlan's voice say *Shall we kiss her?* So that was why Dai and Mailin had flinched at my scars. The kitchen was not safe, the world was not safe, there were paidmen at the door, and behind them Harlan panted. I said, "Why did he do that?"

"For leaving the League," said Dai. "Though he said it was for being slow to pay the tariff on the cow. Twice. First time, a week in the guardhouse. Three of us; had a good time, got to work on those floorboards—no Downshoreman need be bored in lockup. Second time it wasn't the guardhouse. Harlan took me to Detention and gave me this. For cockiness. Did you know Harlan is my Rulespatron? That's like a god-father," he said to Robin. "He can better my character and entertain himself at the same time. Detention's reserved for Leaguemen. We're quality."

"He used that word with me—'Detention,'" I said.

"A girl wouldn't know about it. Detention's up there among his warehouses, but deep in, locks and bars—it's his playground; he keeps his toys there. When he laid the poker on me, he said, 'As I recall, you could never sit still at your sums. Think of the favor I can do you: The next time I see you here, I'll make sure sitting is all you ever do again.'"

"He's mad!"

"Was he ever a rose?"

"He was horrible. But not like that. People don't just suddenly go mad. The League hasn't stopped him?"

Then I remembered that dreadful lullaby, and what was taken for granted by every family in Upslope: that children were to be slapped or beaten or shamed, starved or threatened or locked in the dark, "to teach them to be good." It was in miniature, but it was all there.

"Right after you left, Sister, that's when he began to tighten the screws."

A Rig stole the bride of Ab Harlot's son and carried her off to be his queen under the waves, and Ab Harlot's gone mad with rage. Those wild tales had been telling a kind of truth. I said, "I'm the reason he's doing this."

"Don't give yourself airs, brat."

"I shamed him. I refused his son—"

"Queelic, child accountant," said Dai. "We did our sums together."

"—and I ran away to a dirty native." I turned to look at Nall and saw him grave, intent.

Nondany had been quiet. Now he lifted his hand from the strings of the dindarion and it made that sound—soft, but so deep, I felt it in my bones. Nall sat forward.

"A tidal wave is caused by the snapping of tension that has built for a long time," said Nondany. "An earthquake under the sea. To be caught in a tidal wave is not to be its cause."

"I don't think Ab Harlan would distinguish between a great slight and a small one, Kat," said Pao. "You foul him, as we foul him, by existing." He rubbed his eyes. "This earthquake has been long overdue."

"He said I was a witch, that he must be purged of me."

Mailin said, "When I think what his childhood must have been, to make him what he is, my soul cringes in me."

"My heart's broken," said Dai.

"Was it a happy thing to be a child in Upslope?" said Mailin. "I ask this of you, who soon will have a child."

He looked ashamed. I answered for him. "It was lonely as death."

"Never knew how little Father gave us until I met you," said Dai, nodding at the group around the fire. "Leaguemen aren't fathers, they're power-traders. That's the seed of these bad times; Harlan's just the flower."

"Could we get along with no merchants?" said Mailin. "We have our little shopkeepers, but the world needs traders. The Leaguemen are not—but they could be—like the network of a river, connecting us with other lands, taking and bringing goods and news and songs—"

"On the day hell freezes," said Dai. "On the day I say I love my father."

A miserable silence fell. The flames gobbled at the wood.

Nondany cleared his throat. "It's useful to take a peek at history," he said in his precise voice. He touched the dindarion. This time it sounded a true chord, sonorous. "As a tribe—they would hate to hear me call them a tribe, although, of course, they are—the Leaguemen worship Light. This particular group, in Upslope, has lived on the coast for generations; yet they hate and fear the sea. Now tell me—what lives in the sea?"

"Fish?" said Robin.

But the rest of us stared at Nall.

"Exactly," said Nondany. He played a fluid trill. "The Rigi. Nall, what do your people worship?"

Nall looked from Nondany to the dindarion. Did not answer.

"No matter. We don't know what our deepest beliefs are any more than Robin's fish knows what water is. But to my mind the Rigi worship—"

"Dreams," said Nall, as though he spoke from one. "The deep, the darkness. The moon barely seen. The Gate."

"Ah, the Gate at the world's end, through which all things come to be!"

"You know about the Gate?"

"I am a Downshoreman. Your ancestors danced with mine."

"They talk little here about the Gate," said Nall. "As though it were a place in a story, not real—and always with fear. Except Mailin." He gave her a warm glance.

"The Gate is dark and distant for us now," said Nondany. "As if the Rigi took it with them when they left. That which is hidden breeds fear."

"The Gate is not hidden. It stands in the sea. I saw it and heard it every day of my life, until I was killed. It is right to fear it."

"Fear and worship live in the same house. I was about to say that the League worships the Light—"

"—and ledgers," said Dai with a grin. "For totting up accounts."

"If you like. The Leaguemen worship the Light and ledgers. The Rigi worship the Dark and the Gate."

Nondany held up his right hand and named it, "Leaguemen," his left, "Rigi." Nodding at each in turn, he said, "East, west. Day, night. Light, Dark. Earth, sea."

"Ledgers, Gate," said Dai, enjoying himself. But Nall leaned forward, so absorbed that I felt a twinge of jealousy.

Nondany's hands made fists; they fought each other. Then the left disappeared behind his back, leaving the right hand lonely, palm up. "See? Here are our Leaguemen—especially Ab Harlan—alone now in the wealth and daylight they crave. They have driven away the Rigi, the moon people, the animal dreamers they despise and fear. But along with the Rigi they have driven away their own children." Nondany looked from me to Dai. "I ask you now: Who could live like that and not be in pain?"

He brought his left hand out of hiding, took up the dindarion, and sat back.

"The Leaguemen have lost the Gate," said Nall. Then, as if to himself, "Not only the Leaguemen."

Dai said, "Pretty story, sir. But my kindness is all gone."

Robin stroked his shaved head. "No, it isn't."

"If Harlan's in pain, he deserves it." Dai clenched his teeth. "My god, this last while! Tariffs, taxes, fines—murders, even. Paidmen plaguing the borders. How's a man to get breeding stock? Harlan's squatting on the roads like a spider on its web. Our little shopkeepers are strangled and starving. As if we had money to spend, anyway. . . ."

I remembered the big talk of the Weedrun boy, that if a Black Boot set foot outside the market, he would be skewered. Not with a camp of armed soldiers there!

As though he read my thoughts, Dai said, "Paidmen aren't so stupid as to show their faces down here. All payments are to be made at the guardhouse, if you please. That's the only thing stopping a fight. The rough lads—nay, even the peaceable ones—want a brawl, and after tonight's escapade I expect they'll get it. Maybe you triggered the quake, brat, but it's been building for generations."

"But why should you bear this?" I said. "*Murders?* And Ab Harlan levies tariffs and fines—why do you pay them? You keep saying you're in a trap. Who set it?"

In the firelight each face fell, even Nondany's. Only Nall's was unchanged, intent.

"We did," said Mailin. "Lali Kat, we are not telling you the whole truth."

I looked at Dai. He dropped his eyes, then faced me and muttered, "We owe him money."

"Who?"

"Ab Harlan."

I knew nothing about money. I had never had any. I had grown kale, made cook pots, carded wool, baked bread, raised chickens, and chased crows out of cornfields, but never for money. All the coins I ever handled had been doled out to me by my father, warm from his pockets.

I felt ignorant and ashamed. "But he buys your fish."

"The fishing has been bad," said Pao.

"Other market stuff, then. Vegetables."

"Worth pennies."

"You sell him sealskins!"

"The seals are gone."

"Gone?"

"All gone," said Mailin. "This winter. Withdrawn from us between one moon and the next, the beaches empty. There are no more seals on these shores, Lali Kat."

I remembered how, as he showed me his manat, Nall had said, *When there were still seals.* "Where have they gone?"

"Who knows? We killed so many, perhaps the king of seals has called the rest away."

I turned to Nall. Was he not the king of the sea, and I his queen? "Where are they?"

"I don't know." But his face said he knew something.

Mailin said, "All we know is that there are no more sealskins to sell to Ab Harlan for our debt."

In the silence the kittens squirmed and mewed. I saw for

the first time how shabby the kitchen was, patched and mended, all its goods worn thin.

"It started so small," said Mailin. "And so long ago. A bad fishing season and a bad harvest. Before the Leaguemen came, we would have gone hungry. A few old people, a few children might have died; we would have eaten nettles and cockles and begged from our neighbors. But the Leaguemen—it was Ab Harlan's father then—offered small loans, to families and the council. That got us through until the seal-killing; so we killed extra. But the next harvest was poor too. Who would eat nettles when she could buy corn on credit? More loans, and a little help to the shopkeeper. Another bad year.

"So it grew." Her voice was tired and wondering. "How fast debt grows! We would borrow against the catch, kill more seals—but then we'd buy a little brandy, too. Or cinnamon for the holidays, or ribbons, or a wedding ring. We were hungry for trinkets. You think Ab Harlan has a devil in his belly—what have we in ours? Lali, we are in debt to him for our lives. We have a little corn, some pigs, dried tomatoes—that's all. He has grown cruel now; he takes everything else for the debt. He takes young men when they can't pay, to work off what they owe as road guards—like paidmen but not paid. He took Suni's man."

Pretty Suni, with fat Rosie in her arms, who had sold me fish. "Rosie's father? Oh, no!"

"Oh, yes. A press gang caught him on the road. They carried him far off, traded him for some poor debtor from another village. The League doesn't like pressed lads to be near their families."

Mailin bowed her head. Dai looked defiant, Pao looked

tired and old. Nondany had silenced the dindarion with a hand across the strings.

I turned in Nall's arms, seeing firelight on the sleek of his eye. As if I showed him my scars, my shame, I said, "The Leaguemen are my people."

"You think mine are better?" His tongue played at his broken tooth. "A club kills as dead as a gibbet."

"The Rigi don't have an Ab Harlan!"

"No?"

In his face I saw a story I had not heard. I did not want to hear it. I wanted him to be for me, merry and teasing, the man I had called.

He held up both hands like Nondany and said, "When one hand is sick, so is the other."

"But you don't owe anybody anything!"

"I owe everybody everything," he said. "I owe you my life."

"You do not! Who do you think I am, Ab Harlan keeping books?"

"Nall would fetch a good price," said Dai. "He's the last seal in the place."

"Oh," I cried, "why doesn't it ever get easier? Can't there be a time, finally, when we can just be *happy*?"

"No," said Nall. Then, "Yes." He smiled.

"When?"

"Now," he said, and kissed me.

The dindarion's hum lapped the room like water. Tipping his chair onto its back legs, Nondany said to Nall, "You are a singer, I understand?"

"Yes. But first a listener."

"A seal priest?"

"No. But a listener."

"Explain."

"There are no words for it," said Nall.

As there were no words for the Bear. But the mountain felt far away and strange; this world was the sea, it was Nall's.

"Use the words you have," said Nondany.

Nall rubbed his mouth. Beyond the open door the sea fell—*thud, thud*—on the sand. After a little he said, "In the deep beyond the Gate swims everything that is not yet. Everything: what may be; what will be; what would be. With each tide the world rushes in and out between the stones of the Gate. There one can hear the world coming into being, taking its shapes. *That* is listening."

The fire snapped. Nondany said, "It takes its shapes as songs?"

"As everything. But as it does that, it sings. In words, if one is lucky; I am lucky. The water gives the music."

"Do you find you are as well able to listen here, so far from the Gate?"

"You are the first to ask that."

"Everybody but me has manners."

"I listen in water," said Nall. "I swim and listen. Even here, if I am in the sea, I can hear the Gate, but very far away. Like a known voice. And the words—" He frowned. "I think it is the Gate," he said.

"I should think water your element." Nondany and his dindarion balanced on the chair's two legs, motionless as a dragonfly in midair. "What do you hear?"

"Now?"

"These days. Given the strangeness of your . . . arrival

here, and Downshore's distress, I assume you have listened for what may be coming through the Gate? For all of us."

Nall flushed. I looked aside; I knew I was part of that strangeness and did not want to be. He said, "I have listened. Tried to."

"And?"

The room was as still as that mountain meadow before the Roadsoul girl had sung.

"Something is coming," said Nall.

"A song? A change in the world?"

"The world and a song are the same."

"You have heard what this coming thing will be?"

"When I hear it, I will know."

"Will you sing it?"

"Sing it or live it. Also the same." He glanced around, as though remembering the rest of us. "But something is always coming. From the hour the sea was made until it breaks no longer, the world is rushing in and out through the Gate."

Nondany's chair came back onto four legs with a thump. Dai said, "Misty Rig talk, Brother."

"I was a Rig."

Was.

"Well, now you're a tar-handed boatbuilder," said Dai.

"Not to Downshore folk."

"Aye, to them you're a Rig and an omen," said Dai. He looked at me from under his brows. "You saw the crowd on the beach, Sister. Been needing an omen around here. Folk think this laddie's come from the sea to clear the debt with Ab Harlan, and they're waiting for him to do it. It'll have to be by magic, for he never saw a copper penny in his life till I showed him one."

"I thought it was a fish scale," said Nall. "It smelled like blood."

"Enough prophecy, then," said Nondany. "If you build songs and boats, try this." Smiling, he held out the dindarion.

Nall reached around me and took it. He held it at arm's length in front of us, balanced on his hands, and laughed. It sounded with his laugh; he laughed again, brought it closer, and sang at it.

> See how we dance, love,
> Round the town,
> Then ring-a-rose, love,
> We all fall down.

His voice made the strings of the dindarion ring. When he stopped singing, they hummed on.

"It purrs!" he said.

"You like it?" said Nondany, retrieving it. "Good, for I'm offering you a bribe: Teach me songs, and I'll teach you to play the dindarion. But what you just sang is a Downshore ballad, and that won't do. I'll have some Rig music out of you, Nall, or I'm a Roadsoul."

This bargain must have satisfied Nondany, for he rose and stretched. The first pale light of dawn bleached the windows. "I must go. Remember you have that paidmen's song for me, Half-and-Half." He bent to lay his cheek on mine.

"Get along, Songsparrow," said Mailin. "They won't disappear; I'm feeding them. And may Dai and Robin stay in town with you and your sister tonight?"

"Surely."

Dai said, "Why?"

"Your house is too close to Upslope. We've stirred the hornets' nest—there's no telling what may fly out of it."

"Knew that when we stirred it," said Dai. "Now it's look sharp and pull together. You saw how many were on the beach last night; Shoreman or Least Night guest, they'll all be in the plaza tomorrow, clamoring for council."

"Then you be in the plaza too. Not sitting alone on the border."

"Cow's to be milked."

"Dai."

He made a rueful face. But he nodded, saying to Nondany, "Sorry to be a nuisance, sir. Tell Lilliena we'll be along directly."

"No nuisance. More ears for her to exercise." At this all present groaned; I gathered that Lilliena must be a famous gossip. Nondany pointed his forefingers at Nall and me. "Don't you dare forget anything!" he said. He picked up the dindarion and rattled down the veranda steps as though he were not half blind, as though he had run them a thousand times. Next to the door I saw what he had told me to look for: Mailin's Year Altar, a wall niche filled with rocks and feathers, dried flowers, scraps of cloth. Someone had put there a little seal carved from driftwood; I knew who.

Dai turned to me. "I know who *won't* be in the plaza tomorrow. Harlan. He'll be at the guardhouse with all his toadies, offering a fat sack of coin to whoever will turn you in, Sister. And I know how many offers he'll get." He looked at me from under his brows. "You're a portent, you know."

"I thought it was Nall."

Nall had risen and stood like the otter, poised. "There is nothing in the world that is not a portent," he said.

Dai slapped his forehead. "What did I say about Rig talk? Muck the stall for me, Brother, and clear your head. But see, Kat—if Nall's an omen, it stands to reason you're one, too. I try to tell them you were an ugly baby and smelled funny, but who listens?" He cuffed me gently. "Well, we've bitten the adder back. Things will change now. Glad of it." He hugged Mailin, saying, "You believe too much good of people."

"I've delivered so many babies."

"We'll try to keep you in work."

Robin refused Mailin's offer of a shawl against the sweet night air. "I'm hot all the time," she said, fanning her hands at her face.

I hesitated, then left Nall and followed the two of them out onto the veranda in the hoarse ocean dawn. "Dai, they told me Father's dead."

His sleepy look sharpened. "When?"

"At the guardhouse. Seroy said I killed him."

"You jammed his cart wheel, all right, but you never killed him. He's sick, that's all."

Against all reason my heart lightened. "Sick with what?"

"Just sick. Too mean to die."

I wondered who got Father's dinner now, who scrubbed his hearth. There would be no cow to milk anymore. "Dai, where did you get all those cows last night?"

"Borrowed 'em."

I thought of the scream we had heard. "You didn't *kill* Queelic?"

"Me? The udder warrior? Bull gave him a good fright, that's all. Might clear up his pimples."

"Nobody's ever killed a Leagueman," said Robin with a shiver. "There'd be hangings then!"

"Can't kill 'em. They're like our father: nothing inside but shredded ledgers. Speaking of the dear old man, Kat, I near forgot—I have a homecoming present for you, from him."

"A present? From *Father*?"

"Last time I went to see him, before my—well, my intimacy with Ab Harlan, he threw this to me. *At* me, actually." Dai pulled his round face into an approximation of our father's long, unhappy one. "'You could never manage money,' he says. 'Half of this is yours. The other half is your sister's, should she be fool enough to show her face. It's not for your own use, either of you. It's for my grandchildren. I won't have them raised poor dirt.' So catch, Sister. Love from Dad."

The fist-size buckskin pouch clinked as I caught it, heavier than a rock.

"Dai, it's gold!" In the League that was to say: *It's the Blood of Light—the greatest blessing, deepest truth.* I untied the neck and tipped a few coins into my palm, the old, thick, embossed weights that were saved, not spent.

"Bought the land with my half. Thought I'd use Father's money to raise cows; he'd like that."

The coins were cold in my hand. I said, "It's the only way he knows how to say he loves us."

"He's a stone, Sister. He never loved anybody."

"He loved Mother."

"If that was love, it killed her." Dai pulled Robin close. "This one knows how to love. And doesn't mind teaching."

"You just love me because I'm getting to look like a cow," said Robin, yawning.

"Time to herd you home along the beach. *Barn for my cuddy-o,*" Dai sang.

Robin went back to hug Mailin over her big belly. Dai watched her go, his face so soft that my heart turned in my chest and I said, "I'm glad you're happy."

"You be happy too, Sister." He jerked his chin toward the end of the veranda. Nall had slipped past us as we talked and leaned there on the railing, watching the sea.

"You like him?" I said.

"He's my brother. Don't listen to that truck about omens either." He looked away and said, "When Harlan had me, I thought—well, it crossed my mind, 'If anything happens to me, what'll become of Kat?' But it's all right. You've got Nall now."

I put my arms around my brother. "I love you more than anybody. I'll tell you about our people in the Hills."

"Tomorrow." Dai yawned in turn. "I'm not used to midnight alarms."

"Wait till you have a baby!"

As Dai and Robin walked the beach toward town in the rising sun, their shadows held hands.

I was so weary that my head rolled on my neck. An arm went around my waist. "Bear Spit," said Nall, "are you coming with me?"

I let him take my hand and lead me down the veranda steps, back among the great pilings that held up the house, and into the stall of the black-and-white cow. There I took back my hand and said, "*This* is where you live?"

"In the summer. In winter I go upstairs by the fire."

"I thought—I thought you'd have a little house."

He laughed. Through the slats in the wall I could see a lean-to with the manat in it. Otherwise there was nothing to suggest that a human lived here but a blanket on the straw and a few worn implements on the wall: razor, hammer, axe. The haltered cow chewed her cud.

He knelt, pulling at my hand. I felt as the water in the millpond must feel at the brink of the millrace, when in an instant the roar will begin, the rush into space. I put out my hands against him. "Nall—"

"What?" Smiling, wicked.

"Don't tease me! I mean, I never—" Dealt with cabbage worms. At last I said, "I never slept with a man."

"You slept with me."

"I don't mean *sleep!*"

"But I do." The cow breathed her clover breath; the straw was soft. Past his shoulder I could see the dawn ocean through a gap in the wall. "The night is spent. Come sleep," he said.

I would not take off my shift or untie the deer mouse sash. But I lay down against him in the rustling straw, and his mouth was right where it should be.

He made a little happy grunt, like a puppy nursing. It made me laugh, and in the middle of laughing I fell asleep.

10

Kill! Kill! Kill!
The army's on the hill!
Katyesha's dead
And the worms shall eat their fill!

Children's Game. Upslope.

A FLY BUZZED, and landed on my lip. I woke.

I was hot, with the sick feeling that comes from sleeping deeply in daytime heat. I had had a bad dream, of which I remembered only noise, and trying to wake but not waking. Sunlight glared through the gaps in the cowshed wall.

In a moment I knew where I was, hearing the ocean's breath and breath. I put out my hand for Nall. Touched nothing. I opened my eyes again and saw only the heap of straw.

I sat up. It was afternoon, the flat time. The cow had moved to the back of the stall, away from the barred, dusty light. Desolate and cross, I rubbed my face in the crook of my elbow.

A woman screamed.

A high, raking scream. In the Hills women scream like that at burials. It yanked me to my feet with my arms flung out, my hand hit the haft of Nall's axe and it dropped from its hook like a rock.

I blundered to the doorway. No more screams, but sobbing, a gabbling wild sound, upstairs. I was afraid to go up the steps and ran up them, my shift stuck full of straw. On the veranda Robin knelt with her face in Mailin's lap, arms stiff, braid undone. It was she who sobbed, her body so strange, so big.

I cried, "What!"

Mailin began to speak but Robin jerked up her head, her face swollen, a different face. "They took Dai!"

"Who?"

"Paidmen," said Mailin.

"Paidmen?" The sun shone plain. I was stupid, that was all. "Why would they take Dai?"

Because he had sprung me from the lockup. Someone had recognized him—Queelic, probably. Or maybe just because he was my brother.

I woke completely, awfully. "Just now? They just *came*?"

Mailin said, "Robin. Breathe."

Robin took a breath too big for her and said, "They killed the calf."

"The calf—"

"He had to milk the cow, he's so stubborn, he wouldn't stay in town so I wouldn't either. We went home, we were asleep. They kicked in the door and the mirror broke, they made him put his pants on. I went after them, I shouted and they said, 'Get back, old lady.' The calf was in the pen—she's so little, they pulled her out."

Mailin closed her eyes.

"They stabbed her with their dirks. Again, again. Little white calf. Then they took Dai." Robin had stopped crying. Her face was still with wonder. "They laughed."

I felt only a hugeness. "So then? What happened?"

Mailin said, "Downshoremen have gone to get him back."

"Then it's all right! They'll get him back. Robin, they got *me* out—so easy, it was funny: one, two, three!" My heart jumped. "Did Nall go?"

"Yes."

Still I said, "Robin, it'll be fine. Paidmen, Leaguemen—pig dirt!" It felt good to say those words about my father's people, my own. "When did they go?"

"It's been some time," said Mailin. "I wonder you slept through it. Pao and Nondany stayed in town, but Suni and I brought Robin away."

I turned to see a young woman standing in the doorway. She was as I remembered her, baby on hip, but it was a different baby, and behind her full culottes a three-year-old was hiding.

"Lali Kat." Suni embraced me around the infant. The older child gave a high, tense wail.

I did not know what to do. I knelt and said, "Rosie, do you remember me?"

"No!" Rosie screamed into her mother's knees.

"We're in a state," said Suni. "My brother's gone with the others to get Dai. You heard Ab Harlan took my man? Three months ago." In my mind I saw her man, curly-haired and slender, a paidman in some little town, learning to laugh as he stabbed a white calf.

"How many went for Dai?" The air was still, the surf soft, yet I felt as though I were hearing a murmur rising to a yell.

"Fifteen, maybe. More wanted to go. It's gotten bad since you left, Lali Kat. We aren't warring sorts of folk, but we know what to do in a brawl. Now then, Rose, don't pinch! There was talk of stealing somebody important from up there, to stand hostage. Maybe there were twenty men."

Rosie whined and snuffled; Robin lay facedown on Mailin's lap. The heat was sticky as flies.

I said, "What can we do?"

"What women do," said Mailin. "Wait, and try to calm the children."

The child on Suni's hip began to scream. Suni said, "Rose, did you pinch your brother? Shame, what would your daddy say? Pick her up, Kat, she wants to be held tight."

"No, no, no!" Rosie shrieked as I hefted her, all fists and knees.

"There's a Rosie, there's a Rose." I walked her up and down the veranda, singing a grinding song of Bian's.

> A rose upon the ditch bank grew,
> With a green thorn beside it;
> In one the wind did sing of love,
> And in the other sighed it.

It is so hard to be little, so easy, with somebody big to hold you while you scream. I swayed, saying, "Rosie, look at the sea. Look at the little birds, Rose, see how they run along the water—Oh!"

Suni followed my glance and caught up the baby against her neck. A crowd of men ran along the tide line, making the sanderlings fly. More than twenty men. In my arms Rosie screamed and screamed.

Robin ran to the railing. "He's not with them!"

Nall was. I knew his gait now. As the crowd rushed the stairs, I drew aside and waited for him to limp to the top step.

A new gash split his cheek. I could not reach my hand to him because my arms were full of child.

Robin's low wail.

Like a runner touching finish, Nall laid his unmarked cheek against mine. He stank of bodies, of hate. He turned, he stumbled back down the steps, elbowing through the crowd that poured up; he limped to the tide line shedding breech-clout and knife belt, leaned into the waves, and disappeared.

Rosie's screams had gone to sobs. I turned from the sea, back to the confusion of shouting, weeping, angry talk. The speakers stared at me. Last night they had whispered my name; now nothing mattered but the rage they were in, the relief of it, like vomiting.

Pao and Nondany had come with them. Pao saw me and stooped to take the child, but I held tighter, as if she were all I had.

"Dai's alive," said Pao. Rosie sobbed on my neck, slimy and warm. "He was alive when they left him."

"They left him."

"Too many paidmen. They didn't expect us—peaceable little Downshore! But they're trained to fight, and these boys are farmers, tailors, armed with fish knives. It was bad, they said." Pao closed his eyes. "Did they think it would be sport? The boil's burst now. Trenk's lost a hand and Larrigo's stabbed in the belly. And there's a man dead."

I said stupidly, "But not Dai."

"No. One of them. But a Leagueman, an important man."

"Who?"

"The Axe, we called him. We scarcely know their real names." Pao's face was like Nall's: beaten. "We'll pay for that. We only hated them, and never learned their names."

"The Axe, what does he look like?"

"Lean. Ab Something; their names all sound alike! Ab Harlan's deputy. Pearl cuff links."

"Ab Seroy!"

"Yes."

"My uncle." I felt lust or glee, knowing that cruel man was dead. "But what will happen now?" I answered myself, "Ab Harlan will kill Dai. Or he'll—" Kiss him. The white-hot poker.

Pao looked away. "We," he began, and paused, as though he could not stomach the words. "We took two hostages. Apparently. Both are Leaguemen. That may stay Ab Harlan's hand. But they may be dead by now; the young men had them, and they don't think. There was talk of taking them out to sea. Leaguemen so fear the sea."

I looked at the ocean, pretty blue, with two white sails on it.

"The men will try again," said Pao. "They want food and weapons and more fighters. The town's in a ferment. When night falls, they'll go back for Dai."

"Not until night?" I felt the poker on Dai's body as I had

felt Ab Harlan's hand shove Queelic's onto my breasts, the shape of hate driven home.

"So they said. No chance by daylight. Where's Nall?"

I looked at the sea.

Pao nodded. "Gone to get clean of us. We're a dirty lot."

"You are not!"

"We are. Please, Lali Kat—love us anyway."

Rosie's body, sobbing, was heavy as unrisen bread. I walked the veranda up and down, up and down, singing a lullaby from Creek.

> Loolee, loolee, you're my pigalee,
> You'll be bonnie when you grow bigalee.

A stupid, stupid song. But it was something I could do.

11

God of gods
comes with a flute
dancing
face like the sun
says laughing
Child of mine
betray your friends
or betray yourself
Whichever you choose
will be wrong
Choose
and dance!
God of gods
who comes with a flute
I dance

Flute Melody. The Roadsouls.

NALL DID NOT COME BACK until dusk. I waited for him at the door of the cowshed, sitting in the sand. Rosie had long since wept herself to sleep and been laid on Mailin's bed upstairs, where the talk, the argument, the tears of grown-ups went on and on. From the cowshed that noise seemed distant, like the cries of animals in a wood.

He rose out of the sea, dark against the dark water. He

picked his belt and breechclout out of the sand; holding them in his hand, he limped up the beach.

I could not think where he had been. I was afraid of him naked and did not speak his name. But he saw me, half hidden by the cowshed door. His face had lost its beaten look and he shuddered, shining with wet.

Timidly, I held out my arms. He knelt into them. He was cold as a frog. As I held him, his shivering stopped and I saw him crying—not with sobs, but with tears that came and came, as though he were made of water.

I did not know what to do. I had not known what to do since Robin's first scream, as though that scream had never stopped. "The men are upstairs," I said. "More every minute. Fishermen, and farmers with their scythes. You'll be an army."

His face did not change.

"They're asking where you are."

Silence.

"Nall."

He said, "I won't go with them."

My arms let go of him. "Won't go?"

"No."

"But Ab Harlan will—he'll—"

"Yes. I saw what the lads did to the man with the cuff links."

I stared at him. He stared back. His tears had stopped; his eyes were all pupil.

"You— Is it because of your foot? You can't fight?"

"I was trained to fight. A lame foot is nothing."

"Then what—"

"I'm leaving."

The waves stopped breaking. The night wind stopped.

But it was my breath that stopped, until with a gasp I caught it. "Leaving?"

"I'm going back to the Rigi's land."

My mouth said *No,* with no sound.

"Kat," he said. "Kat. I swam and listened. Murmurs; words that are not words; the voice of water. I said, *Tell me what I am to do!* Then I knew in my heart. I must go back to the Rigi's land, and listen at the Gate."

"The Gate—"

"At the world's mouth, where it speaks clearest. I'll listen to the world being born, singing itself, and I will sing that. Whatever it is."

I said, "A song to sing when Dai is dead?"

"I won't know what song until I hear it."

"A song. But you—but we—we have to get Dai."

"I have to listen."

"Nall, I saved your life!"

He did not say, *And you said I owed you nothing.* He said, "So I must use it."

"And not lose it? Oh, and I kissed you!" I shoved him away, scrabbled to my feet.

He caught my wrist. "Do you think this time is just about you and me? Something is moving. Something is changing. Do you think we are only for ourselves, not waves in the great sea?"

Or threads in the great loom; but I had forgotten that. I had no home but Dai and no room in me for anything but Dai withering in the smoke of Ab Harlan's hate, the safe world withering.

"The world is breathing through the Gate," said Nall. "It wants to be born, it wants listeners. Was it only for ourselves that we sang the Rigi's song?"

I jerked my arm out of his fist. "*Yes!* And what good was it? You come. You go. *Dai called you brother!* What do you care for him—or for me?"

"Come with me," he said.

I stood with my mouth open.

Behind him the foam of the wave tops was blue in the last light. He held out his hand, his face in shadow. "Come with me to the Rigi's land."

I said, "I will die first."

He let his hand drop.

"I'll go with the men and fight," I said. "I'll get my brother back. You—you think you can swim back to your people? Who'll save you there, some pretty Rig girl? You're not a seal, not a man. You're cold, a fish. Swim, fish!"

I turned to run.

He said, "I won't swim. I'll take the manat."

I ran out of the cowshed, up the steps. The veranda was jammed with angry people who paid no attention to me. Men with grins like dogs moved or stood in the dying light, jangling with hatchets and gaffs. They were dressed in festival clothes, they smelled of iron and sweat, they wolfed bread and withered apples and threw the cores over the veranda rail.

Standing with Pao was a fisherman, fair and young, who held in one hand a big knife of the kind used for gutting salmon, in the other an apple that he ate as he spoke, steadily and fast. "We'll be at the guardhouse within the hour. We're a hundred and twenty men!"

Pao's voice was full of pain. "Rosh, you're sure he's in the guardhouse? I thought—"

I heard my own voice say, "He's not in the guardhouse."

Rosh the fisherman heard me. A portent is of no use once the storm has struck; he gave me the sparest nod between bites. "Yes, he is. That's where they dump us when we won't pay the tariff."

"You saw him there?"

"Ha! We were too busy with Mister Prettycuffs, who's taxing the worms now."

"But you didn't *see* him."

"Didn't need to. Wasn't him on the gibbet."

"So you thought he was alive. And you told Robin that." The pins that held the world together were falling away, the shoulder that had kept the demons at bay dissolving like smoke. "They wouldn't put him in the guardhouse because you got me out of it. Has nobody thought of that? He'll be in Detention, at Ab Harlan's place."

Rosh's face said he had never heard of Detention. But he was already fighting a war and said readily, "Then we'll grab him out of there! We're a hundred and twenty men."

"Ab Seroy is dead!" I shouted. "Do you think Ab Harlan's pokers aren't already in the fire?"

Around us the crowd had grown silent. I put my hand over my mouth. Mailin looked old and sick. Robin's face was painted white.

Rosh flushed. His hand tightened on the knife. I had made him a fool; his revenge, till now focused on Ab Harlan, shifted a little to me. "*You'd* know how Leaguemen think, wouldn't you? And where's your pretty laddie? Our Rig, our magic man; no sign of him since the Axe nicked his face."

I said nothing.

"Gone scarce, eh? Rigs are scarce, this one's scarcer." He glared about. "Has the Rig saved us? Been here a year and more, and what's changed? Tell me! We'll save ourselves. It's not magic we need, it's blood!"

Voices tried to hush him. Eyes turned from me to him, then back to me; more and more eyes. The men who had seen me only on the dark beach last night now let their eyes travel downward from my neck, began to back away. Even Rosh looked again, fell silent, edged.

I gathered the torn collar of my shift in my fist. Faltering, I said, "I'll come with you and fight."

Mailin made a little sound.

"No," said Rosh, staring.

"Let me come! I can use a knife—"

"*No.*" He turned to the others. "Let's go. Right now. We'll get Dai! Listen. It's not just for him. If Dai's a martyr, it's for *us*—sucked and bled and spat on, ground in the dirt. We'll kill them." He bared his teeth. "We'll have a little talk with Harlan. Convince him of a couple of things. Those two we took today, they're convinced by now."

Hard, relieved laughter rose from the crowd. Knives chimed, and bodies began to move away from me, down the veranda steps. A voice in my head kept stuttering, *Please let— Please let—*

As if I yanked open a stuck door, I made myself think the thought whole: *Please let Dai be dead. Let Ab Harlan have hanged him, because hanging is quick.*

There was a girl I knew in Creek, younger than I, who had such skill at pottery that they said she would be Clay Keep before she was twenty. One winter morning she had a fever, and the next she was dead.

I thought of her, begun and stopped. I thought of Dai's

cow, Moss, cropping grass—the life of this blade, that blade surely stopped. But that was for a reason: to feed a cow to make milk. But for Dai's life and mine, stopped, I could see no reason at all.

I might have run to Mailin, but she was part of what had stopped. As the crowd streamed yelling down the steps, I went the other way, into the dark room where Rosie lay. Though it was summer, I was cold. I sat on the edge of the bed feeling nothing, smelling the sweet, fusty odor of day's-end child.

Something moved in a corner. My body jumped. And this was the strange thing: it jumped to protect Rosie, as if she were my child.

The thing in the corner was Nondany, sitting in a chair. I had forgotten him. "Half-and-Half."

I leaned away, silent.

"So it is," he said.

I think that was the quietest house I was ever in, after those men had gone. Quiet as a grave, as a winter night when frost snaps in the cistern. I heard the house's pilings groan, and the hiss of the sea.

"That Rig," I said. I did not want his name in my mouth. "He didn't go with the men. He's running away, back to the Rigi's land."

Nondany sat back in his chair. His foot tapped. "Did he say why?"

"He wants to listen at that Gate."

The tapping stopped. Began again. "By life! And what will you do now?"

"He wants me to run away with him. I will not."

Nondany rose, he came over and sat on the bed. Next to my coldness he was hot as a stove. I got up and went to the window. The sea growled; I started back, hugging my elbows.

Nondany smoothed Rosie's blouse, her hair; he picked up her two fat hands. She slept as though dead.

I said, "Detention is in Ab Harlan's compound. Somewhere in there. You go in the main gate—" There was an army camped around that gate. "No. But there are other ways in. There must be. I could find one. A man couldn't get in, but somebody small, like me—" No one could get in there. I said, "I won't hide, then. I'll go straight to Ab Harlan." At this thought my knees turned to water, I had to put my hands on the sill.

Nondany said nothing.

I said in a whisper, "That would be fair."

"Bravely spoken. And Ab Harlan would enjoy it very much."

I held on to the sill as the world jerked and clattered in disorder so evil, I could not breathe in it.

"Half-and-Half. May I ask you two questions?"

I nodded.

"Thank you." Nondany's voice was light, pedantic, a little cold. "One: What were you born for? And two: What will you do about Nall?"

I could not see his face in the dimness. To both questions I answered, "Nothing."

"Interesting stuff, nothing. There's a song about it."

> *Nee, nah, nothing!*
> *Nee, nah, nothing!*
> A wise man ate a seed,
> And it grew into a weed

In his middle, till its roots
Had filled up his boots
And split apart his brain,
So he stood there in the rain,
As happy as a duck in a sweet spring downpour,
singing,
Nee, nah, nothing!

While he sang, he patted Rosie's hands together softly, as if for one of his games. I said suddenly, "Do you have children?"

"One, long ago. Dead with his mother. We all do die." He patted Rosie's hands. "But don't divert me. Another way to ask those questions is to say, It seems Nall knows his calling; what is yours?"

"My calling was that I called him. He came. Now he's leaving."

"So it's meaningless?"

I did not answer.

"How incomprehensible is the world to one with a wasps' nest for a brain!" said Nondany. "You think I'm joking. Yet the world is so vast and I know so little of it, I can hardly judge whether an event makes sense or not." He looked out the window. "I have never been to the Rigi's land."

I looked too, over the soft, repeating waves to the western horizon. The sky there was a little lighter than the sea.

"Half-and-Half, what do you know about Nall and why he came? Other than that you called him?"

I thought, I know he had a great-grandmother. I did not say this.

Nondany said, "Have you asked him?"

"He's a seal. Seals don't talk to people."

"Perhaps he was a seal once. At present he seems remarkably like a man. You are not curious about what a seal man might say?"

I stood stonily silent.

"One wonders whether he is curious about a woman who was eaten by a bear— Don't jump, my dear. You think I'm not familiar with the customs of Creek?"

"It wasn't a bear!"

"I thought not. You were blessed. Be grateful."

I stared at that homely little man. He stared right back and said, "Have you told Nall what it was like to be eaten?"

"No. He's a coward."

"Is he."

"You know nothing!"

"Next to nothing," said Nondany. "Though I have a bit of experience with courage, and with being eaten by things that are not bears. Half-and-Half, you will find it a challenge, this talking about things that have no names. Yet it's essential. As is doing what you must, even when you don't know what that is."

I turned to face him and his riddles, letting the casement hold me up. "I don't know what to do," I said. "What should I do?"

"I have no idea." He patted Rosie's hands together. "But you might begin by appreciating your state. There's a story they tell in Wicker Breaks—you know that Hill town? About a girl who was eaten by her bear, but she didn't become a woman right away. First she had to pass some time as what emerged from the far end of the bear."

"What kind of story is that!"

"What kind of story is this?" He dropped Rosie's hands

and stretched out his own to indicate this world as it is, this life, all of us.

I pressed my palms to my forehead. "What happened to the girl in the story?"

"I never found out. The tale was fragmentary."

"You're crazy!"

"My dear, if I were sane, I couldn't bear to live."

"Then die. Like my brother."

"I shall. That's a promise. But at this moment I'm alive, and I know *my* calling. Therefore, I shall ask you to sing that very silly song you were singing to Rosie on the veranda. About the piggie."

"So you can write it down!"

"Eventually." Bowing his head, he kissed Rosie's hands, left and right, moon and sun, Rig and Leagueman. He patted them together. "At present I am occupied."

I turned my back on him. Over the sea the stars were showing, one by one. I sang the song for him, very low. By the second time through he could sing it with me.

"Thank you," he said.

"I don't know what to do."

"So does it matter where you do it?"

"No."

"Then you can do it just as well at the wrong end of the bear."

"I said I don't know what to do!"

"Who does?" said Nondany.

12

Find a stone that fits your hand.
Carry it for a long time.
Die.
Let the stone roll back into the sea.

How to Hold Beach Stones. The Rigi.

THE HOUSE WAS QUIET. I stood at the bottom of the steps in the
dark. A tiny clatter in the lean-to was Nall, working. I listened
to those light sounds for a long time.

A noiseless shape slipped down the steps: the cat, leaving
her kittens to go hunting. As if her motion moved me, I
stepped across the trampled sand to the front of the lean-to.

In the slatted starlight he bent over the slim hull of the

manat. Gleam of his haunch, blink of a knife blade. I wondered if he could see in the dark.

"Nall."

He jumped. He must have been very intent. He cut a last cord and came crouching along the hull holding his short, curved knife, stroking his thumb along the blade.

"When will you go?"

"Before morning."

"Why did you come?"

Silence. He said, "For what is happening."

"What is that?"

"I don't know."

"Mailin said you came because I called you with the Rigi's song. She said *you* called *me*."

"I must have. I thought I had." He moved a little, like a man in pain. "I listen, then I sing, and live what I sing. All this"—he stretched out his hands like Nondany, toward the world—"it's here, it came through the Gate. I'm part of it, so it must have been in my listening. Like a call."

"I don't want misty Rig talk!" But I heard Nondany's dry voice ask, *You are not curious about what a seal man might say?*

"What does it sound like?" I said. "In the sea, when you listen."

"There's a voice," he said.

"Of what."

"The Gate. Not words. But words cling to it."

He spoke slowly, trying words, dropping them, the way I spoke when I tried to talk about the Bear. I said, "When the world first comes through the Gate, is it good? And if it is, why is it like this when it gets here?"

"I don't know. If I listened, maybe I would understand."

"Would understanding change anything?"

"I don't know."

"Then what good is it?"

"I don't know."

I ground my teeth. I walked away from him, down to the water where waves were coming and coming from somewhere out in the dark. Walked back to him. "Tell me about the Gate."

"I have."

"Only a little."

"It would be a story."

I thought of Jekka brushing my hair. "Tell it."

I would not sit. Neither would he. He set his shoulder on the pole of the lean-to. A little light fell on his face, from the high house where people raged and wept, but his body was dark.

"The Gate stands at the mouth of a bay," he said, "on the west coast of the westernmost land there is: the Home Stone, the island where I was born. The Rigi keep the Gate. They have always kept the Gate."

In his voice I heard another voice, surely his ama's. I wondered what she was like, besides being smaller than me.

"In the beginning," said Nall, "the Rigi, men and women, could put on their sealskins and, as seals, could swim in the water before the Gate, listening to the world being born. Then they took off their skins and were human, and they sang what they had heard. But in time—"

"—they forgot how to put on their skins," I said.

He blinked. Nodded.

"I know that story. Creek calls it 'How Ouma the Bear

Mother Made the World.' It starts out, 'In the beginning . . .' Then the beginning ends. We ruin it, we get lost and can't go back. But go on," I said.

After a moment he went on.

"In time the Rigi forgot how to put on their skins. But there were a few who still knew how, and how to listen; these became the seal priests. That was not so long ago, Kat. When the Rigi still came to Downshore to dance and trade, there were seal priests. They listened at the Gate for the songs of the making world, and at Least and Long Nights they sang them. Those songs were not for the Rigi only, but for the whole world. Even the Leaguemen."

"And the Leaguemen ran the Rigi off."

"Do you think the Rigi themselves had no hand in it? I told you they have their own Ab Harlan: He is called the Reirig, the One True Seal Priest. In the times Mailin spoke of, when Downshore began to kill so many seals, the Rigi screamed for a strong leader—aye, and got what they screamed for! A warrior. He killed the last priests, he named his cohorts 'elders,' and made himself the One. When those League lads killed and robbed the Rig, the Reirig seized the chance to rule a world with only himself as king. He led the Rigi into exile.

"The Reirig has no name, only 'the Reirig.' He is strong; when he begins to weaken, sooner or later some stronger man fights him hand to hand, kills him, and becomes in turn the One.

"Thus the Reirig's face changes, but the Reirig does not change. He is always the One True Seal Priest. The only man— he says!—who can put on his skin and be a seal; who can swim, listening, in the sea before the Gate, return to shore, and sing the truths of the world. Shall I tell you what he sings?"

I nodded.

With the point of his knife Nall counted on his open hand.

"One: The old songs are sacred, never change them. Two: The Reirig is without fault. Three: The Reirig must have this woman for his next wife, and that naysayer must be killed. Four: The Rigi are never to make peace with the seal-killers or the Black Boots or any other beings on this shore."

He folded his hand into a fist and set it on his hip. "Strange, how the voice of the Gate seems always to choose what suits the Reirig."

"The League says that *they* are the chosen, that Light bleeds gold only for them, that they deserve the best goods."

"It's the same lust. The Reirig and his elders take the best of everything—food and shelter and women. Little is left for the people. The Rigi are like water trapped in a tide pool, with no tide returning.

"Kat, they are dying. It's a sickness; they call it *hsuu heo*— 'too much sea.' The fields are spent, the gardens scant, the wild herbs gone. Even the fish have fled. Whole families starve, or die of fevers that fill the lungs with water. Too much sea! Children as thin as grass die in their sleep; babies are born wrong. Girls are barren, their babies never born." Nall turned his face away. "But the Reirig has many wives, many children, all rosy and fat. So do those elders whom he favors, for he feeds them."

"Those he favors, he feeds—but if he feeds them, they'll grow strong and kill him."

"Yes. It sets man against man, all spying and guessing and killing in secret, each soul bound so tight, between need and fear, that it can scarcely breathe. So the sickness grows." Nall turned. "Kat, why would I not come away out of too much sea? Stripped and killed and cast away, would I not swim if I could—east, to a woman all earth, with hair like the sun, who called to me from the shore?"

I could not even weep. I had no brother and no home on earth; I could not remember how it had felt to walk upon the mountain. "I was a little stupid child," I said.

He looked at me. His chin stuck out.

I dropped my eyes. "Why don't the Rigi just come back here? They have manats."

"Manats—but sealskins, too. A Rig bound at birth to a seal-skin does not leave the Rigi. With the blade of his lance the first Reirig scribed a line across the sea: the Ni'Na'—the Changes. No Rig can cross it. I crossed because they unmade me, they burned my skin. I am no longer a Rig."

"What are you?"

"A listener."

Again.

"Kat. Since the Rigi left these shores, no one but the Reirig has listened at the Gate. Except me."

I looked at him then, all right. "You listened at the Gate?"

"Not in the old, true way. I am no priest. I could not become my seal and swim in the sea before the Gate. If I could do that! But there is a rock just landward of it, called Stillness, where the Reirig goes to put on his sealskin. I listened from Stillness."

"And he caught you?"

"No. No one knew I went there." He hesitated. "Almost no one. I had a—I had a clan."

"Your ama."

"And . . . cousins. All of us born to one *arem,* one warren-house: the arem of Selí. Three of us were boys, Tadde and Liu and myself. Liu was like Dai to me. A brother in my heart."

I said nothing.

"All of us were trouble. Tadde was eldest. The Rigi are all factions and quarrel, but Tadde began to pull them together, speaking in secret of return to the mainland. Perhaps we could kill the Reirig—though Tadde was not a killing man—or steal his lance and open a way through the Ni'Na'. Rumors reached the Reirig, and he closed his fist still tighter.

"On feast days Liu and I sang together in the arems. Liu had a wicked tongue—he could make you laugh at your own death! He made a song against the Reirig."

I thought of Nondany. "Sing it."

"It has no lilt in Plain," he said, but he sang.

> Raven comes to Seal, he says,
> "How does one listen at the Gate?"
> "With that," says Seal,
> pointing to Raven's anus.
> Raven backs up to two stones,
> he hears his own dung falling
> and cries, "I know the secrets of the world!"

"Good song, eh?" Nall laughed, not merrily. "That song fled through the clans like wind—but the wind blows everywhere. One night, when Liu and I ran home along the strand, the Reirig's men waited." Nall touched his broken tooth. "It was my—it was Liu's sister who found us. They had clubbed us both, and Liu was dead. They had cut out his tongue."

I went hot and cold at once, as though I stood in snow and looked into a furnace.

"No word was spoken," said Nall. "Liu's death was the

word. By it the Reirig told us, 'Speak, and I shall speak death.' So I knew I would speak. Songs are my speech.

"At the dark of the moon the time came for the One to listen at the Gate. When the sun had set, he left the elders making sacrifice on the shore and paddled to the rock Stillness. It was the intertide, when the currents are slack; I swam after him and crept up among the spires of rock.

"He had pulled up his manat and taken out a little picnic. This he ate, belching and tossing the bones into the sea. He watched the waves awhile, and picked his nose. Then he pissed in the sea, took off his sealskin—it was heavy with jet, surely uncomfortable—took a robe of otter skins from the manat, rolled up in it, and slept. He snores; but I knew that. Any night outside his arem you can hear him snore.

"I clung among the spires of rock. Still he slept. I crept out and looked for his lance, to steal it; it was not there, only his knife. I thought, 'I'll kill him as he sleeps.'

"But there before me was the Gate—the Gate! That petty king blubbering his lips was less to me than bird slime. Should I make myself a murderer for a turd?

"I hid among the rocks and listened. Tide and world rushed in and out of the Gate.

"Near dawn the Reirig woke. He scratched, farted, and splashed himself with water from a little pool on the stone; he never so much as dipped himself in the sea.

"In the intertide he paddled back to shore. I followed, swimming, and by the time I got back to the beach, he was singing the songs he had heard, his head rolling in holy madness. I have told you what he heard."

"What did *you* hear?" But I knew.

"The song they killed me for. The Rigi's song, made new.

The Reirig said I profaned it and must be killed; but he killed me because I sang the truth instead of his lies."

"When you first told me about it"—nearly two years ago, or two lifetimes—"you said you sang for a woman giving birth."

"Liu's wife."

"She had twin girls, you said, and their arms were like a seal's flippers."

"Too much sea," said Nall.

"Then *your* father helped the Reirig kill you."

An uncertainty crept into his voice. "The Reirig would have killed me in the birthing room, as I stood singing that new song. He would have slit my throat. But my father said, 'Is my son's sin so slight? If you kill him that way, he will still be a Rig and swim among the ancestors. Strip him of his seal: Burn his sealskin and his name, and lay him living among the dead. Then there will be nothing left but bones in the surf, for eternity."

I knew I had a rotten father, but this was worse. "Does he hate you so much?"

"I—I did not think so. Until then. My father is— No one knows how he is." Nall looked out at the moving water. "His name is Hsuu, 'Old Sea.' He is like the sea, which neither hates nor loves, but moves for its own reasons. Maybe he wanted to hurt my ama."

"You said your mother didn't cry."

His face went wistful. "Perhaps she was being a seagull at that moment. Or a sand rat, or a shadow. It isn't her fault. She becomes what she dreams; no one can hold her. But she's very beautiful." He looked at me as though to defend his parentage—a strange thing, for that shame was mine. "When I was small, she was my best playmate. She could be a frog, or a flower, or a fish swimming; but then she would forget me and swim off, or grow bored and turn into a cloud. I would be left crying on the shore. Then my ama would come looking for me, she would smack me and curse my parents, and carry me to her own place and make me drink hot soup and talk like a person."

I did not know what to do with all this news. "Did your ama cry?"

"She shouted at the Reirig and his warriors. They knocked her down."

He touched my cold arm. I let him. "You think I am running away from war," he said. "Then you must think that. But the little man understands—Nondany. He knows that *as it is here, so it is there*. The League has no sea, and it has driven them mad; the Rigi have no earth, and it is killing them. Ab Harlan's war and the Reirig's are the same war, pouring through the Gate. And to the Gate I will go.

"Let the Reirig sing his lies: 'This world is mine, and never changes.' A world that never changes is dead. I'll listen and sing the world changing, because it is alive." He leaned to me. I could feel the heat of him on my coldness. "The world moves. It always has. But *we* are not alive with the world. Our tides are stopped, and that is our sickness: too much earth or too much sea. I'll listen for that living change and sing it, though it cost me my life."

"If you do that, will the world be well again?"

He looked at me as though I were crazy. "It will be the world, coming through the Gate. It has always been coming through the Gate. I only listen to it, and sing."

"And if your listening makes no difference?"

"Then it makes no difference."

I did not understand what he said any more than Bian had understood the Bear. I could see that whether or not Nall's listening had made a difference, his singing had: It had gotten him killed. I hugged my hands under my arms, shivering in the summer night.

So what do you do when you can't bear the world to be the world? When it devours brothers like a shark, twists babies, gives wealth and power to evil men? Do you go to where it is being born—if you can find that place—and see whether there, perhaps, it makes sense? Or maybe you just go searching for that place, because if you are moving, the pain is less?

I looked where Nall looked, west. Only darkness. But not empty; something waited out there.

"I'll go with you," I said.

"No."

"But—but you asked me to!"

"Because we called each other. But you have said no. And, Kat—" His thumb still played on the knife blade; he moved his hand as though to put the knife out of my reach. "—if you go to sea in a small boat wanting to die, you do."

I put my hands over my face, that had showed him more than I knew myself. "You said it might cost you *your* life."

"It's not for myself that I gamble with it."

"Nall, take me."

"No."

Tied at my sash, the gold in its warm pouch knocked at my thigh. "I never got to make love to you," I said. "Now I'll never know what it's like."

His thumb flexed; he dropped the knife in the sand with a hiss.

"Take me with you," I said. "I can run and hide now, and then die in bed someday, an old woman wetting herself. Or I can go with you." I laid my hands on his chest. "I have to go with you. Father gave me money for his grandchild. Do you think I'd get a baby with anybody else?"

He groaned, he put his hand to his eyes. Then he pulled it away, staring. "I've cut myself," he said. Blood from his thumb ran down his temple.

"Thumb cuts are terrible," said my own cold voice. "They take forever to heal."

He put his arms around me and pulled me down against the mummy skin of the manat. My knees and elbows knocked against him. "You're bleeding on me," I said. "You always bleed on me."

"Kat, Kat—"

I stood up out of his embrace and said, "I'm coming with you. I'll help you carry out the manat."

I went to Mailin's hearth, where the little group sat holding one another, and said, to nobody, "He's going to the Gate. I'm going with him."

Mailin put her hand to her heart.

They did not ask me why. Maybe, like Nall, they saw something in my face. Mailin rose and said, "I'll put extra in his bundle."

So she had known. In a cold fever I walked here, walked there as she cut more bread and cheese, put more dried meat and tea into the oiled bag. She moved as if she were as old as Hamarry, and when she looked at me, I looked away.

Nondany drifted at the edge of my vision, like the floating

specks that move when your eye moves. The sky had gone pale and Mailin was tying up the bundle before he edged me into a corner and said, "Half-and-Half."

I shook my head.

"No one has gone to the Rigi's land for a hundred years," he said. "Think of the chance."

"For what."

"To learn songs."

I stared.

He peered like a mole with its squinty eyes and said, "I trust you completely. Whatever delights you will delight me. Or," he said, cocking his head, "you could let it all be Nall's journey. He's strong."

I said to the floor, "He knows what he wants."

"You don't?"

I said in a whisper, "I want it to be how it was before." Mailin's calm face, Dai's chuckle, Nall's seeking mouth.

Nondany was silent. When I looked up at him, his face was full of pain and tenderness. "Half-and-Half, it was just like this before. It has always been like this."

I looked away.

"There's a song—," he began, then waved his hand to cancel the thought. "Never mind. I'll give you something for your journey. A token. Not much; tokens belong in the Year Fire. I don't want to weigh you down." He held out his closed fist. "Here."

I did not want anything. But it was rude not to take it. I put out my palm, and he opened his fist.

Nothing.

I thought maybe something tiny had fallen or had stuck to his palm. I looked about. His hand was empty.

He seemed as pleased as if he had given me a diamond. "Don't lose it," he said.

I did not answer, did not need to, because a dark hubbub had begun on the beach. I forgot my gift and gripped Nondany's arm. We went to the kitchen, where Robin crowded against Mailin. Suni ran to the veranda rail.

It was not paidmen storming the steps, but our own men—the world was now our men, their men—without Dai. They were lying, to make their exploit bigger than its failure.

"Almost," said Rosh, the young fisherman. Spittle clung in the corners of his mouth. "They threw us back, but we killed two South Road toadies. Larcody's dead, but he died fighting, and his son swears he'll fight in his stead. The Least Night crowds are arming; we'll have more men tomorrow." He saw me in the press and grinned. "Lord Fat-Ass wants the witch. 'Bring me the witch!' he cries. He won't get her. You're safe with us, sweetheart."

I thought, Am I hearing a Downshoreman? A Leagueman? A paidman? I said, "I am not your sweetheart."

He muttered an apology of sorts. Then, to save face, he said, "Your little Rig's on the beach with his boat. Let him come with us, if he's a man. If he isn't—"

"Watch your tongue," said another. "Luck or storms."

Rosh turned his sneer into plans, boasts, arguments. Soon the mass of them went off, leaving two men moaning on the hearth for Mailin to mend, if she could, and black gouts of blood on the kitchen floor.

I let go of Nondany. I ran away down the steps and along the beach to Nall, who had known, who had not even come up into the kitchen. He stood by the manat, the waves foaming at his feet.

I felt as I had in Creek when I ran up the mountain: that there was only one way open. Every home was closed, and every other way blocked, as if the world itself drove me.

A rustle behind me was Mailin, alone, bringing the food bundle. There was blood on her hands. I took the bundle and held it the way I had held Rosie.

Through her tears she said, "I put in plenty for two."

Nall put his arms around her. They stood so still that a gull strolled up to their stillness and rose with a yelp when they moved at last.

She touched Nall's cheek. "The world I knew is coming apart. All deaths seem terrible to the one who dies."

Her world too, I thought. Yet she could bear it, and I could not. When Nall took the food bundle and she came to embrace me, I was stiff and cold, and if I felt anything at all, it was guilt that I would not stay to suffer a woman's lot, the terror and boredom of waiting.

"War is too big," I whispered at her shoulder. "I can fight with only one person at a time."

"That is the root of all wars—and of all peace." She held me in spite of my stiffness, as I had held Rosie's fists and knees. "Your work is worthy, Lali Kat. Go, fight with Nall and with yourself, as long as you may." Her cheek on mine was soft and old. "All my life I've wanted to go west over the water. Take my heart with you!"

Nall spoke a word in the Rigi's tongue. Mailin sighed. "I'll push you off," she said.

I climbed into the rear hatch. Mailin helped Nall run the manat into the creamy foam. When it was waterborne, he hopped in quickly, for the seas had the wind behind them and the boat wanted to turn broadside to the waves. Soft spray burst up. I watched his working back and tried to match his stroke. When we came through into a quieter space between waves, I looked over my shoulder. Mailin stood thigh-deep in the water, waving, very small, behind her the house full of people to whom I had not even said good-bye.

I had a panicky feeling that I had lost something, dropped it out of my hand. Then I realized it was Nondany's nothing; the paddle was in my hand. Behind me Downshore and Upslope faded to smoky shadows, and we were on the open water when the sun rose.

13

It rises, it falls
It rises, it falls
It breathes
All around us it breathes
It rises, it falls

Tide Chant. The Rigi.

I THOUGHT SOMETHING as big as the sea must make a sound. It made no sound. Around the little manat the huge water tipped and hove, rose and fell as the sun turned it from gray to a cold green like glass, in silence. Only where the sea touched something else—prow, paddle, my dipped hand—did it hiss and crackle, a tiny noise in that bigness. The boat's lashings creaked.

In front of me Nall's shoulders changed from a shadow to a scarred brown back. My paddle kept time with his— right, left, right—as we rode west across the shining plain I had seen from the mule cart, toiling up hills that fell away beneath us and rose again, paddling toward a distant, bare arc of sky.

The manat was so small that the swell rolled under it and passed, as if it were a drifting log. So small; I shipped the paddle, touched the water with my palm. Below my hand the translucent blue-green glass went down, powdery as if with dust motes for the first fathom, then dark.

"How deep is it?"

"I don't know."

"Is there a bottom?"

Chiss, chiss went the blade of Nall's paddle. He spoke over his shoulder between strokes. "Here, close to land, the fishermen can drop their nets and draw them up full of creatures. Crabs, crawling sideways. Dogfish—sharks no bigger than cats. Shrimp with feelers striped white and red. Lobsters." He shook his head. "They drag up a world, and all they know to do with it is eat it."

I thought of the seafloor far below, a cold meadow, beasts grazing on it. "When we aren't close to land anymore, will there be a bottom?"

"I don't know."

A wind came up at our left hand, writing on the water a script that changed and changed. A commotion at the horizon became a cloud of birds.

Nall pointed with his chin. "Those little islands, the skerries—they lead westward. Between them the water is not so deep; creeping skerry to skerry, the fishermen feel safe. But they don't venture west of the last one, for there the water deepens beyond the sun's reach."

"So they can't get at the lobsters?"

The line of his cheek bunched in a smile. My heart made a little lurch toward him. But if I let it move, it would spill its cargo into the sea of pain, so I held it still again, tight and cold.

"There are no lobsters in the deep," he said. "Eaters and eaten both love sunlight; they crowd together in the shallows where it can touch them. We say—*they* say, one may eat the cool beings: fish and lobster, mussel and crab. But not the warm beings: whale and orca and seal. So they say. The Rigi."

We're going to the Rigi's land, I thought. Where the world is born. But I could not feel anything about it. The part of me that thought seemed to work fine; it was my heart that was frozen. I said, "What lies west of the last skerry?"

"The great deep."

"And west of that?"

"The Isle of Bones, where the Rigi lay their dead. Where they laid me."

I saw now the magnitude of this journey, impossible. But Nall said, "When I broke free and swam, the first fetch was the longest. After that I followed the skerries. I ate mussels and drank rain from the rock pools. But the air was colder than the sea, so I swam again."

"Will we go to the Isle of Bones?"

"No. We'll slip past it and on through the islands, west. No one must see us."

"No one?" My first, foolish thought was, *But how will I learn songs for Nondany?* My second was, *Of course the Rigi mustn't see us. The Reirig and the elders killed Nall, they'd kill him again.* My third was, *What would they do to* me?

"They won't see us," said Nall.

I looked at the dim horizon, as if it might suddenly blacken with manats. "Don't the Rigi come east to the skerries? If there are lobsters?"

"I told you about the Ni'Na'; the Rigi can't cross that boundary without the Reirig's lance." He stopped paddling for a moment. "This side of the Isle of Bones it changes."

"What changes?"

"Whatever it is. What won't let them out."

"*You* got out."

"I was dead," he said. "I was no longer a Rig." He stopped paddling and turned in the hatch till I could see half his living face. "Soon we'll stop at a place I know. We'll eat and sleep a little and ready ourselves for the deep." He reached out his hand to me. From that awkward position he could offer it only upside down.

Instantly I was shy, with nowhere to hide on the whole wide ocean; yet my heart was cold. I looked away over the water. After a moment he withdrew his hand. We paddled west.

The manat nosed ashore in the lee of a grassy islet, in a confusion of little waves. Even loaded it was light enough to carry up onto the shingle. Nall stood twisting his back to ease it, while I dug out Mailin's bundle.

"Look!" I said. In the clear water of a tide pool a perfect flower grew, ivory tinged with pink.

I reached to pick it. Nall knocked my hand away. "It has a bitter sting," he said.

With food and a water skin we climbed rocks splashed white with bird droppings, in the sharp iodine smell of seaweed. A notch in the tumbled stones led upward, fifty, sixty feet to a small plateau.

The island was an acre or two, furred with grass that bent, bent in the wind from the west. It was dimpled with corries and stacked with wind-eaten stone, but there was a nook at the top of the cleft where the grass was soft and dark green with summer. Everywhere the sun shone, glittering on the bowing blades. Nall threw himself down and lay looking up at the blue sky.

I sat next to him, my knees drawn up. He pushed one hand through the grass and took hold of my ankle, laid his other hand across his eyes. Above us gulls and kittiwakes mewed and drifted. Wind combed the grass into whorls like a baby's cowlick. His hand slacked on my ankle, and he slept.

I remembered he had hardly slept for two nights, and I felt toward him a cold, devouring tenderness. The world and this journey could not be real; my brother's name could not be thought, much less spoken. All my life and need fixed on Nall.

Right here, I thought, we'll make life new. This is my island, and I name it *Shining*. There will be no grief here, no horror. Just us. I'll wake him and we'll make love. We have to.

I touched his thigh. He woke. "What?"

"N-nothing," I said. "There was a beetle on you."

His mouth quirked. He found my hand and held it, saying, "Wake me when this shadow touches that stone."

So I watched him sleep, driven toward him. The ground got hard; an ant crawled up the back of my knee. I drew my hand out of his, stood, and began to explore my shining home.

Here's where he'll build our house, I thought, reckless as a gambler bluffing with a bad hand. We'll get water from the rain. I'll plant cabbages. Our children will play in that grassy place, out of the wind. We'll have a cat.

I wandered among the boulders, touching them. We could get a kitten from Mailin, I thought. I would not let the image of Robin come. Aloud I said, "And Nall shall have a workshop, looking west."

I walked to the edge of the western cliff and looked down.

Ran back, nearly falling. At the grassy swale I gasped twice before I could cry, "*Nall!*"

He rolled to his feet. I pointed, he ran where I pointed, we stood looking down at the waves that pushed the body of a man to and fro.

Nall squinted west. Empty ocean. He began to pick his way down among the rocks. I followed because I would not be left alone.

It was a Leagueman. He lay on his back, his feet on the shingle and his head in the sea. He was barefoot; his feet looked naked and pitiful, very white. Lazy waves broke across his face.

"It's the clerk who takes the tariff," I said. His eyes were open, brown eyes in a face without expression. The mark of Jake's reins was on his cheek. I remembered the two sails I had seen from Mailin's porch. "He'd be one of the hostages. They left him here because he'd be so afraid of the sea." He's not afraid now, I thought.

"His neck is broken."

When you are hanged, your neck is broken.

"Maybe they threw him from the cliff," said Nall. But I was already climbing like a monkey. From the cliff top I watched him make a quick search of the shore, finding no other human sign. By the time he returned to the grassy level, I had piled the food and water next to the crushed grass where he had lain.

"I won't stay in this place," I said.

We slipped the manat into the waves and paddled out, swinging in a wide arc to clear the western shore. Later we made an uncomfortable meal inboard, passing bread and water over the rocking deck.

All day we followed the string of stony islands westward, stopping only to stand and stretch, and on that whole wide ocean were only ourselves and birds. Once, deep down, a shadow passed; once, far away, something furious chased something frightened out of the water in a shimmer of spray. But I never saw the creatures, if they were creatures, or heard any sound but water's. Everything was shadow and shine. Our paddles dipped and dipped, like fins.

The sky began to be everything, ranked and cliffed with cloud, slabbed and canyoned, green and white and gray and blue. I stopped looking at it. Instead I looked at one place on Nall's back near his spine where there was a dark mark the size of my thumbnail. I thought it was a birthmark and then saw it was a tattoo, blurred and faded, a spiral like the writing on Raím's bowl. I stared at it until it pulled me downward, then at the sky until it pulled me upward. I thought of the desert with the little creek running across it, the sea with the little islands strewn across it—everything backward, like the image on your eyelid after you have stared at something bright. Somewhere there were mountains and flowers, but not here.

Painted white by birds, the skerries were cairns on a

trackless track, each farther from the last. Late in the day we pulled past the last one and came onto the great deep.

We spoke little. At first Nall tried to. But the silence of the huge sky became the name I could not speak; my answers got shorter and shorter, and after a while he fell silent too. Sometimes he sang under his breath, a minor tune.

> Cold sea
> Deep sea
> Green wave
> Under me
>
> Low wind
> Cold wind
> Bright day
> Soon end

His voice was steady, grieving. I thought, He has forgotten me.

I did not listen anymore, but paddled in the song as if it were the sea, for a thousand miles and a thousand years.

The sun had long since hidden itself in low, mild cloud. We went toward that cloud bank seeming to go nowhere, paddling, quiet. Nall paused, his paddle in the air. He turned his head this way, that way, snuffing or listening.

"Here," he said. "Can you feel it?"

I could not feel anything. I would not let myself feel anything, except the paddle in my hand.

He pushed his hand in front of him, pressing at the face of the air. The spiral mark on his spine coiled as his muscles strained, and my bare legs, lying along his, felt him shiver. Something broke across my face, like a spiderweb or the skin of the water when you slide under it.

He let his breath out. *"Ah."* Looked back. "We are in."

Nothing had changed. The light was bluer, but that was the cloud.

We went on, seeming not to move. True, the wind was in our faces, but I thought too that Nall might be paddling slowly, to spare me. My hands were hard from work, but by early evening they had blistered in the soft place between fingers and thumb. My shoulders hurt.

I laid the paddle across the deck. "Nall." My voice was thin between the water and the sky. "Do we keep going all night?"

He stopped his steady stroke and stretched each arm, shook out each hand.

"I'm tired," I said. Hearing the plaint in my voice, I sat straighter. "Not so very."

He made that awkward half turn to look at me. "We'll stop. But not yet. There"—he lowered his voice—"there is the Isle of Bones."

I looked past his shoulder at what I had thought a cloud among the thousand clouds, low-laid and dark. "We have to pass it?"

"Beyond it is another landing, a place to rest. A little farther."

We paddled on through the dimming day. The cloud bank became an island that was one tall cliff, gray and black and rough as a rotten tooth, riddled with stacks and caves and holes through which the sea poured in, poured out. Mist smoked from its ragged pinnacles, where skeins of birds tangled in the late light.

I shivered. Nall's hand was out of reach unless he offered

it; he did not offer. He twisted until I saw his tense profile and said, "Kat. From now on."

I did not ask what that meant. I said, "I'm cold."

"It's the breath from the caves." He swung up his paddle. We went on across the water.

After a long fetch we drew level with the riddled cliff, but south of it, not close. We paddled fast. Birds screamed. I thought of the dead clerk, his face under water. In Upslope he would have been laid in a grave. I thought of my mother's grave and the breath of cold that had risen from it.

I dug at the swell. Still I was cold. I worked and splashed and sweat, but I could not get warm, and we did not pass the Isle of Bones. Panting, I stopped paddling to find that the wind had sharpened in our faces, the cloud bank thickened to bring an early dusk.

West of us I could see the little island we were heading for. Then I could not. Rain, walking over the ocean on gray legs, had blotted it out. Another few minutes, and the rain hit us, too; the wind eased, sheets of falling water flattened the swell. The world became a room with straight gray walls, the Isle of Bones just visible at our right hand.

To be sure of a landmark, Nall pulled the manat closer to the cliff and held it there with slow strokes while the rain poured down. I bailed. Paddling, bailing, we hunched and spat water, wiping our faces. The rain drummed on the skin deck.

Just a summer rain, I told myself. But I was cold. I began to shake and could not stop.

"Rain getting worse." My jaw shuddered. "Go on to that place to sleep?"

"I can't find it now."

"Spend night in boat?"

He half turned, to that unnatural position. "You're too cold."

"Am not." My teeth chattered too hard for more.

But he was already paddling, turning the manat to face the cliff that sloped into the dark.

"So," he said. "We shall ask lodging of the dead."

14

A dark place wants me
and I want it.
Do not tell the man about the dark.
Be the dark.
Be that threshold,
that cave,
that well so deep
not even a dropped stone
knows the bottom.

Women's Song. The Roadsouls.

THE SPLASH OF HIS paddle was drowned in the drum of the rain. He drew the boat toward the Isle of Bones like a cat creeping into a sleeping house.

I tried to help. But I was clumsy with cold, the blades clacked on each other, and Nall hissed, stilling me with a downward jerk of his hand. Among leaden eddies we slipped along the foot of the eastern cliff. Above us hung breaks and caverns, darker in the dark. Posts and shoals of fallen rock trailed out from shore; right under our skin hull, rocks bladed with barnacles sawed up and down in the wash. We fended off with our paddles, making little runs along the cliff.

"Don't like it," I said, my voice too high. "West shore better?"

"Yes. But we need a cave. I can't make a fire in the rain."

"But in the caves—"

"Kat. I would not come here if there were anywhere else to go."

So I kept silent and tried to watch for rocks. We crept around two more rockfalls, the rain boiled up a mist that the waves quenched. Before us a cavern opened its gullet to the ocean, wide and black. Nall swung the manat into a back eddy, and the hull groaned on gravel.

The stony beach twitched, like a blanket with somebody under it.

I sucked in one breath, then saw, in the dim light, that the gravel was thick with crabs. From the cave that magnified sound, I heard, through the rain, the clicking of their claws.

Nall put one leg overside. The boat teetered.

"Nall!"

Emerging from under the blanket of crabs I saw a human foot; two feet; legs. The crabs scuttled like cockroaches shooed from a feast.

He was back in the boat and pushing off, shooting us out too far, rocking and splashing.

"Not that cave," he said, bending to the stroke. "Somebody's using it."

I looked back. The dark throng of crabs was tiptoeing in again. Something white fluttered in the cave's depth.

The manat nosed around bony headlands. We passed two

more caverns without looking in them. The cliff above us rose into darkness, strange eddies tugged at us, the rain drummed down.

At the head of a narrow bay the sea had spit up a gray beach, and over it arched a cave with a sandy floor. Warily, Nall ran the boat alongshore and climbed out.

I huddled, my paddle planted in the gravel. There were crabs, but not so many. He came back from his quick, seeking run and said, "Here."

My hands would not work. I tried to stand; he caught me as the manat tipped me out, swung me to the shallows, and grabbed the boat as it shot toward the sea. My legs were numb from sitting, they dumped me in the water. He picked me out and hauled first me, then the manat out of the rain and into the cave, above the highest tidemark, to cold sand.

He grubbed in the boat for a blanket. It was wet. He put it around my shoulders anyway and began to hunt for driftwood. His face was drawn. I tried to say, *I'll help,* but from cold or horror I could not speak. The sodden blanket was heavy, the coldness in my heart flowed out and turned the whole world cold—there was no warm place. The thoughts I had frozen in order not to feel them grew monstrous, freezing everything else.

Tide wrack lay under the overhang of the cave, and was dry. It was white with human bones. Nall sorted through them, kicking aside skulls and femurs to gather scoured cedar logs. When he came to dump his gleanings at my feet, I shrank away.

He had found two little planks and a straight stick. He whittled at them with his knife. Fetching a length of cord from the manat, he searched again among the charnel-house drift until he found a strong, springy twig, which he strung to make a bow. He turned a twist of the bowstring around the stick, and knelt.

"Watch," he said.

Laying one little plank on the other, he set one end of the stick in a newly cut notch, found a fist-size rock with a dimple in it and used it to anchor the free end of the stick so that it stood upright like a drill, and leaned his chin on it to brace it.

He began to draw the bow back and forth, making the stick spin.

It sounded like a bumblebee, fat and clumsy and flying in bursts—a close, busy sound in the rain and drear. Soon the first thick puff of smoke rose up, smelling of forest, earth, hearth: land things.

He pulled and pulled at the bow until the smoke was white. Then he dropped bow and stick to lift the plank where the drill had been.

The smoke stopped. Nothing was there but a pile of fine black dust.

"No," I said. Even the cedar scent was gone.

"Wait."

Cupping his hand around the dust, he blew. One red coal glowed there, like a seed.

On the sand he had built a little nest of cedar bark, and into that he tipped the coal. Lying on his belly, he blew gently, steadily, without pausing except for breath. White smoke rose around his head. He coughed and blew. More smoke came thick; he blew, and as it wreathed and thinned, I heard the lively voice of fire. He rolled aside to show me, between his hands, the nest of baby flames.

He fed it twigs, then sticks, then branches. It blazed on the jagged ceiling, roared and danced, was hungry, ate everything he gave it. The blanket began to steam and stink; he took it away from me and propped it to dry on three sticks. He dragged a whole tree trunk from among the scattered bones and shoved one end of it into the blaze.

A spark landed on my foot. I did not brush it off. He brushed it off, then sat behind me with his arms around me, putting me between himself and the fire.

My knees baked, and Nall was warm. But my heart was cold as bone.

I felt him sigh. His voice buzzed in my ear, singing a little worn song that Downshore cowherds, mostly children, sing as they drive their cattle home along Scythe Road.

> Barn for my cuddy-o,
> When the day's done;
> Saw a hundred lilies-o,
> Never picked one.

> Barn for my cuddy-o,
> Lily for the lady,
> House for the gentleman,
> Cradle for the baby.

I thought of slow flanks and swaying udders, the tired children with their willow switches. I could not bear that Nall should try to comfort me, when there was no comfort.

Turning my head, I saw his face and knew that he sang to comfort not me, but himself.

Barn for my cuddy-o,
House, hearth, byre.
Supper for my honey-o,
By the kitchen fire.

"When you first came to Downshore," I said, my voice strange and small, "you didn't know what a cow was."

He shifted his eyes from whatever he had been looking at. "I was cold. You laid me against the cow to get warm."

"It wasn't me did that. It was Dai."

So the name was spoken, and I cried.

I had not known you could get warm by crying, but it was so. Crying, I turned in his arms to be warm in front, and felt him shake with his own tears.

The blanket got dry. We forgot to eat, and touched each other's faces. I untied the deer mouse sash. On the warm sand we spoke in whispers, then without words.

The old skulls stared. The fire died down; one of us would rise, naked, to scratch for wood among the cold bones, and then slide back under the blanket to be warmed.

It was the first time laughter was heard in that place, the first time anyone built a fire on the Isle of Bones.

Morning came white, with fog thick as wool crowding the mouth of the cave.

I sat up. Nall slept with his feet in the ashes, his unshaven face peaceful as water in a cup.

I watched the blanket move with his breathing. Then I slipped out from under it shivering, raked up the last coals, and kindled a new fire. When it was crackling, I picked my way through the bone pile to the sea.

Little waves lipped the sand. Crabs tiptoed. In a whisper I told them, "Poor things, you didn't get to eat us."

In the cold salt water I scrubbed all over, even my hair. I crept out with goose bumps, and in my unbelted shift I built up the fire, swept the sand with a twig, and set bread and cheese on a flat rock to make a kitchen. I wished for my honey crock. The skulls, my in-laws, grinned. By poking in the manat I found an old black cook pot. When I brought it back, Nall was awake, kicking his feet over because they were too close to the fire.

He snaked his hand out of the blanket and grabbed my ankle, growling, "Bears!'

"No biting!" Last night I had bitten him, to teach him about bears; the marks were on his neck.

"No mercy." Then his laughter changed and he said, "Hold me." The fire sank neglected, and the washing was all to do again.

Later he reached across me and took up the deer mouse sash that lay tangled in the sand. "This is a pretty thing, Bear Spit. Did you make it?"

"A—a friend wove it for me."

His quick eyes admired the weft. "Can you weave?"

"No. But I can make bowls."

"How?"

"I roll snakes of clay, then I coil them and pinch them," I said. I pinched him. "Then I take a piece of dry gourd, and I scrape and scrape and scrape the clay until it's thin, until only emptiness is left, with a little bit of bowl around it. Then I fire it in goat shit."

"So you can weave, but with earth and fire. *You* are earth and fire," he said, rolling over, pulling me with him.

"And you're water, Mister Long Wave! To make a bowl strong, I have to drive the water out—with burning goat shit. Out! Out!" I pretended to push at his face. He laughed and caught my hands. "I made a crock for you, with wild honeycomb in it," I said, "but they broke it."

"You have brought me nothing broken."

"Only scarred."

"Scars are writing. They are the marks left by stories."

"Can you write?"

"No."

"I can." I liked it that there were things I could do that he could not. He had more scars than I did, but I had stories he did not know about. Like the Bear, which I had not yet tried to explain. And Raím.

I felt secretive, powerful, adult. Examining his scars, I said in my haughtiest Leagueman's voice, "I won't accept this. It's been damaged in transit." He shouted and pounced, until I squealed, "I take it back!"

He rose, chucked a stick on the coals, and followed my footprints down to the sea. Against the mist his silhouette tipped forward as he dove.

I splashed in the shallows. I could touch the thought of Dai with the edge of my mind, like touching a bruise so deep, it had bled through my whole body. But that had happened in some other world. When Nall's sleek head bobbed alongside the rocks, I put my shift on loose and damp, and made tea.

He came out of the water shaking like a dog and stood over the fire. We sat together on the blanket and ate like soldiers after a battle, shoulder to shoulder, not caring whether we saved enough for later. The scalding tea tasted of the leather water skin.

He was serious again. I was not. Creek, Downshore, even Ab Harlan felt far and strange; Nall was real, and here. I pushed my toes into the fire-warmed sand and linked my hands across my knees. The cave seemed homey, the skulls like a row of beaming ancestral portraits.

"I like this place," I said. "Let's rent it."

He smiled, but not quickly enough. The look of peace that we had made together was gone from his face. "We must go," he said.

"It's too foggy." Mist filled the cave mouth. I raked my fingers through the sand, and when I lifted them, they held a ring. "Nall! Look!"

It was heavy gold, carved round with swimming seals. I put it on my finger. It fit.

"Drop it," he said.

"It was just lying here. In the sand where we—right in the sand."

"It belongs to someone. She wanted it with her. Throw it in the sea."

"No! It's for us. Look, there are two seals on it."

"It's not ours to keep."

I closed my hand into a fist, the ring on my finger. "Nothing's ours to keep. Not even a fireplace in a bony old cave."

"That's true."

I took off the ring without looking at it and tossed it into the sea, then got up and began to gather food sacks and kick sand over the fire.

"Kat."

"I know. You told me."

"Kat." He sat on the sand naked, a crust of bread in one

hand and nothing in the other. "I'll tell you my name," he said.

"What do you mean?"

"The name they took when they killed me. I'll tell you that."

He was offering me the name because I could not have the ring. I was ashamed, afraid.

"But you must never speak it."

I did not want the name. I wanted the ring, solid and flashy on my hand. I remembered how I had given Raím the bowl he had not wanted, with writing on it that he could not read.

Nall said, "Shall I tell you?"

"No. Yes."

I knelt beside him. He paused; then he cupped his hand around my ear and whispered.

I flushed.

"Never speak it," he said.

"I promise."

I did not know what to do with the name, where to keep it. It was hot, like molten gold.

He knew it was not the gift I wanted. He was watching my face. I gave him a tiny crooked smile and pushed my finger along in the sand until it touched his thigh.

He said, "I had another name. A nickname. You can speak that."

"What is it?"

"Bij. Say it, Kat."

"Bij."

He held me so tight, it hurt. "My ama called me that. And my cousins. They carried me everywhere; they were glad when I learned to walk."

"What does it mean?"

"A small, very round stone, of the right size to play marbles."

I said, "I don't know what to call you anymore."

"My name is Nall. The boy who had those other names is dead. Kat, among the Rigi I have no skin."

I saw what he meant, that he had nothing to protect him—no name, no sealskin, no custom or family or habit or religion, those things of which human beings make skins to be safe in. He was utterly naked. And I had thought him poor in his cowshed!

"Nall, then. If the Rigi saw you, would they think you were a ghost?"

"*Uhui*—that's how you say 'ghost' in Rig. Maybe I am."

"That wasn't a ghost with me last night!"

"No?" Bullying soft kisses, deft hands. He was going to the Gate, he said. But had he been a moth going to a candle flame, I would have gone with him.

15

Living in the world
by being small
and keeping still.
Like a nighthawk's egg:
fragile, speckled,
laid on the bare ground.

The Nighthawk. Creek.

I RETIED THE DEER MOUSE SASH with its pouch of coins. We gathered bundles and blanket and packed the manat. We left the fire still smoldering and pushed away from the cave.

The world was dirty white fog that coiled like smoke from a snuffed wick. "The shroud of the dead," said Nall. "When we reach open water, it will thin." To our left the sea faded into the dank air; to our right the gray cliff dissolved above our heads. We picked our way along its foot, eyes on the foam that fringed it. The manat was noiseless. Even the drip of water from the paddle blades seemed slow.

We crept past the caverns we had passed last night, dim black mouths that led somewhere upward and back. A cold breath sighed from each, pressing my curls to my cheek. It's only air, I told myself. There must be fissures that go up to the cliff top, and the wind blows down through them.

But the cave we were passing was the one with the body in it. I did not want to think about the wind or any odor that might lie on it. I bent to the paddle, but not before I saw again that flash of white in the pit of the cave, quick and gone.

This time Nall saw it too. He paused in his stroke with a low exclamation.

"It's a ghost," I said. "Don't stop."

"Ghosts are the color of fire."

"Leaguemen's ghosts are white. Nall, it wouldn't be . . . Dai?"

He did not answer, staring into the dark.

"Let's go." As I dug my paddle into the water, I heard a keening whimper, like a gull's cry.

"Something's there," said Nall.

"Don't!"

But he was sculling the prow to face the cave. I felt like the shell of a hermit crab, dragged willy-nilly behind its tenant. "Nall, no!"

The white thing rose among the rocks and crossed the cave mouth, weaving and dipping: It was the ghost of the clerk, in white shirt and dark trousers. *"Ah! Ah!"* it cried. It raised its arms above its head, the way the corpse had lain in the water.

I back-paddled so hard that foam creamed around the paddle shaft. But Nall was pulling forward, left and right; we went nowhere.

I hit him with my paddle. The manat heeled and shuddered. He wrenched around, shouting, "You'll sink us!"

"You think you can take us anyplace you want!"

The ghost stopped waving its arms and stared at us.

"It's a hostage," said Nall, holding his ear. "The other one the fishermen put off. How did they come out so far, past the Changes?"

I lowered my paddle. It was not the clerk—the clerk had been plump. This man was thin and young.

"It's Queelic," I said.

"Who?"

"The one the bull chased. The man I was to marry."

"*That's* the man?"

Queelic waved one arm and said, "Ah?" again, as though he did not know what language to speak.

"He must be half dead with fear," I said. I began to paddle us in. On the second stroke I remembered it must have been Queelic who had recognized Dai on the night of my escape.

Nall stared at his rival, then took up the stroke. We pulled alongshore a few yards out. I looked away from the corpse. "Queelic!"

He looked more boy than man, with his pale, blotched face and nose too big for him. His body jerked, as though he might flee back into the cave. But maybe whatever was back there frightened him worse, for in the end he stood where he was, shivering in his tall black boots.

"Queelic, it's Kat."

He gawked back and forth from me to Nall.

"Did the fishermen leave you here?"

A slight nod.

"When?"

His eyes were on my scars. His throat worked. At last he whispered, "I don't remember."

I wanted to hate him. But all I could think of was the death cave in the rain and no fire. Nall jumped out into the little waves and pulled the manat to shore. Queelic retreated up the shingle.

"This is Nall," I said, climbing out.

"The—the demon king?"

Nall looked him up and down. "You were going to marry Kat?"

Queelic's eyes widened. Then he shut them. "It wasn't my idea. I didn't want her." Swaying, shuddering, he turned to me and said, "Tell him to do it!"

"Do what?" I said. "Who?"

"Your demon. He's got a knife—tell him to kill me quick. I know he owes me."

"*Owes* you?" I imagined a fat ledger like the one my father kept, with entries that were not money and pelts, but slights, insults, murders. "Nobody's killing you. Not us, anyway."

"Kill me! Don't leave me in this place." Queelic's eyes flickered toward the corpse.

Under his breath Nall said, "I will know who it is."

"It hasn't got a face," said Queelic.

Nall stalked to the thin feet that here and there gleamed white with bone and stood looking down. His eyes closed. Opened. He knelt, rummaging.

Queelic swallowed.

Nall rose and returned. "It's Tadde," he said. "My cousin Tadde—I told you of him. Those are his tattoos, what's left of them. *Ai*, Kat, that it should be Tadde!"

I did not know what to say. Queelic stared from the corpse to Nall, his forehead puckering. I told him, "Nall's people live out here. The Rigi."

Then I was sorry I had said it. Queelic shrank, crying, "Rigi? The Rigi aren't real! They aren't flesh!"

The cousin smelled terribly like flesh. And Nall looked real enough, gnawing the knuckle of his clenched fist.

"You mean *here's* where they live?" said Queelic.

"Farther west."

His face followed my gesture. "Is that true?"

"Ask Nall. I've never been there."

"But it's near two years since he carried you off."

"He did not! I carried myself off! Can't you imagine a woman doing anything without a man?" But of course he could not. Two years ago I could not have either. "That's not where I went."

"You should have," said Queelic.

While I puzzled at this, Nall turned to me from his brooding and said, "I told you, something is coming. It is near. Queelic, we're bound west now. You see my boat. There's no room for you."

"Don't leave me here!"

Oh, exquisite revenge! But the ledger with its ranked retaliations. I said, "Nall. We could ferry him to the west side of the island. You said there was a beach."

"He'd still be on the Isle of Bones."

Queelic said, "I know I have to die. I just—I don't want those wet crawling things to eat me."

"If you die on the far side of the island, it will be birds," said Nall.

"I wouldn't mind that. I'd like being part of a bird." Queelic looked west. "Take me to where the birds are."

"There's no room in the manat."

I said, "Take him first, then come back for me."

"I won't leave you in this place."

"It's just your cousin." Because I was too afraid, I walked to the corpse and looked at it. It was bad. Then not so bad— a man turning into bone. There was enough left to see he had been tattooed with smoky blue spirals, like the one on Nall's back, but more and bigger. A crumpled sealskin lay across his breast, silver with a dark blotch the shape of a human hand.

The breath of the cave stirred my hair. "There's a wind coming from somewhere," I said. "We should look back there; maybe there's a fissure to the top."

Nall made a clicking noise with his tongue that meant admiration. "Queelic, did you look?"

Queelic shook his head.

Slinging the strap of a water skin over his shoulder, Nall stowed the paddles in the manat and dragged it above the tidemark. With Queelic stumbling behind we climbed up into the cave and nosed into the current of air like salmon swimming upstream.

It was nasty rock—jagged, with a feeling underfoot of pits and knives. There were pools of slimy wet. When we got back away from the light, the scuttling crabs were fewer, but there were other things: a constant noise of something small and frantic trying to get away. I stepped on a wetness; it burst. The cave was never pitch-dark, never light, but a faint shine that slicked all surfaces came from somewhere ahead of us.

"Up there," I said.

The rocks got drier as we climbed, until we stood in a narrow canyon full of light from a high, bright slit. The rocks underfoot were speckled with bird dung.

"No way up," I said.

But Nall had begun to climb, testing ledges and chimneys. I tied my sandals to my sash and scrambled after him. "Wait," he said. "We must be sure of climbing down again."

With my eyes on that high sunlight I did not want to think about going back to wet things, and the cousin. When Nall said "Come," I followed quickly. He made me go back and put Queelic between the two of us, because he shook.

We made a clumsy chain of our hands and crawled upward. Queelic's slick-soled boots made him nearly helpless; Nall hauled him over ledge after ledge by armpit or collar while I shoved from below. I climbed easily, as if my toes were fingers, and where the stretch was too great, Nall put down his hand, we clasped wrists, and he pulled me up neat as a trout.

On scraped knees we clambered underneath the bright window. It was fringed with grass, and the wind blew in our faces. With a last leg up, a heave and scramble that sent loose stones spinning down into the pit, we dragged ourselves over the rim into a world of birds. Loud with alarm, a nesting colony wheeled in the blue. Nall stood up. Spreading his arms wide, he shouted, "I have never been up here before!"

He had to shout. The birds screamed, the wind blew, the sun blazed on rutted gray stone that sloped to green grass far below, on dissolving mist and the huge blue sea. Away westward, like mountains in a mirage, islands floated on the indigo deep.

"The Rigi's land!" said Nall. He snuffed the wind as though it carried the odors of strange fruits, unnamed flowers. Queelic stared from hands and knees, his pale forelock blown back.

Nall let his arms fall to his sides. He gazed at the shadowy islands until I touched him and said, "Could anyone see us?"

He started and crouched. Shaded his eyes. "No one is here. We'd see their boats."

The Isle of Bones was a huge stone raft, shoved up on the east to form the cave-riddled cliffs. From where we crouched the land sloped west, stony at its height but growing grassy as it tilted toward the sea. Above a narrow beach stretched a green, treeless field in which gray geese were grazing.

I stared at them. The geese became stones leaning in no order, a frozen dance.

"Shrines," said Nall. "Or tombs, they might be."

"Are they old?"

"Yes."

"How old?"

"Who could know?"

In Upslope the tombstones stood in tidy rows, bearing long names that looked chiseled yesterday. In our kale yard my mother's stone said only LOVING WIFE OF AB DREM, with no name at all. Dai would have no stone; I could not think of him alive, of the poker, but on the gibbet the birds would eat him. With what speed he would become part of this wild, flying world!

A scrabble was Queelic, crawling away from the slit that opened downward into the dark. He sat down with his eyes on the west and said, "I guess this is where I stay."

Nall bit his lip. "Go anywhere. Nothing can save you."

"I like it here."

"Behind those rocks you'll be out of the wind." Nall unslung the water skin and set it on the stones.

Queelic did not look at it. He took his eyes off the islands and looked at Nall instead. Then he turned to me and said, "Now I know why you didn't want me."

"Nobody asked me what I wanted."

But he was creeping to Nall on hands and knees. He stuck out his hand. "Nall, I'm obliged to you."

Taken aback, Nall gave his hand a quick shake.

"She went to the best man," said Queelic. "You got her. Enjoy her." To me he said, "I'm glad you're his. I don't know if I'd have liked you."

He crawled off toward the rocks. Nall frowned after him. "Kat, do they all talk like that?"

"Mostly."

He shook himself. "He's as brave as he knows how to be. We must go."

"He forgot the water skin."

"Leave it." Nall swung himself over the lip of the pit, found footing, and raised his arms to lift me down.

"Nall. Do you enjoy me?"

He kissed me. "I only know about joy," he said.

We climbed back down into the dark. It took much longer than going up, an ugly scramble full of false starts, retracings, little falls. The last rags of mist were on the water. The cave was wet; it stank. What was left of Nall's cousin was still there, but the manat was gone.

🖐 🖐 🖐

There was a groove in the gravel where the keel had been dragged. Nothing else. The water lapped and chuckled.

As I stared at the bare beach, my wrist was grabbed. I half fell as Nall yanked me back into the dark fissure, his head darting like a hawk's.

I said, "The fishermen who dumped Queelic—"

"No."

"Then—"

"The Rigi."

He pulled me farther into the dark. The rock was horrible underfoot, like sharkskin, in the shaft he climbed so fast that I panted to keep up, tearing my shins on the boulders.

"Wait for me!" I said.

He waited, but I could see the shine of his bunched muscles, ready to spring up the next pitch. I was so frightened that I climbed right up places where before he had had to help me, as if I had grown extra legs like a spider.

At the last ledge he stopped so suddenly that I banged against him. He motioned: *Stay.* Levered himself through the gap to daylight, vanished. Reappeared, reached down, and dragged me up. The birds screamed.

"Keep low," he said.

The cliff was empty. The water skin lay where we had left it, and I snatched it up. We ran below the brow of the cliff to the pinnacles that made a little shelter. Queelic was not there, either. The ocean was bare and blue.

We lay flat, panting. "Didn't want to be caught down there," said Nall. The muscles stood out around his mouth.

"They, whoever—they'll think we're still in the cave."

"The elders will know of that way up."

"Old men could never—"

"Elders aren't old. My father—" he said. His face was as tight as the skin of the manat. "They've seen my boat, Rig-made but not Rig. There will be a hunt."

"Queelic."

"A Black Boot! Pity him, when they find him!"

Not *if*, but *when*. "They'll think the manat is his," I said. "We could hide while they—" Then I saw my own evil, and stopped.

Nall's look of disgust was for me, or maybe for the idea of Queelic in a manat. To atone for my thoughts, I cried, "But where is he? *Queelic!*"

No answer. Bare rock. Below us on the wrinkled gray-green slope I saw no winking dot of white that might be Queelic's shirt. I thought of my father's board game, War, in which the porcelain pieces—baron, chancellor, slave—were taken away one by one until there was nobody left.

Nall made a hushing motion.

I said, "He hasn't gone and—"

I was thinking of the clerk, broken at the bottom of a cliff. Here was a cliff. I moved to look over it.

Nall grabbed me back and crept to the edge himself, his head barely breaking the line of rocks. Returned. "No boats. But we were slow, climbing twice."

"Did you see Queelic?"

"It's straight down into the sea."

"His shirt in the water, could you see that?"

He was not listening. His glance went right and left, and that animal look was on him. I said, "Listen. We could sneak down past the shrines, to the beach. If they hunt for us"—by "they" I meant monsters, darkness, the Rigi—"if they hunt, they'll leave a boat on the beach. We could steal it—"

Nall said, "Beach."

I thought, He can swim from a beach. I can swim only in a millpond.

"We'll go down." He motioned me to leave the water skin.

"It's all the water we have!"

"It's his. If he's dead, he'll take it with him. Drink first, and thank him."

We drank, spoke thanks into the empty air, laid the skin by the rocks like an offering, and began to creep down the slope toward the green meadow.

Rain and wind had dredged ravines into the island's back, shallow at the top, deepening as they descended. Nall found a steep, boulder-choked channel that twisted left and right. Once in it, we could not be seen, but neither could we see. We had to clamber up, down, around the boulders, like ants. At every bend Nall motioned me to wait while he climbed the rubbly bank and looked about.

I hated that he took the lead. But it was his world: moony limestone, pitted and razor-edged, a scaling, spalling book laid open to reveal stone flowers, insects, fish. It cut my hands. I thought of the red, round-bellied sandstone of Creek, such kindly rock that I had sometimes laid my cheek against it to feel the last of the sun.

Descending, the ravine became a stone-walled tunnel so clogged with fallen rock that we traveled as much sideways as forward. It was cold and smelled like stone; our little scrapes and rattles made big echoes.

Down and down. It was never so steep that I needed Nall's hand to help me; if I spoke, he hushed me; I did not exist except to be signaled to keep quiet, to come quick, to wait. He scrambled far ahead. Above, at the lip of the ravine, short grass ducked in a wind I could not feel.

I rounded a boulder, shrank back. The rift had opened to wide day, gray stones on green grass.

We had come among the shrines.

Though broad, the stones were hardly taller than a man; they looked like stooped humans struggling to stand up out of the earth, pocked and mottled like the flanks of whales. Maybe there were fifty stones in that field. Close to, I saw that each was double, as though it had been split from top to bottom by a single blow, then pulled apart to make a gap just wide enough for a body to squeeze through.

One of each pair was taller. The shadows they cast on each other were without texture. The air between them shimmered.

Nall knelt behind a boulder at the gully mouth. I ran to crouch beside him. Panting, rising, he motioned again: *Stay here.*

I said, *"I will not!"*

He jumped, stared, mouth open.

"I will not stay in these horrible rocks and watch you be killed. If you try to leave me, I'll yell!"

He sank down again behind the boulder. I watched him make his change, back from single-minded beast to man.

He listened about. No sound anywhere. Wiped his face in his elbow. "I go first," he said. "I motion. You follow."

It was what we had been doing already. But I had to know he could speak. "Thanks," I said.

He ducked across the open to the first pair of stones, his body rosy against them. The jerk of his head was sharp and slight: *Come.*

I ran to him over the green grass. It was tussocky and wet with the night's rain. The crack between the stones was like a crease in the air. It trembled. I would not look at it. I crammed against his shoulder. The other shrines leaned in random lines, couples forever a little parted.

I followed him to the next pair. The wind stirred the air like water in a bowl; the short grass bobbed in all directions. From the corner of my eye I saw a pair of stones move.

They moved together, separate and one. I looked again. Nothing had moved.

But as we crouched at the next stone, I saw movement again, and at the next, always just at the edge of vision. When I caught up to Nall, I whispered, "The stones are moving."

"Yes." He breathed hard, but that was from running. He ran on. I followed him, stumbling as though the ground heaved with an earthquake.

When we reached the far side of the field, he turned. I turned with him. The stones that had been following us froze, motionless since the beginning of the world.

Nall said words in Rig. "Tell them, Kat. You must."

"I can't speak Rig!"

"In the Plain tongue, then. 'Until I pass the Gate.'"

My hair stood up. "Until I pass the Gate," I said.

The stones were still. Nall laid his hand on my belly and spoke more words, he dragged me into the mouth of another ravine, we clawed up the side of it, ran across a stony open, and half dove, half rolled through tall weeds into a shallow overhang a few yards deep where a fringe of grass hid us, like a curtain. There he lay gasping, his forehead on his hands.

I lay next to him. When I could speak, I whispered, "What—what else did you tell those stones? "

"Who you are. So they would know you. They're my ancestors." He turned his filthy face to me. "This island is my tomb."

A little wind blew. Beyond the stirring green curtain, crickets began to sing.

Under the ledge some rodent had made a nest of twigs and the delicate bones of birds. The floor was powdery dust; it stuck to our sweating bodies. Nall's face screwed up like a baby's, and he sneezed.

"*Shhh!*" I hissed. Nothing happened, except the crickets stopped. They began again. I said, "You knew this place was here."

There was barely room for him to get up on his elbows. "'Beach,' you said, and I remembered this. The beach lies just beyond."

He spoke like a human. He had said, *My ama would come looking for me and make me talk like a person.* I felt grateful to her. I asked, "Was it here they brought you after they killed you?"

"No. To the caves. The shrines are for families. We came on feast days, to serve the dead."

"I thought your ancestors were seals."

"One must have also a home on earth. For a little while." His voice changed. "Now you have seen it."

"What?"

"Between the stones. Worlds beyond worlds are rushing between the stones of the Gate; death hangs there, like a wrinkle in the air."

"But—those are shrines, you said. Not the Gate."

He gazed at me. I dropped my eyes.

He said, "What happens when we die?"

"I don't know."

"I don't know either. Yet I have died at least once. Maybe it is different every time."

I shivered.

He kissed me. "When I was little, still Bij, my ama brought us to the isle to make offering. The others laid fish and herbs before the stones, but I had stolen something, I wanted to hide it, so I ran away." He pulled one of my curls. "I thought, 'I'll do what Mother does; I'll become some other being, and vanish.' So I dreamed myself into a harvest mouse, and ran off, and found this place."

"You—you turned into a mouse?"

He smiled. "Surely. I was a mouse all morning. Then I ran back to my ama, and she spanked me right where my tail was."

I nudged his shoulder with mine. "What was it you stole?"

"A knife of Liu's. He wouldn't give it to me, so I stole it and I hid it here." He squirmed forward and slipped his hand into a crack in the rock, withdrew it, and laid an oval stone knife on my palm. It was clear obsidian, long as my finger and sharp as glass. One end was snapped off. Over his face, which was full of awe and distance, crept an old guilty look. "It was broken," he said. "I wouldn't have stolen his good one."

The wind shifted, blustering in the fringe of grass. "Thief!" yelled a high, hard voice.

16

I shall have a hope chest, I shall have a ring,
I shall have a white hearth, and marry with a king.
I shall have a baby, pretty as a jewel;
You shall have a monkey child, and sup cold tea and gruel.

Hand Slap. Upslope.

NALL JERKED HIS HEAD BACK and cracked it on the low roof.

"Filth!" cried the voice.

He clutched the back of his head. I clutched the knife and jammed against him, trying to be invisible.

Nothing happened.

He dropped his hands. Crawling to the grass curtain, he leaned on his forearms, listening.

Wind. Crickets. Gulls.

Then the clear voice, not near, screaming, "I will tear out your heart!"

He exhaled as though hit. *"Aieh!"* He shoved me aside, he slid out of the cleft and ran the way a lizard does, on toes and fingers, toward that voice.

I dithered, making little lunges. Through the grass I saw him already far away up a little rise, throwing himself flat. Without caring what happened I ran after him across the open, fell over his legs, and squirmed up next to him as he parted a screen of blowing grass.

Twenty feet below, down a sloping bank framed by the grass like the stage of a traveling show, lay a pretty graveled beach. Our manat leaned on the shingle, and next to it a second skin boat without a deck, like a dory.

Queelic knelt in the seaweed, his arms lashed behind his back. In front of him a slim girl rocked on her toes, slicing the air with a curved flint knife.

She wore a sealskin belted around her hips. Nothing else. Her head was shaved; through its fine, dark fur I could see the shine of her skull. She hooked the tip of the knife in the soft place under Queelic's jaw. "Flesh-eater!" she cried in the Plain tongue.

Queelic tried to raise his chin away from the knife.

"I have your manat," she said. "Let the others eat what they will, and die. No one leaves the caves!"

"Do it," said Queelic through shut teeth. "Stop jumping around and *do* it."

The girl let the knife drop a little, beating away tears with her free hand. "I can kill! I have killed and killed. Otters, and the goat." She set the hook again under Queelic's ear.

Nall was on his feet. *"Aieh!"*

The knife nicked Queelic's throat as she whipped around to face Nall; did not see him; saw him; screamed.

Screamed and cowered. The knife went flying. She snapped into a heap on the gravel, crying, *"Uhui! Uhui!"* in a high bird's voice.

He leaped the bank in three strides that brought down stones. She groveled. He implored her in Rig.

"Uhui!" She huddled her arms across her face.

He turned back to me. "She thinks I'm dead!" he said. His face said, *Am I?*

"You're all right!" I said. "You're here!"

I flung both legs over the ledge and half ran, half slid down the bank. It was too steep; I hopped twice, caught one foot, flipped in the air, and landed with a squawk.

The girl stopped screaming. She stared between her fore-arms, white as shell.

I sat up, holding my behind. That is how the clown enters, and everybody laughs.

The cowering girl pushed herself up a little on her arms, but it was not me she stared at.

"Bij," she said.

Aieh was her name. She was beautiful. Her slenderness and dark shaved head made her eyes look huge; her eyes were silver. Her sealskin kirtle was mottled silver and gray, like the constellation called the Hunter, stitched along the edge with jet.

Flinching, she put out her hand to touch Nall's feet. He knelt. She rose to her knees, and then it seemed she must touch him everywhere, sobbing, crying in the Rigi's tongue.

Now it was Nall who looked as though he saw a ghost, who answered in whispers.

I stood up. They did not notice. I rubbed my elbows and found I still held Liu's knife; it had cut my palm. Nall stared like a sleepwalker. His hands moved at Aieh's waist.

I opened my mouth. But I could not speak those murmurous Rig wind-and-water words; only Plain, or Hill, or Kitchen Hessdish, which sounds like sharpening a hatchet. I did not have brown breasts or silver eyes. My breasts were purple with scars, and a bruise on one buttock was going to match.

Queelic knelt on the shingle like a stunned hare. He cleared his throat. "Kat. Could you cut this rope?"

I stared at the knife in my hand. At Queelic. I said, "I forgot you."

"That's all right. Everybody does."

It was a thick hide rope, but the knife cut it like nothing. I was glad to spoil that girl's good rope. Queelic touched the nick under his ear and stared at the blood on his hand.

I would not look at Nall and the girl. I said to Queelic, "How did you get here?"

"I walked." He seemed cheerful, not quite sane. "Down a big crack. It got too hard, so I climbed out and walked on the grass till I got to those rocks, the split ones. That's where that—that girl got me." He licked his lips. "I forgot to bring the water."

I dropped Liu's knife in the pocket of my shift and dug another water skin from the manat. Queelic's hands shook. I held the skin while he drank.

Without thanking me he wiped his mouth on his sleeve and stared at Aieh. "Who is she?"

"I have no idea."

"I think they know each other."

I looked then. Nall and Aieh had their hands on each other's faces. Their lips still moved in that liquid tongue. I said loudly, "There are two people here who don't speak Rig." As I put the water skin back in the manat, I saw Nall silence Aieh with three fingers on her mouth.

He did not meet my eyes. "Aieh is my cousin," he said.

"Oh." So many cousins.

"Tadde is—Tadde was her brother. Tadde and Liu."

Brothers turning to bone. I closed my eyes. When I opened them, Aieh's hand, soft as a cat's paw, was kneading Nall's thigh. The skin around her mouth and nipples was dusky, as if her blood gathered there, and her dark eyelashes were stuck together with tears.

She pointed at Queelic. "Filth! He ate my brother's flesh!"

"Me?" said Queelic. "I don't even like pork chops."

"Manflesh-eater! Black Boot!"

Queelic turned to me. "Is she one of those Rigi things?"

"I suppose."

He crossed his arms. "The Rigi eat *babies*."

Nall looked amazed. Aieh spat. Reluctantly, I said, "When we're little, they tell us that if we're bad, the Rigi will drown us and eat us."

"The Rigi bring nightmares," said Queelic. "My father has nightmares. That's why he has to drink."

"Lies to frighten children!" said Aieh.

I said, "So where did *you* learn that rubbish about the Black Boots?"

It was Nall who answered, as though dreaming. "From Tadde. He told us little ones, 'Be still, or the Black Boots will eat you. Starting from the middle.' Then he blew on our bellies."

Weeping, Aieh pushed her face against Nall's shoulder. With the palm of his hand he smoothed, smoothed the fine dark plush on her skull. When she murmured in Rig, he said, "Speak in Plain."

"Why have you come back from the dead, talking like a savage and bringing Black Boots to foul my Tadde's body?"

"No, no—Queelic was left in the cave for punishment."

"Not for dinner," said Queelic.

"There were three there with Tadde. I saw their tracks!"

"You see them. Queelic. Myself. And Kat."

Aieh stared as if she saw me for the first time. "That scarred girl? Who is she?"

My wretched blush began; my ears buzzed with it. I looked at Nall, who never blushed, and saw him blushing until last night's bear bites stood out dark on his neck.

Softly as a cat leaving a lap, Aieh withdrew from him and sat apart, staring at the gravel. "Bij," she said.

"My name is Nall."

But he seemed lost. His eyes asked me something, yet his hands still reached for her. I looked away, picking at the fringe of the deer mouse sash. When I looked back, he had a wrinkle at one eyebrow that had not been there before. He looked from me to Aieh. More at Aieh, I was sure of it.

Everything in me drew back from him, like petals curling away from a fire.

He said, "Aieh and I—"

I turned my head away. I had watched my League aunts punish their husbands like that; it worked, too. When I raised my eyes, he was leaning toward me, his face beseeching. I dropped my eyes.

He said, "Aieh and I were—we're cousins."

He had been going to say something else. And why hadn't he reached for me and pulled me into the place she had left? He should be saying, *Aieh, this is my lover. Kat and I called each other; she's what I longed for, a woman all earth. She saved my life.*

I thought of many things he might say. He did not say them. He looked confused, caught.

Last night's coldness came back to me, changed, and I thought, You won't notice me? I'll *make* you notice me!

Driving the nail of one thumb into the ball of the other, I said, "How lucky, to find two cousins on the same day! I'm so happy for you."

He winced. Aieh bridled and flushed; she stared at him. He had withdrawn his hands by then, and his eyes flew back and forth between us.

I said, "Maybe your cousins *called* you?"

He winced again. I did not care. Did he think knives were made only of stone? That I didn't know how to use one? What had last night meant to him? And what was I? No wonder he wouldn't let me have that ring!

Aieh caught his arm. He pulled it away. Her face crumpled, and she said, "Maybe the flesh-eater is that Black Boot girl!"

"Ah—" He crouched like a badger I had seen once in Creek, cornered by boys and stoned; but I had felt sorry for the badger. Not for him.

Then, in a breath, I saw him see a way out: I saw him remember the Gate.

He had a three-day beard, he was as dirty as I was, but a hero's look came over him—distant, relieved. He straightened. "There are no flesh-eaters here," he said. "Nor time to waste. I have work to do."

He sounded so stern and sure that I grew unsure. Why were we making this mad journey after all? Not for ourselves. For the world that was sick, that needed true songs or—or something.

My fury wobbled toward guilt. Nall was on a quest. Why should he have to explain himself to a couple of angry girls? If he gained the Gate, he would be a hero; and a hero does not clean up petty messes. It is the world's big mess he fixes, and then everyone is happy.

Aieh did not feel guilty. "Work to do?" She jumped up and seized the gunwale of her open boat, as though to shove it back into the surf. "When the wind is westerly, our ama weeps, and in her sleep she speaks a name!"

Nall jumped after her and held the other side. "She lives?"

"A broken heart kills only in songs. It is your mother who is dead."

His fingernails went white. "What being did she become, that she could not come back?"

"None! She died in her bed. She coughed, and vomited, and drowned in herself. Too much sea."

"So all is as it was."

"Should it be different? Rage by day and murder by night, singers killed for songs and truth-speakers for truth." Aieh's tears ran down. "What good is truth? It is like loving—death ends it. There was one I loved once, and our ama loved him . . . but they killed him. There was another; he tried to hold back the wave, but you have seen him—the crabs are eating him."

"Hold back the wave?"

Aieh shut her mouth. Queelic, who had been listening with his hanging open, said, "Kat, they talk in riddles here."

Aieh turned on him. "Shall I read you a riddle, Black Boot?"

He had been trying not to stare at her breasts. He said, "I'm terrible at riddles. But I like how you talk."

She looked at him as if he were some new fish pulled from the deep. "Listen, then, Pimple Boy," she said. "I am green and blue, deep as life. I have withdrawn from the shore, leaving the reefs and tide pools bare; fish flap and gasp, and one can go on human feet where before only crabs could walk. I am towering, dark, deadly; piled upon myself, toppling; poised, like a drawn breath. What am I?"

Queelic wrinkled his brow. He put out his tongue like a schoolboy at sums, then said, "Water all piled together. Would it be that thing you just said—too much sea?"

"Such a wise Black Boot! But it has another name."

"A really big wave?"

Nall made an explosive sound. Aieh said to Queelic, "And what happens when that big wave rushes back in upon the land?"

"It destroys everything. There was a wave like that in Wilwherra on the south coast, it knocked over a mill and drowned the workers and cost my dad a lot of money. A *tidal wave*. Did I guess the riddle? If I did, I think it's the first one I ever got right."

"It has one more part. I am a tidal wave made not of water, but of warriors with spears. What am I?"

"There isn't any such thing," said Queelic. "You can't pile people up like that. They— Oh!" His ears went pink. "You mean—the warriors aren't *actually* piled up. They're just so tense and ready that they *have* to rush at something and wreck it, like a tidal wave. I got it!" He slapped his thigh. "They'd hit the land and overrun it, like paidmen. The answer is: an invasion!"

"You have solved my riddle, Pimple Boy."

Queelic beamed. "It's like the words of songs!" he said. "I never understood till now—songs are *riddles*."

"Aieh," said Nall, in a voice I had never heard him use, "tell me what is happening."

"Why? You have work to do."

"Tell me for Tadde's sake—and for our ama's."

She twisted her hands in front of her. I had to keep shutting my heart to what she must be feeling, seeing his living face that she had thought a skull among driftwood. She said in a mutter, "The Rigi will go back to Tanshari."

"*Eh!*" said Nall.

Queelic said, "What's Tanshari?"

"What your ass covers when you are at home, Black Boot!" said Aieh.

"There are no Black Boots in Tanshari," said Nall. "They live above it on the cliffs, in Uslap."

Tanshari and Uslap. "Downshore and Upslope," I said.

"Give them their true names, Scarred Girl!" said Aieh. "The Rigi founded them! We were the first to step onto that shore, the first to take off our skins and be human. Tanshari, the coast, and all the land were ours, its fruits and grains and game. We were healthy then, not as we are now. Why should we not take back what is our own?"

"That was never Tadde's hope," said Nall. "He was a man of parley, not force. Who is it who would invade Tanshari?"

Well, I could guess whose power drove it, the way Ab Harlan's drove the paidmen. Aieh said sullenly, "The factions want this, want that. But there is one thing everyone wants, and that is to be sick no more. To see their children born straight and whole. You think the Reirig would not see that and use it?"

"Tell me what happened."

"Why should I?"

"I cannot think of any reason."

Aieh flushed and turned away. I hoped she would try again to shift her boat and go. But she turned back and said, "Tadde was a fool. A brave fool. He held us together with his good heart. He bribed his way to the Reirig, who drank grass wine among his wives, and said, 'Seal Priest, your people are united in this: Open the way past the Changes! We would speak to the Tansharians, our relatives; if they hear us out, surely they will stop killing our seals. We can join again in the dance, and by traffic with earth we shall be cured of too much sea.'

"The Reirig let Tadde speak. But he said he must first listen at the Gate, to hear what was being born and be obedient to the will of the world.

"So he went there. Then he paddled back, and frothed at his mouth, and rolled his eyes and shouted, 'I have heard the world that is coming to be! In it there is no peace with seal-killers or Black Boots. The Rigi shall return to Tanshari—as *kas*, the tidal wave. *Kas, kas, kas!* Rise, my warriors, arm the manats!'"

"Plenty would go," said Nall behind his hand. "For goods, or glory, or because they are afraid of the Reirig."

"Or to do *something*. Anything, to be no longer locked away. But Tadde told the factions, 'Shall we kill our relatives to fatten the One?'" Aieh's shoulders drooped. "Word of that got back to the Reirig. We found Tadde on the beach, no blood in him. He had gone to dig clams."

"*Eh, mimo,*" said Nall, looking at the sea. "Oh, my cousin."

"One loves fools," said Aieh. "But the fools I loved are all dead. Liu and Tadde and—"

She stopped before she said it. But in the shape of her mouth I saw the name I was never to speak, the name that was mine to have instead of the ring.

"—and you." Her voice rose. "The wave is cresting. Soon half the world will be dead, and the Reirig will feast in Tanshari. He will get more wives there—it seems those women are willing! And I stand here on the dead isle, talking to the dead!"

"When will it happen?" said Nall.

His voice was hard. Aieh caught her breath. "Now," she said. "Now?"

"The manats are ready. Tonight begins the Least Night cycle, and we dance. Tonight the Reirig and his warriors will draw in as many of the factions as they can—there will be fights, and corpses for the caves!"

She gathered herself. "It makes no difference who lives or dies. Were the Reirig to be killed, a dozen men wait to snatch his lance and be the One. The wave has risen; it *will* rush east. Tomorrow at dusk they will set out, with the lance to open the Changes; they will reach the coast on Least Night and kill every soul in Tanshari—seal-killer and Black Boot alike. They will eat land fruit and breathe the wind from the hills, and at the Least Night fire they will dance upon the shore."

In the silence that followed, Queelic remarked in his mad, ordinary voice, "Least Night—that's day after tomorrow."

But I was seeing Mailin's house on the beach and Rosie sleeping, Nondany patting her hands, and paidmen with pikes standing at any escape up the cliffs.

I had left them.

For Nall I had left them. Nall, who did not move at all, even his eyes, but stood holding the gunwale of Aieh's boat while the little waves tripped and fell forward on the stones.

He said, "Where is Hsuu, my father, in all this?"

"At the Reirig's fire."

"Is he shouting *Kas!* with the rest?"

"Hsuu never shouts. He watches. It is the Reirig's lance he wants."

"You are sure of that?"

"He killed you at the Reirig's word."

"He—and others."

It hurt me to see Nall trying to make a good father out of a bad one. Maybe Aieh felt the same, for she said, "You would call a shark a sunfish!"

"My father is neither bad nor good. He is the sea. Was it he who called the seals away?"

"The Reirig says he called the seals himself."

"He does not have that power. The seals would be my father's work. Where are they?"

"Why should I tell you?" Aieh picked a round pebble from the beach. "Bij," she named it, and threw it into the sea. "Maybe you will see for yourself," she said. "Such a busy ghost. Why have you come?"

"I am going to the Gate."

We, I thought. *We* are going to the Gate.

"I have come back from Tanshari to listen at the Gate," said Nall.

Aieh's eyes went wide. Narrowed. "The Gate killed you before," she said. "Spying on the Reirig. Listening to songs that no one can forget even when you are dead. The Gate will kill you again!"

So I was not the first girl to whom Nall had told his tale of listening from the rock Stillness. I was not the first at anything.

"You think you are a seal priest?" said Aieh. "You are a man, that is all."

"Men have listened."

"When they were seals—the heroes in our ama's songs!"

"Songs are made from men's lives," said Nall. "Aieh! The whole world is at war. The Black Boots are killing from the east; now you say the Rigi will kill from the west—"

"Not if you stop them."

"*What?*"

Behind Aieh's shoulders the green waves followed, followed on one another, all coming *here.* She said, "You shall take Tadde's place. You shall call us together. Who better than you? You have been killed once already; what can the Reirig take from you? Among the factions there are warriors enough to face him and snatch his lance. Already they sing your song in secret, the song your father killed you for. When they see you, they will love you: Tadde's comrade, the son of Old Sea, come back from the dead."

"Are you mad?"

She laughed. How beautiful she was! "Mad? Do men rise from the dead every morning? Why should you come back to me—to us, on this day of all days?"

"I am not a leader! I am a listener."

"And a hero, you hope. A man of the great songs. Take

Tadde's place, and you shall be that. Our healer, the man who unites us against the Reirig—"

"Stop!" Nall raised his hands before his face. "I am going to listen at the Gate!"

Aieh's cheeks burned. Queelic watched with his mouth open.

"Truth!" she cried. "That is what you lust for, not women! The Reirig's wave will overwhelm the world, but you are busy bringing back a song: 'How Bij the Pure of Heart Snatched Wisdom from the Gate'!"

"Aieh!"

She turned to me. "He thinks he is a god. But he is a man. I know."

"Oh, shut up!" I said.

To Nall she said, "For all her scars, that girl knows nothing about the world, nothing about you. But *I* know you. You are mad like your mother. You swim out too far." She leaned to look in his face. "You listened before, and what did you bring back? A song. Listen again, and there will be no songs at all, for it is not the Reirig who will kill you, but the Gate itself. Man of my body, *this* is the truth: Your people need you."

"My people! I am a skinless, nameless ghost."

"You are the man I know."

Nall put his hand over his eyes.

"Leave him alone!" I said. "The Rigi would truly kill him!"

"Why? He will lead them," said Aieh. "And he will be with me."

"Nall!"

"Bij, you are a Rig."

"Nall, don't listen!"

"Bij—"

"Nall!"

He leaped away from us, to the sea. As he unbuckled his knife belt I ran after him, splashing into the waves. I caught his arm. "Where are you going?"

"To wash. Let me go." Another face shone through his man's face, like a stone through running water. He shook me off, and dove.

17

Ride to the east,
Ride to the west,
Kiss the girl that you love best.

From a Circle Game. Downshore.

I TURNED BACK to the beach, soaked to my sash. Aieh picked up her hooked knife and said, "You should not try to keep that man from the sea."

I thought, If she kills me, I'll scar her first, with fingernails or teeth.

But she dropped the knife into a sheath at her waist. With

an angry, uncertain face she watched each furrow darken, crest, crash, and dissolve. It was the darkening that made the wave.

Nall did not come back.

I drifted to Queelic, who sat staring west.

"He's left us with her," he said. "And she's got her knife back."

I did not answer. I thought of Dai saying, *You've got Nall now.*

Queelic said, "Is all that true? The Rigi are going to kill everybody on the coast?"

"Ask her."

"I don't like to. I mean, with her bare bosoms."

"She's as dressed as if she had a shirt on, for her."

Queelic unfolded his legs. Stretched them. "I guess they'll kill my dad?"

"Why are you asking me?"

He was musing on something. "When Dad was little and his name was still just Harlan, *his* dad had a special box made, to lock him up in when he was bad. Did your father lock you up?"

"In the woodbox once," I said. "I wouldn't wear petticoats."

"Right. Grandda would laugh, 'Down you go to the Rigi!' Then he'd shut Dad in the box, along with a rotten pig's carcass and a live cat."

I stared, horrified.

"He'd leave him in there for a day. Or two. So you see, Dad doesn't like the thought of the Rigi." Queelic stole a glance at Aieh. Her face looked translucent and she was blinking hard, but she glared right back. He dropped his eyes. "Dad doesn't like the feel of fur—or skin. That makes it difficult when he has his ladies in. He kept the box, though."

"Did he do that to you?" For the first time I wondered what my own father's childhood had been like.

"Oh, no. I have five older brothers; he never paid any attention to me."

"My father would have given his right hand to work for your father."

"So he gave you instead."

I stared again, then said, "I wasn't worth to him near what a hand's worth."

"More than me. I'm not worth shit."

Because that was exactly what I had been thinking, I hurried to say, "That's not true!"

"Oh, I'm fine at sums. Fine, fine," said Queelic, and giggled. It gave me the creeps. "You never said where you got those scars."

"A bear."

"Really? Then you're not a witch?"

"Do I look like one?"

"Don't ask me. I don't know anything." He flapped his hand toward Aieh, then toward the horizon with its dreaming islands. "Nothing's what I thought. Dad doesn't know about this. Dad's not out here at all."

I walked up and down the shingle. Nall did not come back. I could not sit or lie down, with every moment more uneasy; I started to climb the bank, thinking to walk on the green grass by the shrines, but quick as a fish, Aieh stood in front of me, knife in hand.

"Stay," she said.

In Kitchen Hessdish I said to her silver face, "You're a pig's daughter. Your blood stinks."

She replied in Rig. Maybe she said the same thing. I turned back to the beach, trying not to think what I thought: that Nall had gone on, swimming, to the Gate.

Time itself had changed. Queelic had said, *day after tomorrow,* but on that beach there was only this moment, the green wave next after this one. Aieh tinkered at her boat until she ran out of ropes to toy with. She pretended not to look out to sea, but I saw her do it. It was what I was doing. Queelic had fallen asleep and sprawled snoring on the shingle; I looked at him instead. When at last I turned back to the dissolving waves, Nall was wading out of the sea.

I drew breath to call to him. Did not. Neither did Aieh, though she rose.

The water had made him ruddy and beautiful. He stood apart from us both, silent, retying his breechclout. Aieh went to him, speaking in the Rigi's tongue—beseeching, nudging her chin toward the west.

He did not look at either of us. "I am going to the Gate," he said.

So it was me he chose. Not her. I clasped my hands, dizzy with victory.

Aieh paled, she drooped. In a still, dull voice she said, "I must go back to the caves. I went hunting that flesh-eater, and never gave Tadde his rope."

She lifted a fold of the sealskin that shone around her waist. A slender cord was bound above her belt, crisscrossing the silvery constellation of the Hunter. She passed this cord round and round her body, gathering it, and when she had all of it, she tossed the coil from hand to hand as if she did not care. It was like the horsehair rope that had bound me at the guardhouse, but made of exquisitely tiny plaits, braided, rebraided, braided again.

Queelic sat up sleepily. "That's hair," he said in his too-loud voice. Then, "It's *your* hair."

The rope was very long, and slim as a snake's tail; it would never bear weight. But Aieh lifted a length of it and pulled. The muscles strained in her slender arms. "Four days making, never sleeping. I put words in it."

"What's it for?" said Queelic.

"Binding."

"Binding what?"

"You are so stupid! When you die, you will be dirt! But when *we* die, we with skins"—she shot a desperate glance at Nall—"we will be our seals again and swim with our ancestors. This rope will bind Tadde to his skin."

Queelic said humbly, "Other people's religions are hard to understand."

"Do you think this sealskin is part of me, Pimple Boy? I will show you—"

She began to unbuckle her belt. Blushing, Queelic said, "No, no! It's clothes, I believe you!"

"Clothes!" She buckled the belt again. "Only for ceremony. It was bound to me when I was born; the men of my clan chanted for me at the shrines there. They will bind it to me again when I die." She jerked her chin at Nall. *"That* man had no skin to bind, when he died. They burned it."

"The thing in the cave—" Queelic looked peaked. "I mean, your brother. He had a sealskin."

"Marked with the sign of a hand, my Tadde! And he will be a seal. But if no man chants at the shrines, he will not stay with the Rigi. He will swim away who knows where, and someday, when I am my seal, he will not know me."

"Nobody would chant?"

"The Reirig set a watch on Selí; no man could leave. But I am not a man."

"No," said Queelic.

"Do you have a brother, Black Boot?"

"Lots."

"And you, girl?"

"No."

"Then you will not understand. I will not let my Tadde leave me, the way—the way one other did. If I were a man, I would know the chants; but I am not. So I will go to the cave and bind him to his skin with my hair. Only—now I must look at him again."

Queelic got to his knees. "You shouldn't. It's not nice to see. Miss—I mean Miss Aieh—isn't there some other way to bind him?"

"With blood," she said. "But that needs a death. Better the rope, for he cannot have the chants."

Nall said, "I know those chants."

Aieh hugged the rope to her breasts; she threw her arms around him. Snatching at his wrist, she tried to tug him toward the shrines.

"But I am not a Rig."

"Yes, you are! You swam away lost, because no one bound you. But your heart found the way back. And Tadde loves you; how could he not come to your voice?"

Nall turned to me. "I will do this. For Tadde."

Aieh pushed the coiled rope into his hand. "Then he will not need this. I give it to you."

He took it. "We'll be back directly," he said, "and then we must away."

They walked toward the shrines. I saw Aieh's hand slide down his arm and into his hand.

I sat down with Queelic and, like him, looked out to sea.

"Men with muscles," he said. "Women like them."

Nall came back from the shrines as he had gone—with Aieh, and silent. He did not want my help with the manat. He touched my hand once, then began to stow the meager stores, making sure the float bladders were firmly wedged at bow and stern. He had coiled the hair rope tight and small and tied it to his belt with a thong.

He glanced at me now and again, but I did not know how to talk to him, what to say. I felt as though a dark flood had risen, pushing everything askew; my words were all crooked in me.

Aieh's face was tear-marked and bright. She climbed about in her own boat, tightening the lashings and inspecting its greasy, translucent hull, pretending to do what she had already done. All the while she looked at Nall, talking and talking in Rig. He no longer tried to make her speak Plain, though he answered her in it, in monosyllables. Her glances at me were secretive, brief.

Queelic's face had reddened with sun. He sat staring west over the water. Now and then he sneaked a look at Aieh. When she caught him at it, she stared back boldly, and he dropped his eyes to his boots.

I could not bear it. I went to Nall at the manat and said, "Let me help."

He was tying a length of hemp to the bow line of oiled

hide and barely looked up. I thought, *Who kissed me on the sandspit? Who was I with last night? Where has that man gone?*

"I'll teach you a knot," he said. "A knot that will not slip, that ties together two ropes made of different stuff."

I did not want to learn about knots. I wanted him to say he was sorry, that he loved me, only me, forever. I wanted him to explain what Aieh was to him, what he wanted, what I could do. The words sat in my throat. The knot was what he offered, so I learned that, hemp in one hand and braided hide in the other.

Aieh watched us. When Nall paid no attention to her, she stalked toward Queelic, who put his hand to his throat.

Nall nodded at my work. "On the water a rope is safety."

So Aieh had given him safety; my own hair was barely long enough to braid. I handed back the knotted line. "Nall—"

He looked up. My heart clenched around my voice; I looked away and said, "What—what now?"

"The Gate." Then, in an undertone, "Kat, Kat. I wish you had not come."

I hugged my elbows.

"I was wrong to ask you. Wrong to let you. I thought it was meant. I thought—"

"*Let* me?" I said in a half whisper. "Who are you, my father? I *chose* to come!"

"And I let you. I have brought you to ruin. Aieh—"

"Don't tell me—" I began to say, *Don't tell me about Aieh!* but in the middle it became, "Don't tell me what to do!" I put my arms around him, but he felt wrong, all bones and angles instead of the sweet fit of the night before.

He got a soft grip on my curls and tipped my head back to make me look at him. He spoke in Rig.

I said, "I can't understand you."

"I know. And I can't say it in Plain. What have I done?"

"Nothing!" I pulled away and stamped my foot. "*I* called you! *I* chose!"

"You don't know what you chose."

"Neither do you!"

Queelic squealed. Aieh was inspecting him fore and aft as if to see what a Black Boot was built of, ignoring his attempts to beat her off. She peered into his ear and said loudly, "We are leaving. You will come with me."

"With you?" he said, his collar all awry. "West?"

I thought, She'll get him into mid-ocean and help him over the side.

"Oh, I'd love to!" he said.

"If I leave you here, you will foul the shrines," she said. "I will take you to the Home Stone, to a hidden place. There you can sit until you starve, or you can wander and be killed; whichever you like."

I turned back to Nall, but our words had died. Bent over the manat, he said, "The Home Stone has a thousand bays and coves; one could hide there forever. Maybe. Though one must land unseen."

"I told you the landings are unwatched!" said Aieh. "Today every Rig but the sick and the old is in pilgrimage, traveling to the Gate arem and the Reirig's throne. The whole world will dance tonight. But not you, Pimple Boy; you will sit at Linn Cove and tell over every riddle you know."

I said to Nall, "We'll paddle through the islands, then on to the Gate?"

"It will be enough to raise Linn Cove with a whole skin."

"I thought— You said we weren't going to the Home Stone, but past it—"

"To Linn Cove first."

"But they'll see us!"

Aieh answered for him. "There are paths on the water as there are paths in the forest. Do you think we are fools? No one will see us."

Nall would say no more. With my eyes I tried to tell him I would go with him into the mouth of death—but not if *she* were there.

Queelic looked at Aieh's open boat. "I guess I have to go in that?"

"My *voi*? How else? Did you fly here?"

"The fishermen's boat was bigger. They tied me up."

"Shall I tie you up?"

"No."

"You would lie quieter. Your great boots will put holes in the hull."

"He'll take them off," said Nall. Queelic began to tug at his boots. In the end I had to help him; a Leagueman's boots require a servant, or a wife.

His feet were white as grubs and looked crooked. Aieh stared at them. So did he, as if he had never seen them before. He clutched the boots to his heart.

Aieh slipped past me and laid her hand on Nall's breast, saying, "The open sea is ours, and by the time we make the islands, the dusk will hide us." To Queelic she said, "Get into my voi, Pimple Boy. Look where you put your feet."

18

Odor of stars, of dark dew.
The day birds cower.
The night moth plunges
And shivers in the white flower.

Moonlight Chant. The Rigi.

WE PUSHED OFF from the Isle of Bones, onto the blue deep. The wind soughed and buffeted, but the sky was clear.

Aieh had chivvied Queelic into the stern of her boat. There he crouched, clutching the oily thwarts while she rowed quick as a water strider, glancing over her shoulder. He fixed his eyes on the horizon.

I fixed mine on the blue spiral on Nall's back, and paddled. Now I should speak, I thought.

I composed words in my mind. *Nall. I was wondering. . . . Excuse me, Nall—could we talk? Do you mind if we talk? I understand that you— It seems as though— I think I deserve— If you would just—*

Not one word came out of my mouth. We paddled. After a while my thoughts turned into, *Why don't you talk? Damn you, could you say something? Can't you see that I'm— Do you realize that you're—that we're—*

Neither of us spoke. The manat cut the dusky water with a rustle. Once something big rose behind us and exhaled, *phoo!* But when I turned to look, I saw nothing. I thought of nameless great beings, gliding beneath us in the deep.

The islands hung motionless, yet drew nearer. Time went on, we did not speak, until it had been so long that it felt stupid to say anything and I could feel desolate, rescued from having to.

We paddled west. Sometimes we waited for Aieh to catch up—she was one rower to our two—still without a word between us. Slow as a dream, the islands rose out of the sea.

They were cliffs and pillars, arches and mounts, crags and sloping cones, all glinting and dim. They were rounded like bread loaves or pointed like awls, square and crumbling like ruined palaces, or so furred with trees that the shadow forests seemed to rise straight out of the water. Each island wore a ghostly dome of cloud that mimicked its shape.

By then the sun had slid low, turning the blue water to purple, like the heart of an amethyst. When it sank at last, it left its glow in a green sky with the slimmest feather of a moon.

We stole among the islands as we had stolen among the

shrines. Like the shrines, they seemed to move. They swung like boats drifting at anchor; I knew it was we who moved, not they, but my eyes would not believe it. As we crept along the first strait, they seemed to circle us, to loom, to slip behind us, until when I looked where we had come from, the way was closed by shadow.

My heart beat hard. The jerk of Nall's head was tense, quick. On swell or shadowy hillside was no human sign, only water and shapes made by water. Just once did I see, far away along a ripple of reflected light, a fleck that might have been a voi with many paddlers, and once, on a dark hillside, a little orange seed of fire. We passed skerries luminous with brooding birds; here and there a wing stretched, was folded. Dusk rose around us, like water poured into a bowl.

We waited for Aieh in the wave-wash at the foot of a cliff. She came alongside with a one-handed hook stroke that slid the voi sideways. Queelic made a gulping sound.

"He vomited," she said.

Nall said, "Do not speak so loud."

She pointed to a swelling darkness in the west, and in a whisper she said, "Home. No Black Boot has seen it since the world began." Her look said that Queelic and I were dogs, we would piss on paradise. "There are more Rigi than all the Black Boots under the moon, more than all the seal-killers, and tonight we shall be gathered, every one."

Queelic said faintly, "Is that where we're going?"

"*Hai!* There they *would* eat you!" To Nall she said, "Remember to keep wide of the rocks."

He nodded. I did not trust her and said, "Surely there will be boats about, on their way to the gathering?"

"Would we be so stupid as to use a traveled track, Scarred Girl? Besides, the whole world is at the Counting Downward dance."

"Counting?" groaned Queelic as the boats jigged up and down. "Counting" is the League word for "prayer"; League-men carry counting beads. "Counting dance?" he said.

"Not for you, Vomiting Boy."

Nall said, "Before Least and Long Nights we dance the Counting Downward Nights."

We dance. We, the Rigi.

The shell-colored twilight dimmed to black. Nall and his flicking paddle became only a shape, until my eyes grew used to starlight and I could see the shine of his sweat. A greenish gleam dripped from our paddles and marked our vanishing wake.

I saw no other boats. Yet I felt watched. I wanted to make myself small, or stop my heart's beating. The night went on— surely it was midnight; as we crept west through the forest of islands, the body of the Home Stone grew huge before us, more smelled than seen. A breeze turned back from the cliffs, bringing the odor of cedar and night-blooming flowers. Nall stopped paddling to breathe it. Paddled again. Breathed. At the waft of another odor, deep as honeysuckle, he shipped his oar.

Aieh's voi slipped past us. I heard a soft phrase in Rig. Nall started; he took up his paddle and pulled the manat under a dark cliff slit by ravines and draped with shadowy vines.

Waves crackled at a cluster of rocks. Aieh waited to be sure he was with her and then, with the twist of an oar, drove her voi straight into the cliff.

Nall bent his back. A black crack widened in the stone, and the manat dove into it like a fish into a hole in a reef. Rock whirled past my face, a trailing vine brushed my lips, and we were through the gap into a round, steep-walled cove. The sound of water was loud. Cliffs rose out of the sea, clotted with ferny shadow, below them a tiny beach where the prow of the voi stilled in the sand.

Crack—crash—a white goat burst from cover, clattering up an impossible cliff to vanish at the top.

Nall pulled the manat's nose to shore and slid into the water with no splash. I could not see his face. He steadied the hull for me to climb out, then held the gunwale of the voi.

Queelic rose up, fell back. Nall heaved him out and set him in shin-deep water. Still clutching his boots, Queelic tottered up the beach and sat down in the same sprawled position as before.

Nall dragged the manat higher. He took my paddle and stowed it. He did not stow his own, but stood leaning on it, turning his head left and right. So had blind Raím stood, catching familiar air currents on cheek and thigh. I thought of Creek and earth things: clay, cedar smoke, Raím's freckled shoulder.

Nall said to Queelic, "Here is where you must stay."

Queelic nodded, looking around at the trailing dark vines, the dome of starlight high above. Aieh lingered behind the prow of her voi, watching us. Her eyes seemed darker. I thought, As soon as Nall and I leave for the Gate, Queelic's life will be short.

I said to her, "Do you give your word that you'll—" What? Leave him alone until the next lot of Rigi find him? Until everyone in Downshore is dead? Until Nall and I have done what we have to do, which is I don't know what, and can come back to rescue Ab Harlan's son?

Aieh shrugged.

It could not be helped. I looked at Queelic for the last time. He gazed back calmly. As I turned to the manat Nall said, "Kat, you'll stay with Queelic."

"No, I won't," I said. Then, *"What?"*

"Aieh was wise to bring him. He will be company."

"I'm not staying here," I said like a simpleton. "I'm going to the Gate with you."

He would not look at me. "I shall take you no farther."

"Take me? We're together!"

"We were. But from here I shall go on alone, to Stillness before the Gate, and listen. I will come back for you—if I live."

And if you die? I had known I might die—indeed, at first I had not cared—but I would die with him. "I'm not leaving you," I said.

"Yes."

"I won't, Nall!"

"Beyond this there is no safe place for you."

"Safe!" Did he think I would be safer with Aieh and her knife? "What do I care for safety?"

"I care." But his eyes slid away. Surely Aieh had talked him into this, at the shrines. His face was white in the gloom. He said again, "If I live, I will come—"

"My life is my own, to risk as I will!"

He looked at me straight then, with his hero's face on. In a terrible, low voice he said, "But mine is not my own. I serve the world. I am to listen, and I cannot hear; it is 'Nall! Nall!'—all noise and strife. I must have silence! Alone, I will have silence."

So it was not even a desire for my safety that made him abandon me, but my grubby, quarreling heart. Even Aieh looked shocked. It was not to this she had coaxed him, for she was half the quarrel.

I could not bear my shame and fell back on rage. "You never told me that! You never said!"

"Because I am a fool. And how can I tell you everything, in this world that changes and changes?"

"*Everything?* You've told me nothing! Why didn't you speak to me? Have you no tongue?"

"Doesn't grief come soon enough? I would spare you—"

"*Spare* me? My grief is mine! *I* feel it! You rob me!"

"Kat—"

"Oh," I said, "must I remember you like this, with lies in your mouth?"

He put his hand over his eyes.

Aieh said, "Listen."

She was touching Nall's arm.

"There is more than one road to the Gate," she said.

He shook her off. But she caught his hand and held it, saying, "Listen to me. Do not think I say this for the sake of that girl who will be dirt. I say it because I want your happiness, and it seems hers is yours. Hide the manat here and go overland. She can stay with you a little longer so, and drink all the grief she wants." She put her hand over his heart. "Nall!"

He stared, that she should call him by that name.

"Take her to our ama, in Selí. Let our ama see you for one instant; how can you come so far and never greet her, who loves you and thinks you are dead forever? Leave the girl in Selí and swim from there—oh, fool and hero—and then go die at the Gate."

"Selí? What safety would there be for her there?"

"I am not 'her'!" I said. "I have a name!"

"As to safety, there is none. But there are a thousand hiding places in the woods and warrenhouse, and our ama is there alone; she does not go to the dances anymore, now that her nani is dead. And I will watch over that scarred girl. I swear I will not bring her to harm," said Aieh. "By Tadde's soul I swear!"

"The land way is too risky," said Nall, "and I am lame."

"Hey," said Queelic. "Look!"

He pointed at the water. In the waves that washed in rings off the rocky walls a dark head bobbed, round and big and coming.

He scrambled away on all fours like a crab. I backed up the beach, as out of the lipping pool rose a sleek shape bigger than a man. On its streaming shoulder was a dark blotch the shape of a human hand.

Aieh stepped behind Nall with a whining cry. The seal drew itself half out of the water, starlight on its liquid eye. It nosed Nall's manat, tipping it gently on its side; my paddle clattered inside the hull. It put back its head and made a moan, a singing that was not quite, or no longer, words.

Aieh stepped forward, trembling. The seal slid back into the water. As it vanished she plunged in to her thighs, crying, "Tadde! Taddiki!"

Queelic murmured, "It said something."

Aieh turned back weeping to the shore. In the waves, even in the little wind, I heard the echo of those almost-words, a voice trying to speak.

"What did it say?" said Queelic.

Nall, on an inbreath, said, "'Go on beyond the reef.'"

"No!" said Aieh. "He said, 'On, on to Selí!'"

I said nothing, for what I had heard, or almost heard, in the Plain tongue that is spoken by all peoples and has no magic at all, was *Love in the sea of grief.*

Queelic said, "But it spoke Hessdish, like a Leagueman. It said—" And then, "What—what was it?"

No one answered him. Aieh spoke in Rig, wept, spoke, then changed to the Plain tongue as if to share her victory. "He is not lost. Bij, you have saved him to me!"

"Nall is my name. Nall!"

"That name is nothing. Soon Tadde will pass the Gate and all speech will be taken from him, but you heard him: He bids you go the land way, to Selí. See—he overturned your manat!"

Nall swung his head as if to clear it. "Beyond the reef, he said."

"Selí!"

But I had understood something, seen it like a vista lit by a lightning flash: that if it had been Dai listening to that seal, he might have heard, *Lowing upon the heath.* Or Raím, *Loom and the comb's teeth.* And what might Bian have heard? Or Nondany? When the world speaks in its inhuman tongue, why do we hear what we do?

For an instant my misery was pierced and stripped away and I was myself, eager, without rage or confusion. Then I heard Aieh say again, "To Selí! You can take the girl—"

"Beyond the reef. Alone."

Aieh turned to me. Not loud, she said, "You see? He never loved you."

Nall straightened.

"Do as you wish," she said. "I know my brother's voice." She strode away. I saw the whites of her eyes as she looked back, watching.

In a low, driven voice Nall said, "Kat, that is not true." He took my hand and held it to his mouth. But his eyes still

255

went to Aieh's; I pulled my hand away. He caught it again, gripping it so hard that it hurt. "So be it. Have your grief; maybe my ama will give you hers. We will go to Selí."

My hand let itself be held. My heart, hearing even a hint of what it wanted to hear, unclenched a little. On the way to Selí I would make no trouble; he would see how good I could be, he would take me with him to the Gate.

Nall went to Aieh, speaking in Rig. He was angry. I went hot and black with triumph. She stood stiff, her back to him, saying sullenly, "By Tadde's soul I swore!"

He turned away from both of us, righted the manat, stowed the second paddle, and lifted the boat to hide it under vines well above the tidemark.

Aieh did not speak. She went to her voi and stowed gear also, then pulled the boat higher on the gravel.

Queelic said, "Kat, help me get my boots back on."

"I'm not your slave! Did nobody ever teach you to say 'please'?"

"Please."

It was the first time I had heard that word from a League-man's mouth. I bullied him into his boots. He did not need them anyway, to sit on the sand.

He said, "Which way's west?"

"Please."

"Please, which—"

"Ask Nall."

Nall, pointing over the leafy brow of the cliff, said, "That star."

"Thank you," said Queelic. With his booted feet splayed in front of him, he gazed at that star.

ᵔ ᵔ ᵔ

We climbed up the way the goat had gone. A narrow trail threaded the cliff, and a thin rill of springwater ran beside it. I pushed my mouth into that trickle and drank. Moss sprang under my hands, sedge whipped my cheek. Scrambling, sometimes on all fours, I followed Aieh and Nall up through vining herbs whose odors were deep and strange.

They were not strange to Nall. In the patches of starshine I watched him brush his hand here and there, crush a leaf in his fingers. White flowers overhung the muddy trail, more musky than sweet; he pulled them down to his face.

Aieh was climbing ahead; she turned back with a dark clump of something in her hands and held it out to him. At first he shook his head. Then he took it, and she went on. As I came up behind him, I saw he held flowers so black that if they bloomed in sunlight they must be red, their odor half fungus, half perfume. He did not show them to me, but climbed on, holding them, until abruptly he threw them away.

The track led into a ravine, winding and climbing to the cliff top. There the west wind met us, and the enormous, glittering sky.

I could not see the ocean, but I could feel it out there, encircling us. We stood at the edge of a meadow of rippling grass, which like the Isle of Bones, tilted westward, tipping us as if toward a last waterfall, over the brink of the world.

Far down the dark way behind us some animal thrashed in the underbrush. Nall took my hand, whispering in Rig.

"What?" I said.

He shook his head and said in Plain, "Keep to the shadow." His hand was tense and wet. We skirted the meadow, wading thigh-deep in grass until we could duck among thick-leafed bushes taller than a man. I could see no big trees, but I heard wind in branches somewhere—*haash, haash*. When Nall dropped my hand, my fingers smelled of the black flowers.

The bushes stooped away from the wind. Between them the grass was shorter, and from the corner of my eye I thought I saw movement—snake or weasel. Nall moved as though he knew each step by heart.

The copse went on and on, miles, broken here and there by fields of stunted barley, scatters of scrawny plants as cool as cabbage, hairy as squash. There began to be hills around us, crumpled and dim and shivering with leaf. Panting, we paused in speckled shadow. From over our heads came a breathy cry.

I jumped. My whole skin was an ear. Again near-speech, a querulous wail. I thought, The trees are full of souls! Then saw two black stump shapes that bobbed their heads. Owls.

Nall was listening for something else. His eyelids puckered as if in pain. Then he was off again, following Aieh's silver ghost through the grove. The stars were so bright that they cast shadows. We skirted another meadow, where hissing grass leaped in the wind and the land began to fall away on either side.

The rasp of the wind filled my hearing. Then I thought it was my own blood I heard, hissing in my veins. The more afraid I got, the louder it grew, until I covered my ears and it lessened, so I knew it was outside of me.

"Nall!" I said, whisper or shout.

He halted as if shot. I crashed into him and said, "There's a sound."

"The Gate."

"What—"

"Everything rushing through." He jerked his chin in the direction we were going. "In the sea beyond the bay there, beyond the dance."

"The dance—but that's where the Rigi are!"

"I am a Rig—," he said, and stopped. Aieh circled back, looking at him without expression. He shook his head, said, "—and—and I know where we are. Selí lies at our right hand, there. At our left is the dance."

"But—"

"You should not have come."

"I'll stop here, then! I'll go back! If you don't want me—"

He took my wrist and pulled me on, west. I thought he held me so that I would not run off. Then I thought it was for comfort, because he was afraid. Then I could not think, for that sound was everywhere. He let me go, and we ran on into the noise of blood.

We dodged through a wood and out again, onto a broad ridge hummocky with grass, littered with pale boulders like statues in every shape stone can weather to. The rushy roar grew louder, became a giant breath. Aieh flew west straight as a homing bee. The ridge narrowed, but I could see nothing, only stones, and caves under stones; we came to a promontory jagged with spines and slabs, and began to climb among them.

Aieh pushed past us, scrambled ahead. I clambered with feet and hands. Nall's heels flashed at my eye level.

He pulled himself over a high step, reached down, and without waiting for my hand he dragged me up by the slack of my shift. I landed on my belly, rolled into Aieh, jerked away from her, and sprawled, staring west over water.

We lay on a rocky headland, the north jaw of the mouth of

a great, round, west-facing bay. The water in the bay was still and crinkled, but outside its mouth the western sea came marching in rank after rank of waves, an army of water striking the shore, over and over forever.

The sound had softened and grown vast, just noise. Fallen to my left, Nall dropped his head onto his forearms. Raised it.

"*Las,*" he said. And in the Plain tongue, "The Gate."

I followed his eyes. At the bay's mouth a black rock stood in the night sea. It was split in two, like a shrine in the sea.

East before it and west beyond it, shining shoals of water spread in fans too wide, too long to be what they must be: the tide rushing through the break in the rock. That was what made the sound, as though all the water in the bay, in the sea, were tipping through that gap.

The split rock was textureless, quite black. No starlit birds nested there; it was not speckled with nests or dung. Just east of it, the only other rock in the sea, a tiny skerry broke the wash: Stillness.

I was numb. I thought, That doesn't look hard to get to.

Nall's lips moved. I looked at his face in the starlight and I was nowhere in it, had never been in it. He was pure intent, set on that split black rock.

Aieh touched his arm. "Selí," she said, nodding to the north. I could see nothing there, only darkness and waves breaking. Nall's fixed look wavered. "Selí," she said again, but softly. "Ama."

He nodded but did not turn. Instead he began to creep, flat on his belly, to the south rim of the promontory. She hesitated, then crept after him.

I would not be left. I followed the pale soles of their feet, crawled to Nall's elbow, crowded my cheek next to his, and looked where he looked, straight down.

Seaward was the Gate; landward, the bay spread out round as the moon. Below us earth and ocean met in a shining edge. The water side was wrinkled glass, the land side a curving beach thick with rocks. Dark, long, crowded in hundreds, in thousands, the rocks moved, like the shrines.

"*Rigoi*," Nall whispered. Seals. All the seals in the sea.

Big seals, little seals crammed the long beach, singly and in clots and bunches, dark bodies on pale sand. The shifting wind brought the stink of their crowded life, crowded sleep, its belches, farts, moans, and snores. It brought the sound of a drum.

Nall gazed raptly down, as though that fertile, squirming herd were his home. "*Hom meshai*," he said, and his tired, tense face was glad.

Seeing that village of flesh, I knew I stood outside it and always would. I had splashed in the creek; I had run the high mountains and walked the dusty inland roads; but this was a different place. It was too much sea.

Aieh's face was as expressionless as a cat's. The pelt around her waist shone rumpled silver, the sleek fur on her skull made her head look wet. I thought, It's true: Aieh is a seal.

Nall looked at me. He seemed puzzled. "*Dua 'eam?*"

"What?"

He did not answer. Aieh hid a smile. She nudged him to look inland, beyond the seals, where the dark island glittered with fires—red stars that blinked and bobbed to the sound of the drum. The Gate roared.

"*Aremoi?*" said Nall. He stared from me to those starry fires. "Eh! *Aremoi Lasai.*"

Aieh slid back from the edge. *"Im Selí, Bij? Selí!"*

His half-dreaming face. *"Ki nibo—"*

She smiled again. *"Nibo kashoé."*

I said, "I can't understand!"

Nall put his hand on my mouth. His hand was cold. He gaped like a fish in air, said, *"Ovai—ne, ne!"* Tried again: "Or this journey has been nothing. Come with me." Still on his belly, he scrambled sideways. Not north to Selí, but south and east, toward the fires.

I followed him because he asked me to. Because I had to be wanted by him—for certain, forever.

Aieh came with us. We crept down among rocks, toward the drum that beat, monotonous, like something that keeps happening—not urgent, but inevitable.

"Nall—"

He made a fierce gesture: *Be quiet.*

I was quiet, and followed.

Once down from the rocks we pushed through scrubby beach plum and low, sticky weeds that smelled like milk. We crawled up a windy dune on our bellies. The sand was loose and cool. I crowded Nall's heels. Aieh squirmed alongside him like a lizard.

Below the slipping rim he stopped. When I nudged up level with him, he pinned my wrist. So close that I felt the heat of his breath, he said, "Do you want to know who I am?"

Terrified, I nodded.

"Then look."

Slow as moonrise, we pushed our heads over the crest of the dune.

The dance was *there.* Right at me—loud sound, dark motion. Flesh pumped and gleamed; the darkness was fur, it was gaps between shine, whatever was not flesh. Seals dancing—no—I saw legs, teeth, faces human and not human. I could see nothing long enough to know it. Fish in a boiling ocean, haunch and shoulder, groin and straining mouth, dreams grown bodies. Half-and-half and a thousand halves, dark as the woodbox, rage and naked joy: the Rigi.

Whimpering, I ducked my head.

Nall's eyes were all blackness, like a seal's. He rose, he stood. On the crest of the dune he raised his arms and spoke his name, the name of a dead man.

"*Hai!*" cried Aieh. "I knew if he heard the drum, he would remember who he is!"

He froze. He had been seen.

The pulse of the dance went chaotic, like tide rips meeting. From the crowded darkness rose a cry, and the Rigi poured up the dune toward us.

19

Rararanga!
Thunder in the stone!
Rararam!
The house falls down!
Rararash!
Ouma gnaws her bone!
Rai! Rai!
Wailing in the town!

Earthquake Chant. Creek.

I FELT NOTHING. Blankness. Then rushing, and a black weight as Nall threw himself on me.

I thought he would devour me and screamed with my mouth full of sand. But he locked his arms around me as together we were grabbed and swung high, like a turtle lifted by an eagle to be dropped on the rocks.

We were dropped. Just let go of, Nall underneath. Voices

screamed, *"Uhui! Uhui!"* Aieh's voice screamed other sounds, high as a gull's cry and unheeded. The firelight stuttered with running shadows. Nall lay on his back gaping, not breathing. I wrenched myself away from him.

"Get up," I said. Everything was motion and cries, I could see nothing to name. "Get up!"

He did not move.

A white fire rushed up in me, bleaching everything. I scrambled to my feet, straddled his body, and shrieked at the dark, *"Stop it!* Let me see you clear!"

The motion did not stop. But it slowed, like stirred water settling, the sediment sinking down. The drum took up its steady beat. In the hiss of the Gate the darkness circled us counterclockwise, becoming, in brief glimpses, teeth, claws, eyes.

Nall sat up, forcing me to stumble backward. Then he stood, trying in a blind, clumsy way to get in front of me.

The center of a circle has no front. All I could think was, *He has no skin.* His lips were drawn back from teeth as bare as a skull's. I wrestled with him. Fear made me so angry that I shook—furious at his nakedness, his stupidity in bringing us here.

Murmuring, the crowd drew close.

He stopped fighting. I got my back to him and stretched my arms back around him, felt him press against me. Somewhere in the jangled shadow Aieh's voice screamed on and on.

I tucked my chin down on my neck as the Rigi put out their hands and began to touch us.

At first it was a tapping soft as moths at a window. It grew firmer until it was a cat's tongue, the nudging nose of a dog— a caress, insistent and yearning, like love.

Nall shrank from it. I hooked one arm back over his neck, and he hid his face in my hair.

I shouted at the circling shadows. *"What do you want?"*

No answer. Only the pressure, restrained and urgent, of many and many hands. The drum still beat. I saw the shimmer of sealskins; the claws were necklaces of claws, the eyes and teeth belonged to wild masks. The instant I recognized them as masks they were lowered. Behind them were wild faces.

I let go of Nall. He slid to his knees. Among the nudging hands I pushed back with my own hands, saying, "Stop it. Don't touch him. Tell me what you want."

The faces belonged to women, men, children—thin and windblown, mostly naked, half covered by the glittering skins.

They are not nightmares, I thought. They're people.

I looked and looked, at brown skin and pale skin, hook nose and broad nose, hard mouth and sweet mouth, belly and breast. They moved to the beat of the drum, as though they dreamed. I looked at the hands that touched me, and among them I saw Nall's.

I looked again. It was his, the hand that had caressed me in the death cave, but gone the color of shadow. When next it blinked past in the circling press, I took it and held it.

"Hsuu," I said. "Old Sea."

The circling stopped. So did the murmuring, and Aieh's wailing voice. I looked at the father who had killed his son.

I had expected a cruel face. It was not. It was Nall's face grown older, neither happy nor sad, on a hard, small, graying man who was naked except for a worn sealskin over one shoulder. Every plane, every ridge and crevice of his body was written over with dark spirals that by daylight must be blue.

From the edge of my eye I saw Nall's face, stunned and open, so like his father's in shape and set that I thought he must be sucked right into the other like a raindrop into the sea. There was nothing to put between them but myself. This I did, shouldering up big like a bear who sees the hunter near her cub. The Gate roared.

Hsuu's face was expressionless, full of all expression; it seemed to ripple, like windblown water. Sweetness, outrage, fascination, fear—each moved him, none stayed. The sum was a dangerous stillness.

I said the first thing I thought. "I brought back your son."

He pursed his tattooed lips. "My son is dead."

"He is not!"

"I killed him."

I pressed Nall's face to my thigh. "You did not! Here he is. I called him, and he came to me!"

The crowd murmured, shifted. Away behind them a chutter of motion had begun.

Hsuu said gently, "I killed him with the hand you hold."

I dropped that hand. I grew huge, enraged like a mother bear. To get Nall safe I devoured him, and tore Aieh with my claws. "If you killed him, I gave him life again! I called him and I named him. He belongs to me. I am Ouma the Bear!"

"Bear," said Hsuu.

He would not know what a bear was. I raised my hands and raked them through the air, then pulled down the neck of my shift to show my scars. "See *my* tattoo? I made this world, all of it! I made your son—I made him new. His name is Nall now!"

The dreaming faces of the crowd turned to one another. *"Nall, Nall"* went whispering round.

Hsuu made a slight move forward, like a seal that noses its dead pup. I blocked him with my body. I felt so strong that I thought, Bian was right—it was Ouma herself who ate me.

As Ouma, I drew breath and roared like a she-bear.

But what came out was *"Me-e-eh!"* A bear cub's squall.

I put my fist to my mouth.

Hsuu stood patiently. Was he curious? Loving? Angry? These feelings crossed his face, did not linger on it. Nall's face was empty and growing emptier, the face of a man in a sinking boat who throws everything overside, everything, as he tries to stay afloat.

Hsuu said, "This man you own—"

As he spoke, a grove of spears clattered out of the crowd, upright and rattling like bamboo in wind. Running men held them, fierce in skins and silver earrings. *They* were not dreaming, or perhaps their dream was war. When they saw Hsuu, they stopped their pressing and low shouts and straightened, in deference or uncertainty.

Hsuu withdrew a little. The spear thicket wavered, parted like grass before a snake. The crowd muttered, *"Reirig, Reirig,"* they drew their sealskins round them and stumbled aside, as from among the spearmen stepped a man with a lance.

The sealskin over his shoulder was sewn so full of jet that it was all ornament—I could scarcely see the fur. The lance was long. In my mind I had made the Reirig fat and old, like Ab Harlan. But he was young and tall and naked, the most beautiful man I had ever seen.

He was tattooed in bands across his calves, groin, and breast; his shaved skull was tattooed, and his mouth. He was beautiful in spite of this, or because of it. I had to look only at the tattoos, because if I looked at his body itself I felt terror, as one might before a god.

He planted the butt of the lance in the sand. The jet on his sealskin chimed. He had high cheekbones and long, light eyes that I could not meet.

The crowd had scrambled back, all but Hsuu. The Reirig scratched himself and yawned, his teeth sharp behind his tattooed lips. He was tense as a bow, but he feigned laziness as he prowled toward us. With the sandy butt of his spear he prodded Nall's shoulder. He spoke to Hsuu in Rig; his voice was deep and without inflection, like a dog's bark.

Hsuu answered. The Reirig gripped Nall's hair and bent back his head, twisting until I thought Nall's neck must break. I let go of him just as the Reirig did, and he fell backward like a cloth doll.

Then it was my hair the Reirig gripped. His body gave off heat like a horse after a race. He tucked the spear into the crook of his elbow and used one hand to tilt my head about while he ran the other down my bare arm. He put his hand to his blackened mouth, wet his fingers, and drew them down the lines of my scars. Past his shoulder the faces of the crowd were half hidden in smoke from the fires.

"Look at me, girlie," he said in Plain.

I looked at him. My father had called me "girlie," and the dead Seroy.

His long eyes narrowed and he smiled, his white teeth peeped. "Girlie, where have you come from?"

I did not speak. I no longer heard the Gate; its roar had become my mind itself. I could not think, or reason, or get away from the noise.

The Reirig shortened his grip on the lance and held the

blade at my throat. Like Liu's it was obsidian, black glass.

I whispered, "Creek."

He did not know where that was. He did not like not knowing. His smile faded to black; the lance point slid from my chin to my breast.

"In the mountains," I said. "East. Where the sun comes from."

He rubbed my curls between his fingers. "You have come from the sun?"

Oh, then I remembered it, like a dream in a dream: the sun shining in Bian's kitchen window, glittering in the fur of bears, traveling sometimes from dawn to sunset across a cobalt sky without one cloud. "Yes," I said. My tears welled up, spilled down. "From the sun."

He was not listening. He had found the pouch tied at my waist. He hefted it. "Gold." His lip flared like a cat's. "Do you think I need gold? I who will own the world? I am the One!" He let it drop against my hip. He fingered the spear shaft, fidgeted. He seemed to forget me, flushed with possession like a child with too many toys. Two of his guards were speaking in low voices; he sprang at them, snarling. They cowered. He turned away satisfied, saw me again, sauntered back.

"Girlie. Why have you come from the sun now, on this very night?"

"To—to—"

I need not have spoken. He knew the answer. He knew all answers; he did not even need to listen at the Gate. "To show the world that I am king," he said, "and that the plans of those who covet my lance always fail."

He looked at Hsuu, a glare like an ape's. "A man's son wanted to kill me once. That man was loyal—perhaps. So loyal that for my sake he killed his own son—perhaps. Or did he have other plans? Because that son has sought to return from the dead, on this night of all nights, to kill me." He pushed Nall's body with his foot. "But see—he is dead again himself, and he has brought me a gift besides. The plots of my enemies always fail."

He bared his teeth at Hsuu, grin or threat.

Hsuu seemed no less moved by this, and no more, than a wave by rain. He pursed his lips.

The Reirig glared about at the crowd. "The world is made ready. The wave rises, the towering waters shall fall upon the sorry shore, and I am your priest and king!"

Turning back to me, he wiped my eyes with his thumb—not as Nall had done on the sandspit, but as if he cleaned a dog's eyes. "I am the Dark Moon," he said. "Do not cry anymore, Sun Girl. You shall be my wife. Moon shall have Sun, and the world shall be whole again." He stared around at the crowd. "Its warring parts shall be one, because it shall be mine. All of it. I am king of the universe," he said.

His laugh was sincere and easy. I had known men in Creek who laughed like that, who hunted bears and women and got them. Raím had been such a man, once.

The Reirig took Nall's arm and jerked him to sitting. Nall lolled; I knelt and held him up. In front of his half-open eyes the Reirig swung his lance like a pendulum, butt end, blade end.

It thrummed. The black blade twinkled. He spun it; its glitter and hum made spirals in the firelight as his hands, like a juggler's, tossed and caught the shaft that seemed to squirm like an eel, to fill the space around us as whirlpools fill a tide race.

I stared in a trance. I could not even be afraid. Nall raised his face to the sparkle like a child with a pinwheel, and in that instant the blade slithered past me and brushed his breast. *Zik!*

He did not flinch. The Reirig snatched the lance out of the air, grounded the shaft, and leaned on it.

This happened between breath and breath. Left to right, a slender wound crossed Nall's heart, and a tiny rivulet of blood ran down over the nipple. He did not move.

Hsuu looked on, pursing his lips.

The Reirig smiled behind his tattoo. He reached to play with my curls again; they pleased him. He used them to pull me up, so that I had to let go of Nall and stand. "Girlie, come along to me."

I tried to shake my head, *No.*

"Come along," he said. But when he let go of my hair, I knelt, gathered Nall out of the sand, and held him.

The Reirig laughed. "That is dead, girlie. Leave it, and come along to me." He took my wrist, as one might coax a child to lay down a dead kitten.

"No." I could see the pulse in Nall's neck, his eyes racing behind closed lids.

The Reirig's pull at my wrist grew harsh. "You want that, girlie? Bring it. I give it to you. You may keep it until it stinks. Come along to me now." He swung the lance point to hang at my neck.

I stood up, lifting Nall as well as I could. "Get up now," I said, wheedling like a mother. He was mine; everybody said so. "Come on, sweetheart, let's go."

He rose, staggering. The crowd whispered; I had forgotten them. The Reirig turned toward the drum, motioning me to follow. Nall's legs buckled. I could not hold him up, and fell with him.

Softly the crowd closed behind us. A hundred hands raised us, they held us up and touched us forward, we were carried by hands like driftwood on a wave.

In the press was Aieh, her insolence gone. She stared at Nall, her face all horror. I threw her a look of hate and pulled him safely past her, through groves of human shadow, between shining fires, along the beach to the edge of the seal colony, its stink and roar.

The seals were restless as tied dogs; they groaned and squirmed away—even from Hsuu, who trotted behind us. Those closest to the water plunged into it, then jerked and came back, invisibly tethered.

Nall reeled like a drunk. The drum got louder until it was only loud, and then I saw it, like a whale's back on the sand. The arms of eight drummers rose and fell against the smoky sky.

Seaward of it, the seals moaned and snaked their necks. Landward, firelit ladders stood out of the earth, flames leaped, piles of rocks smoked red in a clutter that sprawled uphill into the dark. It was the inferno, the fiery place to which—so my cousins said—my mother had gone.

Then I saw that the ladders stood in hatchways that led underground; the smoking rock piles were chimneys for underground rooms, the flames were firelight. There was a rack with drying fish, a thatched frame that sheltered a loom, a little cradle. Thin women and children moved among their meager goods, cooking at the fires. Not an inferno but a kitchen: an arem, a warrenhouse.

Before it stood a pavilion built of the rib cage of some

ocean leviathan, softened inside with furs. This too was the mouth of an arem—a fine one, for the women who peeked from it were plump and coy, and fat children hid behind their knees. When they saw the Reirig, they scuttled away below like mice. Before the pavilion was a throne made of an enormous jawbone with blunt teeth. The Reirig tossed his sealskin down across it.

A knot of men greeted him. Nall had said that an elder need not be old; many were younger than the Reirig. They wore jet-edged sealskins and ivory anklets; they were hardy and nervous and armed. Like wolves of second rank they watched their leader every instant, reading him for any weakness.

He showed none. He prowled among them. His elders did not grovel but inclined their heads a little, watching him from the corners of their eyes. Some were half tranced with dancing and moved with the beat where they stood.

Hsuu had gone to stand among them. Wherever the Reirig was not, he was, like a fish that moves without a sound. The elders watched him, too.

I stopped walking. The hands that held Nall released him and he fell, pulling me with him onto the trodden sand. We were not far from the throne, next to a little skin lean-to where a guard might shelter from the rain. A bony dog lay there; it rose and licked Nall's face. The drum beat. I could not hear the Gate as sound but only as fear; I could not feel anything, or think in words.

The Reirig muttered with the elders. Whatever he said, they did not like it, and one who wore a bandolier full of flint knives dared to raise his voice. Quick as a wasp, the Reirig snatched a knife and put the tip of it under the man's ribs. The blood ran down, and he had to stand on tiptoe not to be gutted. The Reirig held out his hand. Gasping, the elder pressed that hand to his forehead, and the knife was withdrawn.

Hsuu watched. Sometimes he looked at me or at Nall. Sometimes he looked over the heads of the crowd, west, toward the sea.

The Reirig left the elders and came to where I crouched with Nall. He tossed aside the bloody knife and smiled. "Curs," he said. "What is there yet to do? Only to dance the best dance, then go east and kill."

He took my chin between finger and thumb. When I pulled away, he laughed; it was not even cruel laughter. "Pretty woman," he said. "It is no use to love the weak. The strong will give you strong children. Leave your pet, and come along in to me." He gestured toward the pavilion of fur and bone.

"No," I said. But it meant *yes*, for I had nothing to make it *no*, only Nall across my lap like a corpse.

The Reirig laughed again, so sure of himself that his shoulders dropped, relaxed as a child's. He took hold of my hair, turned up my face, and kissed me.

In Creek a man had kissed me like that once, as if he had the right. My mind was too frightened to help, but my body remembered and I writhed away.

The Reirig thought this even better sport. He caught my elbows, pulling me to him. "This salmon fights me?" His teeth, sharp as a ferret's, snapped at the air before my face, my neck. He dragged me through the crowd of elders and warriors that parted to let him through, to the mouth of the bone pavilion made soft with furs the way a spider's hole is lined with silk. It smelled of heat down there, of food and blood. I heard soft laughter.

Then I heard, over the drumbeat, a different commotion. The elders heard; they shifted their gaze from the Reirig's prize-taking.

He heard it too. He liked commotion, it seemed, for he let me go and stared over the warrenhouse fires, the swaying crowd.

Something white flashed and flapped there: Queelic's shirt. Queelic was in it, carried high on hands and shoulders, shielding his face with his arms.

20

Fire! Fire! Fire!
Katyesha's a liar!
Say a prayer, pull her hair,
Roll her in the mire!

Children's Taunt. Upslope.

QUEELIC'S BODY FLAILED in the air. I heard his muffled squeak
as they carried him toward the Reirig's throne, saw the hundred hands upon him like the crabs on Tadde's body.

I was hot with terror, with the Reirig's snapping teeth and
my body that had said *No!* when my mind could not. But
when he let me go, something else did too. I ducked under
his elbow and ran toward Queelic, yelling.

I thought the Reirig would kill me and did not care. I ran to Queelic's tormentors and shouted, "Put that down!" As if they were dogs and Queelic a stolen roast.

They were young men, with bone ankle rings and faces like blades. They looked at me, at the Reirig, at Hsuu, who had checked the Reirig's leap after me with some murmured word. They put Queelic down. Not gently, but at least he was on the sand, making no effort to get away. "Queelic!" I said.

He lowered his arms. He was smiling.

"Kat!" He sat up, trying to straighten his shirt. He had lost one boot. "I thought you'd be here," he said. "I started to walk west, and I ran into these folks. I think I got here about as fast as you did!"

He dusted his sleeves. The forest of sinewy thighs moved to the drumbeat as the Reirig stalked toward us, showing his teeth. I grabbed Queelic by the arm and said, "This is my brother! Don't touch him!"

Queelic waved me off with his bright, demented smile. "It's fine, Kat. They all speak Plain. We talked as we came along." He looked shy. "It's nice of you to call me your brother."

The Reirig brushed me aside. Queelic beamed at him. Clambering to his feet, he stood in his one boot and held out his hand. "You're the boss, I guess? I'm Queelic, sir."

The Reirig sneered at the hand. Queelic said, "I'm afraid 'Queelic' will have to do. I told these fellows my full name, but it seems in your language it means something rude. I'm a Black Boot."

"Black Boot," said the Reirig.

"I'm down to one boot, though."

"Black Boot!"

Queelic put his hands in his pockets and grinned. "Born and bred," he said.

The Reirig had laughed before, but not like this. He rocked on his heels; he roared. His spearmen began to nudge and chuckle, and the elders tittered—all but Hsuu.

Queelic laughed too. "Kat, these folks do love a joke. They told me some good ones already, but, well, they're not nice. Oh, I forgot—" Turning to the youths who had carried him, he stuck out his bare ankle and said, "Weren't you going to tie me up?"

They looked at one another, at the mirthful Reirig. Shrugged. Someone produced a length of rope and tied one end to Queelic's ankle, the other to a stake, as if he were a pet parrot.

"Thanks," said Queelic. "Kat, where's Nall? Did he go already?"

I made a little gesture.

He peered. "That's Nall? Doesn't look like him. Hey, though—there's Aieh!" He waved. "Aieh!"

Aieh knelt beside Nall, his face in her hands.

I ran to them. "Leave him!" I slapped her hands away. "Haven't you hurt him enough? He's mine!"

"Never!"

"He is!"

"Ask him whose he is!"

"He can't answer. You killed him, tricking him into this. Oh, I don't mean that," I said, embracing Nall. "You're all right, I'm here, I won't let her hurt you—"

"He is not your child!"

"Who else will save him?"

"Himself," said Aieh. "If he is able. Think of that, girl, before you strangle him with the rope you throw."

Her hands darted to take Nall's face. His eyes kindled a little; I knocked her hands away, and he sank again, out of reach. Weeping, she withdrew, leaving me in possession.

The Reirig watched all this, as pleased as a child at a puppet show who waits for the part where they chop off the clown's head. Clearly, he could not decide which toy he wanted: me to play with in his fur pavilion, Queelic to humiliate, Nall to kill, or the wild dance itself. He stretched his arms wide, threw back his head, and howled.

Something like a dogfight broke out in the crowd to his left, a yarring and worrying, but of human voices.

The Reirig sniffed like a hound. Then he sprang away from the elders and gestured to his men; they joined him at a clattering run. The lot would have passed me without interest—it seemed the Reirig liked blood even better than women—but he saw me from the tail of those long eyes and paused to crow, "*Thus* are the Black Boots? I am the man the universe loves! Enemies come to kill me, and they are all fools." He kissed me because the other men were watching. "You like dead men and their kin?" he said. He knew who Aieh was and did not care. "In two days' time I shall give you plenty!"

He rattled off to his quarrel. I had an instant clear of nightmare, like the one I had had after Tadde's ghost spoke. In it I thought, That man is not half-and-half. He is all one simple thing—himself—and he is *happy*. All that his happiness costs is everyone else's.

So then I had only to kneel in the sand and keep my arms around my property. Nall's eyes were closed. The trickle of blood from his breast slowed and dried. The Rigi danced. Under the drumbeat I could feel the wave rising, standing, the wave that must topple and break.

In glimpses between the men's bodies I saw Queelic in the crowd of younger ones, cross-legged at the end of his tether. It was no youth who sat closest to him, but Hsuu, his tattooed head inclined, like a sea god listening to prayers. He seemed to ask questions.

Queelic seemed to listen, and to offer cheerful answers. He did not look parrotlike, but like a big, bedraggled eagle.

I gave up calling Nall's name. Not even his baby name moved him. Once I put my lips close to his ear and began to whisper that other name, the one he had given to me; he withered like paper in fire, and I stopped in the middle, saying, "No!" I sat against the lean-to without feeling or thought, numb with the drum.

Together with the Gate's roar it filled every space, the way heart's drub and blood's hiss fill the body. At first it was just a thump, endlessly repeated. Then I began to hear other rhythms playing off it: ticks and clacks, trills and flourishes.

These came from the crowd of dancers. A smiling woman knocked a gourd with a spoon. A young boy whacked two bones together. Everyone with hands clapped and slapped their own or others'. I had never had a community that was mine—not Upslope, not Creek, not even Downshore, where I had lived for one day—but the thought came to me, That drum is the drum that beat for all of us in the first home of all, through nine changes of the moon. No one is a stranger here. Not even me.

Tricking and playing with the drum's rhythm were rasps,

rattles, clappers, castanets. There were no stringed instruments; I began to crane and look for them, but there was no dindarion, no wood and wire and gut bridging the gap between the world of things and the human voice.

But voices there were. Songs and songs, in Rig mostly, but sometimes in Plain. The singers dreamed as they sang, yet they looked at me—strangers' faces, kind or angry or timid or wild. Somewhere, sometime, a person whose name I could not remember had told me to listen for songs. So I did.

> Love me, loose me,
> Grip me, fly;
> Sea on stone grinding,
> Bird in the blue sky.

A young man with bone bracelets sang that, treading and sliding. He threw me a kiss before he spun away. After him a sad, slim girl came chanting.

> I am she who will use life.
> Give it to me.
> I am she who will drink it up.
> My mouth is ready.

The crowd streamed past, masked or barefaced or with sealskins pulled up like hoods. Clans and factions: well-fed men in skins heavy with jet, the Reirig's; lean men, quiet or quarrelsome; women with thin faces and strong feet; old women; old men. Each had to touch me, touch Nall. I stopped pushing away their hands.

"Nall," they said, singing. Knuckles brushed his lips. Sometimes a voice said, "Bij," but never that other name. Women with sharp cheekbones, their hair unbound to the ground, came singing and stroked my face. Men with faces like hatchets sang as they touched Nall's feet.

They brought their children, naked and few: a newborn tiny as a cat; toddlers sleeping in arms or blinking with eyes too big for their faces. Twin girls, each dressed only in a string of beads, leaned on me weightless as wrens and kissed me before they were lifted away.

A skein of children danced, diving under one another's linked hands.

> One comes in and over,
> Two go out and under,
> Three come in and sigh,
> Four go out and cry,
> Five come in and stumble,
> Six go out and crumble,
> Seven come in and groan,
> Eight go out alone,
> Nine come in like spring tide
> Over the green bright lands—
> *Deep water, lover!*
> Ten start it over.

They kissed, clapped hands, and let each other go. Their bare feet wrote in the sand as wind writes on the water.

No one moved to help, none to hurt. All eyes looked through me. Sometimes one would come with direct eyes, whispering "Selí" or "ama" or "singer, singer," but those always said "Aieh," too, and I would not listen. I held Nall tighter and they went away.

I clung to the songs like a swimmer to a floating log. The twin girls played hand slaps; I saw their mouths move but could not hear for the noise of the drum. I thought, That drum is the grandmother of all hand slaps.

I heard a song I knew.

> I am the ash that snuffs the fire,
> I am the knot that halts the loom,
> I am the tangle of desire—

The Rigi's song, but Nall's new words. I would not listen, not to that! Nor did Nall seem to hear it. I wondered whether a messenger had run to Selí, to tell an old woman her singer had come home.

The Reirig's wives and children did not dance or sing or touch me. They crept in and out of the furred pavilion, staring. Once the Reirig himself came, striding like a roebuck on his long legs and dragging a man by the hair. Away in a muddle of shadows another snarling, gnarring fight broke out, louder than the last; he bounded after it. If the Reirig was not divided, it seemed the Rigi were.

Nall's eyes shifted, candles moving in an empty house. The noise rose like a fever, drawing the singers back into the dance until Nall and I knelt nearly alone. I looked for Queelic. The knot of young men had closed around him like a clot of ants on a wounded mouse. I could tell where he must be only by following the rope. Seeing no flash of blows, I thought, They're touching him to death.

I shifted my arms on Nall's waist. Under my fingers I felt the slippery loops of Aieh's hair. I did not want to touch it and moved my hand away. The thong that tied the coil to his belt was half undone.

A rope is safety—but this rope was drowning him. I thought, That's it! She has bound him to her with her rope.

"Nall." I pretended to rouse him by tugging at his belt, but it was the rope I tugged at. It came away in my hand. I said, "Nall, look there, it's Queelic." With my free hand I turned his face toward the knot of warriors. With the other I slid the coil of rope under my thigh and sat on it.

His face stayed where I had turned it, though he did not seem to look at anything. The crowd of men around Queelic rose and melted into the dance—all but Hsuu, who squatted at Queelic's shoulder like a blue toad.

Queelic saw me. He rose to hands and knees. Hsuu moved to block his path; Queelic spoke. Hsuu stood aside, and Queelic came to me crawling like a child, dragging the rope.

He reached the limit of his tether where I sat. He peered at Nall, then whispered, "Excuse me, Kat. Would you help me get this other boot off? Please?"

I shook my head in despair. Then shrugged. Why not? I let go of Nall, and Queelic put his booted foot in my lap, his tied ankle pointing toward the stake. As I wrestled the boot off, he said, "You knew about this!"

"What."

"All of this! The Rigi. That's why he brought you to be their queen."

"I'm nobody's queen." I threw the boot aside and put my arms around Nall again.

"I never knew about this. Nobody ever said. They wouldn't, though. Nobody says much about the world. I think that's strange." He looked again at Nall. "Kat, is he all right? I thought he must be praying. But he looks odd."

"He's fine, they knocked him out by mistake, it's taking him a while to get his breath."

Queelic looked doubtful. But he said, "I'm fine too." He patted himself here and there. "I tried to get away at first. But how do you run away from these folks?" He stretched his arms, stared at the sky. "Look at that. So many stars! Kat, do you remember playing kickball? Well, you wouldn't, you're a girl. But that drum's made me remember what you're supposed to say before you start the game. It goes,

> Kick in the ass,
> Kick in the eye,
> How many stars are in the sky?

Did you ever wonder how many stars there are?"

"Not really," I said. But I was thinking, He's gone mad like his father; now I have two babies to look after. As if I spoke to a four-year-old, I said, "An awful lot of stars."

He frowned. "Did you ever wonder what stars *are*? Are they holes poked through to a bright place? Or are they fires up there?"

"I don't know. Nobody knows."

"I could find out. If I paid attention and didn't lie." His face hardened. "That's what I do at Dad's place, when I'm not on customs duty. I use numbers to lie. I fix the books so people will think they owe us more money than they do.

Like Downshore—they owe us a lot, but not half as much as we say they do. If they'd learn accounting, they'd figure it out. But they won't—they're afraid of money, so they trust us. They shouldn't trust us." He looked at me with clear eyes. "I'm shit, like I said. Because numbers aren't to lie with. Numbers are truth." Laying his hand on my knee, he said, "Hear me, Katyesha Marashya N'Ab Drem! I won't lie anymore. Not ever."

He gazed at me, grave and straight. With a shock I realized he was perfectly sane. He had just fallen through, all at once, into a deeper layer of himself—as if he had crashed through rotten floorboards into the basement.

Maybe he read my thoughts. He said, "I think I'm a little crazy. That's all right. I was crazier at Dad's. There I was tied to a desk, now I'm tied to a stake." He laughed and shook the rope. "These folks live like birds or fish. The way Aieh does, just her skin on. And that old blue man, he's the one to watch out for! The fancy boss is kind of stupid."

He leaned in and whispered. "If you ask me, Hsuu's the real boss. A strange one. It's like he's watching, waiting for something. I asked him about those stones we saw—the split ones? Split with one blow, it looked like, and I couldn't think how they did it so I asked him. He goes like this"—Queelic pursed his lips—"and he says, 'Each being is a gate.' He talks in riddles, see, the way Aieh does. The way songs do.

"So I said, 'Maybe the answer is: You split them with a wedge? You get a little crack started so the balance is off, then you press there and *snap!*'" Queelic snapped his fingers.

"So Hsuu smiles to himself. He says, 'And what would that wedge be?' And I said, 'Ice? A tree root?' But he shakes his head. He says, 'What splits every stone in the universe is *longing*. There is no other force. The tide longs for the shore; when it touches the shore, it longs for the sea again.'

"See—he answered his riddle with another riddle!" Queelic laughed. "So I said, 'I give up!' and Hsuu says, 'That is wisdom.'"

These words frightened me. There was no one I trusted less than Hsuu, even the Reirig. But Queelic said, "That old man is deep."

"He's Nall's father."

"His father!" Queelic stared at Nall. His look grew hesitant. "Kat, honest—I'm not sure Nall's all right."

"He is! He will be! It's just—it's like a dream to him. As if he were a ghost."

Queelic nodded. "They're dreamy. I'll bet they're different in the daytime, though. More like people. Like Aieh." Queelic turned the name over on his tongue. "Aieh. And right now they're working themselves up for the invasion. There are different clans and whatnot—I don't have the shape of it yet—but some of them like the boss and some don't. It's the same as at home, really." He did seem to feel at home, smiling. "I hope I get to see them by daylight, before they leave."

"When—did they say when they'll go?"

"To kill everybody? I didn't ask. I wasn't sure it was polite." Queelic looked at Nall again. "*He* knows how to dream. That's why you love him. Aieh does too. I thought it was his muscles."

He crawled off a little way and sat thoughtful, watching the dance and playing with the knot at his ankle. He could have untied it, but he did not.

21

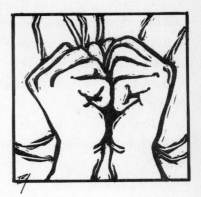

The rose it has as bitter a thorn
As ever from a stem was torn,
And love it has as bitter a sting
As ever knife from heart did wring.

Love Song. Downshore.

"NALL." I WANTED HIM to raise his head and look at me. I wanted him to tell me Aieh's love meant nothing. Queelic's strange sanity had waked me, like a drenching with cold water.

But behind Nall's abandoned face he was sinking, as if he held a stone that he would not let go of though it dragged him under.

Out of the whirling dancers Aieh came creeping back.

Her eyes were fixed on Nall. I began a lunge to stop her, but I remembered the stolen rope and had to keep sitting on it. She put her hand under Nall's chin. He raised his head and looked at her.

As before, I lifted my hand to slap hers away. Then I saw Nall's straining face with no desire in it, no hope, and stopped my hand in midair.

Without a glance at me Aieh spoke quickly in Rig. Nall mumbled an answer. He groped at his belt where the hair rope had been.

She saw the empty thongs. "His rope!" *Now* she looked at me. "Where is his rope?"

So I knew for sure that the rope was the magic by which she was drawing Nall back down among the Rigi, binding him to herself. I spread my empty hands to show her the rope was not there.

Nall pawed at the dangling thongs. Aieh seized my shoulders and shook me. "Where is it? You have thrown it somewhere!"

"Maybe the oak brush pulled it off as we ran."

"You have it in your bodice!"

I pulled down my shift.

"Your scars are no use to him. He must have his rope! Can you not see I must bind him?"

"I'm sure!"

Aieh made a desperate sound. I laughed in my heart. I had the rope now, and Nall would stay with me.

"So be it, then," she said. "Even so." She spoke to Nall again in Rig, seeming to plead.

He put up his hand and fumbled at her mouth. With almost his old strength he wrenched away from me, lurched to his feet, and put his arm around her. For shock and rage I would not rise and snatch him back; besides, I had to sit on the rope.

He put out his hand toward me. I would not take it. Aieh tugged at him. He laid his arm across her shoulders and, with her, shambled into the crowd that opened to receive them, then closed after them. I heard his voice above the drum, speaking in Rig.

I took the hair rope from under my thigh and beat the sand off it. I put it in my bodice, above the deer mouse sash. It was all I had left.

I lay down against the lean-to and pulled my knees up to my chest. Something sharp hurt me: Liu's knife in my pocket. But I did not move. If I made a sound, nobody heard it.

I must have slept, because I woke. The stars had shifted. The Gate roared, the drum boomed, the Rigi quarreled and danced. I was curled tight, like a sheet that has been knotted wet and left to dry, and I remembered only the taste of a vicious dream.

My eyes were swollen. I opened them a slit and saw what had waked me: a creature hairy and black, with a groping claw. Whining, I shrank from it, then saw it was Nall.

A sealskin covered him, even his head. Beneath the seal's empty-eyed face his own face looked out at me vivid and driven, his own, as it had not been since we hid in the little shelter by the shrines. "Kat, Kat," he said, looking this way and that like a hunted fox.

He smelled of blood. He smelled musky, like a woman, like Aieh. The skin was Aieh's.

I struck his hand away.

He pulled the sealskin around him. "There is no time. I must leave you—"

I sat up, rotten with dream, full of vileness like a cup. "Again?" I said.

He drew back. I thought with relish, Feeling better, eh? I'll bet you are. So listen.

I said, "You went off with Aieh. Where?"

"Not far—"

"'Not far.'" I put into my voice all the filth I felt. "Just out of earshot?"

His face went tense. I rejoiced and said, "Was it nice to be home again?"

He took my arm. "Oh, love—"

I jerked away. I heard my own voice shrill and shrewish, like my League aunts' voices when their husbands came home drunk. "Don't touch me! Did you think I loved you? It's a man from Creek I love! The one who made my sash. He's a handsome, big hunter—his eyes are blue." I gasped and said, "When I was in his arms, I never thought of you!"

The drum beat. I heard the distant sea.

"It was a lie, then," said Nall, his voice so soft. "All but the Gate."

He stood up. I stood too, twisting away from him, shouting. "*Aieh's* your damned Gate!"

He turned and was gone, limping along the shore between the humans and the seals.

I stood where I was.

Queelic came creeping to me across the starlit sand. He plumped himself at my feet and rolled up his sleeves.

I sat down next to him. What else was there to do? In his face I saw my father's as I wished I could think of him: not evil, just young, doing the best he could.

Unbidden, my hand reached out and touched his.

He let me touch him, then withdrew his hand and said, "Why did you do that?"

"I don't know."

"They were lovers before. Nall and Aieh. They look at each other that way." He slid me a glance. "You think I'm a little boy, that I'd never notice anything like that."

I had bent my face to my knees, my hands clasped against my body, against the hair rope. Clumsily, Queelic patted my shoulder. "Kat, don't cry."

I said, "I wish I'd married you after all. I wish I'd listened to my father."

Queelic dropped his hand. "You don't really."

"Yes, I do." I raised my head and pushed back my hair, staring at him. "When you're a kid, you don't know what you want. You go after something, and in the end it's worthless—there's no way to live your life."

"I know what you mean."

"No, you don't. Suppose you loved Aieh."

He ducked his head and said, "Well, I kind of do. I *do*. You think I'm not a man. But she"—he raised his hands together, like a cup—"she's like that water you brought me, when my arms were tied."

"She's lying with Nall."

"I know. I don't care. That's part of her. She didn't get to be Aieh by being like—like my aunts or something. The same with Nall. You women, you're all alike! Except for Aieh."

He tucked his chin down on his chest, as though I might jump for his throat. "I'm a man," he said, "and I know. You won't let Nall be Nall unless it's nice for you. You want him in a box. So what if he can't explain what he's doing? You think it's easy to explain to women? It's easier to be a hero than explain to women, especially when they're mad at you. So Nall doesn't know how to talk to you? Well, you don't know how to talk to *him*. I've watched him try, and you wouldn't listen—you had to get your licks in. You can't be bothered to wonder how it is for him. But he's amazing. I wish he were my brother. Even if he's got muscles."

Queelic raised his chin. "So now you wish you'd married *me*, because you think that'd be easier. Well, it wouldn't be. And I wouldn't marry you, not for money. Not even money."

I sat still.

"Don't bother me," he said. He crab-walked over the sand to the extreme opposite of the compass of his rope.

Starlight bathed me. I was made of porcelain, thin and breakable, like a player in my father's game of War, or like an eggshell, smashed with the baby bird inside. A voice in my head said, *It's not my fault, it's not my fault,* until my tears fell hot and my crying, perfectly silent, felt as though it would shake me to pieces. Queelic crept back, saying, "Kat, don't."

Then in a different voice he said, "Kat—"

I looked up. I saw Aieh slipping along the edge of the crowd. She was completely naked. Queelic looked away from her, looked back. Through the dreaming dancers she crept, hugging her arms around her waist—not to hide herself, but as though she were cold. She came straight to us and knelt with her head bent, so slim and slight that she seemed part of the night.

"Aieh," said Queelic.

"He has gone, then?" she said between the blows of the drum. "He said he must bid you good-bye before he left."

I said, "Left."

"For the Gate." Aieh's face had caught some of Nall's

sleepwalking; her eyes did not focus. "Girl. Kat. I begged him not to go. But there was no stopping him."

"The Gate?" I said. "The actual Gate?" Then, "I thought he'd gone to *you*."

"To me?"

I said it out loud. "You made love."

Aieh looked down and away. "I could not hide that."

"No."

"But it is you he loves."

"He said— He told you that?"

"Of course."

I looked at Queelic. "I'll try to listen," I said. "I *will* try. But that he could say that and then—and then go to her!"

"Just now?" said Aieh. "You think it was just now that we made love?"

"You said—"

"It was long ago we were lovers," she said, dreary. "Before he was killed. What—you think I would make love with him now? In the evil I brought upon him?"

"Then he didn't—"

"The man whose name I used to speak is dead. I knew that man; you never will. I wanted— You saw what I wanted. But this is some other man."

"Where did you take him, then? Just now?"

"I gave him my skin." Aieh looked up with a face as wistful as Jekka's. "I tricked that man we love into the tide of the drum. When he had no skin! He was dying. I could not right my wrong, but I could give him my skin.

"I sent for our ama in Selí. I thought maybe her love could bind him. But she is so old, she walks slowly; he would be dead before she came. I might have bound him to the skin with my hair rope, but it is lost. There was no time to search or quarrel, so I bound my skin to him with blood." She unfolded her left arm to the firelight. On the creamy inside of her elbow a gash like an open mouth ran blood; it had printed an answering mouth on the pale skin of her waist. At her movement a new rill ran down her hip.

Queelic made a choking sound.

I pulled the rope out of my bodice. "I stole your rope."

"So I supposed."

"Aieh!" said Queelic. "What will happen to you?"

"I shall die."

"From that little cut? It's nothing!"

"I shall die because I have no skin. The spell of binding wants a death; and I need to die. I did wrong." She huddled down smaller. "Perhaps that man will come back from the Gate and give me my skin again. But I do not think he will come back."

"He came back before!" I said.

"He was a different man then. Now he is possessed. It is a priest's work he wants—but he is only a man. The Gate will swallow him." Aieh looked beyond us. "These are great times, when the wave rises and the tide turns on one water drop. Such times want lives, they want souls, and one gives them, like a gift."

Queelic clenched his fist. She turned her huge eyes to him. "You are so strange! Day-colored, like her. I wish I could have seen your land." She smiled a little. "All night long Tadde's kin and mine have been starting fights, now here, now there, so the Reirig might have our blood to entertain him, and not yours. We are a quarrelsome people, but not like this."

I said, "I have killed you."

"You are not important enough to kill me. By blessing or rope or blood, I would have given that man my skin and, skinless, died. And I sent him to Tadde's manat, on the beach there beyond the seals' beach, for fear he was too weak to swim."

"I gave him nothing. I gave him dirt."

"When he said he must speak to you, I thought, 'At least he will go in good heart.'"

"I filled him with poison!"

"Never think it is only you," said Aieh. Her face looked older, and so sad. "Think how I have been!" She put her hand on mine. "That man will wreak upon you what he has upon me, just by being who he is. You and I are braided together, tight as my hair rope."

"Aieh. It takes a little time to rig a manat, maybe he's still on the beach. I'll run. I'll give him your rope and beg his pardon—"

"Do not try to stop him!"

"Never. Never again." I was running already, with no thought that anyone might stop *me*. I turned back. "Aieh. When he took your skin, he knew you would die?"

"For all of us. As it is for all of us he listens. Even the Black Boots." She said dryly, "We shall be heroes."

"Sister—"

"Go ahead, Kat," said Queelic. "I'll take care of her."

He was unbuttoning his shirt. It was dirty and torn, but he held it out to Aieh like ermine. "Come here. I mean, please come here. Put this on." His body was bony and shining in the firelight, a few gold hairs on his chest.

She stared. Then she crept to him. Queelic helped her

arms through the full sleeves, pulled the shirt straight, and buttoned it up. Then he who had never put his arms around anyone put his arms around Aieh.

"Listen, please," he said. "I'm going to tell you about numbers, and the stars."

22

Star at the world's edge
sinking
White stone through green water
sinking
Whale in the blue deep
sinking

Chant. The Rigi.

I COULD NOT TELL what I was running in, but it felt nasty—
offal or excrement. I slipped, caught myself, and ran where
Aieh had pointed, straight through the seal colony toward
the far curve of the beach.

Nobody stopped me. I was too fast to stop. They were dancing the wave higher and higher, and I was one water drop, no
more. Another snarling quarrel began; I ran straight through it

under the Reirig's startled face, as though a spell had broken.

The seals groaned and squalled, they recoiled from me, trying to flop away. The bulls terrified me, male mountains with necks quick as snakes. They were rousing, bellowing. I stepped on a fat calf, it bawled, I fell and was up again in the same roll, dodging through the spaces the seals kept around themselves in order to tolerate one another. At every instant I was inside some body's boundaries, and that body screamed.

I thought, If I live, I could learn it, maybe—this stink and press and fear and all this rage. But I won't live.

Closer to the beach my running drove the seals into the sea. Like sand crumbling at the edge of a flood, they fell into the water, a wave of frightened shapes that swam a little way and turned back, bound to the shore. The splash of big bodies muddled the sound of the drum. I heard the shouts of the Reirig's men behind me, but they were few; no one dared to plunge into the chaos of panicked seals. Abandoned calves squalled. One lay shuddering; a bull had flounced over it and broken its back.

Against the distant west the Gate was black. It roared. Next to it I could see, faintly, the jagged skerry called Stillness.

The calf with the broken back lay motionless. So did hundreds of black seals at the far end of the beach. I looked again and saw they were manats laid out in rows like weapons, death ready to race east. Nall would be there, rigging Tadde's boat.

I ran. But when I came to the empty boats, he was not there. No one was; all were at the dance. There were tiny manats like rolled leaves, made for one person, but I did not think of those. I chose a two-hatch boat because it looked like Nall's. The paddles rattled in it as I dragged it to the water.

A strict, practical part of myself had taken charge. It was

my father in me, and for the first time in my life I praised him, seeing worth in his orderliness. As though I knew what I were doing I made a lightning check of the gear: air bladders full, bailer in place, even a water skin that I shifted to the front hatch. I snatched a second skin from another boat so mine would steer as if with the weight of a second paddler. I could not believe how wise and skilled I was. As the Reirig's men came howling round the end of the seal colony, I shoved off from the beach into the waves, barely wetting my legs, fending off with the paddle.

I was a bird that had learned to fly. The manat breasted the water like a gull in air, perfectly balanced. I took up the stroke and swung into the bay, traveling more quickly than I could have believed—so quickly that I laughed, thinking that on the journey west Nall must have made us go slowly on purpose. Glancing back, I saw that I had truly won away: No manat followed me. In palest dawn light the gesticulating dark figures of the Reirig's men stood together on the beach.

The sea was mine. In no time I was in the middle of the bay. There was Stillness, its ragged crest a little south of the Gate. With easy strokes on either side I pointed the bow toward it.

As though from a trance, I woke to two things. One was that Nall's comforting torso was not between me and the sea. The other was that the manat was going quickly—too quickly—toward the Gate.

I wanted to go to Stillness, where Nall had gone in Tadde's manat. Not to the Gate.

I pulled with the right-hand paddle blade to swing the nose of the boat south. It turned, but not enough. The manat still went fast, but sideways. It was incredible how fast it went, sucked west. I saw why no other manat would dare that sea: The whole ocean was leaving the beach at once, pouring out through the Gate.

I began to paddle in earnest, pulling and pulling on the right. Sideways and helpless, I went nowhere but west, in the grip of the tide. *Right, right, right,* I dug in the water, straightening the boat a little, going broadside and a little forward, hearing a roar in my ears.

Panic rushed over me, blotting out the stars. I saw my foolishness: Puny and stupid in a two-person boat, I was rolling like a minnow down the gullet of the sea.

The thought of Nall fell away from me as if he were dead already. Like a demon I paddled crosswise to the race with no thought but *Get me out, get me out, I promise I'll never leave the shore.*

The world became a roar. The water felt different and I thought, This is it.

I glanced around, still paddling, to find I was out of the main rip into slower water, drifting sideways toward Stillness.

My whole will was for shore, for life in its cranky commonness, morning and workday and no glory. I knew Nall at last by what sucked him from me, a force like ocean; it had nothing to do with my silly human desires.

He was not for me. I would win back through the islands, east to the mainland and then to Raím—I was bad enough for Raím, I knew that now.

I wrenched the bow east. The sky was light.

But the sea was too strong. Paddle as I might, I went nowhere, fighting and fighting the crazy dimpled water of the race on my left now, hearing behind me the roar of the Gate.

In the end my arms gave out, and the drift began.

I could not bear to be swallowed from behind. Planting the paddle, I swung the boat around and saw Stillness only a few strokes away, water creaming against its shoreward side.

From somewhere I dragged the strength for those strokes, brought the manat abreast of the rock and crashed into it. I dropped the paddle; it surged away in the sea. With both hands I grabbed a knob of rock, lost my grip, fell sideways and grabbed another, hauled myself out of the boat, and flung myself across a ledge.

The lightened hull leaped after the lost paddle. But I was only half out of the hatch; I hooked my foot and caught the coaming, grabbed downward and crooked my elbow through it. I lay flat on the ledge with the boat trying to yank me off until a wave lifted it. I scrambled sideways into a crack in the stone, dragging the manat like an extra body. Once on solid rock my legs found a life of their own. My hands did not work, but with my elbow crooked I could drag the manat upward, out of the sea. It wedged itself upright in the crack, gear and ballast thumping down into the stern.

With mad logic I decided the crack was as good a place as any to dock it. I unhooked my elbow, pawed at the bow line, and carried it to the top of the rock, looking for something to tie it to.

I found a wave-scrubbed hole in the stone. A rope was tied to it already but there was room for another. I nursed my arms, fed the line through the hole in the rock, and with my hands beginning to wake again I tied such a clumsy knot that I tied a second for safety. I was seeing more clearly and tied the knots by the pale light of morning.

I looked down at the manat where it stood on its tail. My

numb reasonableness dissolved, and a wail squeezed out of me into the dawn full of roaring.

I remembered why I had come. I looked down on Stillness. The strange rope in the boat hitch led to a little manat hardly longer than a man, tucked into a horizontal ledge that seemed made for it. Tied to its forward deck under crossed thongs, empty eyes staring, was Aieh's sealskin.

Nall's breechclout was tied with it, and his belt and knife. Nall was not there.

I looked again. I clambered down, around, everywhere on the rock. He was not there.

The wind blew; it tossed spume over me. Through flying water I looked west, and saw the Gate close and clear for the first time.

It had taken shape in the dawn light, but west of it the night was still dark. The line of air between the stones had no color, and it trembled.

I dropped my eyes to its foot. A black cone of water, shapeless at the gap, rushed through it into the dark. Before it a field of chasing crosscurrents boiled white, and in the middle of that field was Nall.

He was swimming toward the Gate. In the opal light I saw his dark head, his arm flung up, flung up, regular as a drummer's.

It is a priest's work he wants. Greater risk means greater truth: He would not listen from Stillness, but from the sea itself, like a seal priest.

I knew the pull of that current. A swimming man would be sucked instantly into the dark. So he was not human.

Then I saw in the water with him a seal, weaving and div-ing, meeting him and parting, bearing him up. They played; the seal rose, it carried him landward a little, twisted, dove again.

He was at his work, in his element, with his people. How beautiful he was! And how foreign; the longer I watched, the stranger he became. I was right: I must go home to the Hills.

I looked again. Stared hard.

He was swimming, or trying to swim, *away* from the Gate. The seal that played with him stayed him, bore him, lost him, rose under him as he slid away. The dimpled black water sucked west.

"Oh—," I said.

I had told Aieh that I would never stop him, would never interfere with what he chose for himself. But how could I know what he had chosen?

I scrambled to the top of the rock and stood with the east-ern light behind me, staring over the hissing sea. He swam like a human swimmer, plodding, drawing nearer, falling back as the seal wreathed and dove around him. He was no nearer. I knew the shape of his arm.

Then the paler flash of his face. He stopped swimming, was sucked backward. The seal caught and carried him, lost him. He swam again, faster. His face flashed, flashed. He was looking; had he seen me? Was his arm swimming or signal-ing? Was the seal playing with him, kind and kind, or trying to bear him east?

He stopped waving—if it was a wave—and only swam, dragged west.

"What shall I do?" I said. If he had seen me, it was not to

recognize me, only a human shape against the whitening sky. Maybe he did not want anything, there where he played, alive in the water with his own.

But that laboring stroke, trying and trying to pull east.

"I don't know!" But my body had decided for me. I scrabbled at my boat for the bow line.

It was nothing, barely ten feet long. I dug in the loose gear fallen into the stern: water skin, second paddle, bailer. Here was more rope. I scrambled to the tiny manat and searched that, too, finding only the bow line, which I cut with Nall's knife. Back on top of the rock I looked for him in the crazy water.

There he was. Still swimming, stroke and stroke, but farther away. The seal was with him, I could not tell whether its dance was rescue or the game a cat plays with a mouse. The Gate pulled them west. Nall's head rose for an instant; he was dragged back.

I tied the lines together. Back at my own boat I yanked the air bladder free of the bow and tied it to the end of the rope. From the crest of the rock I screamed, *"Nall!"*

He could not have heard me. But as his face blinked toward me, I raised bladder and rope against the lightening east and threw them, aiming a little in front of him.

He saw. He lunged forward in the water. He wanted it.

But where the rope should have landed was nothing. The wind had caught the bladder and blown it back. And the rope was not long enough.

He was losing ground. Perhaps he was losing heart; he must have seen that the rope was too short. He fell back, he took up his dogged crawl but it had gaps in it, as my paddling had broken when exhaustion came on.

The seal rose below him. Their dark bodies made one for a moment, plunging eastward until Nall slipped again into the wash.

I hauled in the rope in wet loops, ran to my manat, and again scratched frantically in the stern. There was no more rope.

Only then did I remember Aieh's hair.

I pulled the coil from my bodice. Its fine braids shone in the rising light. With the knot that does not slip I tied the hair to the end of the wet rope—twice, three times, because it felt so fragile. The knot held, or seemed to. To the end of Aieh's rope I tied the deer mouse sash, then the air bladder.

I looked for a stone to weight the bladder in the wind, but Stillness was scoured bare by waves, Liu's knife was near weightless, and there was nothing in the boats, neither stone nor sinker.

Nall's stroke was failing, he was falling back. The seal could not hold him; a seal has no hands.

To the air bladder, by its purse strings, I tied the pouch of gold. Coiling the combined ropes, I screamed *"Nall!"* across the boiling ocean. Then I threw.

The wind blew the bladder. I had to haul it back, re-guess my aim, and throw again. But the rope was long enough. The little swimmer flailing the water saw it go over him, grabbed for it, missed. He stopped swimming and let himself drift.

I thought, He doesn't want it. He wants to go to the dark.

But he was only letting the water carry him within reach of the floating bladder. I felt the drag on the rope, and began to haul him in.

I used my back, I got under the rope and leaned my whole body to swing each coil around a jag of rock. I was in terror that the hair rope would break, the knots part. They held. I hauled him closer. He had the bladder clamped under his arm, and he kicked, not strongly. Beneath him the seal's dark body rose and rose.

I dragged him to the rock. He slammed against it in the water. He did not climb out, but held the bladder and let himself be slammed against the rock. I put a last hitch around the stone, climbed down, and grabbed him by the hair.

A wave lifted him, or the seal did. I got him under one armpit and heaved.

He came alive and resistant, a willful, angular weight like a crab held by the carapace. He swung his arms as if to grab the rock, and hit me in the face. I dragged him right out of the water. He was much heavier than a manat.

He clung to the rock, then to me as if I were the rock. I thought his living grip would kill me. I stared over his shoulder into the boiling water as the seal rose and dove, rose and dove. I saw the mark on its shoulder, the shape of a human hand.

It turned west, breaking the foam, dwindling in my sight until it entered the glassy cone of water, became wholly seal, and passed out through the Gate.

He was as cold as the sea.

He clutched me. Then he seemed to see where he was, who I was, and rolled away from me. I thought he would roll back into the water, and grabbed after him.

With the hand he had waved for rescue he pushed me away.

I pulled my hands back to my chest. He heaved himself onto his elbows, gasping, shuddering. He stilled. Gape-mouthed, he looked up.

"You," he said.

"I'm sorry," I said like a fool. "I am so sorry."

He turned his face back to the Gate.

I gabbled as if I had just run next door. "Listen—Nall—I was horrible, hateful, a shrew. Nall—don't forgive me, how could you? But I had to come, to tell you." My voice trailed off. "Then I saw you in the water and . . ."

"It doesn't matter," he said.

"Yes, it does!"

No answer. Below him the black waves raced.

"Nall!"

The mad night was fading, yet it stayed in him: His body had a darkness. Without passion or grief, like his father, Hsuu, he said, "I killed my Aieh for nothing."

"What do you mean?"

"It doesn't matter. Aieh is nothing."

Yesterday how I had wanted to hear those words! Now I was bewildered. "She is not," I said.

"She's nothing. You are nothing. The world, it's nothing."

"That's not true! It's right here, it's the same as always."

The same as always. The world where brothers are tortured, daughters sold, lovers hate each other. That world.

"Nothing matters," said Nall.

Over his body a blueness crept.

Like fronds of frost on pond water, it began at the tattooed whorl on his back and grew like ice crystals, spiraling over his shoulders and haunches, calves and hands, even the curves of his ears: the sea's tattoos, no mortal color.

He turned his hero's face to me. I watched it change, letting go of its human quirks and loves, becoming his father's: impersonal, inhuman, the sea's.

All the waves in the world were draining west.

"*Nall!*"

Once I had warmed him by holding him against my body. But now he had blocked me with silence, I had paid him back with spite; we were equals, all right, but not lovers. Just a shrewish girl and a man with a cold face.

"It's true," I said. "Loving is hopeless. It's nothing."

I could watch him die as I said that. Blue waves poured across his back. I touched him; blue spirals crept onto my own hands. I pulled my hands away; the spirals faded, but my hands wanted to go back there, to wear the tattoos he was accepting. It was all a lie, as he said. Everything came to this, to nothing.

His face began to enter that greatest peace, death. All but his eyes, which looked at me across the widening gap that filled him with sea.

I thought, When his eyes go peaceful he will have passed the Gate. Then I will follow him, one last time.

Nee, nah, nothing!

Nondany's merry, nearsighted glance, his hand held out empty.

I said aloud, "But he gave it like a gift."

Nall's eyes were not merry. In his face, as it died into nobility and peace, his eyes were bright with rage.

I had a thought so terrible that I smothered it. Something never to be said to a lover, a dying man.

But I felt it real as a rope's end in my hand, and I could have beaten the man to death if he had not been dying anyway.

"You *liar!*" I said. Not shrewish, just furious. "You say it's all nothing—but you *hate* me!"

He flinched as if struck.

"And you won't say it!" I said. "You won't say *anything*. You coward! If you can't scrape up the guts to speak when it's that bad, I don't *care* if you die. You think I'd waste my life chasing all over this damned cold ocean after some silent hero? I'd rather make love to a *fish*."

His mouth opened, panting. I was too angry to care. I threw away my stupid childish dreams, letting him go. Let him swim on his own, damn him! And I would too.

"*You* were the one who told me to swim for myself!" I jumped up. "Do it, then! Roll back into the sea! But you'll have to do that yourself too—I won't push you. Swim through the damned Gate if you want, and be peaceful forever. You won't have to talk to anybody there!"

He drew a huge breath. His face contorted, he rose to his knees and screamed, "For *you* they killed me? For *you* I came back from death? I sang, I broke the bonds, I swam—for what? A *witch*!"

"*I am not a witch!*" I cried, stamping my foot. "Or a portent or a goddess or a—a—whatever you thought. I'm a *girl*. You had a girl already, why didn't you tell me? Bouncing her breasts under your nose—*she* has no scars!"

"I've had plenty of girls," he shouted back. "D'you think I'd lie alone? Am I a stone? You slept with that hunter!"

"I did not—you know I didn't! I kissed him is all, I wish I were kissing him now! I wish I were anywhere but here with you!"

"*You hurt me!*" He raised his fist.

I raised my own. "*Don't touch me!*"

He stared at his fist. Dropped it. He fell to his hands and knees, vomiting water and bile. I was crying by then, the ugly kind that twists your mouth and makes you blind, until I had to sit down on the same rotten rock that he was on, listening to him retch and spit and sob in that horrible way men do that sounds like tearing something apart, tearing it open.

"I can't," he cried. "I can't bear it."

"I know." Because how can anybody bear it?

Except we were. Weeping and puking and bearing it.

I raised my blubbery face and blinked till I could see him. "You're all pink," I said.

He looked at himself. The blue frost had faded. He was bruised and clotted and common, like a beggar's baby.

He said a word I had never spoken, one for which my father would have locked me in the woodbox for a week. My father was not there, though. So I said it too.

He stared at me. Hiccuped. Stared.

I stared back. In that moment I heard a sound heard only in stillness: the wing-flick of a bird changing direction in the air.

That dawn bird I never saw, nor knew what it was. The stillness was the sea; the whistling suck of water at the Gate had slacked, beginning to turn back toward the land.

His hand was still a fist. He fumbled it out to me. I took it. He opened it.

Then, scrabbling on the rock, we held each other so tight we made new bruises; we shook, we gasped till the horizon swam. In my arms his body went warm as a cat's.

Holding him, I thought, Who is this man? All I know about him is that he lives, and dies, and lives.

23

What great stone drops?
What unseen hand slaps the bowl of sea?
What breath, drawn and drawn,
swells what breast,
stirring the whole cold sea
to lift and surge,
to rise and roll,
to break, and break, and break
upon this shore?

Wave Chant. The Rigi.

AND IT WAS MORNING, on a stone in the sea at the end of the world.

The water did not roar. It murmured and chuckled, dark emerald patched with foam. A gold mist lay on it, and on the Gate that loomed in the endless waves from the west. I thought I heard the drum, but it was my own heart.

The man in my arms pushed away a little. The dawn air

moved between us. I felt shy holding him, as if he were a stranger.

All around us was the sound of water: plish and sigh, chirp and lip, muffled by mist. Under it hung a resonance like the fading hum of a gong, so pungent that I could almost smell it. I raised my nose like a bear.

"Thirsty," said Nall.

Me too. I thought I would die of thirst, in the middle of all that water. I rose, tottering as if I were a thousand years old, and dug in the manat I had stolen. In my search for rope I had thrown one of the water skins overside, but the other was still there, wedged in the stern. I dragged it out and brought it to Nall.

He held it in both hands. Did not drink.

I licked my lips. "You were thirsty?"

He blinked. Stared at the water skin, at the manat docked on its tail. He said, *"That's* how you got here?"

I nodded.

"Bear Spit."

I was comforted that he remembered that name, that he made me drink first. His hands did not shake, but when it was his turn he took the skin clumsily, as if he had never held one. He had that look a newborn has, of lopsided bafflement.

The mist coiled around us. Except for the dim, cleft shape of the Gate we might have been on a drifting raft.

The rope was still wrapped in bights around the jag of rock, its far end floating in the sea. I pulled it in. The air bladder was gone from it; so were the deer mouse sash and the pouch of gold. The raveling end of Aieh's braid had unmade itself into wet dark hair.

I untied it from the bow lines, coiled it, and brought it to

Nall where he sat staring. "I stole it from you. I'm sorry."

He took it, with a waking look at Aieh's sealskin, folded as if for ceremony on the deck of the tiny manat. "My Aieh—"

A few hours ago I would have flown into a rage at her name. I could still feel in me that being who wanted everything for herself; she squealed and bit, but I held her tight like Rosie, and in the end she wept.

I thought, Who was I last night? And knew the answer: I was myself. One of my thousand halves. Not one I liked, but mine.

Nall watched me cry. He held the rope bunched against his breast. "What's his name?" he said.

"Who?"

"The man you kissed."

"Him? Oh. Raím."

"Is—is it true what you said? That he's the man you love?"

"It was then." I wanted to touch him. But I remembered how I had tried to own him and pressed my hands together. "I said it to hurt you."

"And I hurt you with silence." He drew back his arm and threw Aieh's rope wide of the rock. It uncoiled in the air, hit the surge with a whipping sound, and sank. "It doesn't matter," he said.

I stopped crying. I rose and took his wrists, as I had taken my father's once to stop him hitting me. "Didn't we just fight about that? Why are you still saying it?"

He turned his wrists slowly, until I had to let go. Then he took my hands and held them, looked at them as if he had never seen hands before. I was ashamed of my broken fingernails.

"No words for it," he said.

I knew how that was. Like Nondany, I said, "Say it however you can."

He turned toward the Gate. Only then did I remember why we were there.

"You listened?" I said.

"Yes."

"What did you hear?"

"Nothing."

"I don't wonder. Who could hear in that water?"

"No. Not that kind of hearing. I listened and heard in the way I can—the way I could. To that voice. Not a voice. Something; I don't know what it was. Is." He rubbed his face. "Swimming as a priest swims, listening, I heard—nothing. I hear nothing still."

"You're talking to me!"

"I mean, I still hear what I heard as I swam: the sound the whole world makes as it rushes through the Gate. And it is: nothing."

"The fight we just had was nothing?"

His rage seemed to have burned clean through him, like a forest fire. "Fight, yell, hit, that's real," he said. "Isn't it? It must be. A fist, isn't that real? But when I listen beyond that place, to where it's all being born—it's nothing." His gray eyes on me, baffled. "That's what is real. Nothing. What then can matter?"

The big, dreaming stone was split now by tendrils of mist. The sea had begun to eddy landward through it, the surge made a sound like an old man humming. There were many sounds in it; certainly not nothing. I half thought I heard laughter.

"It's shock," I said. "My boy-cousin hit me with a bat once. I couldn't hear out of one ear for days."

"No." He set my hands together as Nondany had done with Rosie's and said, "Kat, *I heard nothing*. Nothing the way nothing sounds."

"It makes a noise?"

"No. Yes. No. A sound is something. This not. Yet there is—" He sat so still, I could *see* him listening. But the words were not there.

I said, "Don't listen like that."

"I hear what I hear. It used to be I heard each living thing singing, and it was she I heard."

"Aieh?"

"No. My mother. Stone, minnow, cloud as she was—all sang, I listened. Now . . . I can still hear them, but under and beyond them is that other sound, that is no sound."

A sound that is not sound; a Bear that is not a bear. Like Bian, I was afraid in my turn and said, "It's because when I—when we were both being so horrible, you said, 'I must have silence!'"

"No. Silence is something. This is nothing. Why couldn't I hear it before? I think it has been there always. From the beginning of time." He put out his hand and stubbed it on my arm, stared at it. "At the end of the world, at the beginning of the world; under the sea and over the sky; at the root and crown of the universe: nothing. At all. That's what I heard. What I hear." He leaned forward. "Do you understand?"

"No."

"It doesn't matter."

"Stop saying that!"

317

"It's so. I can stand before my father now with no skin, and he can't drink me up. I can stand before the Reirig. They are nothing, and so am I."

Hsuu, the Reirig! The world rattled awake. Yet around us was only water. I put my hand on the new wound over Nall's heart. "The Reirig's lance would pierce your breast!"

"And I would die. And that would not weigh a breath more than my living."

"But you wanted the rope, you grabbed it. You *fought* with me!"

"I'm a creature, and afraid. But if I had not grabbed the rope, the balance would not have changed: nothing to nothing."

He did not say these things in anger, or bitterness, or grief, but with awe. He laid his palms on my cheeks. They were warm.

"I invited you into my body!" I said. "Was that nothing? And you were jealous of Raím, and you made me drink first from the water skin!"

"I'm a creature," he said again. "But nothing is the truth. The truth is nothing. I heard it at the Gate."

I was ready to fly into my usual rage, but his stillness stilled me. I thought of Raím, groping at a world he could not see, and my fury turned to strangeness. I thought, Are all the men I love blind or deaf? Or are they just men?

I said, "You must believe what you believe. But so must I, and I say the world's not nothing! It's full of noise, right here: birds and winds and foam and the water splashing and us quarreling. Nall, it's *loud!*"

He pushed back my curls and set his forehead on mine.

"That you called me and I swam to you—maybe it was a good thing."

"*Maybe?* By life—jump back in the sea and drown!"

"No," he said, as the staccato patter I had thought to be bursting bubbles became, in the mist, the sound of many paddles.

24

A mountain,
A lake of fire,
A glass mirror;
Less and less he made it,
Slimmer and slimmer;
Until it fit at his hip,
In his hand,
In his heart.

A sliver of glass,
Clear as
A black tear:
Nothing!
From it death gushes,
Filling the world:
Death stands,
A mountain.

Obsidian Knife. The Rigi (sung serially or antiphonally).

I THOUGHT NALL might leap to cover himself with Aieh's seal-skin, or to get his knife. But he only rose to his feet, still holding my hand. Without the deer mouse sash my shift fell loose, as though I too were naked before the spears upright in the boats below.

One voi and a swarm of manats had taken shape in the

mist. In the first manat, dragging whorls of dark water around his paddle shaft, sat Hsuu.

He sprang onto Stillness on the landward side. He had laid aside his sealskin; he wore a breechclout of the same indigo as his tattoos. Lightly, he climbed the rock.

Nall drew me to stand a little behind himself. There was not time for thought. Though it had come to nothing, we had done what we came for.

Hsuu looked at the two manats, at us where we leaned against each other, at the ghostly Gate. I wanted to lay my ear on his chest to find whether I could hear a heartbeat there, or only the suffle of salt water. His neck was wrinkled leather, like a sea turtle's. How could I have thought he was like Nall? Hsuu was *old*.

Old as the sea, with no mercy in him. No cruelty, either, or affection or hatred or joy, though as he looked at us a tenderness crossed his face, like a cloud shadow. It faded. From his son's manat he plucked the knife and, after a long look, Aieh's sealskin.

"He waits," said Hsuu. We all knew who. He motioned us to the voi, turned his painted back, and began to climb down to his own boat.

Barely moving my lips, I said to Nall, "Liu's knife is in my pocket."

He said, "Shall I kill you?"

I had not thought of that. "No." Because I would not leave him. "But do you want the knife?"

He shook his head.

We clambered down from Stillness. If Nall's listening was changed, so was mine; perhaps I had found what he had lost, for I swear the barnacles and crabs and weeds on that rock made a noise together that I could hear, a sound like the smell of iodine.

A hard-faced man in a threadbare breechclout lifted me into the voi. I could not tell whether his scowl was anger or uncertainty. Another man tied Nall's wrists in front of him; it seemed we had grown more dangerous since last night.

Nall looked about like a child amazed by bluebirds. Nobody tied me; perhaps they guessed I could not swim like them. I crept into the circle of Nall's bound arms, and he looked at me as if I were a bluebird too.

We knelt together in the prow. I felt every breath he took. With each pull of the oars the bow wave drummed on the hide hull; I heard the birdlike chirp and crow of some animal deep in the water, unknown until a dolphin leaped, smiling its perpetual smile.

"It's singing," I whispered to Nall. He did not answer. I thought, He is listening to that soundless sound.

We rode the changed current eastward, back into the bay. The seals on the shore, penned and miserable, wailed songs as dreadful as the smell they made.

Never before had I stepped, waking, back into the domain of a dream. But it was day—the mist was fading, the sun shone. On our left was the ridge we had run last night, with Selí somewhere beyond it; the bay-front dancing field that had been chaotic as nightmare now looked like a military camp, an anthill, a bowl full of knives. Tiny figures flourished spears that twinkled like antennae; they crawled among the lines of ready manats drawn up on the beach where I had been last night, just north of the unhappy seals. *Clink, clink* was the sound of stonesmiths finishing knives and spear-heads. The Rig host did not look like what it was, a wave poised and toppling. It looked like a paidmen's camp, like any army in the wicked world, and it rustled, like the crabs on Tadde's body.

Beyond the busy camp a clutter of arems—warrenhouses with their little settlements—rose toward the goblin-stone hills that were half hidden among wisps of cloud and windtwisted trees. Smoke from many cookfires rose and tangled. Smaller, brighter figures were busy there: The women and children who had kissed me in their dreams were awake now, feeding an invasion. The women would be stirring the copper cook pots, the twins who had played hand slaps begging for scanty scraps. I could almost hear them.

We pulled toward the ranked manats. The shore thickened with warriors. We drew in under the spears, and I could no longer see the cooks and children, only men. I looked for the white patch that would be Queelic's shirt, on his back or Aieh's, living or dead; nothing in the Rigi's land was so white as that milled, bleached, tailored League linen. But I could not see it anywhere.

The manats made the shore first. Then the voi grounded and tilted. Many hands grabbed the gunwale, and lean, brown faces frowned above them. Some men wore sealskins or breechclouts; some were naked; they were Nall multiplied a hundred times, and not one of them was like him.

He raised his tied arms to free me, leaned his forearms on the gunwale, and climbed out onto the sand. I watched him search among the faces, as last night he had not. Sometimes he knew one, for his eyes would stay on it with that new astonishment. Surely they knew him too, but no one spoke to him. Once or twice I heard a murmured tune, the words all blurred: the Rigi's song. But were these not the Rigi?

They were the wave poised to crash, the Reirig's men.

No one touched me. I held Nall's forearm; no one jerked my hand away. Only sometimes, as we trudged through the sand behind Hsuu and the armed male horde parted before him like ants from beneath a treading foot, a hand reached out and touched my hair.

Lame, hands tied, Nall rolled in his stride like Mailin's parrot. His shoulder kept knocking mine. I wanted to whisper *I love you*, to get it said. But if I was nothing and he was nothing, what was love?

I looked again for Queelic. I needed his simpleminded League talk the way a swimmer needs land. I saw only armed men. Hsuu tossed Nall's knife and Aieh's skin into the crowd; they vanished with hardly a ripple, as though he had thrown them in the sea. Someone set a spear in Hsuu's hand.

The shoving male bodies parted to reveal the Reirig's throne. His sealskin was spread across it, and he across the sealskin, casual and furious. He toyed with his lance. The bony mouth of his estate was empty, now ringed not with peeping babies but with shields, spears, hooks, and knives, hastily hung. No Queelic. No Aieh. Only soldiers.

We jostled to a halt. The Reirig allowed himself to look at us. Under the boredom of his manner his face was that of a dog that will bite, that is restrained only by some caution for itself.

As in the night, he was clad only in his tattoos—by daylight not blue, but black. I could look at him now. I was not in my own nightmare anymore, and anyway he had a hangover; his face was like Seroy's after late carousal, the skin sagging from his eyes. I had not seen him drinking and wondered whether it was a hangover from too much of himself.

When he tired of ignoring us, he stood to his great height, using the shaft of the lance to pull himself up. The new sun on the oiled planes of his body made him look younger than his spoiled eyes—younger almost than Nall, so scuffed and lopsided and still.

He yawned his leopard's yawn. Turned on us; whirled the lance, spun it whining into the air once, twice; and when he grabbed it back, he brought the glass blade to rest with its tip over Nall's heart.

Nall did not move. He looked at the lance as if it were a buttercup, a star. But I looked at the blade, longer than Liu's before it was broken, and at the curve of Nall's breast that moved with his breath.

Hsuu looked too, fingering the shaft of his lance. I could not think except in pictures: the Reirig's blade sunk in Nall's heart; Hsuu's blade in the Reirig's; a blue yell coming from that old man's mouth, and the wave of boats pouring east behind him, the new king of the sea.

King of the sea. And I his bride?

I broke into a sweat. The Reirig's blade quivered, slid sideways to hang at my neck instead.

Breath. Breath. I turned my eyes to Nall's. His were clear and steady, his lips parted.

The blade was withdrawn. The Reirig leaned on his spear, casual and cruel and frightened, and asked Nall the thing he had to know before he killed him.

"What did you hear?"

The warriors hushed their buzz. Behind their silence I could hear the distant chant and chatter of the women and children excluded from the Reirig's show, and the sound of the sea.

"Nothing," said Nall.

Hsuu pursed his lips.

The Reirig's eyes went slits. "You heard nothing?"

"Nothing."

The Reirig showed his perfect dog's teeth. He swung the butt of the spear to Nall's shoulder and shoved. Nall staggered, straightened. His face was open. He was not in trance, not gone away as he had been last night. He was *there*.

I thought, He is himself. He will live and die as himself, and so shall I.

"The plots of my enemies always fail!" said the Reirig. "This dead man, this ghost has laid his dirty ear to the Gate of the universe—and what has he heard?" He shook the lance. "Nothing! And why? *There was nothing left to hear!* I heard it all. I am the One Priest! The whole world is mine!"

He thrust out his arms and howled. A babble of comment or assent rose up. He turned to Hsuu, who gazed steadily at Nall, lips pursed. "Behold your son!" he said.

"My son is dead."

"But this rotten sack was once your son."

Hsuu's eyebrow quirked.

"He was of your blood—see what strong blood it is! So I shall honor you; I shall not kill him quickly like a Black Boot, like that idiot pale worm who came among us."

So the Reirig had not kept his pet. He had killed Ab Harlan's son, new lover of riddles, the boy who wanted to be a bird. But what about Aieh?

The Reirig prodded Nall again. "This wraith was a Rig once. Let him fight me as a Rig!" Grinning, he laid aside the lance and clapped his hands.

The elders scowled as if at an impiety. But without a word Hsuu gave his spear to be held, came forward, and loosed

Nall's wrists. He did not cut the thong, but untied it and rolled it, as if he used it often.

Nall rubbed the old scars. The elders fidgeted. A screech and yammer began in the crowd behind the warriors: women's voices now high and loud. Hsuu cocked his head like a fox, and spoke a low word to the Reirig. He had to say it twice, for the Reirig was grimacing and flexing with great show, as if preparing to defend his harem from an insolent contender. When at last he heard Hsuu, he laughed and said, "Better still! Let her see her nani now."

A narrow lane opened in the crowd of warriors. Even leaning on a stick, she could barely hobble down it—the tiny woman with flyaway white hair around a brown face clean as a bone. She wore her sealskin kirtle, brown freckled with silver like a doeskin; her breasts lay flat on her chest, and she rolled as she walked, as lame as her great-grandson. And why not, when she had walked night into morning, all the way from Selí?

"Ama," said Nall.

With one finger the Reirig signaled her to come to his throne. She paid him the attention she would a fly, planted her stick, and turned her fierce old eyes on Nall.

He leaned to her like a leaf to light. But she stood glaring, letting him remember what she had told him: *You must not meddle with the Gate!*

A laugh like a sob squeaked out of me. She glared at me instead. Stamping with her stick, she set out toward us across the sand.

The Reirig snarled. She ignored him. Two warriors clattered out and took her by her skinny arms; a murmur of displeasure went through the crowd. Shamefaced, the men lifted her clean off her feet and set her down where the Reirig pointed, to one side of the throne.

To struggle was beneath her. She laced her old fingers on the knob of her stick as I, too, was seized, carried, and set down beside her to make the women's side: the harmless watchers and mourners, and I the lazily garnered prize.

When they set me down, I stumbled. The ama's old claw steadied me, knucklebones under soft, loose skin. Her voice was for me only—slow, as though she did not often speak Plain.

"He would not be stopped," she said.

"No."

"He keeps his word."

"Yes."

"He has brought women only grief."

"Not only grief," I said.

Her eyes were blue; she was Bian and Mailin and my auntie Jerash in one. She looked me up and down. "Has he got you with child?"

I did not answer. My face, my whole body prickled with heat. Because he might have. It might be so.

In the ruck and passion and madness I had not thought of that. Not once. I had thought only of myself. And now Nall— *Nall*—stood before me like a wildcat bound at the altar, awaiting the priest's stone knife.

That old woman gave me the stare, no fooling her. "The world is weighed against one grain of sand," she said, in the frayed voice that had sung so many lullabies. "For every birth, a death."

I hated her. I would not hear it. When I had seen no way out, I had been half at peace with dying. But if I was carrying

Nall's child, I could *not* die, nor him, either. It could not be.

And the world went on just the same.

The Reirig clapped again, a lively sound. Mincing like a stag, he moved onto the pocked sand and crouched, motioning Nall to come to him.

I thought Nall would not go. If nothing mattered, then let the Reirig come to him.

But he gave me one last look, and his ama another. He limped across the sand to the Reirig's posturing and offered himself into a formal fighting hold, his hands on the taller man's arms.

The crowd sighed.

Hsuu had his spear again.

The muscles strained in the backs of the two naked men. Nall's stance was as crooked as his walk. The Reirig looked around with a smirk and in one quick turn threw him, hard.

A grunt from the crowd.

"Up," said the Reirig.

Nall got up.

"Here."

Nall went to him, laid his hands on the other's arms again, was thrown again. Perhaps the Reirig had intended to lay him down with a flourish, but a lame man does not use his weight as his attacker expects; Nall fell crookedly onto the point of his shoulder, and rose slowly.

He took the offered arms again. A mutter ran round. I stood heavy, a bowl poured full. *My life is my own,* yes; but what if it was not just *my* life?

They grabbed, grappled. Nall had a doggedness; it was not enough. The Reirig flashed his style, letting Nall nearly toss him before he leaned onto Nall's lame leg and threw him down.

Nall rose. The Reirig showed his canines, slapped his thighs, inviting the smaller man to another fall. Each time his grip was crueler. I saw what he wanted: to play with Nall like a cat with a vole, then tear out his throat with his teeth, or break his back.

Beside me the ama rocked a little, closed her eyes.

Nall's patient, fumbling grabs. Sometimes he took a hard fall, as though he were willing. Sometimes he slipped from the Reirig's hands awkwardly, like an armful of fruit or a spilled toolbox. He moved oddly. He was not doing the things a man does to protect himself; he was wide open, unpredictable.

The Reirig looked confused, the elders puzzled. On Stillness, Nall had been astonished to feel my hands, because they were nothing; under his hands the Reirig was nothing, too.

It seemed the Reirig felt this, and did not like it. The Reirig was *something*.

He got angry. He began to snatch and clutch and throw more cruelly, yet every throw was half bungled because Nall fell, or stumbled, or fumbled from his grip, or snagged the Reirig's leg or tipped him sideways and, though he had not the weight to throw him, spoiled his form.

The Reirig began to fight in earnest.

Like sharks smelling blood, warriors and elders leaned forward. Hsuu fingered his spear. Nall hit the ground, rolled, struggled to rise. Fell. Rose.

A low hum began.

I thought it was inside me, rage and despair made audible. But it was the ama keening, a soft, minor wail as at a midnight wake. Almost words; almost *Love in the sea of grief.*

I could not bear it. Nall fell. Stumbling as he fell, he pulled the Reirig into a clumsy spin that threw him onto one elbow and sprayed sand in his mouth. The elders panted. The ama keened. The Reirig, greased with fury, did not wait for the formal stance but leaped up and grabbed Nall from behind.

Nall twisted half out of his grip. Not far enough; the Reirig fell on him full weight, his hands around his throat, squeezing, cursing as he squeezed.

Nall's face went black. The ama's keen rose to a shriek.

I snatched Liu's knife from my pocket, ran four long steps across the sand, and sliced down across the Reirig's snarl.

Blood burst out. I met his furious eye as he loosed Nall and swung his arm, hit me in the chest, and sent me staggering. Nall squirmed like a lizard; like a lizard he seemed to scamper over the rock of the Reirig's body as I sprawled back and the Reirig, following the motion of his arm, fell forward. Nall set his knee between the Reirig's shoulders, hooked one arm under his chin, and flexed his back.

There was a little sound, domestic and accidental, like setting a bowl down on an egg. The Reirig's head no longer finished the curve of his back but stood at an angle to it. Then it dropped. Nall dropped on top of it, both hands in the sand.

A roar. The elders, the warriors shouting with bared teeth, shaking their spears; then men with knives running toward us yelling, Hsuu running, raising his spear; the ama's finishing scream.

Then silence. Only Nall's sobbing breath.

Nothing moved.

Nothing.

Around us the elders hung in mid-leap, mouths open. The warriors, statues of a battle, held knives that shone, motionless, in the sunlight; they ran, and did not. Like a fly in amber, Hsuu reached for a stride that never came, his lance raised, his mutable face frozen in joy.

I crawled to Nall. The sand crunched under my knees. No sound but that and his racking breath—not even the sea, for every wave stood still, crisp at its untoppling edge.

Shuffle, shuffle in the sand behind me, an old voice crying the name I was never to speak.

"Get up! Foolish children! Come!"

Nall rolled off the Reirig's body. Half rose. Fell. I plucked at him as in a dream when you must run, run, and cannot. I did not know where I was—in a frozen forest, a picture carved on a vase. Motionless in the air a kittiwake hung painted, each feather bright.

"Get up!"

I got up, reeling. Nall was standing too, clutching me, the ama like a little dog worrying at us, snapping and tugging, yapping, "Come, come!" The world was glass, a glacier that had frozen an army—all but a crease in the air that hung, trembling like the crack between two halves of a stone. As if the world itself were stone.

"There!" She bundled us toward it. I shrank from it, clinging to Nall. She screamed, "Idiot children, *go!* He rises!"

A bubbling sound: the Reirig's breathing, as, against the stopped world but no longer ruled by it, he lurched to his feet. Blood poured from his slashed face. His head bobbled to one side like a plum on a broken twig, and his dead lips made a snarl.

"*Ama!*" said Nall.

But her gnarled monkey hands pushed him, pushed me; he threw his arm round my waist as we fell through the stillness into that trembling line, it pressed us together and delivered us into the dark.

25

A very little ghost for such a long life,
She was child and girl and maid and wife,
Mother and grandmother, cripple and clay.
Her little wraith dissolves in the bright day.

Year Altar Offering. Downshore.

FALLEN ON SAND, my face pressed to Nall's neck. I was afraid
to open my eyes. I did not know what I might see: nothing, a
place without being.

His pulse beat at my temple. "*O he, Ama!*" he said.

I opened one eye. Looked past his shoulder into darkness
that was incomplete, there were shapes in it. Smelled earth
and stone. So quiet. I held him tighter. "A tomb!" I said.

"*Ne, ne.* O heart! She has given us into Selí."

I raised my head. It hurt to move. The place where we lay was no darker than Raím's bothy; pale morning light glowed at a smoke hole. I began to see an underground room round as a basket, its carved stone walls, the lintel of a door.

An old woman's tidy daybed of rushes and furs was spread against the wall. Next to the fire pit lay the reed mat where she had sat to spin. Driftwood for the fire lay to hand, with three loaves of bread, a basket of berries, three dried fish lapped in a cloth—the tails stuck out—and two water skins. Someone had worried that she might want, the stubborn old ama who would not go to the dances now that her nani was dead.

I whispered, "Are we alive?"

"Yes. But she is not."

He half sat up. I was afraid to let go of him, I did not know where I might be swept to. I smelled the honey of a beeswax candle. There was no human sound, but on some unseen beach the sea said *hush, hush,* like the voice in a shell.

"*O Ama!*" he said. "She pulled us with her through some gate—away from my father, first, and then from that dead man. She pulled us away with her death."

Those old, unflinching eyes—the heart slapped on the counter like money, and keep the change. Like him, I said, "*O Ama.* But, Nall—what will happen to her? Wherever she is, *he* is there too."

"I don't know. I can't get to her." All the layers and worlds of the universe were piled around us, but we could not see them, we could not find their gates. We clung to each other like children waked in the night. "Kat, who are we? What are we?"

I could only hold him.

Whispering, I said, "*When* in the world is it? Is it still now?"

"I don't know." A shadow at the smoke hole became a gray cat looking down at us. Nall held out his hand to it; his hand shook. "Tinga!" he said.

The cat ran away. "Not Tinga. Tinga had a white breast. Maybe it is still now." He drew his hand across his eyes and stared at the bed, the worn mat, the empty goods pole with no sealskin on it. His face was desolate. "I think it is now."

I sat up, holding tight to his arm.

"I never killed a man before," he said. "She snared rabbits for the pot. My ama did. She broke their necks. She taught me how. The rabbit is alive, you move your hand a little and it's dead." *Hush, hush* said the waves. "I am killing and killing. That dog man, and my ama, and Aieh and Queelic. You, nearly."

"Only the Reirig for certain," I said. I was sure I was alive now. The light grew brighter. The carvings on the walls were like those on the ring I had thrown away, seals frozen in play. I said, "Is—is the world still stopped?"

"It never was. She pulled us out of it."

There was no way to think about this. "Then—your father is the new Reirig?"

"Someone is."

The earth I had mislaid, of dirt and bread and common daylight, came back in pieces. "The tidal wave, the Rigi. Will they still—"

"A crested wave must rush somewhere. If one leader is dead, they will find another."

"Then we have to go. Now." I got to my knees. "It's only morning; they won't leave until tonight. We'll go ahead of them and warn Mailin."

This was impossible. In stories the hero travels forty

days and forty nights, through every danger and travail, without rest; in stories. I looked about at the old-lady clutter of spindles and yarns. "O, Ama! Couldn't you have pushed us out in Downshore?"

Nall got to all fours. What if Downshore was nothing to him now, and did not matter?

He tried to rise. As on the wrestling ground he fell back, then grappled himself to his feet. Clinging to a beam of the low ceiling, he looked at the bed, at the stone cupboards with their meager stores. At me. Took a breath. "To my manat, then," he said.

I helped him gather the bread and berries, the fish and the water skins. He took a stone sheath knife from the wall and belted it around his naked hips. I said, "Must we run back the way we came last night?"

"Not if there's a manat where there should be." He put out his hand. I set mine in it. He said, "Kat."

I thought it was a question, and waited. But he only held my hand, in this room he must know by touch. The beach wind whuffed at the smoke hole. I thought I could hear every dream ever dreamed in that place, every lullaby sung.

I began to draw my hand out of his. He would not let me. He pressed aside the hide curtain over the door and pulled me after him, into the warrenhouse of Selí.

The corridor was narrow, lower-ceilinged than the room and lit by gaps in the overhanging slabs. It smelled of wood smoke, of roots and grass and midden and the sea. We crouched along it, feeling our way on stone walls that were carved like Hsuu's body in spirals and whirlpools, all soft with time and smoke and groping hands.

Room after room; I thought of the warrens of hopping rats in the dry hills of Creek, where I had lain at dusk to watch the big-eyed, whiskered tenants creep out and dance. Branching corridors, nooks, niches, stone cupboards, deep shelves—what a house to be a child in! Sleeping rooms spread with straw, storage rooms with shadowy alcoves, heart's hide-and-seek.

"Nall!"

He froze.

"Someone's singing!" The tune was melodic and dark, a faraway ballad heard on a nighttime street.

He strained to listen. "Moles," he said. "Digging and singing. Nothing more."

"Moles can sing?" I was enchanted. *Root, root for food,* they sang, grumping and mumbling. *Bug and grub and slug.* "Nall, they speak Plain!"

"Come. Come," he said, like the ama.

It was a maze. We turned left, turned right, doubled back. I began to panic; I saw dim light as from a tunnel, Nall ran for it, I shot after him so fast that when he stopped on the threshold I bounced off him and sat down. In the wall by the door was a stone split down the middle, the halves set left and right to frame a niche.

"Year Altar," said Nall, panting. "We should leave something. But—it doesn't matter."

"Yes, it does." I had nothing left to leave. "Give me the knife." I cut a lock of my hair, of his, laid them on the altar. "Say something?"

"You."

"Blessed, blessed," I said, all I could think of as he yanked me up the tunnel toward the light so fast that I had just a glimpse of what else lay there: a carved fish pierced with a bone lance, a child's bracelet, a withered plum.

Like hopping rats we pushed our noses into the whisper of blowing sand. I looked for Selí and saw only random chimney stones, ruinous as the Tells of Creek. A second look showed a stone quern, a driftwood drying rack, a basket like one of Mailin's but frayed and faded, set down on a rock. All silent.

Not quite; as Nall pulled me into a run, I said, "There *is* singing! It's not moles!"

He did not even slow down, bobbing one leg short like Pao's fox, through scrub that lined a path worn deep by bare feet. He ran toward the singing; it was a quick, pattering ditty like a hand slap sung so fast that the words were blurred.

"Nall, there are people!"

He shook his head, pulled me into a looming green thicket and down the bank to a little fast creek overhung with evergreens and a tree like a river poplar with shivering leaves. All the branches leaned east, away from the wind.

I still heard singing. Nobody was there.

I had been to a fair once in Ten Orchards, when on the packed midway a fiddler roamed from booth to booth; I never saw him but I heard him, his thread of melody caught and then lost. That was what it sounded like. Surely Nall could hear it?

"Birds," he said. He rummaged in a hedge thick with white blooms that bent to touch the water. "The little gray ones that go in flocks."

"But those just chirp." *O lark, o leaf, o sweet lea, never leave me!* sang the tiny voices.

He dragged a battered manat from beneath the hedge,

waded into the water, and leaned on it, searching. "Leaks. Always did. Get in front, you'll have to bail. Kat! Get in."

A cloud of mouse-gray birds fled from the evergreens. I said, "Everything is singing!"

"Get in!"

I got in. While he scratched among other half-derelict boats for paddles and bailer, I refilled the water skins from the stream. The water was sweet and slightly warm, it eddied around my wrists—creek water, not the infinite sea. The populars sang *shhh*, the evergreens sang *ahhh*.

He gave me a paddle, warped and gray. "East."

"You're sure where east is?"

"I can smell east. Comes with being a Rig." He pushed us off, jumped in. "Or whatever I am now."

Nothing.

I saw his face and thought, Until now you've always known who you were and were not. Are you really nothing? Or are you just finding out that you have a thousand halves, like me?

He was not used to that. I was. In fact I almost liked it, this listening for everybody's songs but wearing nobody's tattoo.

For the first time in my life I saw an advantage in being who I was. A strange ease crept over me, like feeling the pain leave a burn. I turned to look at Nall and found for myself how hard that is to do from the front hatch of a manat. I gave him my upside-down hand instead.

We slipped from the creek mouth. Mist crowded us to the shore. We worked our way north, or east, or south, I could not tell—anywhere but west. With food but no hands free to eat it, Nall paddled and I bailed, for the sea came in fast.

"To my manat before we founder," he said. I broke a lump of bread for him and he tucked it in his cheek like a squirrel, still paddling. I heard voices in the water but they were little ones, monotonous and bright—fish, probably. I was so tired and hungry that I wept as I bailed, wiping my nose on the shoulder of my shift. I was afraid to speak what I feared: that Nall's manat had been discovered and was gone.

We picked our way along the half-seen shore. A soft, conjoined bubbling was a chorus of clams. Now and then we swung out so far that the hiss of surf on a beach could be heard but not seen. In that leaking boat it frightened me to lose the land, but Nall said, "An arem, there on the shore. Out of sight is safest."

I made him name each settlement. *Lissliss*, "Sand Walking." *Hoyroynoy*, "Logs Roll at Night." *Saiaushu*, "Needle Eel Whistling." *Kaskas*, "Tidal Waves."

The sound of the paddles became *kas, kas, kas*. I bailed. In a trance of sweat I saw in my mind Hsuu riding that wave, whirling the Reirig's lance, but its movement was spiral and I could not tell where his blow would fall. I did not know what he wanted or intended, only that the sea, his sea, had risen and would follow us. He could loose even the seals against us. I wondered what our leaking manat looked like from below, to a bull seal.

After we passed each arem, we returned to tracing the coast. The cliffs rose higher. Sheltered from the west wind, the trees in the riven clefts grew taller, thick-trunked and bearded with moss. They sang a deep melody, spicy as pine.

"The trees are singing," I said. I tried to catch the words.

"Bail," said Nall.

We ran in under a looming cliff, slipped through foam and

then through a cleft in stone, a trailing curtain of vines. I woke out of the trees' song, saw where we were and thought of ambush, a shower of blows. But there was only the cove in daylight stillness, waves splashing the tiny beach.

Everything lay as we had left it. Nall flew at the manat, swapping gear, flinging spare provisions out of Aieh's voi. I stood listening. The cove was full of the voices of flowers and bees, roots and buds, hidden birds. I could not untangle the melodies and listened to them whole, like part-singing. Our footprints still marked the sand above the tide line, as though we had been carried off by eagles.

Nall ran his manat into the sea. "Get in."

"Look!" I pointed to Aieh's footprints, naked and slender. I thought I could hear her voice.

"Get in!"

"They'll be gone with the next high tide—"

He grabbed me and swung me into the front hatch, steadied and shoved the boat in the same motion, jumped in. "Work," he said.

We shot out of the mouth of the cove, our faces stroked first by vines, then by the sea wind. A kittiwake dove away, squealing something funny. I laughed. Nall said, "To the Isle of Bones."

"We have to go there?" I had trouble paddling. I was distracted by songs. Deep in the water something thrummed like a plucked dindarion.

"We have to pass it," he said.

"Can't we stop and rest?"

"Not till we pass it."

"It's far!"

"Yes."

The sound of the water dripping off my paddle was round as grapes; I wanted to eat that sound. "Aren't you hungry?"

"Give me another hunk of bread," he said. "You take one too."

It was not bread I was hungry for. The whole sea was to eat, the sky was ripe with words just out of reach. I could almost sip, almost taste as they slipped by me, passing and passing. I listened. Sometimes I remembered to paddle and listened to that—*kas, kas* or *chass, chass,* which in Hessdish means "lust, lust."

Sometimes I forgot to paddle. The sea hummed. Not like a dindarion but like a great drum; keeping time with it, I paddled again, and the sound it made became *toom, toom,* almost below hearing. I went on and on. I forgot hunger. I could boost the boat along with sound.

Behind me Nall worked and said nothing. But I did not need to talk anymore, that big beat was under everything, heaving it along, making the world pour in, pour out like rising tide, falling tide, bright, dark.

"Kat."

"Ah."

"Did you eat?"

"Ah."

"Kat!" He put his cold feet on my thighs.

"Ai!" I cried, turning in a fury.

He withdrew his feet, pulled a loaf from Mailin's oiled bag, broke another hard chunk, and gave it to me. His face poured sweat. "Put it in your mouth. Don't listen."

I put it in my mouth and said through it, "I can eat and listen."

It was true. The bread itself spoke. I heard the voice of the woman who had made it, kind and worried like Bian's, and the little piping songs of the barley grains. I laid the paddle across my lap so that I would not lose it while I listened, but I heard the paddle singing and was so astonished that the bread fell out of my mouth. We had come into the lee of cliffs, not close; at the edges of my eyes, left and right, Nall's paddle flashed black. It sang back to my own paddle, a song like the big trees but higher, like wind in branches, then a pant-song that went *change, change.* I could not quite get the words, but I knew that was it. Things changing, dying, being born.

A high keening, birds and mourners; a low chumbling, crabs and worms. No words, just a tearing apart. I smelled dirt, I smelled warm flesh, I heard a voice singing and knew whose it was, felt a warm arm.

"Sit down!"

But I cried, "Oh, Ma!" and rose in the hatch to step out into her arms, onto the thrumming drumhead of the sea. The black edge of Nall's paddle came singing from the corner of my eye, and all the singing stopped.

26

The earth is round. The sky is round.
In all directions, the world is round.
　　Days come and days go.
　　Years come and years go.
　　The world grows light,
　　Dark,
　　Light,
　　And it is still round.

Circle Game. Downshore.

SILENCE. NO MOTION. Hot sun.

　My lips lay against salt. Against flesh, my mother's breast; her hand stroked my hair. I had stepped across, and she held me.

　I moved my face against her and smelled Nall's skin. He held me in his arms, my face on his shoulder. I had drooled on him.

I woke weeping. My head throbbed and spun. He held it still against him, whispering, "I hit you. I hit you hard."

"She was there, I heard her!"

"They're all there. Traces in the air, voices from dreams. I had to keep on. I was afraid I would hear my mother."

"Not—not your ama?"

"I wouldn't be afraid to hear her."

We held each other, bereft. The sun burned hot. I opened my eyes on brilliance and shut them, wincing. "Where is this?"

"A little island east of the Isle of Bones."

I had thought there were no islands east of the Isle of Bones, not until the skerries; but my head ached. "You heard—*them* singing?" If Nall could have been a little slower . . . If I could have heard Dai's voice. . .

"Yes."

"Why didn't we hear them when we were in the cave?"

"We weren't the same as we are now."

"What has changed?"

"I don't know. Be still." He wiped his eyes with his wrist.

Through slitted eyes I saw looming driftwood logs, wide and tall as houses, with giant root wheels tilted in the air. Their flanks made a little room, and in it we huddled. The walls were wave-scoured, with shells and little stones wedged in the wood; the floor was sand, the roof was sky.

"Where's the manat?"

"We're leaning on it. Hush."

I was afraid to hush, for fear I would listen again and be drowned. But I could not help it. I heard my ear ringing as it had when my cousin hit me, then wave-hum, then a chipper singing that might have been sand fleas. The songs were still there, but they did not possess me as they had. I could listen or not, and I could sort them a little. Deep and peaceful, those old logs were chanting *hoyroynoy*.

I stopped listening, to prove I could. The world went more ordinary. I said, "Are we still in the Rigi's land?"

"We aren't out of it."

I pondered this, dull-witted.

"We're in the Ni'Na', the Changes."

I remembered how, when we came, he had pushed at something and said, *We are in*. That was all; no islands; but if the voices of the dead had changed, maybe the boundary had.

"Somewhere in the Ni'Na'," he said. "It doesn't matter."

At these words my mind began to move a little. "Nall, are you still hearing—that? What you heard at the Gate?"

"Yes."

"Nothing." I would say the word, at least. "Tell me what it sounds like."

For a long time he did not speak. I thought he was not going to and tipped my head to see his face. It too had changed. Still his, certainly, but older—gaunt and quiet.

"Like a sea whose waves are not waves," he said at last. "Like a sky full of stars."

I thought of Queelic. "Stars make a sound?"

But he was not listening to me. "It's so big," he said. "Or so tiny." He tilted his head like a listening dog. "No words, no music, no tongue, no rhythm. Only space, but full; a rich emptiness; nothing. Not even the beat of the drum. What was there before the beat of the drum?"

The place where all patterns came from, before the world was made. But how could that be nothing? I thought of the way the patterns on Hsuu's face had canceled themselves to make stillness and said, "It's your father getting at you."

He shook his head.

"Then you need to eat something, that's what." I sounded like Mailin. "Where's the food?"

I started to get up. He caught me back. "Sit down!"

"It's *nothing*," I said, feeling the goose egg behind my ear. It was sticky with blood. "Don't hit me with nothing too often."

He grinned. That had changed too, to a wry half grin that matched the wrinkle at his eyebrow. He rose and began to rummage in the manat.

Right away I tried to stand. The log room tilted like the sea. Nall turned back with his hands full of bread and meat; he threw these down cursing, picked me off my feet, and sat me on the sand again. "Sit still! Eat."

I was not used to hearing him swear. I said, "No fair! You're stronger."

"In some ways. Kiss me."

I already had bread in my mouth, and looked up at him startled. He kissed me bread and all, then sat down and put his shoulder against mine. There was only room enough to sit close, like harvest mice in their nest of grass.

The bread and fish were tough and tasted better than anything I had ever eaten. We worried at them like dogs. The creek water from Selí was fresh and holy.

I said carefully, "Do you remember last night?"

He hunched his shoulders. "The taste of it. And Aieh."

"Did you know Queelic was there?"

He stopped with bread halfway to his mouth. "*Queelic!* At the drum?"

"He walked west and they caught him. They brought him to the Reirig."

"Did the Reirig kill him?"

"Not then. The warriors tied him to a stake. He talked with your father for a long time."

Nall whistled softly. "What is afoot in this world? Were the Rigi to join forces with the Leaguemen—"

"Oh, never!"

"Queelic is Ab Harlan's son; power makes strange marriages. And my father is a strange man."

I did not think Ab Harlan was strange, only fat with sickness, like a boil. "Queelic is dead, I think. Nall, he—" I wanted to tell him how Queelic had tried to save Aieh with his shirt, but it made me so sad, I could not. Instead I said, "He liked your father." How odd that sounded. "He liked your father a lot."

"I loved my father once. Hsuu." In that sighing name I heard the ocean, restless on the world. "Here is what you can't know about my father: Is he working for you? Against you? Does he care for you at all? Does he have plans, or is it that he moves like the sea, flowing here, flowing there, changing as the sea changes?"

He spoke as if to himself. "He killed me without killing me. When he took my skin and my name, he gave me death— and one narrow chance. I took it. Maybe I was the chip of wood he cast on the water, and how chance played me might tell him how the great current of the world flowed." He glanced at me. "Maybe we are that for him still, you and I."

"He has no heart or soul, then!"

"Why should he? He is the sea. The sea doesn't love. It *is*."

I remembered that blood is salt, that we all bleed.

"He watches how the world flows," said Nall, "then he chooses."

"Maybe the world itself is choosing," I said, "and we are its decision."

He was not looking at me. "Kat," he said. "About Aieh."

I pushed sand grains around with my finger.

"She was crazy for a child. But . . . barren, like so many now. There was nothing I— Anyway, I was crazy too. For—I didn't know for what. For the east, the sun. Something calling and calling." He put his finger on mine. "Aieh and I fought like bobcats."

I nodded. Raím and I had fought like that. And the fight at the Gate had been a bobcat fight, but with words instead of clawing and snarling. I wondered whether, if I listened very hard, I would find that bobcats speak Plain.

"Then Liu died and I was even crazier. The new Rigi's song, the one I heard on Stillness—do you remember the last line?"

I had heard it last night at the drum. I sang, *"I am the child. I come, I come."*

He looked at me straight. "It wasn't Aieh's child."

"How did you know?" I burned all over.

"I knew. And that was the end of Aieh and me—or it would have been, but the rest happened so fast; they caught me and killed me. She never knew."

"Poor Aieh," I said, and meant it.

"And there on the Isle of Bones, with both of you—" He bowed his head. "I have dragged ruin behind me, I have destroyed the people I love. For nothing."

I wanted to say, *You haven't destroyed* me! But he had said I was nothing.

Instead I said, "How do you know how the universe works?" I put my finger in the middle of his palm and rubbed the hollow of it. "You know what *I* think is strange? Queelic.

Born to a mad father, kidnapped, marooned, his throat near slit, roughed up and tied up, and now I suppose he's dead. But, Nall—last night at the dance he seemed completely happy. How can anybody know whether what they've done is good or bad?"

His hand curled around my finger, let it go.

I said, "Before they killed you, your hair was long?"

He looked up, puzzled. "Never cut."

"Did you braid it?"

"One or another of my cousins would braid it. Or my ama; we braided each other's."

"My cousins wore three-fours and rake-rows and hand-me-overs. I was the one who had to braid them. There's a chant you say to make the plaits lie smooth.

> The sun crosses the river,
> The moon crosses the river,
> The water runs down
> And the light rolls over.
> Braid me up tight, Mama,
> Comb me out free.
> Birth me, bury me.
> So let it be.

"I think the world is like a little girl's braid," I said, "bound up and combed out, over and over. How can you say of it, 'This hair is good, this one is bad!' 'This hank is evil, and that one's holy!' It's just a braid, loosed every night and plaited up new every morning."

Nall pulled one of my curls straight. "Did your cousins braid your hair?"

"It was never long enough. Don't you remember?"

"Yes. When I raised my head on that cold beach, it was just dawn. I saw a little being with a stick, singing. Then I saw your hair and I thought, It's the sun!"

"But it was only me."

"And only me. Hero of nothing."

Gulls sang jeers, high up. I do not think gulls like people much, except their garbage.

I put my arms around him. "Aieh said, 'One loves fools.' But there's nobody else to love, as far as I can tell."

We held each other. The surf sighed. After a little I sighed too and said, "We'd better go."

"If I go like this, I will fail in mid-ocean. I must rest, if only for an hour. You too. The tide will soon touch us; we'll wake and be gone." He rose, packed what was left of the food into the manat, and lay down in the sand. He tied the bow line of the manat around his wrist. This made me uneasy, for who was there to steal it? But I was too weary to ask. I squirmed down next to him and laid my arm across his waist.

His eyes were still open, looking and looking.

"Nall. What are you thinking?"

"Nothing."

"Stop it."

He laughed, grim, and shut his eyes. His body gave a little twitch, falling asleep. Then I could sleep too. I dreamed that something big and old and quiet came, and watched us while we slept.

Water touched my hand. I had fallen through that quiet dream into black sleep, and when the tide touched me I thought I was in deep water—that I had tipped over the manat, I was pressing the sea with my hands and they went right through.

I woke with a gasp that sucked salt water, coughing and clawing at the sea. I got right, found the sun, scrabbled upward, and bumped the bottom of the manat. Saw Nall's legs, his underwater face streaming bubbles, his hand grabbing. Then both of us were bobbing next to the manat in the blue, empty ocean. The bow line was still tied to his wrist.

He cursed, spat water from his sleepy face, and clutched the slack of my shift. "I thought I had hold of you," he said.

"What—"

"It changed. I feared it might."

"Changed—"

"The island. They do."

I hung on to the coaming. "Have we died?" I said. Or maybe I had dreamed the white sand, the sunny logs.

"No. It's the Ni'Na'," he said in a more awake voice. "The island changed while we slept. I shouldn't have stopped there, but I'd hit you; there was nowhere else. I thought it would hold." He rubbed water from his face and looked around at the sea that was empty of islands.

"Was it— Did something wash us away?" A tidal wave. *Kas.* The Rigi.

"No. It changed. From an island to—to whatever it is now. Get into the manat; we must go."

Stunned, obedient, I tried to pull myself up by the coaming and nearly capsized the boat. Even with Nall as counterweight I could not climb from fluid onto solid, nor make that house of giant logs into this bare, bright sea.

"Wait." He swam sideways, pulling the manat by the bow line. I clung to the stern. A shadow underneath us became a dark shoal. I thought it was the back of some leviathan and said, "Nall! Don't—"

But he was standing on it, waist-deep and then knee-deep, steadying the boat. "Get in," he said.

I would not put my foot on that black thing. But it came up to meet my thrashing knees and was black sand, opalescent where the sun could reach it. Surface currents had made ripples on it, and a school of tiny blue fish swam over it, each the size of a pea.

"Stand up," said Nall.

"It's not real. It wouldn't come rising up like that, all alone in the middle of the ocean—"

"Stand up and get in! Hurry."

I stood up dripping and stepped into the manat. He slid in behind me. The boat turned gently, and I saw around us a ring of islands, of which our shoal was one.

None of them had white sand or drifted logs. They had black sand and green trees that crowded down close to the lazy surf, draped with vines and yellow flowers.

I gazed and gazed. A flock of fork-tailed birds wheeled away from one isle and nipped across an inlet to another.

"What—what islands are these?"

"Just the Ni'Na'," he said, and drove the paddle deep.

"But there was only sea."

"Yes."

"Did we pass them before? When we first came, when it was raining so hard?"

"They weren't here."

"Where were they?"

"Somewhere else. Or maybe they were here, but being something else. I could feel them, as we came."

"Can you step on them?"

"You just did. And we slept on one."

"But that was real!"

He said, "What is real?" and pointed with his chin. I turned and saw, just under the surface of the water, a sad little fat boat sunk on a reef—surely the fishing boat that had marooned Queelic. A shadowy shape, two, on the deck: drowned men.

We made haste away from it. When I looked up, the island on our left had grown a round green hill, soft with meadows. A host of voices, birdlike, sweet.

"Nall, can you hear them?"

"Yes."

"What are they saying?"

"*Su! Su!*" he said. "I am! I am!"

It was a contented, beelike hum. I picked out one voice, then lost it. "Is it still the dead?"

"The unborn." He dug at the water. "So they say. Waiting to come among us, to be given names and be told there are things that never change. To be taught that the shoals they stand on are real."

"But you said the unborn wait beyond the Gate."

"Not our dreams of them."

I thought of the child I had dreamed, burning in fire. The manat shot eastward along the flank of the island. A drift of yellow butterflies floated over the shining green, and beyond the dipping grasses I heard a laugh so delicious that I thought, A child is chasing those butterflies.

I got to my knees, I turned around and grabbed Nall's fists with the paddle in them. "Stop. Listen!"

Chuckle and chirp, that crow of laughter.

"They'll be thrown to war," he said. "One after the other, like roses to the Year Fire. And the sea will break on the rocks just the same, and the moon will rise, and the world will rush in and out through the Gate."

I looked again and saw no island anymore. We had won free of the Ni'Na', yet that busy, relentless song went on.

He kissed my hands and pulled his own away. "Paddle, Kat," he said. "Let's go home to our war."

27

The work that night and day
goes on in darkness,
the strength that is always there.
That strength is the boat
that bears me, weeping,
over the black flood
that does not cease;
that work is the slow blow
after blow of the unseen
maul that makes me.
The god I worship is dark,
patient,
strong.
He made this wood.
He made this sea.

Boatbuilder's Chant. Downshore.

WE WERE TINY on the big sea. The sun was fierce. The wind blew
from the north and pushed us broadside; we wrestled with it
and pulled east, east. Behind us a knot of cloud gathered to
become an indigo wall, hazy where it met the sea. Glancing
back, I sometimes thought it nearer, sometimes farther. I heard
a flock of cranes high up and squinted to find them; they flew
over us crying, and I thought they were fleeing from that cloud.

I heard grief in their cries. But maybe it was my own grief. *Why do we hear what we hear?*

My listening was not the same as it had been before we passed the Changes. Then I had heard actual voices, sometimes words; now what I heard as we paddled was like the sound made by Nondany's dindarion: wordless, a hum and sparkle that was the sea itself, the sky itself, the little quick boat creaking and splashing.

If I listened to this—as if with my skin, not my ears—I could make out a pattern. Not of sound, exactly, nor sight, nor taste, nor any one sense, but of all of them together, piecing out the shape of something the way blind Raím might learn the world from touch, smell, taste.

Sometimes I thought it was some great fish singing, deep down. Or the boat itself singing as it sped along, or a horizon cloud putting down legs of rain, or the blister on my palm, or everything in chorus. I saw with my mind's eye, heard with my heart's ear, felt with my soul's hand, and because I had no name for this, I had to say, *I saw . . . I heard . . . I felt . . .*

At the edge of vision I saw Nall's black paddle flick, flick, flick.

I thought, Jekka would shape a bowl to be this boat, Raím would weave a cloak to be that cloud. They could fit clay or yarn around what they hear-see-feel, but here I have neither clay nor wool. I have words—but not for what I feel.

Well then, I thought as I dug, and dug, and dug at the water, I'll use the words I have.

So it was ordinary words that came as we swung eastward on the skin of the sea. Not in Rig or any holy tongue, but in the peddlers' cant my auntie Jerash called Pigsty Plain.

Shining sky,
Shining water.
Oh, be joyful,
Father's daughter!

It was good to paddle to. It even grew a little tune. Nall behind me neither sang nor spoke. I turned to see him still-faced, pulling stroke and stroke and stroke like a crane's wing in the air.

"Nall." I spoke his name twice before he looked at me. "Do you want water?"

He licked his lips, nodded, and shipped the paddle. We bobbed on the circle of ocean, under the circle of sky.

I passed him the water skin, got to my knees to stretch my back, and knelt facing him. He drank without spilling a drop. When it was my turn I wet the front of my shift and snorted water up my nose.

"You're better at water than I am," I said, and sneezed. Each quarter of the sky had different clouds, that dark bank still in the west. Nall had his back to it, but I knew he knew it was there.

I said, "I want dry land. Roadsouls singing rude songs around a campfire—that's what *I* want to hear."

He gave me that crooked new grin. It made lines around his eyes like the sun's rays, yet there was such sorrow in it. I did not want to ask, but I did. "Are you still—"

He nodded.

My heart swelled with grief; I thought it would burst my shift. What happened then was what always happens: I got angry.

"You just stop that!" I said. "You've forgotten how to hear

the world, that's all. That damned Gate sucked it out of you. I'm going to tell you how." He opened his mouth to speak, but I tumbled on, kneeling backward in the manat. "Remember that flock of cranes? High, high up, keeking and churring? You look for them, but they're so high, the sky is so deep and it has so many layers to it, you can't find where to see. Then your eyes get it right, and there they are, tiny and thronging, beating their big wings. *That's* what listening to the world is like," I said. "Isn't it? Or seeing, or feeling, or however you name it. There's no right word for it. Listening, and suddenly, *there.*"

He put his forefinger at the base of my neck, in that little hollow place. "There are no layers in nothing, Kat. No birds, and no sky."

And no child? What if there already is a child? Is that nothing?

"*Be* a stone, then!" I jerked back around and sat down. "Some old Rig stone, split down the middle forever!"

I paddled. He did not. The manat was like a dead body; paddling felt like running with both legs broken.

Then at the corners of my eyes I saw flick, flick, and the manat flew again like a bird.

"Kat."

I would not answer.

"Kat. Turn around."

I would not turn around because I was crying; I did not want him to see that and know he had won. I kept paddling. The manat went dead. I dragged at it awhile, then wrenched around onto my knees again, shouting, "You just let the Rigi come, then! While we sit here in the middle of the ocean *talking!*"

He held his paddle crosswise between us. "Kat. What you said about the cranes—that's heart-true."

"Then *do* it! Once you find where the world's songs are, and you listen to them, they get louder. Louder than anything. Why can't you listen for *them*?"

He turned his face away, a gesture I began to know. "Between the cries of the cranes, between all the voices of the world is—that. It hums so loud, Kat. I can't not hear it."

"Is—is it death?"

"It's greater than death."

I tried to think of something greater than death, and could not.

He said, "What if that sound is the only sound there is?"

"It's not! There are cranes! I could hear them and so could you—don't tell me you couldn't!"

That crooked half smile. "I can hear *you*."

"Listen to me, then!"

He put his hand on my angry face, next to my mouth. "So tell me something."

"What?"

"Whatever you like. Paddle and tell."

"I'll tell you the story of the merchant's ugly wife," I said. "*That'll* teach you that nothing's stronger than death."

I turned around and took up the stroke. Over my shoulder I told him the story my boy-cousins used to tell to scare the breath out of me, about the merchant who is tired of cooking his own breakfast so he tries to get his wife back from death. At the part where the wife shows up with her guts all rotting out, I made Nall make puking sounds the way you are supposed to—*uullghgh!* When I looked back at him he had his grin on, the west all dark behind him.

So I told him another story, from Creek this time, about how Ouma the Bear Mother got her husband, Trouble. Then a little one about bats. Whenever he was silent for too long, I looked back and saw his eyes looking at nothing, as if he were listening to it; so I told another story, or I remembered some wicked joke of Jekka's, or sang a skipping rhyme.

I taught him a goat holler from Ten Orchards. I sang a hoeing song of Bian's. I yelled all the taunts my cousins and I had ever heaped upon each other. Sometimes he smiled, or warmed his feet, while I squealed, on my thighs.

But there are gaps you cannot fill with talk, and spaces between stories. In them I had to let him go, to drift toward that other place; and it seemed the closer we came to the mainland, the less he spoke.

At first I was terrified and chattered faster. Yet his paddle still bit the water in its rhythm, and sometimes I could trust that. Then we were both quiet, hearing only the hiss of wind and the *chiss, chuck* of the paddle blades.

"Nall."

"Eh."

"What do you want most in the world?"

Chiss, chiss, chuck.

"To shave," he said.

Chiss, Chuck. Men are strange.

"Kat. What do you want?"

I want my brother, whom I never loved enough when I had him. I want peace. Home. Children. You to be the man I called, happy the way you were before so that I can be happy, so that I can love and possess and be safe in you forever and ever.

Chiss, chiss, chuck. I said, "Hot corn bread with butter and honey."

He caught the back of my shift, he rose on his knees and twisted me back and kissed me all stubbly until my mouth burned. The wind blew us sideways. "Damn," he said, sat down, and took up the stroke.

We flew on and on. I thought, Where is the shore of nothing? Do I stand there? What is it I gather, and braid, and tie with the knot that does not slip, and throw into nothing for this man to catch—if he wants it?

Is it myself I throw?

I did not think my rope of songs and stories was greater than death. It did not need to be. Songs are like butter and honey—they are for when you are alive.

28

The ruddy peach, love,
Cold frost shall wither,
The cherry's cheek, love,
Be dust forever.

The mountain's sides, love,
Shall valleys fill;
Though it beat quick, love,
Your heart shall still.

From a Fiddle Tune. Downshore.

ONE BY ONE we raised the skerries out of the eastern sea. The sun went down behind us, night rose before us, and the stars came out, winking one and two and countless. They were clear to follow. We flew over the dark water all night or all my life, a thousand lives, under the dome of stars.

Dawn came pink and tender in the east. We worked in

trance until a moment when, between stroke and stroke, we had to rest or die.

We had raised my shining island. How tiny it was! The body of the clerk was gone, already become eagle or fish. We drew up the manat for an hour, no more; we dragged ourselves to the circle of grass where I had wanted to make love to this man with dark smudges under his eyes who fell asleep with bread in his hand, who whined in his sleep like a dog and woke out of nightmare with a shout.

"What!" I said, waking too.

"Nothing. It's nothing."

We struck eastward and sank that island in the sea. From the front hatch of the manat I watched the mainland rise.

First I saw the circle of the world, all water as it had been, and pillowy white clouds. Then distant sea cliffs drawing a pale, broken line that sank and rose as though it were the cliffs that moved, not we. Then bluey foothills. I picked out the prominence that was Horn Loft. On shore it seemed so high, but from the sea it was just a bump on the long line of cliffs and hills, all obscured with a haze like smoke.

Then I saw it *was* smoke.

Nall stopped paddling. We caught a faint tang of burning. Along the line of cliffs a dozen pale threads were combed up, leaning south a little, tangling their ends into the haze that smudged the Loft.

"What are they burning?" I said.

"They are being burned."

"Have the Rigi—"

"No. Ab Harlan."

At the sound of his voice, more than the words, I knew what I was seeing: a white-hot poker laid along the thigh of the land. From the lift of the swell I could see, at the base of every thread, a tiny dot of flame.

I rose to my knees. Behind me Nall's paddle said *chiss, chiss* quicker.

I had never before come to Downshore from the deep sea. It took me a moment to recognize the gray stone town, the smoking docks, the beach south of it with tiny people on it—and the flames.

"Nall. *Nall!*"

"Oh, heart, be steady."

For one flame was Mailin's house.

The white-gray smoke swelled and streamed, the orange flames were almost dark in the bright midday. A fat billow rose up as something collapsed—walls, or the long veranda—and the base of the column of smoke no longer had the square shape of a house, but only fire.

Nall said, "While I listened at the Gate."

Chiss, chiss.

"We," I said. "*We.*"

I shook. I could not paddle. Then I stopped shaking. Still far out, we turned broadside to the shore because the men running on the sand were not bright-shirted but dark, like beetles.

I did not dare think, or ask, or listen. Then I knew that if I did not do those things, I would float offshore until the manat sank, and I became the sea.

I took a vow then for always: *I will think, and I will ask, and I will listen.* I spoke the worst first. "Have they killed them? Mailin and Rosie and him," for I was too distraught to remember Nondany's name, only his hand held out.

"Maybe."

"Or captured them?"

"Or run them back into town. There's no smoke from town."

We had not yet been out four days. I felt like a mother who takes her eyes off her child for an instant only, and when she looks up, he is gone.

Chiss, chuck.

I spoke over my shoulder. "Where to?"

"Horn Loft."

We angled south. The water turned from blue to green. High on the cliff I could see my father's house, the color of a grazing sheep. As we paddled closer a wind held us off; it brushed up the nap of the waves and pressed bolsters of smoke onto the water. We coughed. We began to see floating trash, broken barrels, a crate with a hen perched on it sailing out to sea.

The foot of Horn Loft was a ridge of bare rock, the harbor's south breakwater. We drew the manat in as close as we dared, like a mallard hugging the shore. We were hidden from town, but neither could we see it, only billows of smoke.

"Hold it there." Nall vanished overside. Then he was leaping up the rocks of the breakwater, streaming like an otter. At the ridgetop he peered through gaps in the smoke, then leaped down again and into the water. He hung from the prow by one hand, making the manat dip a little.

"They are besieged," he said. "Alleyways barricaded with felled trees and broken chairs, paidmen running or standing— two hundred, maybe. None within bowshot of any window, so there must be archers within, not yet out of arrows." He blew water off his lips. "Kat, I know a way into town. I may win through, or I may die. Do you come with me, or no? From here you can paddle south, past the sea marsh—"

"I'm coming." I thought again of the winged child in the fire, and laughed aloud.

He stared up at me, all spangled with seawater. "So be it," he said. He hove himself into the rear hatch. We paddled to the north end of the breakwater; beyond it we would be visible from the docks. He climbed out onto the rocks and motioned me to get out also.

I could see for myself, in glimpses, that the hodgepodge gray stone town had been made an impromptu fortress. The walls that turned the winds now turned the spears and black arrows of the paidmen who tramped round them, keeping a no-man's-land one bowshot wide. They looked like ants. Like the Rigi.

They had burned the wharves, or tried to. The pilings stood, but the boat sheds were gone and the heavy decking of the piers smoldered. So did the hulks of boats torched to the waterline and set adrift. The little harbor was a midden of deliberate ruin: drifting hulls, smashed carts and wagon wheels, a child's hobbyhorse, a dead sheep—the world made garbage.

"Let us be ruin too," said Nall. "Dead already." He stored the paddles and rolled the manat to float belly-up. Bouyed by the air bladders, its hull looked like a dead porpoise adrift in the trash. "Duck under, Kat."

It was like being inside a dindarion. The oiled skin dome glowed amber, echoed with water noise. I held on to the coaming, my feet hung down over the deep. Behind me Nall said, "We can move a little, kicking. But not fast. We are flotsam. Here and there we drift."

We kicked, drifted, edged. The waves were long and low, and once we were inside the breakwater they stilled. Nall ducked in and out, rose like a seal to spy, slid back. Debris brushed the hull. A broken tree limb snagged my ankle; a bed weirdly vertical in the water thumped us like a horse. The stripped body of a man nudged the prow, his dangling arms seeming to embrace the sea.

Hidden behind half-swamped dory or reeking hulk, we tipped the manat for new air, then became a dead seal again. We worked our way toward the smoldering wharves until we were under them, adrift among the slimy pilings.

The prow bumped rock. Seaweed undulated, fading into the dark below. Nall ducked out, ducked back. "Come."

The ledgy rock on which the piers were built was jagged with barnacles; I cut my shins and never noticed as I dog-paddled from the manat to the stone. There I clung among the weeds, the sea still covering my mouth. Above us here and there the decking had been burned away, but most of the planks were so thick and wet that they had borne the fire. The cracks between them cast on the oily surge a warp of sunlight that blinked with moving shadows, and the water echoes under the pier were broken by angry South Road Plain. "—wish to shit I was home fishing the Coora, not burning kids and damned witches in this—"

I turned my eyes to Nall. He was sunk in the water like a frog, little more than his eyes showing. Those eyes looked upward, not at the paidmen, but at a black hole among the rocks, square and so ruinous that I thought the sea had made it.

His hand met mine underwater and put the bow line in it. Slow as a hunting snake, he eased out of the sea. When a shadow passed above, he paused, then moved again. He disappeared into the rocky hole, the knife in his hand.

I clung to the seaweed. The water plucked and tugged, the manat tried to pull me away. Many breaths. Then Nall's face in the black rift, his hand saying, *Come.*

I raised my hand with the bowline: *What do?*

He opened his hand: *Let go.*

I let go. The line sank away. The overturned manat drifted, its prow turning dreamily back to sea. I crept up into the smoky air, taking weight on my feet as the water gave me up. The Bear's foot upon the mountain.

The tunnel stank of drains and fear. I could not stand straight; each step was slippery. The smoky reek of day turned to dank underground night, not sewage, but slime and lightless moss.

Nall went quickly, but I had to run my hands along the stone so as not to fall. Under my fingers I felt, all dressed in algae, the links and whorls of Hsuu's face.

"Nall." He splashed back to me, let me guide his hand. The spirals trailed away down the dim corridor. I said, "The walls of Selí!"

"Of Tanshari. Buried deep. Once a lineage house, now a drain."

"No, it's a root." The alleys and walls of Downshore had sprung out of the ancient warrenhouse in a tangle, looking for light like vines. The turns and doublings, the round chambers and worn lintels were abandoned and wet. I could see that Nall had come and gone by this road many times. I had a thought, that he had been a person in Downshore while I was a person in Creek; yet that made me uneasy, as though it could not be real.

From where we crouched two curving halls branched out.

The end of each hall branched in turn, then branched again, these thresholds visible as faint lines. The air teemed with sounds of shadowy life: scrapes and thumps, muffled speech, the thin wail of a child.

My hair pricked up. "Ghosts!" I said.

"No. The living. The old warrenhouse is a sound box for the town above."

I felt as though I were inside the body of a being. Then I was afraid. Some sounds separated from the rest and grew clearer, then clear: hoarse male voices, splashing feet. In the forgotten arem of Tanshari a red light bloomed like false dawn.

Nall grabbed me backward, down a corridor, around a corner pierced with broken stone tracery. Through this we watched the spirals on the walls grow ruddy, smelled the incense of pitch, and heard, as on the burned docks, a growl. "—split his stinking heart. Kill enough to—"

Paidmen. Worms at the root. But Nall leaned forward and called through the tracery, "Mec. *Mec.*"

Splashes, grunts. Silence. The tunnel went fiery with a torch. Beyond it eyes and teeth glittered in faces as drawn as demons', a huddle of men stripped to their breechclouts and carrying boatbuilders' tools: knives, chisels, slicks.

Nall leaned into the light.

A gasp. They jostled back, the torchbearer making a sign in the air.

Nall stepped clear. "Mec," he said to the glaring leader. "Mec, I am no ghost."

Smoke filled the tunnel. I coughed. They cringed back. Nall held out his hand; I took it and crouched out to join him.

"The witch! It's the witch!" Mec raised his knife.

Nall pulled me behind him. "Who calls her witch?"

"The devil does," said Mec. "*Is* it you, man? Where've you been? Mailin said you went—"

"To the Gate," said Nall.

They were silent, staring. The hall grew smokier. Mec said, "She said that. But the living don't go there. Where did you go?"

"To the Gate."

"Hunh." Disbelief.

I could wait no longer. "What—what news of Dai?"

Mec's knife wavered. "None. Devil's still got him." Maybe he began to believe we were not ghosts; he looked away as though ashamed and said, "That raid we made, when you two ran a—when you left; we didn't get so far as the guard-house. They were on us like wolves."

"Where are you going now?" said Nall.

Mec looked at us again, his face still black with suspicion. But he said, "Out. To kill paidmen. They've stopped our eyes and mouth, but"—he gestured down the way we had come—"they forgot the asshole."

Grim laughter. The men let their weapons drop a little, rubbed their faces.

I said, "We saw Mailin's house—"

"She's above in the plaza, tending the wounded."

"And Pao? And Nondany?"

"Above. Harlan's burning the field from the verge inward, driving his rabbits into the net."

"He says he can burn what he owns," said a boy, maybe twelve. He held a long knife newly honed. "I'm going to cut out his tongue."

"We're ship's rats to him," said Mec. "It's you he wants, Lali Kat."

I leaned closer to Nall.

"'Give me the witch!' he cries. They bring him down in his chair, there beyond the alley mouth; he has a speaking-trumpet. 'You've taken my boy, my precious child,'" said Mec in an unctuous whisper. "'My baby, my dearest son. Yet I'll forgive you if you bring me the witch girl. Bring me the witch! I'll forgive your murders and call off my hounds.'" He spat in the water at his feet. "Doesn't much want the son back, it seems. Good thing, for he's gone, and my brother and his crew with him. It's you he wants."

"You told him I'd gone?"

"Why would he believe us, Lali Kat?"

To be *lali* again, a sister, made me cry. At that the men crowded round; the smoke got thick. "Fighting, fighting since you left," said Mec. "Some of the festival folk won free, but plenty came on into town, for the hills and roads are full of his creatures, raping, burning. Where does that devil get gold to hire so many? Folk have come in from the steadings—he's burning them one by one. We watch from the rooftops. Yesterday they burned the boats. They've closed the way to the river. There are wounded and dying in the plaza, the wells are near dry and we can't get water."

You shall have water soon enough, I thought. You shall have *kas*—too much sea.

"In the name of day," said Mec, "where *did* you go?"

"To the Gate," we said together.

A change came in his face. "Then something will happen," he said. "Good or ill, so be it, only that it come." He gestured back up the tunnel. "To Mailin, then? And may I live to hear your story, that's all."

The men turned from their killing mission to lead us up the tunnel. The lad with the knife came reluctantly, looking back.

Here and there light fell from a high grate, greening the slime that furred the walls. I saw the worn remains of stone shelves and cupboards like those in the ama's quiet room. We came to the bottom of a shallow shaft where steps went up and light fell down. In the wall was the Year Altar, a split stone niche, nothing in it but a green weed looking upward at the light.

We looked up too, heard voices and children's crying. It was the children, peering, chattering about the armed men they had just watched go down the hole, who saw us climb out of it. Like sky beings around a window in the clouds they stared down, they shrieked, "The witch! Mailin's witch!" and ran for their elders, who ran and shrieked with deeper voices as we clambered over the threshold of buried Tanshari, into the plaza of Downshore besieged.

I had known that plaza since I was old enough to go to market, scuttling furtively in kerchief and cloak. Now, as I climbed out of the dark in my filthy undershift, I could see how the square had begun as the open-air courtyard of a warrenhouse.

Once cookfires and looms had been busy there while children played, women ground barley in stone querns, men mended nets. But now the square was refuge for frightened families harried from outlying farms, Hill and River and Lake folk driven from the festival fields, Roadsouls in painted wagons—all camped almost waterless in the midday sun.

It was festival in reverse. The striped awnings that should have sheltered the pie stands shaded tight-faced men with bandaged thighs; girls who should have been flirting sat stunned and dull, fingering their torn bodices. Children wailed and clung to their fierce mothers. And an old man who should have been hawking turkeys and grumbling about watered rum was not there at all.

Smoke hazed the square. The sunlight fell straight down and cast no shadow.

As we stepped into the terrible light, a cry went up, and the crowd scrambled away shouting. But when nothing happened—neither curse nor miracle—they rushed forward again in a roar of voices. They pressed, gabbled, turned in a slow dance with us as its center. It was broad day, the people spoke Plain and wore colored shirts, yet they milled, stared, groped like the Rigi. Like the Rigi, they seemed to be in a dream, but it was a nightmare.

Mec led us among them. Like the Rigi, they touched us. Though Nall was naked except for the knife belt, it was his turn to put me behind him. I fixed my eyes on the blue spiral on his back as the word "Witch! Witch!" hissed around us like fire in dry grass.

But mingled with that word were others. We had been their doom; yet their hands caressed. "Lali Kat," they murmured. Young voices called as if to a comrade: "Nall! Nall!"

Then Pao was there, too big to shoulder aside, and Mailin running behind him with a face so glad and so unhappy that I broke away and embraced her as she wept. Then Nall's arms were around her too, so that she was between us, as if she were our child.

"This way," said Pao. The crowd pressed but did not snatch. Their eyes looked inward. I remembered their watchfulness on the beach that first night and thought, They expected this. If not this, then *something*; they knew the balance was wrong, that they must pay.

I wondered how folk prayed, in this place.

They stared at my scars. I clung close to Mailin. Near the north colonnade was a Roadsoul cart with tattered canopies; a brazier cast up heat ripples above a dinted copper pot in which a little water boiled. Round it, over cobbles speckled with blood, women moved among the damaged, wrapping wounds and giving what comfort they could. Robin was one of them, big-bodied and slow.

I could not look at her. I looked away, and saw a boy with no feet.

He had been born with feet, of course. Now he had none, just bandages torn from somebody's green-checked shirt, oozing pinkish yellow. His legs were eerie to look at, nothing on the ends of them. He was the age of the lad in the tunnel, twelve or thirteen, and motionless on a blanket—a Downshore lad by his dress, but it was a Roadsoul woman in blue silks who fanned his face.

The crowd must have been warned away from the wounded, for they milled beyond an invisible line with their big-eyed thirsty children, their bloodied faces watching, us silent as stars. In the shade under the cart two dirty little Roadsoul girls played hand slaps as if this were an ordinary summer's noon.

I said, "Nondany?"

"In the hall under the east colonnade." Mailin pointed. "The worst wounded are there—it's cooler."

"Wounded?"

"His hands are burned. Badly enough."

"Was he saving his papers?"

"Papers? No! He dragged an old woman burning from her tent on the festival grounds; the paidmen came at night, they threw oil and lit it. She died, thank goodness." Mailin looked from me to Nall. Tears stood in her eyes. She said, "I did not think to see you again."

"May we meet with you alone?" said Nall. "Now?"

He spoke in an undertone. The Roadsoul girls under the cart pricked up their ears like puppies. Mailin threw them a sharp look and said to Pao and the rest, "Wait on us one moment."

She led us away from the chaos and stares. Back under another bit of canvas she sat down on a crate as though she were too weary to stand. She looked this way, that way. "Now," she said.

Nall knelt and put his mouth to her cheek beside her ear, as though to kiss it.

"The Rigi are coming," he said. "If the wave that has gathered breaks—and it must break—they will be here this night, to kill us any way they can, and take Downshore again for their own."

A tidal wave is coming. A forest fire is coming. Death is coming—what will you do? Mailin sat still, her head a little inclined to catch Nall's whisper. A shiver went over her.

"Well," she said. "It seems they will find us right here."

Nall leaned back.

"Kat?" said Mailin.

I started. I had been looking at Nall's face, feeling the strangeness that I had felt since I put my foot again on solid earth. What was he feeling? If the world was nothing, did this matter to him?

"They're coming in manats," I said. "Hundreds. We saw them."

Mailin slumped a little. "My great-grandfather had a manat," she said. I had forgotten she was Rig kin; surely she knew we stood on a buried warrenhouse. "Is it in pursuit of you two they come?"

Nall shook his head. "We fell into the middle of it. We could do nothing."

You killed the Reirig! But he had only killed a man. The Reirig still lived, only now perhaps his face was Hsuu's.

"But—you won through to the Gate?" said Mailin. "You listened?"

He nodded.

She looked wary and puzzled, like a woman whose son has come home from war a stranger. "What did you hear?"

He let his silence say it. That silence grew long.

When still he did not speak, Mailin put her hand on his chest, next to the gash made by the Reirig's lance. "There is no one in this life I trust more than I trust you," she said.

A shadow crossed his face. He did not speak.

She did not press him further. She turned back to the plaza and said, "So, then. For every birth, a death. For Long Night, Least Night. The elders run up the debt, the children pay. How shall I tell this to my friends, who are already half dead with grief?"

I had drawn a breath, hearing the ama's words in Mailin's mouth. I said, "I'll go to Ab Harlan. It's me he wants."

I felt Nall flinch. Mailin looked at me, and for the first time since I had known her I saw her angry. "It's not your debt, but ours."

"I'm one of you," I said. Then I thought, What if I am choosing not just for myself, but for a child?

Mailin took my hand. "For your generous heart we will thank you all our lives, however long those may be. But Ab Harlan isn't healthy like a beast, that he can be satisfied. We could gorge his maw with witches until the seas dried, and he would still lust."

I knew this. Not just of Ab Harlan, but of the League: profits never high enough, kitchens clean enough, children good enough. The swarming, untidy world was not manageable enough, nor would be until it was dead—until they had killed it.

I thought of the obsidian cone of water sucking out through the Gate. With every tide it reversed, poured back, and so made balance; but Harlan was a gate that sucked one way only, a mouth without a stomach. I felt awe, and pity.

Mailin had begun to rise like an old woman, using my hand to help. I said, "The Rigi have Ab Harlan's son," and she sank down again onto the crate, openmouthed. "It's Queelic, the boy I was to marry. He's dead by now, most like." I told part of the tale, adding that poison to the wicked stew.

But Mailin said, "Ab Harlan's son in the Rigi's land? Oh, my children! Say what you will, something is changing." She straightened her shoulders. "We'll call the council. Pao!"

I said, "May I see Nondany?"

"Robin will take you. Robin!" And before I could protest, Robin was there, holding out her hand.

"To Nondany," said Mailin. "We'll send for you all as soon as may be. Nall, help me."

He turned to go with her. I had a strange feeling, as if he

might vanish. I caught his hand and said, "I'll come right back."

His hand was firm, with scabs on the knuckles. He nodded. Robin tugged me toward the colonnade.

I looked back. He was still there. The shrines on the Isle of Bones had moved only when I was not looking at them; I felt that if I were not looking at him, Nall would not be there at all.

Behind us the Roadsoul girls, squatting in the wagon's narrow shade, were counting out.

Icey, dicey,
Tricey, fusty,
Nasty, hasty,
Pusty, pee.
Whinery, shinery,
All in her finery,
Eightery, ninery,
Out goes she.

29

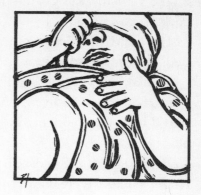

Dancers! Dancers!
We must have many dancers,
Or the seals will forget who they are!
Dancers, robe well.
Pull the shell necklace over the head,
Pull the coral bead
To rest in the very center of the heart.

From Least Night Dance Chant. Downshore.

IT WAS NOT FAR, but it seemed far. I was afraid of the crowd, of the whispered "Witch!" and the hands that touched me. What was to prevent some terrified soul from throwing me to Ab Harlan like a bone to a dog? Yet Mailin had not seemed to think that a danger.

I could not look at Robin's face, but her belly was so big

that I had to think of Dai's baby there, swimming unknowing under the bump of her navel.

She was saying, "If it's a girl, she'll be Lisei, for your mother. We don't—we didn't have a boy's name yet. But maybe Nall." She squeezed my hand. "Nondany's in here."

The hall had a stone door, with a blue blanket hung over it to block the heat. The lintel was carved in spirals, scavenged from the arem. I was afraid the crowd would follow us in over the threshold, but we entered the darkness alone.

In Creek I had stepped from brilliant day into the dim of Raím's bothy and felt, until my eyes got used to it, that I was as blind as he. I felt so now. But I could hear.

The suffering was not loud. No shrieks, only incessant, irregular moans, mutters, sighs. Somewhere in the dark a child wept on and on, a tiny, puling, exhausted wail.

Toward that sound Robin led me. By the time we got to its source I had better eyes for dark and could see a child of three or so, the upper half of its face wrapped in leaking rags. Nondany sat next to it, patting it, as it twisted to get away from the pain it could not get away from. He patted with the back of his hand, also wrapped in rags. In a cracked drone, as though he had sung all night, he stared into the dark blur of the world and sang.

> Loolee, loolee, you're my pigalee,
> You'll be bonnie when you grow bigalee.

I knelt and put my arms around him. He started, then embraced me without hands. "Half-and-Half!" The hair was burned off most of his head, his eyebrows and eyelashes too, making him look expressionless, like a fish. "My singer, my weaver!"

I'm not the singer, I thought. That's Nall. And the weaver is Raím.

"Are you all right?" I asked. Stupidly, for he burned with fever.

"Passable. Nall?"

"He's with Mailin."

The child writhed like a maggot. In a fierce, weak voice it cried, "Pigalee!"

Nondany began again to pat it. "He's clinging to the song. He will live because of the song you brought me. See the great gift you have given!" He stank with the sweat of pain. "Your journey?" he said.

The wrong end of the bear. *Kas*, death, nothing. "I've brought you some songs," I said.

He beamed.

"Pigalee!" said the child.

"Later you'll sing them for me." He licked dry lips and began, "Loolee, loolee . . ."

"Go get a drink. Rest. I'll sing."

I nudged him over and took up the song as I had taken up the stroke in the manat. Nondany gathered himself. I whispered between verses, "Where is the little one's mother? Are his eyes all right?" and was not surprised to see Nondany's mouth make, soundlessly, the words "dead; blind." I wondered what had become of the dindarion and his papers—if they were burned, or only half burned like the child.

He got to his feet by stages, Robin helping. As at Fenno Pass he said, "Would I were seventeen!"

I thought, You've forgotten what it's like to be seventeen.

Robin followed him to the door. There she dipped a little water from a bucket and held it to his mouth. He looked toward me, then shuffled out under the blanket into the day, leaning on the wall with one elbow.

Robin came back. "I sent him to Mailin, for the council. We should go too."

"But the boy must have the song. You're my pigalee . . ."

"I'll find somebody to sing." She ducked out into the light.

I patted the boy and sang. The blanket at the door shook, and two men carried in the footless boy by the corners of a pallet. In the blink of daylight I saw on another blanket Rosh the fisherman, one-legged now. The next blink brought Suni; she made her way through the wounded, her baby on her hip and Rosie by one fist.

"Here's your auntie Kat," she said.

I hugged Rosie's bunchy body. "Suni, it shouldn't be you! Not in here, with the children."

"It's the same in here as out there, only cooler." She settled by the whimpering child, her baby on her lap. Rosie leaned on me, quiet for once, three fingers in her mouth. Suni said, "Rose, we're to sing a song for this laddie. Auntie Kat's song."

Rosie took her fingers out and said, "Pigalee."

"That's the one." Suni began to pat the boy. She looked up at me, dark-eyed in the dark. "You went to the world's end with him, they said."

"Yes."

I thought she would ask, *What was it like? Tell me the story!* But she said only, "It's burning so big, Lali Kat. Surely the green grass must come springing."

Rosie sat down. "Pigalee for the lad," she said.

I left them to it. It could not be right that the world was

nothing. I could feel every one of the somethings, so many that they were cracking the gates of my heart.

The crowd at the door was daunting. Suni had bid me wait there, saying Robin would come for me; instead the one who came was a gaunt stevedore in a torn breechclout, dirty burlap folded over his shoulder. It was only by his eyes that I knew him—Nall, all black with charcoal.

"We shifted a burned beam," he said, throwing the burlap aside. "The paidmen fired lit arrows."

See? I thought. He hasn't disappeared. Yet I could not shake the feeling. I made myself look at the common dirt on him, the scars.

"Harlan is at the gate," he said.

"The Gate!"

"The town's east gate. There beyond the alley mouth."

I began to sweat. "Can he be seen?"

"They say so." His eyelids were smirched with black; it made his eyes look pale. He was thin as the last of the moon. "The council is near gathered."

"I want to see Harlan."

We pushed through the throng. They made way for us, as if they knew where we were going. A woman in a flowered blouse said, "Don't go out to him, Lali Kat!"

Murmurs of assent. "He'll drink you up!" "He's the devil!" "Lali, he'll eat you and then eat us, too!"

I started to cry. "We're not going anywhere," I said. "We're here."

"Ain't we all," said a rueful voice. A muttered laugh went up. The parting bodies showed us a crooked stairway that led up behind chimneys to a crowded lookout, where the watchers, seeing who we were, edged back and made room.

There was a pretty view of summer fields, hedges, dry-stone walls. Wraiths of smoke rose from the burned farm-steads. On the road, a bowshot east of us, a clot of men milled around a black sedan chair.

I knew that chair. I had seen it every week at the Rulesward. I hardly needed to look now, but I did.

The small door was thrown back. The gold-headed cane was thrust out. The plump, puddingy body struggled after it, head darting as the man glared about. As I watched Ab Harlan climb out of the black sedan chair, all I could think of was a little boy crawling out of the box his father had locked him in. And Queelic; I thought of Queelic.

Ab Harlan was a blot, white-faced. His paidmen straight-ened his cape, brought him a black speaking-trumpet. I watched his heavy body tense, heard his reedy words in Trader's Plain, which sounds like breaking glass.

"Give—her—to—me." Tiny words in the wide, smoky day. "I will make your life easy. Give me the witch, and I will smooth all your roads."

"He'll smooth our necks," said a voice in the crowd behind us.

Another said, "We sold ourselves. To that."

Ab Harlan said nothing about his precious, his irreclaimable son. Perhaps he had tired of that tack. The thin cry, smaller than a marsh bird's, wearied of cajoling.

"I'll press the iron to you! Live mute as beasts, die mute! Beware the dusk!" and many more such things, taunting like my boy-cousins. I wondered how old he had been, in that box. Now he was grown—and rich enough to make a six-year-old's revenge real with pike and fire.

His tiny pale face had gone red. As in the guardhouse, he cried at last, "I shall purge myself of you!" He threw away the trumpet and turned to reenter the chair, but he paused there with his back to us, bent over, shaking with rage, vomiting.

I shrank from my own skin. I watched him climb back into his box, be lifted and trundled back up the road.

Around us people sobbed. "'Beware the dusk!' he says. Oh, life, what will he do? Lali Kat, you see that he's mad? He'll make us pay the balance in blood!" I thought, but did not say, What you don't know yet is that you must pay the balance two ways.

Half carried by the crowd, we ran back down to the street. The word "council" flew from mouth to mouth. The sun had sunk westward; the colonnades cast bars of shadow on the yellow walls. Nall made a way for us through the pushing hands. A tribe of little boys followed us because we were something about to happen at last.

The Downshore council room was a street inn. Awnings shaded its sidewalk tables, but we passed under them into the greater privacy of a kitchen that smelled of garlic and stale beer. A table had been carried in from outside and chairs and crates dragged from here and there by sweating, white-faced people.

League councils are all men. They have a saying: *Women and devils speak only evils.* The Creek council is all women, and they say: *A man is a boy with a bigger stick.*

In the Downshore council there were men and women,

old and young, poor and prosperous; there were farmers and mothers and sailors and cooks, and for all I knew, there were hens and kittens, too. It seemed to me so mixed, bizarre, ragged, and chaotic that, being League-bred, I thought, It's a native mob.

Jostling for the makeshift chairs and leaning on the walls were Lake women and River men, lads from the canyons and the sand plains, Shorefolk of every clan, and even three shocked, angry women from Ledges, which is not far from Creek; I knew the style of their tattoos. There were plenty of tattoos in that room, and braids of every twist, earrings and nose rings and toe rings, and any color and cloth of summer costume you could think of, even a Roadsoul woman with full skirts and naked breasts. She gave me a bold, mocking glance, as if this world full of roads belonged to her.

There were fifty or sixty people, and everyone talking. They moaned, shouted, argued, wept. A baby screamed. In this tumult who could debate anything?

Mailin and Pao sat at the battered table. Nondany perched next to them on a tipped crate, eyes closed, leaning against the wall. Robin stood beside Pao; I could look at her now.

I followed Nall through the crowd. The shouters stopped shouting; their faces turned to us like sunflowers. We pushed to the front and squeezed in between Mailin and Nondany. The room began to be hot.

The lines from Mailin's nose to the corners of her mouth seemed carved by tears. She laid the flat of her hand on the table in front of her.

That was a soft sound, yet I heard it, because every voice had gone silent. Looking around, I saw that folk had had the gist of the news already.

"Neighbors," said Mailin. Every eye in that room was on her, and I knew without being told that this council had met every day since we had left, in spite of raids and rage and burning. They knew one another.

Mailin said, "Each part risks and gives to the whole, according to its calling. These two no less—Kat and Nall. What little I knew of their task you have heard already."

So that was why we had come home to a welcome, and why I had been safe in the throng. "Now hear it from them," said Mailin. She raised her hand from the table and held it out to us. "Be brief," she said.

The council muttered. They did not want us to be brief. They wanted the stories, all of them; they wanted to go on that journey with us, to see what we had seen and stand where our feet had stood, so they could say that the news we brought was not true. Nondany watched from half-closed eyes. It was so quiet that I heard, closer than the hubbub in the plaza, the chirp of a finch on the windowsill.

I tried to catch Nall's eye, to ask without words who should speak first. But he was speaking already.

"I went to listen at the Gate, where the world is coming to be," he said.

"The Gate," said whispers. The lost Gate, only a story now; the Gate where the living do not go.

"I went to hear whatever it was we needed to hear," he said. "That was my calling. Kat came with me, from love and courage—"

"It wasn't courage," I said.

"—but we fell into the hands of the Rigi. This was through my own weakness—"

"It was not! We were both—"

Mailin said, "Lali, let him speak."

I shut up. Nall said, "Among the Rigi we found a plan already laid. You are sick with Ab Harlan, but the Rigi are sick with exile—and resolved to end it. We found them poised like a toppling wave, warriors in their hundreds ready to pour east—to kill you, who are the seal-killers, and take Downshore for their own."

Brief enough. A murmur like a moan went round. "But you got away. Living, you came back—"

"I was rescued. The price for that being the lives of a girl and an old woman." One of his hands was a fist. "With the help of Kat, in her strength, I could return to tell you that if the invasion happens as it is planned, the horde follows us by not many hours. Most like it is my own father who leads it."

Movement in the crowd. Mec the boatbuilder said, "But did you listen at the Gate?"

"Yes."

"What did you hear?"

"Nothing," said Nall.

Nondany's eyes flew open.

Nall took a breath. "Everything—" Then stopped, shut his mouth, shook his head, stepped back. Finished.

Mailin looked grieved. Pao, astonished. The council groaned. I thought, That's all? That's all you have to say?

But Nondany pulled his shoulders away from the wall; the crate came down with a bang. In his clear voice he sang:

> If I must be pressed
> From east and west,
> May the wine wrung from me be good!
> Drink up, friends!

In the silence that followed, he said, "Drinking song. From Hearth Hill. Grape's point of view."

Folk began to weep and shout. Little groups fell into panicky argument, and the heat of the room went intolerable, laced with the stink of smoke, until I thought Harlan was burning us already.

"Storm the main road!" said a burly butcher. "They'll kill plenty of us, but we'll kill them, too, and the rest will win free."

"Surrender to him! He'd never—"

"But the man's mad!"

"Burn the town, and ourselves in it! I will not see my children in that devil's hands!"

The pitch of the quarrels grew higher. Once again Mailin laid the flat of her hand on the table.

This time the sound of it could not be heard. But it was seen. Those close to her fell silent; they hushed their neighbors, until in the end the silence itself was heard.

"Lali Kat," said Mailin, "it's your turn. Tell us what you know."

What I know? Had I not just spent four days finding out that everything I thought I knew was wrong?

My ignorance stood around me. Mailin, whom I had thought strong and eternal, looked defeated and old. Her haven home was ash. Dai was dead, or worse. The people of Downshore, whom I had thought hale and wise, were bloodthirsty, disorganized debtors who had sold themselves to a madman. And Nall, for whom I had deserted family and friends and lovers—who was he? Nothing, he said, and so was I.

The people looked at me, waiting. I hung my head. In a tiny voice I said, "I went with Nall because I didn't know what else to do. I abandoned you. I still don't know what to do. Except—"

I shuffled my feet. I had worn a hole right through the sole of my sandal, and I could feel the flagstone I stood on, still cool.

The Bear's foot upon the mountain. Upon the maze of habitation that lay under this town, carved in spirals like roots and tendrils climbing up to make the grove that was Downshore: a forest full of birds calling in many tongues, creatures crying in many tongues. With my ears which were the Bear's, which, like it or not, had listened at the Gate, I heard them all singing—a racket at first, then drawn into order by a rhythm like a heartbeat.

"Oh!" I said. My hands flew up, clapped once, twice. "The drum!"

Nondany let out a held breath.

I said, "I don't know anything—except that they're *people*. The Rigi. I thought they'd be monsters with claws. Even after I met Nall, and he didn't have claws."

Nobody laughed.

"There are great-grandmas there. And little girls, and babies. There are men with spears; they can kill you, but they're *men with spears*, they're not devils. They founded this town, they used to live here. They miss it, they're sick without it, their children are dying. The Rigi *named* Downshore. It was called Tanshari."

It went round in a whisper: *"Tanshari."* Of course they knew the name. There were old songs.

A huge impatience overcame me. Maybe it was impatience to find out what death was like, since life had been so different than anybody said. Or maybe it was trustfulness, like Nondany's, or just my rotten temper.

"You people of Downshore, you keep *saying* you were one with the Rigi once. Why don't you act like it? Get out your big drum, the Sun Drum. The Rigi have one too. When they hear yours, I mean ours, maybe they'll like it. Welcome them! If they kill us, at least we'll die singing.

"You have no idea how lucky you are!" I said to their worn, startled faces, Nall's among them. "You grew up *singing.* The Leaguemen are people too, same as the Rigi, but they're—*deaf* or something. Deaf in their hearts. I don't know what's the matter with them. I cannot tell you how *stupid* it is to grow up with nothing but jump-rope rhymes!"

Into the astonished hush I chanted, loud.

> Hinky-jink! You stink!
> Bring your father meat and drink!
> If you don't, he will beat you,
> And the Rigi roast and eat you!

Silence.

Then such a laugh filled the room—Nondany's, too big for his little body. He beat the table with both elbows, curled his tongue, whistled like a wrestler's mountebank, and shouted, "Half-and-Half!"

Only I knew what he meant. But Mailin's face softened. Pao's eyebrows went up. Old women nodded at one another.

My little courage trembled, and I said, "If Ab Harlan hears the drum, he'll be angry. It will make him fierce!"

"So it's time to be fierce," said a young man in a smith's apron. "Not with the swords we don't have, but fierce for life. I stand with Lali Kat. I'll die singing!"

"Though we die tonight," said a tall woman, "let's send the sun on its journey."

"If we are to dance once more only, why, let's dance our best," said a little tailor. He jumped onto the table and rapped out a step, *nack-a-nack-nock*, for he had clogs on. "Those Rigi—maybe they think we've forgotten Tanshari. That we've forgotten the songs and the Cauldron and the dances of the tribes. Let's show them we remember!" A shout went up. He cut another step. "Let's teach Ab Harlan to dance!"

"Dance, Harlan!" The council rumbled with laughter, dark and bright as coals. "We shan't abandon the sun. Though it be to the square and not the shore, call the clans and bring out the drum! The drum!"

There was no need for Mailin to lay her palm again on the table or to make a plan. Downshore knew how to celebrate Least Night, how to organize the dance called the Cauldron that lasts all the shortest summer night. Indeed, they had been almost ready when this trouble began. Folk turned toward the door, springing to the tasks they knew.

At the threshold they stopped, for a girl had put her arm across it. She looked fifteen, the age I had been when I found Nall on that winter beach. She had curly hair and freckles; she looked like me as I might have been and spoke as boldly as I might have spoken then, if I had not been born my father's daughter.

"Downshore is burning," she said. "Let's throw it in the Year Fire! That name and time is done. Our name is Tanshari now."

"Tanshari! Tanshari!" flew back and forth across the room. With no more words the council pushed out through the inn, back into the plaza, where the shadows were lengthening.

The young smith kissed the freckled girl and swung her to his shoulder. She clutched his hair as he ran, both of them laughing as if days, lives, worlds had no end.

The last one out was the bare-breasted Roadsoul. She raised her empty palm and gave me a secret, sidelong smile.

30

These sounds will outlast us:
water striking earth;
the feet of moths on blossoms;
the feet of birds on wet stone—
cold, quick, small.

Pennywhistle Music. Tanshari.

MAILIN, PAO, AND ROBIN all knew what to do for Least Night. It had been half done for weeks. I did not know how to look at Nall, as if by offering my own plan I had voiced my doubts about him in public. I looked at his feet. I wished I were that other girl, so easy with her smith.

"Lali, take care," said Pao. "This is a kind of madness."

Nondany's eyes were closed. When I touched him, he

jumped and said, "The sensation of burning—one can't look straight into it. Well. I ought to help with the drum, but I must go back to my little lad."

He rose with difficulty, holding his hands close to his chest. Nall moved then; without a word he and I left the others and walked ahead of Nondany, making a barrier of our bodies, fending off the jostling arms as we nudged along the plaza to the blue curtain that hid the wounded.

We should have gone straight in to Suni, but we stopped on the threshold and looked back at the square, in awe of what was begun. The chaos was too great for talk. Nall backed against the wall, on his face the drowning look it had worn among the Rigi.

They were bringing out the drum. I wondered where they kept it, it was so big: round as the moon, broad as a whale, dark with smoke. It rolled on its side, a ponderous wheel with hundreds of hands to help it on. I was afraid the children would be crushed, but they scattered out from under it like mice.

When they had trundled it to the center of the plaza, the hands tipped it on its side. It fell almost lightly, striking the flagstones with a boom that echoed off the stone walls. An old man carried four long drumsticks. The two drummers took their places: the girl and her smith. They limbered their backs, looked at each other, and raised the drumsticks.

A palm was laid on the drum rim; Mailin's, of course. The crowd went almost quiet.

She lifted her hand, and the sticks came down.

In the closed canyon of the square the sound was enormous; it stopped everything but itself. The stark, sweating faces of the crowd froze, and Nall, at the first stroke, covered his ears.

I thought, Tell me *that's* nothing!

Then the people swarmed and shouted. Booths, bundles, carts were hauled back to clear a dancing space. Standards and masks appeared from closets where they had been guarded and mended all year; there were quarrels over who would carry them. Folk were in haste to dance, driven to dance as though the dance would save them—from the Rigi, from Ab Harlan, maybe from themselves.

Boom. Boom. The wind would carry that beat to the paid-men who waited beyond the no-man's-land with torches and dirks. I wondered whether any of them had been pressed from little towns that danced the solstices with a Sun Drum. In my father's house high on the cliffs, each summer and winter, I had heard that deep beat. Ab Harlan would be hearing it now, in his grand mansion.

Fiddles were brought out, and cymbals and flutes. An inner circle of dancers began to move clockwise round the drum, an outer circle counterclockwise. The plaza was already half in shadow.

I had danced one Long Night, Nall must have danced many, yet neither of us moved from the doorway. At Long Night the faces had been merry and open, sometimes drunken; now they were frightened. But as the beat went on and on, calling the people into trance, that fear was washed away by sadness, or longing, or only depth. The world went simple, as the beat divided it into two things: sound, no sound.

"Here," I said aloud. "And not."

Nobody heard me. The thunder was too great. Nall's face was rigid. I guessed that he was back in his nightmare at that other drum, and I did not know what to do for him. I did not see how the wounded could bear the terrible noise.

I pulled his head down and spoke into his ear. "Too loud for Nondany." He nodded and followed me in under the curtain. His limp was worse.

In that close darkness the sound was a horror. Some of the watchers had already carried away their wounded; Rosh was gone, and the footless boy was a corpse, uncovered and alone.

"Pigalee . . . ," sang Nondany. Rosie jumped and shouted, her hands over her ears. Suni ran to us, her baby screaming.

"Thank goodness, Lali Kat! I can't carry all of them, and Nondany's not fit—such a racket! He wants to take the laddie to Lilliena's house, quiet at least, and it has a window to the sea. He wants to see them come."

"He told you, then."

She hefted her shrieking son. As Nall helped Nondany to his feet, she nodded at them and said to me, "Remember when you found Nall? When you brought him to us here in Downshore, and we were dancing? I told you then, a Rig brings luck or storms. You can't choose. Get you to Lilliena's, and I'll dress my two for the dance. We're Badger clan, like Nondany."

The stone room quivered with sound. "Quite a beat," Nondany shouted. "Glory. Yet I think I prefer smaller music." Nall gathered up the boy so deftly that he only whimpered and kicked one foot.

We went out into the plaza. We could not enter it, for the crush in the open was too dense to cross; we edged around it, keeping to the colonnades. There all life wept, it howled in the dance, it screamed in rage and despair and love.

I thought, I have been here before, but in a dream.

I tried to shield Nondany with my body, saw Nall hunched

head down, one hand spread over the child's face to ward off careless knocks. It was I who had said *Dance!* yet I never hated humans so much as I did on that endless, jarring journey sunwise around the plaza that had been Downshore's, as it became again Tanshari's.

We gained the west side and stumbled down an alley. The crowd thinned, becoming mostly children.

I could call them that because they were younger than I, but wild with the drum and too big to be controlled by adult threats. They knew Nondany and came thronging, girls and boys. They knew Nall.

Prancing backward in front of us, they said, "Are you going to Nondany's eyrie? Will you watch there for the Rigi?" They reminded me of hedgehogs, which in the Hills are called urchins: prickly, suspicious, full of life. "Those old people have to dance, but we're going to see the Rigi come!"

Nondany tipped back his head to peer at them, for they were taller than he. "If the Rigi are singing when they come—"

"We'll listen! We'll remember for you!" A big-eyed girl with a gold ring in her nose ran alongside Nall, saying to him, "And *we'll* sing for *them*. We'll sing that song you taught us. My father's clan is Seal, but my mother's an Otter. Can they tell? Will they kill me?"

"I don't know," he said.

At the west end of the alley a blockade had been flung up: hay bales, driftwood, smashed chairs. Next to it a shop's tiny window displayed crockery and tin spoons.

"My sister's shop," said Nondany.

The door was locked. He had the key. I turned it and forced the stiff bolt, the urchins shoving and telling me how.

"Lilliena's in the plaza with her little dog," they said. "She's telling Otter clan the right way to carry their standard and showing Badger clan how to dance. So she's not here."

"Life is merciful," said Nondany.

The urchins wanted to come in with us. More had gathered, as though they had a signal network. But Nondany said, "Leave us to be old, eh?"

"*He's* not old," said the girl with the ring, pointing to the child in Nall's arms.

"Ah, but he's wise," said Nondany. "Get along now, loves. Be joyful."

"All right!" She jumped straight into the air with a squeal of energy, terror, delight. The urchins scattered down the street. We entered Lilliena's tiny shop and shut the door.

The room's wide shelves held scanty goods: a bolt of milled cloth, cheap toweling in lengths, a new kettle, the mirrors and spices and ribbons traded by my father's people—Tanshari's unpaid debt. "Through the back," said Nondany.

We came into a walled courtyard open to the sky. There an old apricot tree overhung a rose garden, a table, a few chairs. You could hear the sea break beyond the wall. At the west end the doors of the rough-walled house stood open to a kitchen and to a spiral staircase.

This we climbed to a second story, then to a squat tower. Nondany lurched on the stairs. At the top was his eyrie: a tiny room where a window looked out over the water, its shutters thrown open to the summer evening. It held a chair, a table with inkwell and quill, a nightstand, a narrow bed. In the wall next to the doorway was a Year Altar, on it the striped pebble and the wasp-nest brain.

On the bed, like a napping child, lay the dindarion. All strings but one were broken. The varnish was blistered, and the neck, like the Reirig's, canted at an odd angle.

Nall looked down at it, then nudged it aside with his elbow. It groaned like a living thing. He laid the boy down in its stead and straightened the dirty little smock. The child's chest moved with quick breaths.

We heard the drum, but distantly. The waves were louder. I moved to look out the window, but Nall snatched me back, pointing to the floor: A black arrow lay there, its iron tip shattered on the stone wall.

He eased his face around the window frame. Searched up and down the shore. Nodded. As he moved the chair for Nondany, I looked out over the sea.

That quarter of Tanshari did not overlie the old arem, but had been built out onto a low, rocky spit. A strip of beach stretched below us, but it was empty, washed by the falling tide, without even footprints. Birds picked at the shining sand. In the west the black cloud bank that had pursued us had rolled closer, waiting to swallow the falling sun.

To the north on the smoking docks I saw the clustering tiny figures of paidmen. South, on the beach below the ruins of Mailin's house, another lot had built a pale daylight bonfire and were tossing into it broken furniture and other rubbish, as if it were a Year Fire.

"Pull the bed to the window, will you, my dears? So I can see, and tend my laddie too."

"Beware any movement on the beach," said Nall. We shifted the bed. I pulled the dindarion away from the boy's feet. He lay still, sleeping or fainting.

Nondany lowered himself into the chair with a grunt. "This is my specialty," he said. "Watching wars from a height. A slight height, as I am not tall."

The nightstand held a clay cup and water jug, half full. I looked around for something to use as a towel besides the skirt of my dirty shift, remembered the toweling in the shop, and sent Nall to fetch it. He was slow to return. I stripped the case off the pillow and used that to wet and wipe Nondany's face, then the boy's hot arms and legs. I gave Nondany water from the clay cup, then drank myself. I filled the cup for Nall, but he was not there.

Western light lit the Year Altar. Nondany bent over the boy. I put down the cup, stepped to the landing, and looked down the dark stairs.

Nall was not there. I thought, Has he gone? To swim and listen, to get clean, to get away from us?

I had a vision of the water pouring out through the Gate, the line trembling in the air between the stones. I clattered down the stairs and shot into the courtyard.

He was there. Just standing, seeming to stare at nothing in particular. He held the toweling in his hands. When he saw me, he started. He looked at the cloth, held it out. "I was coming," he said.

I took it from him. The rose garden smelled like smoke and babies' faces.

"Stay here if you like," I said. "If we need you, I'll call."

"I'm coming," he said. He did not move.

"There's water upstairs." I turned away and left him to come if he would. It was the sea he needed. All I had was a water in a clay cup.

Nondany had angled his chair to look west over the ocean, south over land. Waves wrinkled the empty sea. At the bonfire the little poisonous figures of the paidmen strode about in the smoke.

"Well, well," said Nondany. "So here we are."

He did not ask where I had gone, or where Nall was. He laid his bandaged hands on his lap, palms up, and tipped the chair back. I thought of my auntie Jerash, who whenever I tipped my chair had whacked my head with a spoon. She would be hearing the drum now; so would her daughters, my girl-cousins in their gray gowns who rocked their dollies to threats and frightened one another with taunts about the Rigi. I saw the door of the black box bed burst open, the childish nightmare come alive.

There was nothing I could do.

I could only be. Away from the fever in the plaza, away from the unknowing girls who even now were being chivvied out of their dresses, settled in their box bed whining and pinching, giggling after the doors were shut, or shivering, silent, at the sound of that drum.

So I did nothing. I sat in the high, quiet room with Nondany and the child, and listened to him talk.

About chickens. How they have personalities, which I knew already. He taught me a little song from Graygardens that will make the hens come, every time.

About mudpies. In Arkelina even the grown-ups make them, on the day of a certain saint who ate mud in penance and died of it. The children sing for cakes that day and get them, and their parents get stones for raisins.

About wind. You would not believe all the songs and stories and hand slaps and riddles there are about wind!

Here is the same wind blowing over all of us, and it seems as if everybody has to grab a handful and make a song of it.

"We had a wind skip," I said. "We weren't supposed to say it." But I said it now for him.

> The wind blows hard
> The wind blows true,
> The wind blows backward—
> It's you! *Peeuw!*

He laughed. "My Half-and-Half! I'll just make a note of that—" Grimacing, he groped at the air and said, "I forgot. I can't hold a pen."

"Where are your papers?" I asked at last.

"Ashes. Like some of the children. We had discussed that possibility." He sighed. "Work to do over."

"I'll help you," I said.

As I spoke those words, I felt a little click, exactly as when, on my journey from Creek, I had slid the Weedrun boy's bowstring into the nock. I said slowly, "I know so many songs and stories now. And tattoo designs, and dances, and embroidery designs, and chants and taunts and hand slaps and jump-rope rhymes. I know a little bit of everything. Because I have a thousand halves."

I saw that I was both inside and outside of many tribes: Downshore and Creek and the League, the Rigi and the Roadsouls and all the peoples I had met on my journeys, and thousands I had not met. Women are a tribe, I thought, and so are men. Children are another. Warriors are a tribe, whether paidman or Rig or fierce lad with a fish knife. Creatures are tribes, like the singing moles and the birds; maybe even things are, like the old logs that chanted *hoyroynoy*. They chant and dance, and many of them paint and weave and embroider and make pots and tattoo themselves where their aunties wish they wouldn't.

"It's all tied together. Everything that we make, that we are. It's the loom of countless threads; I saw it when I was the Bear," I said, and burst into tears.

"So, so." Nondany patted me with the back of his hand as he had patted the child, as I had seen Dai pat a cow that had just calved. Proud, relieved. "Half-and-Half, All-and-All. There! The world and I will be glad of your help. And never think your calling has to do only with songs! However, I am an exacting master," he said, as if he had just hired me to begin in three days, when Least Night was done and everybody had hangovers.

Sobbing, I said, "But I can't spell!"

"By life! As if that mattered," he said in a sensible voice.

I stopped crying. I felt light and strange, as though I walked in a meadow full of every sort of flower under heaven, all mine for the gathering. Then I looked at the door to the stairway. It was still empty. "But Nall," I said. "He's changed."

Maybe Nondany did not hear me. He had bent over the boy and was lifting in his bandaged paw the brown boy's hand with its grubby fingernails. "Deaf and blind and burned and lame, one goes on," he said. He laid the little hand down. "That gift I gave you, Half-and-Half—what did you do with it?"

I did not know what to say, but looked at my empty palm.

"Good, you've still got it. I have a task for you, your first in
my employ. Will you remember this song for me, please? It
was among those that were burned. I had it from a Roadsoul,
though I'm sure its origin is Rig."

He tipped his chair and sang.

> At the gate of the great deep,
> Souls are finding bodies,
> Hearts are finding words.
> Nothing turns to every shining thing, and rises
> Like a flight of birds.

He waited, cocking an eyebrow.

"Oh—," I said.

"Do you understand?" said Nondany. "Do you see?"

"Look! Look!"

For I was leaning out the window, pointing. The waves
writhed, drawing shoreward. As far as I could see, across the
wide horizon, the bright sea was alive with seals.

31

Both rose and briar
Shall to the fire
Fall. From burned thorn
The year shall be reborn.

Year Altar Song. Tanshari.

"NALL! *NALL!*"

He rattled up the stairs and slammed into the room.

"Pigalee!" the boy wailed, waking. But the three of us were crammed at the window, staring at the sea.

It boiled. Seals bobbed, twirled, tumbled together, seeming to dance in the water. In the lucent surf their big bodies wreathed and darted, broke surface and splashed until a fine mist rose, gold and turquoise in the falling sun.

The mist rose in spirals, twisted like snakes. Oily, heavy coils piled link upon link, rising to dissolve, collapse, rise again.

"Nondany, can you see?"

"Enough." His face was smooth with wonder. He leaned out so far that I grabbed the back of his shirt. I thought of the black arrow and looked north and south along the shore to the gangs of paidmen.

The glinting black figures crowded together, they pointed at the writhing columns of mist. Under the boom of the drum I heard the cricket chirps that were their yells. Seals thickened the water between the pilings of the docks, they shot into the shallows and raised snaking necks, they moaned and bellowed. What must have been thunder—the paidmen's boots pounding the earth as they ran east, up the foreshore—I could not hear at all.

The coils of mist became a living forest, shimmering pink and emerald, thick as the trunks of trees. *"Hoyroynoy,"* I whispered. Tiny screams were from the paidmen at the bonfire running, falling, scrambling up to run again.

Nall was a man watching the moon rise. He raised one hand with fingers spread. From the base of the raking fog, like leopards stealing out of a forest, slipped host upon host of black manats.

A school of black fish, a flock of night birds, a swarming darkness that glittered with spears and new-edged knives. Black paddles flicked. The seals sank away, or maybe they turned into manats. Nall stood motionless. Nondany's shoulder pressed mine as we watched our death come to us like dusk across the water.

The men fleeing along the shore saw the manats. They dropped their weapons and ran faster, clotting and struggling east up Scythe Road. It did not matter that they could run and we could not. It was our debt to clear, our fate to finish. They were paidmen.

The drum boomed without pause. The dancers could not see the manats. Perhaps they did not care; they were dancing to their death—the drum would shout and shout and shout until the drummers died.

But little figures were running down from town.

"The urchins!" I said. Darting through the fleeing paidmen like sparrows through thorns, the half-grown children of Tanshari were running down to the beach unarmed and wild, throwing their hands in the air to welcome the Rigi and die, celebrating the end of the world.

They ran to the bonfire like moths. I thought they would hurl themselves into the flames like altar goods, like roses. But they caught hands in great shifting rings and began to dance round it, stamping to the rhythm of the drum.

The men in the manats saw the fire too; they flew to it. On the bed the burned lad gave a nightmare scream.

The urchins raised their joined hands, they sang.

"I'm going down," said Nall.

"Then I'm coming with you."

He looked at me. "So be it."

I turned to Nondany, who wept. "Thank you," I said. For the life I had had, all of it; for the pain and confusion that were gifts now, for he had given me a bowl to put them in. "But you—"

"Me? You may not fuss over me! Get down there. Loolie, loolie, mannie. Go— By life, not *that* way!" he cried as we dove over the windowsill. "You'll kill yourselves!"

The walls were rough-laid, with plenty of toeholds; it was no worse than the shaft we had climbed on the Isle of Bones, but I was clumsy, I fell the last pitch onto Nall and knocked him sprawling. He sprang up and yanked me to my feet, we scrambled down the barnacled wet rocks of the spit to the beach and ran toward the fire.

The sand was hard, still wet from the retreating tide. The drum boomed. The bonfire surged high; the urchins were hurling in driftwood and dry wrack to swell the blaze. Mist dimmed the sun. The waves were pale green bands broken by dark manats that did not roll or turn, but dove straight as bees to the hive of fire.

Nall stumbled as he ran. I gave him my shoulder for a crutch, and he used it without thanks. We ran south on the trodden sand until we came between the children and the boats.

"Nall! Nall!" cried the urchins, stamping and clapping, fiercer than the fire.

He did not answer, but faced the sea.

Quick as a needle, the first manat darted through the flattening waves. The rest hung back, but the paddler of the first leaped into the knee-high surf and lifted his little boat to land. His sealskin was tied across his shoulders. In his hand he carried, point forward, the lance: the One's lance, which had opened the way through the Changes. Hsuu's face writhed without stirring, like the sheen of oil on water.

Nall walked toward him. I followed. Nall made a gesture that said, *This is mine.* I fell back, but only a little.

Hsuu looked about. At the fire; at the gangly children grown still; at the smoky town. At the two of us, standing before him a little parted, as we had been at the ama's last scream: *here* as we had been *there,* as if time and space were not real.

Hoarse surf, the roar of fire.

Nall limped toward his father. The point of the lance, held level, stopped him.

"Who kills the king is king," said Hsuu. "Until the next king kills."

"There never was a king," said Nall. "Nor a priest, nor an elder. Only each one of us listening, and the world rushing in and out of the Gate."

"Yet at the Gate you heard—"

"Nothing. That a king is no greater than a grain of sand, nor life than death. Tell me, Father—does that have another name?"

Hsuu pursed his lips. As though to himself, in answer or prayer, he said, "The great deep."

He raised the lance away. But Nall's lame leg half buckled; it gave him to the rising blade so that it nicked his breast as it rose, canceling the Reirig's mark. As he found his feet again a line of blood ran down over his ribs, into the waist of the patched breechclout.

Hsuu held the lance upright. Nall went to him. He laid his hand on his father's heart.

Brown hand, blue breast. Neither man spoke. Maybe the hand meant *Stop.* Maybe it meant *Father.*

Hsuu lowered his head. Looked about. Turning from Nall, he walked to me and put into my hand the lance, warm as a paddle shaft. "That is not mine," he said, "and my son will not have it. Let it be yours, Bear."

The smooth shaft, the ponderous, balanced weight. I looked east over my shoulder. The urchins had the same thought and opened a path for me.

I ran to the fire and hurled that beautiful bullies' tool into the middle of it.

I had never thrown a spear; I chucked it as if it were a clothesline prop. It rattled on a burning bedstead and tipped a fish crate before it sank into the heart of the flames. Heat made the air ripple—or maybe it was the boundary charm, dissolving forever.

I came back to Nall and Hsuu. They looked alike, all right, both mouths open. Then my own opened as I saw the boats that sculled in the cloudy light—truly saw them.

Manats, yes, but also vois, full of people. Small people, even. Children. They were singing.

Hsuu closed his mouth, pursed his lips. As he raised his hands to wave them in, he said, "We have come to speak with the father of the eagle."

"Eagle?" said Nall. He had begun to shake, fingering the nick at his breast. I was afraid he would fall, and leaned on him so it would look as though I were the one leaning.

"Keeo the eagle," said Hsuu. He nudged his chin toward the boats diving out of the dissolving mist, through the long waves.

"Keeo?" Nall stared. He clutched me with his bloody hand. "It's Queelic!" Then, *"Aieh!"*

A voi had grounded and heeled. Its oarswoman leaped into the waves, but her passenger wobbled on a thwart, grabbed at the air, and fell into the sea.

Nall steadied himself at my shoulder, then ran.

I let him go. It was easy, like letting go the hummingbird

you have found stunned and held in your hand a moment to marvel at.

He ran to Aieh. His leg folded, he fell into the surf. Aieh wore Queelic's shirt over her sealskin, tied by the sleeves; I watched her try to pluck Nall out of the sea with one hand, Queelic with the other, until both men got to their feet and Nall had Aieh in his arms the way he had held me sometimes, and I had to watch Queelic flounder to the beach instead.

He tottered toward me, went dizzy with earth, and sat down. "Kat!" he said, waving. "How did you get here?" He stood up, sat down again. "The land moves," he said. "That's odd."

It was Nondany's earthquake, nobody left standing but me. Queelic sat splay-legged; Nall and Aieh knelt in the surf as though knit together; Hsuu stooped to pick up a handful of sand. All around us boats heeled; wild, warlike men sang as they bent to the ropes, steadying their craft to haul them in.

"Queelic." I did not think he was real. In an instant I would wake, flailing, in deep water.

"If you don't mind," he said, looking shy, "they've given me a new name."

Hsuu heard him and said, "Keeo," the eagle's cry.

"That's it. I never liked 'Queelic.' I'm not going to wear boots anymore either. They were making my toes look strange." Cautiously he stood. He stared at the hazy cliffs, the gaping urchins, the gathering manats. "Did Hsuu tell you? I've invited the Rigi to talk to Dad. I didn't think so many would come, but that's best, isn't it? More folk to speak." He sniffed the smoky air. "Are we interrupting a feast or something? I heard they have wild parties in Downshore, but I never went to any."

"'Talk to Dad,'" I said like an imbecile. "Your father is burning Downshore."

"*Burning* it? It's real estate!"

"Burning and killing."

"Well, well." In Queelic's suddenly soft voice I heard an echo of Ab Harlan's, and shivered. "Then we're getting here just in time, aren't we?"

Manats thickened on the sand. Singing rose in the air. Boats sliced the foam, row on row, tilting in the shallows. Lean, armed, windblown men leaped out singing; they lifted others out: old women, young women, old men, all singing. Children the age of the urchins who, behind me, were singing too; and all were singing the same song.

> I am the sigh that stills the scream,
> I am the word that frees the dumb,
> I am the light that ends the dream.
> *I am the child. I come, I come.*

I stood in the breaking wave, remembering Aieh's words—*Already they sing your song in secret*—and then the urchin's: *We'll sing that song you taught us!*

I looked for their teacher. Aieh had helped him to his feet, and he stood swaying, his arms around her. I wondered how much Nondany had understood, peering from his window.

Nondany was not the only watcher. Other eyes had seen the manats dive in, the paidmen flee; they had seen Nall walk to meet the lance and me fling it into the fire. The heaped barriers at the town's alley ends had been torn down, and little shivering figures crept out.

But one was running: Mailin, followed more slowly by

lame Pao and Robin, ponderous in her new weight. *"Alele! Ai alele!"* Mailin cried in the tongue of her Rig ancestors. As Hsuu turned to look, she held up what she carried: her own ancient sealskin, saved from the fire.

Behind her, all along the beach, the people of Tanshari were stumbling down to the sea.

Old women, hobbling on feet already sore with dancing. Old men, their hands trembling. *"Ai alele!"* they said, weeping. The urchins went to meet their grandparents, singing, drawing them to the fire.

The smaller children came; their parents tried to snatch them back, but they were like minnows slipping through the fingers, running to the thin, wild Rig children as they were lifted from the vois, smooth head to tousled head. The smallest were afraid to go alone; they dragged at their mothers' hands, and their mothers swung them high and came.

I looked at Hsuu, who could call seals. His face was as always: serene, mutable.

The men had hung back, dazed with war and the dance; now they hurried after their families. The Tansharians and the Rigi met, they touched. They began to speak and call in the Plain tongue; looking from face to yearning face, I could see no difference, one tribe from the other. In the gang of children on the beach I saw the twin girls who had kissed me; they were dressed in all their best: one string of blue beads and one of white. They had found the Roadsoul girls and were shoving, laughing, running in circles. Somebody had already slapped somebody. There were tears.

"Queelic," I said. "I mean, Keeo. How did you do this?"

"Do what?"

I waved at the heeled manats, the wild-haired children.

"Me?" said Queelic. "*I* didn't do anything. They were coming anyway. We talked, that's all—Hsuu and me and the rest, the younger ones. And one old lady. Nall's grandma she was, and Aieh's, too."

"Their ama! When did you—"

"After you left for the Gate. The boss was in a *fit*—men with spears all over. Nobody noticed Aieh and me. We went up the hill to those campfires, and this old lady comes stumping out of the dark." Queelic spoke in a torrent, as all about us the human torrent rushed and mingled, poured and withdrew and poured again in eddies like the surf where it mixes with sand, only the sound of this surf was singing.

Queelic said, "Was she in a fury! She could speak Plain, but she wouldn't. Aieh had to translate, and I thought, 'Look out, Nall, if she catches him!'

"So it's getting light—we see them fetch you in the boats, but we can't get *at* you for spears. Then all of a sudden they're calling for grandma, and off she goes, cursing gibble-gabble under her breath. The spears let her through—but, Kat, you'll have to tell *me* what happened next, for I can't cipher it."

"Say what you saw."

"Couldn't see *anything*—that's why I'm asking. All's pretty quiet; then there's a great set-to, all noise, like a dogfight. Howls. The crowd breaks like the wind blew it, and there's grandma and the fancy boss stone dead, and you two vanished, and everybody yelling 'The end of the world!' and Hsuu running around trying to keep the muscle men from killing each other. And then—like magic—"

"What?"

"Here and there, and then all together, the Rigi start to sing. That song they're singing now, about the child. It's

Nall's song, did you know? The Reirig hated it, but everybody whispered it anyway, Aieh says, and they just got fed up and belted it out loud. I wish you'd heard them. Seemed they were all of one mind for once, even Hsuu—"

"*Hsuu* sang that song?"

Queelic nodded. "His voice—you can't describe his voice. But it seemed an opportunity. You know how the League is about opportunity, so I just edged in and suggested that the Rigi come see my father. Since they were already packed. Aieh! Ask Nall to explain what happened."

She had her hand in Nall's, drawing him stumbling through the crowd. The Rigi wanted to touch him: their singer, the man who had killed the Reirig.

"We talked a lot," said Queelic. "Aieh and me, and Hsuu, of course, and the young men. The Rigi shouldn't be shut away out there. The babies are getting born with club feet, the barley's got some disease, and the men are fighting each other. The kids are too thin. I don't want the Rigi to die out. I like them."

Aeih said, "You talk as if we were creatures. Birds."

"I know. I want to learn to be one."

Nall took his hand out of Aieh's. Queelic greeted him; Nall seemed not to hear. He came to me and held me, awkwardly first, then hard, as at the Gate. The wound across his heart still bled, and the blood seeped through my shift, first warm, then clammy as he leaned away. He did not look at me; he gripped my arms above the elbows. I could not read anything in his face but endurance.

I thought, We are all neither more nor less to him than a king or a grain of sand.

"No," he said.

I did not know what that meant: *No, you're not the one I love* or *No, it doesn't matter. Nothing matters.*

"No. It's not over," he said. "The wave has not broken."

I thought it had broken. I did not know if I could bear it to break more. But Queelic looked around at the crowd as if it were commonplace, a fair. He looked at the smoking ruin that had been Mailin's house. "Best be getting home," he said.

"To whatever's at home," I said. "Paidmen."

"They might kill me," he said. "I'd rather be killed than go back to what I was doing—cheating with the books and frisking henwives for the tariff." He shaded his eyes to watch the activity on the beach. "How beautiful! All human life is numbers, like the nests of ants or bees."

"My father used to say, 'War is numbers,'" I said.

"Everything is numbers. War also."

"And love? And sex? And singing?"

"I don't know. But it might be there in the middle of them, like the stone in the peach." The low sun lit his face. His pimples were clearing up.

"Numbers," said Aieh. "What you showed me—that 'nothing' has a name: zero. An egg."

"But of what bird?" Queelic smiled, and I had a glimpse of the eccentric charm he would grow into. "Well, I'd better not show up at Dad's place half naked. Kat, Aieh took me swimming before we left, and I've got a sunburn I won't say where. I couldn't swim, either. Aieh, may I have my shirt back?"

She gave it to him. He shrugged it on unbuttoned and rolled up the sleeves. She yanked it around on him, like a mare that licks her colt until it staggers. "Keeo, you need a better skin."

"This isn't my skin, you know that."

"Therefore you need one. Your real skin is so pale, like a

bird's." One full sleeve unrolled and fell down over his knuckles so that their hands, for an instant clasped, were hidden.

At Aieh's waist the shirt had been a white rag, but on Queelic's back it was a Leagueman's shirt, and Queelic a Leagueman. The pressing, impetuous crowd began to stare, and a low snarl rippled through it. A group of young men from Tanshari gathered, chanting "Black Boot! Black Boot!" in time with the drum. "Keeo! Keeo!" cried the Rig warriors, whipping out knives. The Reirig's men were wolves again.

Nall broke away from me. Empty-handed, he ran between the gangs, his arms outspread. I ran after him; Aieh joined us, then Mailin and Pao. Queelic himself came, settling his shirt; the rivals fell back from him, or maybe it was from Hsuu, who padded beside him like a lion.

Leaning to Hsuu, Queelic said, "Can you make everybody listen?"

"I?" said the man who could call seals.

Nothing happened. Then the roar became a querulous gabble; we could hear the surf again. The dog men of both factions hesitated, looked sullen and puzzled.

Queelic put his hands on Aieh's shoulders and said, "Shout her name."

All together we cried *"Aieh!"* and found what a yell it made. Nall knelt to make a step of his thigh and Queelic clambered onto it, waggling about, yanking at Nall's hair until he could stand straight. "Hello!" he shouted. "Excuse me!"

The quarrelers stared at him, at one another. Over the knock of the drum Queelic said, "Maybe you know me? I'm Ab Harlan's son."

There was a roar then! The throng seethed. Queelic flapped

his hand at it, like a cook strewing cold water on a broth. It settled. Teetering on Nall's thigh like a young eagle on a branch, he shouted into the hush, "I promised the Rigi we'd talk with my father. You Downshore people, you come too." He wobbled, fell off his perch, climbed up again. "If there's fighting, we can't talk. Don't fight."

Pao said, "Does he think he can stop a war by telling it to stop?"

Mailin said, "It hasn't stopped for anything else. Why not have a little boy tell it, *Stop*?"

I said, "He's not a little boy."

Queelic nodded at warriors and fishwives, Roadsouls and butchers, grandmothers and brewers and smiths. "Let's go, then. Did anybody see where the paidmen went?"

"Ran up the cliffs," yelled Mec. I thought about walking to Upslope under a rain of black arrows.

Queelic scratched his jaw. His beard was coming in red. "If you're afraid, don't come," he shouted. "But I'll walk in front, and if you want to talk with my dad, I'll do my best to make sure he sees you."

He lost his balance, fell off with a yelp, climbed back up, and said, "Keep the children at the back. And could somebody loan me some shoes? I can't walk that far in my bare feet."

What had been a riot became a muttered argument about shoes. Two impossibly ancient amas came shuffling hand in hand, one a Tansharian in shawl and culottes, the other a Rig in a sealskin worn to the hide, her breasts wrinkled and flat.

"This is my own auntie's child!" the Tansharian said, weeping and clutching her cousin. She shook off her purple carpet slippers. "You take these, boy. We're going to sit right here on the beach and talk."

"Thank you, ma'am." Queelic climbed down from Nall's thigh and put on the slippers, saying in a low voice, "Kat, I'm ashamed. You know how it is—I've taken tariffs and all, but I never was in Downshore in my life. How do we get home?"

"Scythe Road." He made it sound so easy that I believed it: just walk home and talk to Dad. "Or the cliff paths—they're quicker."

"Would you show us the way? Please. But we ought to walk through town; I need to see what I'm talking about."

The real estate. "I know only one path," I said. The one Dai had carried Nall down, so long ago.

"I'll lead you," said Mailin.

Mec said, "They'll shoot us from the cliffs!"

Hsuu showed his strong teeth. "One stops a wave with arrows?"

It was too late to stop anything. It was almost too late for fear, as in the reddening sun the tide of bodies began to nudge and roll east toward higher ground.

Pao said to Robin, "Don't come."

"I'm coming."

Nall had not spoken. Again I had the feeling that if I looked at him, I might see nothing. But there he was; he, and all the Rigi. When I called a man out of the sea, I had called a nation.

The improbable column of walkers began to stir and flow inland. With the children of all tribes running and wrestling behind us, the current flowed up the beach toward Tanshari and the drum.

32

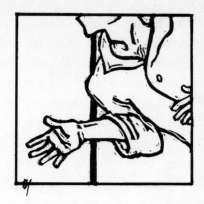

Do not kill those upon whom your business depends.
Do not steal from allies.
Beware of animals and women.
Know your balance.
Watch your back.

From The Rules. Upslope.

THE BARRIERS AT the alley mouths had been scattered. Next to one of them lay the swollen bodies of two paidmen, killed with a hatchet and left to the summer heat.

Aieh stared at the tall stone walls. The Rigi ducked into alleys and doorways, nosed like fish into every hole in this gray stone reef. In the plaza the girl and her smith still beat the drum, and as the strange crowd poured round them, half neighbors and half seeming ghosts, they did not falter. Sweating, mouths open, they worked in a trance.

Streaming above their buried warrenhouse, the Rigi touched the fountain, the worn stone benches where gossipers had sat, the market stalls, the stone pillars grimed by the hands of children. The trees were loud with panicky grackles kept from their night roosts.

In front of the makeshift hospital Suni stood gaping, her baby on her hip and Rosie by one arm. Rosie tugged like a terrier on a leash. "Rose, be still or be spanked," said Suni. "Oh, Lali Kat!"

With a squeal Rosie broke away and dashed into a flock of little girls. Suni ran after her.

There was no time to look for Nondany. The crowd broke out of the east gate; it passed the place where Ab Harlan had shouted through his trumpet. The sinking sun turned the fields green like a vision. The smoke from the burning farmsteads had thinned, it drifted over the river of people who jostled and wept and called, who leaned forward as though in a race. We left the road and took to the crisscrossing cattle paths, narrow and many, where there could be fewer ambushes. The hill was dark with bodies, like a plague of crickets.

We climbed past outlying farms and orchards. Chickens scratched in abandoned yards. Robin pointed: "Our house." A cock crowed there, though his dunghill belonged to a heap of smoking stones. The cowshed still stood, forlorn, and I saw Nall looking at it; mostly his face was set. The drum kept us distant company, as, like migrating antelope, we left a trampled swath that led to the rocky cliffs.

Anything might wait for us above. When we came within a

bowshot of the cliff's crest, we would be easy targets. Queelic flapped along in his slippers, and I thought, He should take off that white shirt.

He pointed and said, "Up there."

A dozen Rig warriors broke ahead and ran straight up the cliff like bobcats. I saw them against the stone, then against the evening sky. They vanished.

I said, "But you told them not to fight—"

"Wait," said Queelic.

The mounting surf of walkers paused and spread. From the cliff's edge one wiry arm waved, then another.

All clear. Come on. Let the tide pour in.

The crowd spread up the trails. Those who could climb swarmed the cliffs by toehold and foothold; the rest swept steadily up the paths, pooling at the top to stand, squinting, in the violent light that poured almost level over the western sea.

Queelic said, "I know the way from here."

The plain I had crossed with Jake the turkey man was empty. Nothing moved on it that was not moved by wind.

To the south the scattered buildings of Upslope looked like a child's abandoned blocks. Away by the cliffs I could see my father's house; nearer, the modest graystone where Ab Jerash lived with my aunt and his daughters. The guardhouse stood by the road well to the north of us, glowing in the low sun. A dead-fly bundle swung from the gibbet.

"This way, please," said Queelic.

Shuffling, he led the river of walkers south toward the stone cluster of warehouses, accounting hall, Rulesward, and mansion that were Ab Harlan's estate, barely a quarter mile away, hard angles set down in blowing grass.

Off among the inland hills I saw faint movement, like deer in flight.

Pao gazed there. "Mules," he said. "Men on them. More men afoot."

"Only men?" said Queelic. If all Upslope had fled, there would be women, children, wagons. But there had been no time for that.

Aieh, sharp-eyed but foreign to mules, looked and said, "Only men. Riding great black hares, spears and bows in their hands."

"Paidmen," said Pao.

"It's not their home," said Mailin. "Why defend it from such an army?" She looked back. "We are so many!"

"As many as the seals in the sea," said Pao. Robin walked with her hand fast in his, her face turned away from the guardhouse.

I knew where my own people must be: locked in their houses, abandoned like the child's blocks. I knew of no Leagueman who could use so much as a kitchen knife. They had always bought that work.

With a rustle like water, we walked through grass and scrub toward Ab Harlan's mansion. We began to pass Upslope's houses, set apart each with its low wall, its flower-less kale yard, and its stone walk. All windows were shuttered, all doors locked. No smoke rose from the chimneys.

The Tansharians shied from those houses, but the Rigi rattled the garden gates, they leaped the walls to finger cabbage leaves and rap on the shutters. The drum throbbed, the late wind soughed in the grass. As we passed Ab Jerash's house, I heard a child's stifled weeping.

At Ab Harlan's estate the walls were taller and topped by

spikes. There was an iron gate with a latch bar as wide as a man's hand, but it stood open; the paidmen had not cared whom they left vulnerable. We crowded through it into the heap of buildings intersected by wide, empty streets.

The streets had always been mostly empty, designed not for loitering but for hurrying down on business or to the Rulesward. The walls were long and blank, the corners sharp. Our rabble ran down them like water down gutters. At the central square, now in shadow, our footsteps echoed from the bare stone walls.

For as long as I could remember, I had passed through here every Rulesday with Dai and our father, my aunts and uncles and cousins, to sit on the hard benches of the women's anteroom and listen to the dry, unintelligible murmur of the men reciting the Rules. The square had not changed.

There were no trees. No bandstand. The few windows that overlooked it were shuttered. All doors were flush with the gray walls, leaving no cubbyholes for whisperers, for kissing lovers—not that there would be lovers here, under the gray brow of the Rulesward. There were no bushes, no benches, no fountains, no flowers. No beer-sellers, no strolling singers, no cookie-hawkers and so no sparrows, no aimless dogs. From a parapet one impassive cat stared down. A pigeon clapped its wings.

The feet of the multitude were loud and hushed at the same time.

"Queelic." My voice came in a whisper, for I had been small in this place. "Maybe Ab Harlan ran with his paidmen?"

Flushed and calm, Queelic shook his head. "His money's here. I know where he'll be."

Around us the square filled with beings, thickened with

shadow. Queelic led us toward the accounting house, which with Ab Harlan's mansion formed the west side of the square. It had tall, many-paned windows—sunlight is cheaper than lamp oil—all blocked with ironbound shutters, pinned from the inside.

Queelic climbed the stone steps and banged on the studded door.

No one answered, of course.

He banged again. "Father! It's me. Open up!"

No sound.

"Dad, I've got the key." And Queelic, from his battered trousers, produced a ring of jingling keys.

Inside, the crash of a bar being dropped across the door. Then silence.

Queelic put the keys back in his pocket. "You ought to open it," he said through the crack above the hinge. "If you don't, I'll ask these folks to break the shutters."

At that a big Tanshari fisherman ran up the steps, pulling from his sash the hatchet he had hidden there. "Let us at them, sir!" he said. A crowd I recognized as the Reirig's men came with him.

"Just a minute, please." Queelic leaned left and right, trying to peer through the shutters.

The crowd shifted. A Tanshari girl of seven or so squirmed between their thighs and pattered up the steps. She was bare-chested, having swapped her blouse for a string of seashells, and she was quick; dodging the hands that grabbed after her, she patted Queelic's elbow.

He frowned. "You're to stay at the back."

She tugged him down and whispered.

"Well now, thanks," he said. "I hadn't noticed. This way,"

he said to the crowd as the girl, dragging at his sleeve, led him down the steps and around the corner to an alley. Out of earshot of the big front door he said, "Her mother washes the floors, but not today, because there's a war. She says there's a servants' entrance; it doesn't have a bar."

"We'll smash the lock!" said the hatchet man, struggling forward. But when we had padded round to the grimy little door, we found it propped open with a mop.

"That's *our* mop!" said the girl, and grabbed it. "Mother left it. If you don't let the air in, you get mildew."

As she spoke, a stout young woman came panting, snatched child and mop, spanked the one with the other, and dragged them both back into the crowd.

"Oh dear," said Queelic.

He turned back to the door. Aieh said, "Keeo, be wary."

The door was narrow and exhaled a musty breath of metal, paper, ink. Queelic stood gazing into the dimness.

Over his shoulder I saw the dusky cavern of the high-ceilinged room where, being neither man nor servant, I had never been. It was crowded with the shapes of high tables, tall chairs. Faintly ruled lines of sunset marked the shutters on the west wall.

The crowd jostled from behind. Still Queelic hesitated. "He has bodyguards," he said. "Paidmen, but well paid."

Aieh ducked under his arm and listened into the dark, sniffing like a vixen. "Only one man," she said. "Very frightened. He was here, but he has gone."

"He's got a hiding place farther in," said Queelic. He motioned with one hand. "Come on in, folks. Quietly, please. Most of you will have to wait outside. But don't worry," he said. "We'll send him out to you."

The tide flowed after us into the accounting room. The big front door was opened, and the shutters were thrown back to let in the stain of sunset and the thump of the drum. The crowd poured in among the ledgers and pens. They stroked and fingered, picked up and put back, snuffed and listened. I thought, They're all Rigi now.

Nall touched nothing. I looked for Hsuu, could not find him. Robin crowded forward between Pao and Mailin; as she looked around, the grief in her face grew mild with wonder.

"Did he work here?" she said to me. "Dai."

"Not long. He was terrible at it."

"I'm glad he got to have his cow."

Queelic nudged his way to the back of the room. We followed him to a small door with a plain stone lintel, shut.

"He had it built in case of trouble," said Queelic. "It's where he takes his ladies." He rapped politely. "Father! We've come."

Silence.

Then, from the other side of the door, a barely audible voice said, "I'll give them money!"

"Ah," said Queelic. The crowd riffled, a school of fish turning.

"We don't want money, Dad."

Silence.

The Rigi could be still as owls; the Tansharians, too, grew still.

"We?" said Ab Harlan.

"We."

Silence.

"Queelic."

"That's not my name anymore, Dad."

"Son!"

"Yes."

"Get in here!"

"Come out, Dad."

Some moments passed. I wondered whether it was dark where Ab Harlan was, a closed box.

Then the voice, a little higher, said, "What army is that?"

"It's Downshore and—"

"Bright boy!" said Ab Harlan. "Twisting the old man's arm! I'll give you Downshore's business!"

"I've got it."

"I'll give you the profits. All of them. It seems you can deal with those folk, go do it! You know how I—"

"It's you they want to talk to."

A monosyllable behind the door.

Queelic said, "There are quite a few of them."

"It was the paidmen," said Ab Harlan. "Out of control. I tried to stop them but they were mad dogs, 'Bring us the witch girl, or we'll kill you,' they told me. They hate women—horrible, they'd have torn her apart but I held them back, I said we'll reason with those natives, reason's what distinguishes us from them. Singe 'em a little, they'll get some sense, eh? Nobody likes to be hurt. A few injuries of course—can't play with knives without a nick or two, now can we? Eh, heh!" Pleading laughter. I thought of his soft big body pressed at the latch in the dark, the smell of him. "I wouldn't have hurt her," he said. "She's Ab Drem's daughter."

Silence in the accounting hall.

"Queelic. Tell them we'll have another look at the books. What the devil are you doing, meddling with natives? Tell them we'll iron out any discrepancies. It's impossible to do any amount of business without discrepancies."

"It would be a good idea to go over the books."

"We'll go over them together! Line by line, fair and square. Tell them—"

Mailin said in her clear voice, "Ab Harlan, we owe you money. What we owe, we will work fairly to pay." She looked around at her townsfolk. Their faces were ashamed, defiant, as though to say: We've paid that debt already, in children, in ashes, in heart's blood.

Yet there were nods here and there. Backs straightened. Mailin said, "We will pay. I promise for all of us."

"What the hell?" said Ab Harlan. "Queelic—are you in business with a *woman*?"

"Several," said Queelic.

"*I* know who's in there!" said a clear, childish voice. The cleaning lady's daughter had escaped; she held the mop and pointed with it. "That fat man!"

"For god's sake!" said Ab Harlan. "*Kids?* Queelic, you bloody dolt—I thought you'd brought an army!"

Bang and clatter behind the door. "Get back," I said. Slams, profanity, the clink of metal. Nall slipped to the doorjamb and flexed his back, ready to spring.

The door swung open under Ab Harlan's left hand. With his right he was restoring the authority of his cravat. He said, "Let's talk."

His face went slack.

His little eyes, shrewd in their fat, darted left and right; his open mouth made a black hole in his face.

"I've brought the Rigi, Dad."

Ab Harlan tried to slam the door. Nall had his knee against it. Ab Harlan made the sound a knife lets out of a pig. Then, "Get out!" he said. "Get them out!"

"You know about the Rigi."

"Rigi!" He was seeing us all now: Nall, gaunt and scarred; me in my ragged shift; Aieh, naked except for her silver sealskin; Queelic, tousled and sunburned and bootless; and, crowding behind him, women and men in fur, shadowy, with shining eyes. He smelled pelt and skin. He shrieked, "There's no such thing as the Rigi!"

"They're as real as the stars, Dad." Queelic's voice was pure, exultant. "As real as zero."

"Get them out! Get them out!"

Queelic looked over his shoulder. "You wanted to talk with my father. Here he is. His name's Harlan."

"*Harlan,*" said the Rigi. The people of Tanshari made way for them to move forward, as if Ab Harlan belonged to them.

Queelic said, "Where's Hsuu?"

Ab Harlan had backed into his hiding place, a small, dark parlor full of everything a Leagueman publicly does not have: cut-glass decanters, silk daybeds, goblets of rhinoceros horn. The Rigi slipped in after him, like dogs sticking to a scent.

"Harlan," they said. They touched him. Night with its dreams was coming; they could hear the drum. They fingered his hair, stroked his face. "*O Harlan!*"

He screamed, a high, gibbering squeal like a monkey's. They soothed him with whispers. He had been lost, was found; they did not so much take hold of him as absorb him, passing him among themselves as if drawn by an undertow, out of his little box, through the high room, and into the night.

Queelic watched. "Ah, Hsuu," he said. "There you are."

Over the sea of bodies I saw Hsuu beyond the outside

door, small against the darkening square, his arms outstretched like a lover's. It was toward him that the current of
hands flowed, like tide to the Gate.

Ab Harlan's pale face bobbed on the waters. Our eyes met.
"Ab Drem's daughter!" he cried. "Call them off! *Call them off!*
I'll give you back your brother!"

33

Fire upon the water,
Fire upon the wave,
Light above the grave,
Light upon the stone,
Alee, alay, alone;
Until the hand that plays
The watery fiddle lays
It down upon the chair,
And the winged mare
Crops mortal hay,
Alee, alay,
Be still this day.

Charm to Calm Demons. Tanshari.

ROBIN SCREAMED. Ab Harlan flung up his hands. Queelic said, "What does he mean?"

For no one had thought to tell him. Not even me.

"In Detention," I said. "Dai—to pay for Ab Seroy."

"Oh no, Kat!" He dragged his eyes from his father's drowning face. "Come on," he said, and ran.

Nall said to the Rigi, "Keep," as one might tell dogs to

guard a goat. There was no need. Ab Harlan's eyes were rolled back white. Hsuu spoke his name.

"This way," said Queelic. Next to the bunker was a low, thick door. He had the key. It opened on a narrow corridor, and we ran down it, even Robin big as she was, striking against one another in our haste, against the walls. We ran down steps. Through grated side doors we saw the gloom of storehouses— kegs and crates and sacks, sealskins bundled by the hundred. We came to a second door, narrower still. I ran not wanting to run, not wanting to come sooner to what Dai might be, chant- ing over and over in my mind, *I'll love you still, I'll love you still.*

Beyond the narrow door was a passageway smelling of metal and stale air, lit by windows high and dim. To left and right other doors led into tiny rooms, each windowless, cramped as a woodbox. Metallic sheen of screw and hook and blade. In one room only a plain black box.

I'll love you the way Nondany loves the maimed boy. I'll love you still.

The floor was polished; the slap of our feet was loud. Someone was singing.

> Sweet cow, my honey,
> Let down your milk.
> I'll give you bright money
> And a gown of silk.

We piled into the end of that blind, barren chute. Queelic had a key. He wrenched open the door of the last cell, to reveal Dai huddled naked in a corner, head down, singing Detention into a cowshed.

He looked up blinking. "Dream," he said. Robin's arms

went round him. "No," he said, and burst into tears.

I tumbled in after her. They held each other, so I had to hold them both. He seemed whole; he did not smell of seared flesh, only of shit. "We thought you were dead," I said. "We thought you were racked and hanged!"

When he could speak, he said, "Father stopped him."

"Father. *Our* father?"

He nodded against Robin's cheek. His head had been shaved again, and on his skull, more naked even than Aieh's, every childhood scar showed clear.

"Sister, listen." He freed one hand to grope for me. "Had the iron in the coals, Harlan did, to put behind my knees. Comes Father, how he walks now, bent. 'Don't touch him,' he says. 'That's my son.'

"'So it is, old man,' says Harlan, 'and I'll kiss him.'

"'I'm dying,' says Father. 'You touch my son, I'll rise from my grave and find you. You fear the Rigi? Fear *me*! Harlan, I'll kiss you for the rest of your putrid life—I'll rot your guts with dreams!' Harlan looks furious. Sick. But he throws down the iron. Father turns to go. Then he looks at me and says, 'I see you finally shaved that beard.'"

For the first time Dai looked about; beyond Queelic's shoulder, skin-clad Rigi were nosing along the corridor. In a whisper he said, "What's happened?"

"We don't know yet," said Queelic. "I'll find out." As he turned, the dark crowd seeped forward, like water through a crack.

Dai pressed closer to Robin. "Who are they?"

"The Rigi," said Queelic. He began to make his way through the press, saying, "Let me by, please. Thanks. I'll just slip by."

"Who's that?" said Dai.

"Ab Harlan's son, Queelic. Remember him?"

"That's not Queelic."

"I know," I said. "But we'd better go with him."

Robin helped Dai to his feet. He stared like a man who wakes to a different world than the one in which he fell asleep.

In the narrow corridor, in the storerooms, in the accounting hall with its main doors open—the Rigi were everywhere. They poked into corners, stroked locks, murmured among themselves.

I expected theft. Saw none. In Ab Harlan's parlor a handful of gold crown weights lay spilled across the floor, jeweled quills stood in silver holders, untouched as though a dream spell lay over all. It had to be Hsuu's doing. Only a Roadsoul child slipped in, nicked a silk throw from the daybed, and stuck out her tongue at me.

Outside, the sun had set and the high sky shone with a pearly, eggshell twilight.

The Rigi filled the square. Among them Queelic's shirt was luminous, seeming to float on the pool of beings who crouched around Ab Harlan in his silk cravat. The Leagueman's body was lax as a fallen marionette's, his head propped on Hsuu's blue thigh.

"*Shu-shu,*" Hsuu whispered.

Ab Harlan's skin was not blue. Nor was it its usual pallor, but pink and damp. He seemed to stare at the clear sky; tears poured from him, and the exhausted wail of a child, too frightened to cry, who cries at last. The right side of his face jerked.

Hsuu pursed his lips. "Keeo, give me a knife."

Queelic had none. Nall drew his knife and passed it to

Queelic, haft first. Queelic held it for a moment, then gave it into Hsuu's blue hand.

Hsuu laid the knife against Ab Harlan's throat. No one moved to stop him, under that clear, dim sky.

He cut Ab Harlan's silk cravat. He sliced the waistcoat and shirt down the front, cut the cruel band of the tweed breeches. Ab Harlan sprawled. His wails went to sobs, and he seemed to stare at the new moon, curved like a cradle in the sky.

Hsuu handed back the knife.

Queelic said hoarsely, "You said you'd talk with him."

Hsuu rubbed his hand across Ab Harlan's face and held up his wet palm. "Salt water," he said. "The oldest tongue of all. Harlan, you are one of us."

"Then so am I." Queelic stumbled as he turned away. "What shall I do now? I only wanted to show Dad that the Rigi are real. I never thought past that." He looked at the scattered houses where whole families crouched, terrified, in the dark. "What about the rest of us?"

Robin and the others came fording the crowd. Dai was still naked; he looked hairy and noble, like a bear. Robin said, "If this were a story, we would tear down these walls!"

"Is that the story we want?" said Mailin. "Give me the truths of stone, of fish and tree and child. They don't conquer. They *are*."

Dai said, "The League would never buy it. No profit."

"No profit without it," said Mailin. "If the world's in ruin, where's your business?"

"Rebuilding is always profitable," said Dai. "Ruin us, then loan us cash for mortar, hey." I knew then that he was not whole after all, and that I must love him as I had promised.

"Let the damned League crouch in their houses," he said. "Let them puke with fear!"

Robin said, "There are children in those houses."

I thought of the child's sob I had heard, of my uncle's face at the grate of the guardhouse cell—anguished, as if I had been his daughter. "We could go to Ab Jerash's house," I said.

Queelic's face lit. "Jerash is decent," he said.

I was in a rush to try it, in this strange war where dreams came real, where you walked up to your enemy's door and knocked on it. I wanted to say, *Nall, come with me!*

But I felt uncertain. Since the instant my foot had touched solid earth again, nothing had felt real. Perhaps this cresting wave had washed the Gate from Nall at last; but I was afraid to ask. I said, "Queelic, would you come?"

But Queelic would not leave his father—his fathers, speaking to each other in the oldest tongue. Dai, too, shook his head, still stunned.

Nall said, "I'll come with you."

He sheathed his knife and fell in beside me. We padded down the echoing streets. I stole a sidelong look at his face and said, "Are you still hearing it?"

A nod.

"But—all this, and Ab Harlan, and Dai!"

He shook his head. Maybe he had no words. Maybe nothing mattered.

I did not know what to say.

34

Shut the doors, lock them tight.
Light shine on me through the night.
Round about my little bed,
Ghosts and demons darkly tread.

From A Box Bed Prayer. Upslope.

THE DUSK WAS as peopled as Soulsday midnight, when the
dead rise up. The drum beat on the wind, the streets and
paths were full of beings weeping and laughing and singing.
I was not sure if they were living or dead, if maybe this invasion had raised souls from Tanshari's old arem.

They moved about the gardens, leaped the low walls,

called at the windows in voices half song, half cry. They touched the closed doors. The houses stood like stones.

Ab Jerash's gate was open, his door shut. Nall said, "Will he be armed?"

I almost said, *Does it matter?*

"No," I said. Jerash had six daughters; he had married off two of them, but the rest needed dowries. "He can't afford paidmen."

"Still." Nall whistled into the night. Three shadows came running, not ghosts, but warriors in sealskins with bone ankle rings—clan brothers, maybe. They spoke together in Rig. The warriors' teeth gleamed; the anklets rattled on their strong feet. I was afraid all over again and said to Nall, "If Jerash sees these, he'll never let us in!"

I had spoken like a Leagueman, as if the Rigi were dogs and could not understand human speech. One of them, a lean lad with a nicked ear, grinned at me and said, "Bear, we shall be the wind—heard, never seen." They sifted back into the dark. I heard chuckles, and the sound of someone making water. Nall and I crept up to the door of Graystone House.

The front stoop offered no cover, only bare stone steps that I had scrubbed a thousand times. The door, whitewashed to ward off devils, shone blue in the starlight. I knocked on it like a Rulesday visitor and said, "Uncle Jerash! Auntie!"

No one answered. But I had learned a lesson at the accounting house and whispered to Nall, "Come round to the back." The kitchen was there, and the box beds.

We slipped through the garden. The shadowy Rig warriors ran with us and nipped over the wall into the blackberry bushes. I heard soft laughter; they had found the ripe berries.

We crept under the shuttered windows to the kitchen steps.

I had scrubbed those, too, and knew where the wooden bucket would be standing overturned to dry. Nall did not, and kicked it. It fell with a bang, and when I put my ear to the door crack, I heard that muffled sob and the snick of a latch.

"Uncle!" I cried at the hinge. "Auntie! It's me. Katyesha."

At the sound of that name, everything I had been when I wore it began to seep out of that house, turning me back into the girl who scrubbed the stoop. I hunched up my shift to cover the scars.

With Nall's breath stirring my hair I said to the door crack, "It's just me. And—"

And a demon, a beast. What else could he be, to them?

"It's just me—and the beggar boy with the moon for his white mare."

Silence. Then knocks and scrapes, my uncle's voice hoarse and indistinct. "Katyesha."

"Hello, Uncle. Are you all right?"

Silence. More knocks, voices too low to understand. I waited, my cheek pressed against the jamb. I smelled cabbage soup with onions.

My uncle's voice, close to my ear this time but higher—for he was tall—said, "Have they killed him?"

No need to ask who. "No. But they have him."

"Who are they?"

"The Rigi."

The silence on the other side of the door stretched so long that Nall shifted on his bad foot. "There's no such thing," said Ab Jerash.

"I wish you'd stop saying that!" I said. "They're all over the place. They're eating Auntie's blackberries and pissing in her kale yard, and you Leaguemen keep saying they don't exist!"

After another, shorter silence my uncle said in almost his normal voice, "We're concerned."

I had grown up with language like this and knew it meant *We're terrified.* "Ab Harlan's been killing people," I said.

"He's excessive," said Ab Jerash in a rush. "We've agreed he's excessive. He stayed within bounds at first, and then— We could say nothing, Niece. They're his paidmen. We've been afraid—" He stopped himself, having used so straightforward a word. "Afraid for our children. For our wives. I've sent for a delegation from Rett. Secretly, of course. When Seroy was killed, I sent word; I said, 'Harlan's excessive, he's out of bounds, we're losing important customers here. Setting a poor example.'"

My cheek was still against the jamb. There would be a crease down it. "Do you know what the paidmen have done?"

"We couldn't stop them. Harlan has the money. I sent for the delegation; they'll be here tomorrow or the day after. Powerful traders—"

"Will they bring paidmen?"

"Yes," said Ab Jerash, very low. "I said there was trouble. But they won't be an army. Not like— We saw that army on the sea. The League—we're businessmen, Niece! We don't make war. We defend trade."

I thought of the boy with no feet. "How is that different from war?"

"A local difficulty. One little village . . . ," Ab Jerash began, and trailed off.

"Men's daughters are raped. Their children are dead and their houses burned."

"There must be reparation." He did not say what the children and houses of natives were worth, or who might pay. "Niece, are all the paidmen dead?"

"Run off."

By his silence I knew he was doing sums: how many paid-men the delegation might bring, plus how many met running on the road who might be persuaded to come back to Upslope and at what price; who would pay them, with Ab Harlan lost; how many warriors were in the army of his nightmares. At last he said, "We might call a council with Downshore. If they will."

"And with the Rigi."

Silence.

"As soon as the delegation comes," I said.

Silence. Then, "Could it be done?" Silence. "Perhaps so."

"You're such a good man!" I said before I thought. For he was; as good as he knew how to be. "Oh, Uncle, let us in!"

"I don't— The one with you—" *The devil king of the sea, the demon you ran off with, Niece.* "I'm afraid," my uncle said.

I knew what this honesty cost his pride. I suspected what it had cost him in money, with Ab Harlan. "If there's to be a council, Uncle, you'll have to know who you're talking to."

"I'm afraid for my girls."

I turned to Nall and soundlessly mouthed, *You try?*

Nall put his lips to the hinge crack. "Ab Jerash. Will you speak with us?"

More silence. Ab Jerash said, "He speaks Plain?"

"We all speak Plain," said Nall.

"How can it be that we did not know this?"

"There has been a separation."

"Yes. Yes, there has." Ab Jerash was at once more at ease talking to a man, though a native and a demon, than to me. He said, "Sir, good sir—can you understand that I'm afraid for my wife and daughters?"

"Yes."

There were rattles on the far side of the door; it was unbarred and opened a handspan. My uncle's pale face, hatless, appeared at the crack. He had braced his body against the door. After a moment he stepped back and said, "Come in."

We slipped into the kitchen; he slammed the door and barred it again. Even distraught he spoke the formal welcome of a League host: "I am in your employ." It was to Nall he spoke it; it was not said to women. "Wife, turn up the lamp."

The dark shape that was my aunt moved to the bead of light and raised the wick until the glare lit her hard, frightened face. Around her, as always, the flagstones gleamed slick as mirrors, the pots shone on the wall, and the hearth, which I had so often scrubbed on my knees with a chunk of pumice, was white as bone.

I realized that my head was uncovered, my hair uncut and uncombed, and I was dressed in dirty underwear.

I could not look at her. The more I blushed, the more I knew that I blushed, that I was naked, that she could see my body and my mind, every crime and shame and sluttery I had ever committed. I remembered being slapped for picking my nose.

"Good evening, Aunt," I said. I waved my hand a little. "This is Nall."

She had bent upon me a steel gaze. Then she looked at him, and her eyes went furtive, flinching.

I looked at him too. Narrow-hipped, nearly naked, he was as I had seen him first: a man, dark and desired. The lamplight slicked his thighs. Then I could look neither at him nor away from him, until at the edge of my vision my aunt's shocked face burned and blurred.

He held out his hands to her.

She put her own behind her back, like a little girl saying, *No!* Tears sprang to her eyes, and to hide them she turned away.

I had never seen her cry. I did not know what to do except to cling to the old courtesies. I said, "Auntie, I've been with my mother's sister in the Hills. Her name is Bian. She sends her kind regards."

Without turning around she said, "If you think you're going to—"

"Wife," said Ab Jerash.

She stood still a moment, then faced us with her eyes downcast. Her cheekbones stood out sharp. "My respects to your aunt," she said.

I said, "Are the girls all right?"

She did not answer. But Jerash said to her, "Are they any safer where they are?" He went to the biggest of the box beds. "Daughters, come out. We have guests." When the double doors were not unlatched from within, he said, "That's twice," in the tone that meant what it always had: *Stop doing whatever you just did, or get a beating.*

The latch rattled. Ab Jerash swung the doors wide to reveal four girls clutched together like mice in a nest, sobbing soundlessly, their fair braids rubbed into haloes. The littlest had buried her head in her sisters' skirts, and I saw only her pink fists, tight as buds.

"Missa, it's all right," I said. But it is never all right for girls in wartime.

"Get up, get up," my aunt said. "Lazy besoms! Your cousin is visiting."

They scrambled out, clinging and trembling. Then they saw Nall, and would have stampeded back into the bed if their mother had not blocked the way, saying stone-faced, "Greet our guests."

They bobbed like a covey of quail, whimpering, "Good evening, Cousin Katyesha."

I did not know what to feel. I did not love them, nor they me. But what if the world had gone differently and I had been among them still, cowering in that bed? What if it had been Jekka in there?

"Cheer up, ratlings," I said.

They startled and scowled. So did Auntie Jerash, who had smacked us for that word. Yet such is the power of insult that they composed themselves and truly looked at me.

And at Nall. Bodices were straightened, gowns shaken out, hair smoothed and tucked. Lila put her shoulders back. Ominya bit her lips to make them pink.

My aunt said sourly, "This is your cousin's—this is—Mister Nall."

Missa curtsied and piped, "Good evening, Mister Nall."

Then she did something she should not have done, that in that house had never been done. She stepped forward, holding out to him her small, pink hand.

He took it in his brown one. I heard my aunt's intake of breath. But she had named us guests and could not deliver smacks till later. "Missa," she said.

Missa turned her eyes to her mother with no obedience in them, withdrew her hand, and hid it in the folds of her skirt. She stepped back among her sisters. A glance went round among them.

Ab Jerash broke this awkwardness with another by asking, "Sir—Mister Nall—what ought we to do?"

His wife and daughters stared at him. A Leagueman had asked a naked native demon what to do.

The demon, by a glance, passed the question to me. I said to Jerash, "Where will the delegation be housed?"

"At Harlan's home. That was the plan. But, sir, Mister Nall, if Harlan—"

Again Nall glanced at me, and I said, "Send them to Downshore. Someone will find a place for them. They need to see for themselves what's been happening. The rest of the League here—are they in hiding?"

"The unmarried fled with the paidmen," Jerash said to Nall, but this time he caught the forwarding glance. Turning to me, he forced himself to talk seriously with a young, half-breed female in dirty underwear. "For the rest of us there was no time. We thought— We saw it coming over the water, that darkness, then those—" He rubbed his mouth. "Ab Harlan's sons have fled—all but your betrothed. He was taken hostage and must be dead. And Seroy is dead, and Dairois your brother is—"

He would not say the word "tortured." I would not tell him otherwise. Let him sit with it awhile.

But he laid his hand over his eyes and said, "We have brought ruin on many. *I* have brought ruin on many. Hear me, Niece! And you, sir, though you are a stranger. I saw what that man was becoming and took no action. You may say the blame falls on many souls, but no less on mine, for mine is the only soul I audit."

My aunt took a step forward and laid her hand on his arm, as if to say, *I stand with you.*

"Well." He looked up. The sweat stood on him. "Here we

are. Now. Niece, you say that a town council exists in Down-shore?"

"In Tanshari. The name has changed."

He corrected himself without question. "Tanshari has a council?"

"Yes, and I think you would be welcome," I said.

"I think I would be killed."

"These people are sick of killing. They want justice." In a bitter part of my heart I thought, Justice—and cinnamon, and rum, and ribbons. After a month on the mainland, won't those little twins want better than a string of beads?

As if he read my mind, Ab Jerash wiped his face and said to Nall, "There's a myth that the Rigi—that your people used to come to trade."

"We did."

"Perhaps we could help them out a little, eh? For example, we import cook pots—everybody needs cook pots. And your people must have things to sell. Until recently Downshore provided us with—"

"Sealskins," Nall said dryly.

"Exactly! Though that seems to have fallen off lately. Surely there are other items. Weaving? Pottery? And there's always a market for dried fish. I could speak with the council. Nothing like trading ties to smooth things over." He slid a glance at his wife. "A splendid opportunity."

I thought, He'll fetch up soon enough against Queelic, Hsuu, and zero.

If it was for money that he stayed, so be it—if only he stayed. If this spotless kitchen might see new visitors, if these pale girls might sit, sometime, at Mailin's table. I thought, We must build Mailin a new table.

"You're brave, Uncle," I said.

That pleased him. He was still afraid, but mostly for the girls, and rightly.

"Stay here for now. Keep the doors barred," I said. It was not much protection; but Ab Harlan's spilled gold had lain untouched.

This did not satisfy my aunt, who drew Jerash aside and must have begged to take the chance and flee inland, for he told her sharply, "We stay. The delegation must be housed and fed."

She bent her head, then looked around as if to be sure she had her saucepans.

I said, "Auntie, I'll help cook."

"I am perfectly capable of managing my own kitchen!"

But my cousins looked at me with faces hopeful as sunflowers. For I had gossip—really good gossip. I had stories of love and passion, of adventure and far places; I had secrets of romance and men and sex. I had jokes and new recipes and clandestine songs—and I could tell them all this in their own comfortable tongue, Kitchen Hessdish.

Oh, please! their eyes begged.

I said to my aunt, "I still make your cream dill sauce."

"*Tcha!*" she said.

I thought of that sauce, in the blue porcelain gravy boat that had come all the way from Rett by muleback, packed in wood shavings in its own little box. It had been a ceremony to make it, to hand the blue boat round and hear my aunt say, "Lila made the sauce this time." "Missa made the sauce." I had had my turn the same as the rest.

"Oh, Aunt," I said, "I'm sorry I caused you so much grief! I was the wrong flower for your garden, but you tended me anyway. How could I do anything but thank you?"

"Thank your father!" she said, and turned her back.

"Is he at the house?"

She made a little assent, but a clatter outside made her gasp and grope for her daughters.

A familiar voice sent Ab Jerash, after a moment's dithering, to open the door. The wind blew into the house, full of the sound of the drum.

It was Dai shouting on the doorstep, with Robin by the hand. Somewhere he had found tweed breeches and black boots, but nothing more; he looked half Leagueman, half bear.

"Dairois!" said Ab Jerash.

"Good evening, Uncle, Aunt! You're all right, then? Quite a night, eh? Don't think you've met my wife."

When I heard the mischief in his voice, my heart eased for him. Then Robin sidled in round as a bun, and who could resist her? Ab Jerash bowed. The women curtsied.

"We're going down to the beach to dance the Least Night," she said, beaming. "The Rigi are carrying Harlan down to the sea."

I heard the music, faint on the wind: the drum still steady, the fiddle, many voices singing.

Soundlessly, my uncle's mouth said *sea*.

"To bathe his feet," said Robin. "He asked to go."

Asked, said my uncle's mouth.

She turned to Auntie Jerash. "Won't you come? We'd love to have you."

"We've knocked on a few doors," said Dai. "Ab Niram's gone with the paidmen. Ab Saison, too—they're bachelors, nothing to hold them. But Ab Hiun's baby is sick, so they stayed; they're with Mailin now. Ab Spelmar is passed out drunk; his wife's there, but she's terrified—won't open the door. Been talking to her through the crack—Queelic has. I mean Keeo."

"Queelic," said Ab Jerash.

"He seems to have things under control. He's loading carts from the storehouse and sending them to Downshore, I mean Tanshari. For the festival."

"I need to think about this," said Ab Jerash.

"Me too," said Dai. "Damn. But come with us, won't you? We've got another lot of doors to knock on. They'll know your voice."

"I won't leave my family."

"Bring them," said Dai.

Ab Jerash opened his mouth. Left it open. Music drifted in through the open door.

"Girls," said Auntie Jerash, "you heard Dairois. Get your cloaks and bonnets."

They fairly scrambled for their cloaks. "Wife!" said Ab Jerash.

"Ab Hiun's baby is sick. Ab Spelmar's wife is terrified. Would you desert your neighbors?" She had her own cloak on and was looking for her basket. She shot me a glance like vinegar and jerked her chin at Nall. "Men!" she said. "You'll find out soon enough."

From Ab Jerash's door I could not see Tanshari or the beach, only a glow of fire beyond the cliff's edge. The wind was full of blown music; it billowed the cloaks of Auntie Jerash and the girls as we ushered them toward Ab Spelmar's house. Missa threw back the hood of her cloak, and the wind tweaked wisps of her light hair from its braid.

Dai held Robin's hand. My heart was so huge that I could not contain it, I wanted Nall to put his arm around me and hold me tight so I would not burst with this glad and terrible collision of souls.

He did not. I did not know who he was, this man with the changed face and worsening limp, to whom, if I believed him, nothing mattered. Not even me.

For there was, after all, a ghost in the wind, of a lonely girl who had longed so deeply that she had called a man out of the sea; yet she had not gotten what she wanted. There had been some mistake. She had longed for a lover like the one who had kissed her on Mailin's hearth, and this was not he.

I did not see that little ghost because she walked exactly in my shoes. I only felt hollow and cold and drew away from Nall a little. Still, there ahead of us was Dai, alive and merry; and it was our father who had saved him. I thought, I have a loving father.

"Dai!" I said. "Father won't know what's happened."

"Won't like it, either," said Dai. Then, shamefaced, "Wait till morning, Sister? Come morning things will be quieter. I—I have to thank him."

"I want to go now." I wanted everything healed, finished, safe. Maybe if I made everything right, everything, *then* I would be given my heart's desire?

"May still be paidmen about."

As if I cared, who had journeyed to the world's end! "I'm going," I said.

"Wait till one of us can go too."

"I'll come with you," said Nall.

I did not want him to come with me. I did not know what

I wanted, except the man I had longed for. But Dai did not seem to notice any change; he embraced Nall and said, "When that woman's mind is made up, look out! Sister, give Father my thanks. Tell him I'll be there tomorrow to say that in person. I'll bring a mule and take him down to Mailin, she'll set him right." He touched my arm and said, with difficulty, "Tell him I love him."

"I will."

Nall and I turned aside from the group, toward Father's house. We took the goat paths that I had so often run, in the high scrub near the cliffs.

Here the ghost of my old self was even stronger. It wore heavy clothes, confusion, a blind longing for something I could not name. Here I had sung into the wind, *Come to me! Come to me!*

Now I said nothing. Neither did Nall. We walked under the uncountable stars. We left the weeds and stunted pinelands and came to the cliff's edge where the wind bit, and we looked out over harbor and sea.

There were many fires. Burned house and bonfire smell the same, and I could not tell whether the faint cries I heard were joy or mourning. The drum beat dull as a heart. The little ghost practiced what she longed to say, to make it true by saying it.

Father, I'm home! The world is made whole. You were mistaken: Here is the man you cursed and sent away; he is my true love, and all is well.

The house was shuttered and dark, for Father was a miser with fuel. Dai's cowshed was roofless, my garden thick with weeds, the cistern clogged with windblown trash. But the dooryard was trodden, and at one shutter's edge clung a crumb of light.

I knocked. Got no answer. Knocked again.

"Father?"

Silence. Nall beside me silent. I wrestled with the latch of the outer door. He moved to help me, but I shook my head, and in the end I kicked it open as I had used to do when I brought water from the cistern. It hurt my foot. The vestibule smelled of mice, by which I knew my old cat was dead.

The inner door was shut, of course. I knocked on it. "Father, it's Kat."

Silence.

Nall held the outer door open for starlight to see by. "Shut it!" I said. I was never to leave both open—it let the wind in. I felt my father's cold glare already, the same he had turned on Nall sprawled and bleeding on the hearth, as he shouted, *Get it out!*

Nall shut the door. I heard his breath in the darkness. I fumbled at the inner latch until it grew a long crack of candle-light, and pushed the door open.

"Father?"

On the mantel the last of a candle guttered in the draft, sending up a ribbon of smoke. In that still, cold room all was in order: chairs set to the table, meager crockery washed. Fine hearth ash had settled on everything—even on Ab Drem my father, stretched on the hard black settee with one hand fallen, the other at his breast. His face had sunk in on itself, empty and calm. His mouth, no breath in it, hung open.

I stood without speaking.

Something touched my back—Nall's hand. I knocked it away. I could not breathe or speak.

Motion to my left: Nall, kneeling to pick up the only object out of place.

Fallen from my father's hand was a trinket case, of the kind sold by Roadsoul artists at country fairs to hold a coarse painting of your darling. Nall held it up to me.

It was worn with carrying but not with opening, for the leather of the spine split as I spread the covers apart.

Smiling up at me was myself, not myself: Lisei my mother, her red hair braided and pinned high like a crown, mischievous and guilty, fearfully in love. Into the frame was tucked a lock of hair that was two locks: one red and curly, one straight and gold, braided together for half their length.

The air around me grew thicker, or thinner, or clearer, or colder; charged, like lightning air. I closed the trinket case.

I was afraid to touch my father. But I lifted his fallen hand; I laid it on his breast with the other and folded both over the case. They were cold, the skin on them soft and loose, his fingers not yet stiff.

The candle made a sound like moth wings.

There were words in my mouth. *Father, Dai loves you. Oh, Father, thank you! Remember Nall? Remember me? I've grown up. So much has happened. I'm proud to be your daughter. I love you.*

There was no one to speak them to.

I drew a great breath, as if to breathe the words back in. They stuck in my heart, there was no room there. Turning, I saw in the guttering light Nall's face as still as my father's, listening.

I knew what he was hearing. The non-sound of it filled the room, empty as the space between two stones.

My breath came in cool, went out warm. I said, "To be alive is not nothing."

He sat back on his heels.

With my warm breath, not loud, I said, *"I am not nothing!"*

I turned right round. I opened the inner door. There should

have been a Year Altar so I could leave something, but there was only the whitewashed wall.

I looked back. "*Be* nothing, then! That's easy. It's being alive that hurts!"

His eyes opened wide. That was something, anyway.

I slammed the inner door, kicked open the outer one. For the second time in my life I left that house with one man standing in it.

35

Round as an eye, round as the moon,
Full as an egg on the first of June,
Empty as a nest on the first of September,
I am. I am not. Forget me. Remember.
What am I?

(Zero)

Riddle. Tanshari.

I THOUGHT he would follow me.

He did not.

I ran, then walked on the goat trails high above the sea,
and Nall did not follow me. The last trace of day had gone
and the night was huge with wind, the hollow arch of the sky
was full of stars, the earth full of songs and fires.

I would die. I knew this for the first time. It would be me cold on a settee with my mouth fallen open.

I was not afraid. I did not need to make time stop, or clutch and hold it. I just had to breathe and keep moving, walking down the goat path in my broken sandals. I breathed the night.

Little fires dotted the line of the beach, the Least Night bonfire in the middle like the hub of a wheel. Year Altar or not, I had thrown something in that fire, and one of his names was Nall.

The music was working into a good roar, but distant, like a carnival in the next village. I had no thoughts. I only felt the bigness of the night around me, as if it were alive.

I came to a cattle path and turned toward town. There were people on it—Tansharians, roving and calling and looking to see whether their houses still stood, and with them a few Rigi, men mostly. Some of these revelers were already drunk.

I did not want to meet anyone, or speak. The dim roar of the crowd made my shoulders jump with dread. But if I did not go back, Dai and Mailin would think I had been raped by paidmen, or worse. I began to pick my way toward town.

I did not know where to begin to look for Mailin, but I headed for the bonfire on the beach. I had danced at the Long Night fire, so the Least Night fire would be as familiar as anything in this new world. Suddenly I was uneasy to be a woman alone.

Once down off the cliffs I found the woods above the strand full of shadowy movement, lovers trysting under the low trees. I hurried without listening to the laughter, the soft voices in Rig and Plain. Above the beach, almost running, I caught my foot on a hank of grass and sprawled in the sand.

Someone lifted me up, a fair, curly-haired lad as big as Raím who said, "Trying to fly? Fly to me, sweet lass!" He began to dust me off with caresses, but by the distant firelight he saw who I was and stopped, ashamed or frightened. "Lali Kat, forgive me!"

He looked about—for Nall, I suppose. Not seeing him, he was tipsy enough to lean closer. "We thank you! Downshore, Tanshari thanks you!"

"Don't thank me. The world changes by itself—"

He was not listening. "We bless you! This is a night to be happy!" He kissed my cheek, and when I did not protest, he gave me a beery wet kiss on the mouth.

I said, "Be happy, then!" and sprang away, like a tranced rabbit that starts and runs. He would find another girl before the night was out. I ran between cookfires just lit, the cooks bustling around them. I tried not to look like myself. Sometimes I slipped past unnoticed. Sometimes there were cries of "Lali Kat!" or "Bear!" and I smiled and ran faster. Carpenters were setting up makeshift booths for food and music, for when did humans let war interrupt a party? Before Hsuu's magic and the beer wore off, there would be fights and resolutions of fights, black eyes, love babies, new brotherhoods. Flocks of children flitted from fire to fire.

Near the main bonfire it was crowded, and I had to slow down. People took my hands and kissed me, asking, "Where's Nall?"

I said, "Where's Mailin? Have you seen Mailin?"

A woman snatched her little daughter out of a cloud of children and charged her with taking me to Mailin. I would sooner have trusted a mayfly; the girl wore borrowed silks and was wild with night, shrieking, all eyes. She took my hand, and I swear she flew instead of walking, like a june bug on a thread.

She pulled me away from the crowds, along the beach to a lean-to cobbled from a canvas awning and the turquoise Roadsoul cart. There the wind flattened a wide fire, throwing shadows so fitful that it was hard to pick out Mailin and Robin, and Suni on a blanket with her children sprawled in her lap like sleeping puppies. Pao wrestled with the awning, sharing a hammer and shouts with an old Rig and a Roadsoul lad. A shadow in the lean-to was young, dark-clad Ab Hiun, crouching against his wife as she held their child close. He had his big hat off, fanning the baby's face.

When we came into view of this, Mailin's new house, I stopped. My child guide took this as dismissal and slipped my hand, flitting back to her game of tag. I stood alone outside the blustery circle of light.

Ab Hiun waved the wide black hat. Then he set it aside and did what I had never seen any League father do: He held out his arms, and his wife put the baby into them.

He looked terrified, as if he might break it. But he got it held, and his wife took up the hat and fanned. Ab Hiun gazed at his child's face. He nudged back the blankets and touched its sweaty hair.

I stepped into the shifting light. Mailin saw me, then the rest, all their glad faces. Ab Hiun and his wife shrank around their child. Robin came to draw me to the fire, saying, "We were worried! Where's Nall? Did you talk to your father?"

"Father's dead," I said. "Lying on the settee. The candle was still burning."

They stared, dumbfounded. Robin said, "Oh, Kat!" and laid her cheek on mine. "Where's Nall?"

"He stayed at the house."

Mailin looked at me sharply, but Suni made an answer for them by saying, "Will he bring Ab Drem away?"

I imagined my father's body in Nall's arms and shuddered. "Tomorrow will be soon enough. That house is cold even in summer." As though Father were meat.

Ab Hiun said from the lean-to, "Ab Drem is dead?"

"Yes," I said. "Alone."

"He was long ill," said his wife. She looked at her child, and two tears tracked down her cheeks.

Mailin touched her shoulder. "Lali Minashya, the fever is nearly gone."

The woman I had known for years without knowing her name, Minashya, nodded untrustingly. When for my father's sake her husband began to murmur the words for the dead, she snatched the baby from him with a look of horror.

Before they could ask more about Nall, I said, "Where's Dai? And Queelic and Aieh and Hsuu? Oh, where's Nondany?"

Mailin looked at me as though she could see through my skin into my heart, an empty room with a guttering candle in it. "Nondany's at his sister's house. Robin can give you news of Dai. Queelic is off on some errand—Lali, that lad gives me hope for this life. Aieh went with him. Hsuu is down on the beach with Harlan."

"It was hard to get his boots off," said Robin. "Harlan's. He was afraid of the little waves at first and screamed, but then he giggled. Dai's gone to our house. The house is gone, but you saw the cowshed is still there—and Moss is in it! She'll be

in pain from the milk; Dai went to her as soon as we heard—
What's that?"

The drum had beat so unvaryingly that we had stopped
hearing it. Now it stuttered; there was a change in the commotion near town, and I could run out with Pao to look and
not be questioned.

A fuss of shadows heaved at an alley mouth, as if something were trying to get born there. Then the great, round,
rolling shape of the drum emerged, bumping down the path
to the beach, helped along by a host of hands. It was still
being beaten in an approximation of its rhythm—I could not
see by whom, only hear *thump, thump* and happy yells.

"Taking it down to the strand, as is proper," said Pao. We
went closer. The drum rolled between the fires. People danced
as they walked, whole and wounded, Rig and Tansharian,
some with grieving or bitter faces, but mostly merry.

"Look there!" said Pao.

It was Ab Jerash, in shirtsleeves. Queelic walked beside
him. Aieh followed Queelic with both hands on his waist,
and two more bare-chested Rig girls followed her the same;
they were doing that line dance where you kick your feet
out all together, left and right. Ab Jerash glanced nervously
at the girls and waved his hands to the music. He even
jigged a little in his boots. He was a diplomat.

"Lali Kat," said Pao, "can your heart encompass what you
have set in motion, like that rolling drum? You and Nall."

Time collapsed like a folded fan. In one breath I was walking with Nondany on the road to Downshore, eager and
secretive, holding Nall's face in my heart; in the next the
world had turned over, and in place of that man's warm face
was nothing.

I turned and saw Mailin's fire through the shadowy shape of the cart. Her face blinked into the light, then the Roadsoul woman's, then Ab Hiun's. I remembered Nondany saying, *If things get too surprising, Half-and-Half, you're welcome at my sister's house.*

"I'm going to Nondany," I said to Pao, and before he could ask another question, I ran again, into the dark.

Ran and ran. I had hurried from Creek, eager for Nall; hurried to the Gate to save the world and then raced back to warn; hurried to confront Ab Harlan, then to rescue Dai, next to knock on Ab Jerash's door; hurried to my own old house, knocking and calling *Father! Father!*; hurried to open the door, to arrive, to be safe, like a fleeing deer that does not see the cliff until there is nothing under its feet, falling, still running as it falls.

I ran toward Nondany's house through the windy scrub, limped over shell middens on my worn-out sandals, climbed the path to the alley mouth where the drum had been rolled out.

But it was not the alley with Lilliena's shop in it. Right away I got lost in the maze of streets. The lanes were full of broken furniture and crockery, crushed flowers, lost shoes. People came and went through this ruin as if it were not there, except for one old woman who swept her dooryard in the dark, tidying up after war.

The starlight did not reach to the bottom of the alley. Whenever I heard voices, I stepped into a doorway or behind a lilac tree; there were as many hiding places aboveground as the warrenhouse had had below. I thought of Selí, of the ama's quiet room that smelled of honey and sand and peace.

I thought, If she were here with the rest, everything would be all right, she would tell me what to do. But she was dead, and Father was dead, and I ran.

I came to the plaza. Without the drum it was as quiet as a body whose heart has stopped. Starlight silvered everything; the trees, shielded from the wind, were still. I could hear the voices of all the people who had ever lived there, Rig and Tansharian and Lake and Hill, all dead. Then the ghosts turned into lovers standing close in a doorway, a sad man scratching in the trash, a cat.

I turned down the alley I thought was Nondany's. Wrong again. I went back to the plaza and tried another. Everything felt changed. A trio of drunks burst upon me, singing dirty and talking big; I kept still and thought myself invisible, like a nighthawk's chick on its nest of stones. They rolled past. I was left still holding my breath, so quiet that I heard, faintly, a voice singing in some inner garden.

> Love and rose are red as blood
> When their blooms are in the bud;
> Ah, but each droops pale and wan
> When its flower has blown and gone. . . .

I opened my mouth to shout, "Nondany!" But the revelers still bellowed in the street; I held my tongue. I climbed a cobbled buttress and ran along the tops of the stone walls above empty patios, following the voice to a shadowy court where I looked down on the garden cool with roses, and on Nondany's untidy head. He had a chair and a little glass lamp, and he held the broken dindarion across his lap. A little, hairy dog crouched at his feet. The burned boy lay

unmoving in a mess of blankets on a stone wall bench, the
rags that covered his upper face white as bone in the lamplight.

> Oh, heart! That love so soon should fade,
> And that sweet flower in dust be laid . . .

He could not strum the broken dindarion; perhaps it was
comfort to hold it.

"Nondany!"

He jumped, looked everywhere but up.

Because it was not the piggie song, I was afraid the boy
was dead. I ran along the wall to the apricot tree, swarmed
down it, and dropped into Nondany's outstretched arms.

"Half-and-Half! Falling from the sky, by life! No magic—I
saw how you two dove out that window." He embraced me
with his elbows, holding his hands away. The little dog
bounced but did not bark.

"The boy?" I said. I could see now that he slept. His pout-
ing lips trembled with the ferocity of his dreams.

"Better, I think. By life!" He put me back from himself, his
face furrowed with weariness and smiles. I wore my living
breath around me like wind, thinking: Father is dead—and
I'm alive.

I put my hand on the lad's little, hot one. He spread his
fingers and sighed.

"Don't wake him!" said Nondany. "I'll have to sing that
song. It's only justice that at the great change of the world I
should have to sing some damned silly song ten thousand
times."

"So you know what's happened—all about it?"

"'All about it,'" he said. "By life, there's a goal for me. Where's Nall?"

I took my hand off the boy's. "I don't know."

Nondany peered at my face. Raised both eyebrows. He sat down again, lifted the dindarion with his wrists, and said, "I don't think you've met Lilliena's little dog? I rescued him from a horrid fate: He was about to be eaten by Roadsouls. I'm convinced he remembers it, for he is voracious. His name is So It Is. Say hello to the lady, Sotis."

The dog wagged and put up one paw.

I did not shake it. I said, "Nall and I. We went to my father's house, to tell him—to talk to him. He was dead. On the settee. With his mouth open."

Nondany watched me, silent. At last he said, "I have noticed, over the years, that the dead resemble one another more than they do their living relatives. I know that open, empty mouth."

"I never saw him asleep." That seemed like a mystery, almost the core of it. "He slept alone, in his box bed."

"Nall was with you when you found him?"

"He's still there. For all I know."

"You quarreled?"

"No." A quarrel has two sides, like the fight at the Gate. When nothing matters, there are no quarrels.

"Well, well," said Nondany, tilting the chair. The boy whined in his sleep. "Not that it is any of my business. In the middle of this grand, this *loud* time. When I have sung that asinine song until my stomach is upset. And have chattered with a thousand people, including, I believe, an aunt of yours."

"She came here? Auntie Jerash came down *here*?"

"With an entourage of daughters—very frightened, and with good reason. I was worried for them. But it seemed she had plans. She was laden with cloth and medicines, ready to do good. I nearly lost my laddie to her. I'm a cynic, Half-and-Half, but I'm persuaded that she was making such amends as she knew how to."

"If she came down here, in the dark, that's enough. More than enough."

"So I felt. And here you are as well. But Nall—"

"I am not nothing!"

"No. Not only nothing."

You are either nothing or you are something. I turned away, to climb back up the tree and keep running.

Nondany lifted the broken dindarion. Under his breath he whistled the song he had sung in his eyrie right before the Rigi came.

Some part of me must have been paying attention then, for now I turned back and said, "How?"

"How what?"

"If it's true nothing turns to every shining thing, how does it do it?"

"If I knew that, Half-and-Half, I would be king of the sea and of earth and sky besides."

"If I could turn nothing into every shining thing, I could have anything I want."

"Ah. But that isn't what the song says. It is not we who turn nothing into everything. Nothing does that by itself."

I whispered, "But I don't like what it does."

Nondany touched the boy's feet. Someone had washed them, and they were perfect: fat brown toes to kiss, to pretend to eat. I thought, He'll be able to dance someday. If he wants to.

Aloud I said, "If nothing can turn to everything, then it wasn't nothing."

"What would you call it, then?"

"There'd be no word for it! There couldn't be."

I thought of Tadde's seal speaking, how the four of us had each put different words in its mouth. How we all wonder at the same world, yet we explain it with different songs, tattoos, hand slaps.

Who could say for sure what Nall had heard, or name it? Each namer is different, each name has to be in some language and not another. I said, "We use whatever words we have."

I did not look at Nondany. Maybe I dared look, at last, into the gap between the stones of the Gate.

I saw how you might come to believe that your own word for this namelessness was the truth. The way my aunt Bian had to believe that what had eaten me was a bear—it just had to be. The way I had to believe the man I had called was the perfect lover I longed for—he just had to be.

And Nall, trying to name a mystery too big for naming, was able only to feel how unnameable it was.

Like the Bear that was not a bear. I said, "It has a big letter."

Nall had heard Nothing that was not nothing—that is Everything. Everything: nameless; whole; rolling toward the shores of the world to be cast up and named, for a little while—"heart," "fish," "mountain," "Kat," "child"—and then dissolve again to Nothing.

He had said, *I hear Nothing.*

I could not hear what he did: that Sound that was not a sound. But I could feel the waves from its earthquake, the wind from its wings. Like him, I could call that "listening." If I coiled my little words around what I felt, like clay around the emptiness that is a bowl, I could make songs.

Aloud I said, "'Everything is Nothing,' he said. *That's* the place all patterns come from. But to see it or hear it, you have to dress it; you can't make songs from Nothing until it's wearing words."

Something wet lapped at my ankle.

I jumped. The little dog was licking and grinning. It was the ugliest dog I ever saw; its bottom teeth stuck out.

"For shame," Nondany told it. "Interrupting the artist at her work."

I stared around at the world that was changed and not changed, more vast than the sky. Nondany teetered in his chair.

I said, "I walked out and left Nall with my father."

"Ah."

"Father hates him."

"Not anymore."

"But I left him with a corpse— And his ama just dead—" I wrung my hands. "He keeps saying nothing matters."

"You have just told me that Nothing matters a great deal. And you might have some compassion for him; while you have been finding your calling, he has been losing his. Or so he thinks."

"But I don't know who he is now."

Nondany tipped his chair.

"I'm not even sure I like him."

His foot tapping.

"I don't know what he's *feeling*."

"By life!" Nondany roared. "Youth is something I no longer understand. Here you are, with a sound body and sound hands, a pretty face, and all the energy in creation, and what do you do? Think up yet another reason to stall. In my experience, which is not slight, the way to find out what another person feels is to *ask* him!"

A wail rose from the wall bench.

"There now! I've waked my laddie. Husha, husha, mannie."

"Ting piggie!" wept the little hoarse voice.

"I deserved that. I must forgo tirades." Nondany began to pat. I heard someone moving in the house beyond the patio. "You said Nall might still be with your father?"

"Maybe. No. He wouldn't stay there."

"Where might he have gone? 'Nall'—by life, that name confounds me every time. In the dialect of Welling, *nall* means 'nameless' and is one of the appellations of God."

"He's not a god!" I said, and saw that I had made him one. "I have no idea where he's gone."

That was a lie. For in my heart I saw where Nall had gone, clear as a morning dream.

I saw him standing in that still, cold room, unmoving, while the candle flame jumped on the last of the wick and went out. I saw him drag his lame foot to the door—his hands were stronger than mine, he could lift that latch with one thumb—and let himself out into the damp vestibule, then into the forlorn dooryard, shutting each door behind him.

I saw him in the big night, breathing the west wind; saw him walk to the cliff's edge, press through the scrub pines, and, lurching a little, pad down the steep path to the beach. It would be quiet there, the footprints of paidmen long since washed away.

On the sand where I had found him, I saw the man I had called to me strip off his knife belt and breechclout. He rubbed his face, pushed back his curls, stretched his toes into the sand one last time. Then two strides; his shoulders leaned into the waves, and he was swimming west. In the sea he was not lame. He did not follow the line of skerries this time. Just swimming and swimming, into the dark.

As he drew closer to the nothing that he heard so clearly, I saw two shadows come nuzzling up from the deep: a seal with a mark like a human hand and one freckled like a fawn, welcoming him, drawing him down. Surely he would not be lonely forever. Surely they would find him a new skin.

I saw this.

Nondany watched my face.

I said, "What else could I have done?"

"Nothing," said Nondany. "Nothing that I know of. Pigalee."

A little round woman—Lilliena, no doubt—came out carrying a teapot and saying, "What's all this fuss and shout? And who is this lass, our very own Lali Kat?" She chattered and bustled as if this were any night on her patio, exclaimed and fretted at me, at Nondany and the boy; she knew I was the witch but not a witch, really, such a pretty lass, she'd seen me at the market all these years and wasn't it a fine one, dried apricots cheap and plenty on a good year, but good years only one in seven?

"I have to go," I said. There was only one place, one person left to run to.

"Go? Poor little wren!" she said, laying the lad straight. I could not tell whether she meant the boy or me or the dog that wagged at her feet. "Go, like that, all alone into the night with drunks about and dreams, those Rigi, and to be sure we'll have none of that Rig nonsense, we're Badger clan aren't we, short legs and ill tempers, eh, Songsparrow?"

"Pigalee," sang Nondany.

"That song, will we never be done with it! Try him with

the kitty song, the mewly one. Ah, my lamb"—she meant me this time—"stay till morning, won't you? There's work in every house, herbs to be pounded, and have you had any sleep at all? I thought not. Poor bunny! Songsparrow, don't muss the laddie's shirt about. Lali Kat, aren't you thirsty? You'll need a drink, a dipperful, I've never been so grateful to have water again, we don't appreciate what we've got until it's gone. Where are you going? Songsparrow, does she think she's a bird?"

"She's a Kat," said Nondany as I fled up the apricot tree and onto the wall.

"Kat, stop, poor kitty—"

The boy kicked out his legs. "No pigalee!" he said. "Ting kitty song!"

"By life!" said Nondany. "Great day!

36

Deep in the east,
Under the sea's brim,
Under the world's rim,
Dwells a fire,
A hearth, a pyre,
A woman, a beast,
So fierce, so bright,
So red, so white,
That sleeping night
Stirs with a dim cry,
And she comes to him.

Night and Day. The Rigi

I RAN THE TOPS of garden walls, Tanshari below me like a maze. The gardens were mostly deserted wells of dark, but here and there folk were gathered, speaking or singing. I was a sky goddess floating above the world, listening to human prayers as they rose.

I found a branchy olive and climbed down to the street. Footsore, breathless, weary beyond thought, I ran out the gate through which we had walked toward Ab Harlan's. It was like one of those nightmares in which you have to do something over and over until you get it right, and I could not get it right. I could only run to Dai, the first of all, and the last.

Dai was with the cow. Dai would know what to do. I ran as if I could escape what I had seen, the man stripping and swimming into the dark. Like a fox that smells the spittle of the hounds, tastes its own blood in its mouth, I ran fast and faster, up the cattle path to Dai.

A wraith of smoke marked where his house had stood. But some last paidman or reveler strode down the starlit path; I half fell behind a scrubby oak, trying to breathe without gasping, and not until he was nearly past did I hear "—*cuddy-o*—"

"Dai!"

He whirled and crouched, lips in a snarl. Then he jumped and caught me, embraced me, but just as soon was shaking me, saying, "Running around alone—you little chit, what are you about? Where've you been? Sweating blood with worry, all of us, d'you think you're the only person in the world?"

I clung so tight, he had a hard time shaking me. I had no breath left, could not even say, *Dai, Father's dead*. But it was huger than that. The whole world we had grown up in had died, and Nall with it, like a wave that is not a wave anymore, only sea.

He plucked me off and held me away. "Spit it out, brat. What the hell is going on with Nall?"

"Nall!"

"To hear him talk you'd think it's over, that you've ended it. *Ended* it? So you fought, whatever—you think Robin and I don't fight? Cats and dogs, makes the love good after. You called him out of the damned *sea*, Sister. What are you think-ing of?"

"How do you— You talked to him? Where—"

Dai jerked his thumb over his shoulder. "In the cowshed."

The cowshed!

But I had seen him lean into the waves. He was gone.

Dai shook me again. "Told him, 'Get some sleep, you idiot!' but he won't sleep, won't go down to Mailin, won't go after you, either. Strung up like a bow, and no wonder—when's the last he had any rest? What am I supposed to do, knock him out with my fist? Left him a candle lantern for company. I said, 'Make yourself useful, for god's sake. Here's Moss with her little one dead and days unmilked, now there's grief! Cow helped you once, now you help her.' I was coming down to find you, smack some sense into you. It's like his heart's not there at all. What happened?"

I clasped my hands over my own heart. "It's nothing—," I began, and then laughed, grievously. The world rocked like the manat. "Dai, if I never married—if I never married *him*, would you still love me?"

"Yes. But I'd think you were crazy. Already think you're crazy, so it's no odds. What's going on?"

"I don't know."

"You never will. You think *I* know? But I know when I'm lucky."

"Maybe I don't."

"Then ask me, I'll tell you. All that man wants is room to be the disaster he is, same as the rest of us. Now get in there. Slap some sense into *him*." He faced me up the lane and gave me a shove. "Come to a conclusion I like, or I'll kill you both."

I took two steps in the dust. "Dai, our father—"

"Dead. Nall told me. Now there's a life to emulate. Poor old man. Sweetheart and husband and father, and never a loving word spoken under the eye of the sun."

I thought of the portrait case. "Not *never*."

"Never to me. And now never from me to him. Well, I know one child who's going to hear plenty. I'm going down now to my own lass, Sister, but I'll see you up that path first. Get you to that living man."

"I—"

"Wrong word," said Dai. "No wonder the two of you can't get it right. Try 'we.'"

Dai watched my back, standing in the path with his arms crossed. There were new trees planted on either side of the way, apricots, and when the path bent among them I was hidden from him. I could have slipped away into the dark. Some of the little trees had been trampled, the stems snapped, the wood showing white at the break.

Where the house had been was a dark heap that stank of fire. Two walls still stood, and part of a window, but its ruin made the little shed beyond look big as a house. It was built of stone like the one at Father's, but its thatch was thick as a pelt, and I could not think how it had escaped burning except by that chance of war in which one child dies, another lives.

The door was shut.

I had stood once before outside the closed door of a cow-shed, knowing Nall was in there and maybe dead. I had stepped close then, and entered, and there he was.

But this time *Nall was not there.* The Nall I had dreamed and called and named had swum back into the dark. I knew this the way I had known when a baby tooth was gone and I could put my tongue in the gap.

Who, then, was in the cowshed?

I stepped closer. Heard nothing.

A glimmer showed me the chink in the door. I stood for a long time, feeling my clasped hands touch each other. Then, quiet as my old cat, I slipped to the chink and looked through.

I saw Moss's shadowy neck, her soft eye in candle-glow. Heard a harsh, repeated clang. A hand with barked knuckles came into the little illuminated world. It scratched Moss's forehead.

"Sweet cow," said a man's voice. "You shall have another child."

The hand went away. Clang and scrape. Somebody was shoveling manure.

I leaned my cheek on the jamb. Heard the clank of the shovel being put up, rattle of a dragged stool, growl of the first stream of milk into the pail. Through the crack in the door I could see him, his forehead pressed on the cow's flank. Tousled brown curls, gaunt face hazed with beard, a mouth whose corners tucked back as if they had secrets. Behind him a heap of straw shone like gold.

An owl called on the hillside. I raised one finger and tapped at the door.

He looked up frowning, reaching for his knife. Stood. His shoulders blocked the line of candlelight, and the door opened.

I put my hands behind me, like Auntie Jerash.

After a moment he let go of the door and stepped back. Candlelight gilded him all over: scars, worn face. His leg shook. He sat down on the stool.

The thousand things I might have said.

I said, "I— We—" Then, "Where—where did you learn to milk?"

"Dai taught me."

He turned away, began to milk again. Moss swung her mild head.

Hish, hish, milk in the pail.

The wrinkle at his brow was there for good. His ribs stared like a street dog's. To the cow's flank he said, "I don't know."

Odor of beeswax, new milk. He looked up. Deep inside I felt a soft clutch like a hand closing. Milk spurted into the foamy pail.

I said, "I don't know either."

He nodded.

I wet my lips. "In the Hills, when I was herding goats, it was so dry that sometimes I'd dig a hole in the sand, to get down to where it was damp. So I could smell water."

He rose. He fetched a clay cup from a nail, dipped it full of milk, and held it out. I stepped onto the gleamy straw, took the cup, and drank half.

It watered me right down to my heels. I gave him the other half. He tipped back his head and drank it off, filled the cup again, held it out. "There's plenty," he said.

I took the cup. He returned to milking. I could see only half his face. He said, "What was it like there?"

At the Gate? In my dead father's house? In the world without you in it? "Where?" I said.

"In the Hills. When you were gone that long time."

Such a long time!

"It's dry," I said. "And high, and clear, and lonely."

"Tell me."

I sat down in the heaped straw. My feet were so grateful.

"They call them hills," I said, "but they're mountains, really. So high, they have patches of snow on them even in summer, and in winter they're white as ice. Nobody has ever climbed to the top. But you can go up partway. You follow the creek."

"Is it snow makes the creek?"

"I don't know. The creek wells out of the mountain. Maybe the mountain itself makes it, like tears." I drank the milk, listened to the hush of foam, smelled cow and clean straw and him.

"Down on the plains the creek is lined with river poplars—huge old trees with green leaves always moving. That's where the village is, my aunt and everybody, my cousin Jekka. She and I brushed each other's hair."

His hand touched mine; he took the cup away and refilled it for himself. "The creek," he said.

"By the village its banks are red sandstone. There are big trout there if you know where they hide. But when you start to climb the mountain the stone changes to granite, all gray and sparkling. The slope gets steep. You might see a deer, or a weasel, or a skunk. Even a bobcat."

He turned on the stool to rest his elbows on his knees, his head bent over the cup.

"Then it starts to be high up, and greener because of the snows. The trees are aspen instead of river poplars—white slender trunks and little round leaves glittering and rustling. Along the creek there are meadows, and if you're lucky, you might see a bear."

"You never told me about the Bear," he said to the cup. "The holy one."

"I've only been back five days," I said, amazed. "I'll tell you sometime. If you want."

And I'll tell you what I know about Nothing, but I'll find a different name for it; maybe I'll call it the Mystery. I'll tell you how the Mystery sent a lover to a lonely girl, for her to dream and name; how that lover leaned into the waves and gave himself back to the Mystery.

I'll tell you that things between us might get easier. Maybe. Never easy; we are not easy people. But I see the mistake I made, to think "Nothing matters" meant "I don't care." I've been afraid of being left with nothing, but what I'm left with is the Mystery; safe in it.

"The Bear is a big thing," I said. "I can't stand any more bigness right now."

"No."

"I could tell you about bears, though. Just bears. On the mountain."

"Yes."

I reached to take the cup from him. He would not let go of it; I knelt in front of him. "Right before I came back to Downshore, I saw bears, up the creek. Three of them."

He looked up with a listening face.

I started to speak. I could not. I had to put my hands on his thighs and say, "I ran away from you again. Probably I always will."

"I know," he said. "I went silent on you again."

Probably you always will. "I know," I said.

He set down the cup. He put his hands over mine. "Tell me about the bears."

Kneeling between his knees, I thought about the bears and the meadow and the mountain—everything earth is—and peace. "I was digging wild celery for my aunt," I said.

This time the rope I threw to him was not borrowed or

stolen or cobbled out of other people's. It was mine. It braided itself as though it had already existed—like a baby who has been swimming just beyond the Gate, wanting to get born.

"I'll tell you with a song," I said. "It has no music, though. Just words. Listen."

> Summer is coming up in thyme and foxtails,
> The aspen meadow's knee-deep in columbine and
>   daisies.
> Here you come snootling with your big fur coat on,
> Honey-lover, my fat lady.
>
> You turn the logs over with your shiny claws,
> You munch up beetles, wreck the shrew's front room.
> Your two cubs follow you, slapping each other
> And falling down, squalling over bones.
>
> You whack the big fish out of the splashing water
> And strip the blackberry bushes. Your scat is full of
>   seeds.
> Your cubs catch stinkbugs and jump on speckled frogs
> In the slow backwater where the killdeer wades.
>
> When the sun goes down, and the big moon rises
> Over the mountain's back all black and silver,
> You snort and settle your babies at your belly,
> To sleep until the short summer night is over.

He slid from the stool. He held me so close I could not move. With no words at all he said, *Never leave me!*

But I would leave him a thousand thousand times. As he changed with every morning, I would leave him with every breath; and someday I would die, and so would he.

I leaned away from him and let my eyes speak.

He heard what I did not say, and let me go.

With his hands still firm at my waist he drew back and looked at me, the way a seal rises from the sea to take a breath. I watched his face go smooth, intent, for an instant immortal; then he sank as if into a current rushing outward, giving up to it.

Come with me.

Yes, I will.

The tide came in, wave after wave, on all the beaches of the world, and one after the other we let go of the shore.

37

Rocking in and out,
Boat upon the water,
Baby in the cradle,
Bird upon the bough.
Rocking in and out,
Birth, death, living breath,
Over the threshold of—
Kiss me now!

Baby-Dandling Song. Tanshari.

I WOKE TO OTHER WAKINGS. Naked, as on the hillside after the Bear; tucked into the curve of Nall's body, as long ago on Mailin's hearth. His arm lay over me heavy as water. Under the old blanket that covered us a cat was curled, purring, against the back of his hand.

I lifted the blanket to look at her. She was black with white feet. She blinked and began to wash between her toes.

Smell of cow, ashes, morning damp. Because Moss was haltered we had let the door stand open, and beyond it I could see a misty thin light.

I tried to sit up. Nall held me tighter and grunted. I wriggled out and gave him the cat instead, but he scowled and groped, and she ran out the door with her tail straight up.

He opened his eyes and looked up smiling, still as a pool. I leaned down to be kissed by the last of his dream.

Speaking from it, he said, "I was the cup and I was the water. When I knew that, I was neither. And this: I lay asleep, and one word woke me."

"What was the word?"

"I don't remember. But the voice was yours."

His eyes were so clear I could have tossed a gold ring into them and watched it sink.

Outside, the noise that had waked me without my knowing was repeated, a knocking like someone kicking a log with his boot.

Dai shouted, "You two get it worked out?"

Together we yelled, *"No!"*

He laughed. His hand appeared at the jamb, tossed the cat back in, and pulled the door shut. "Breakfast's on the beach," he said.

The drum had stopped. We walked down to the sea handfast, in silence.

There were many bathers. The children were bare and screeching and blue. Fires burned up and down the strand. Kettles steamed.

"There!" I said.

At the end of a sandy spit, bare as the children, Ab Harlan stood in the sea, a stick in his hand.

"*Ooh! Ooh!*" he cried, smacking the water. As the next little wave came in, he bent, closed his other hand on the crest, opened his palm, and looked into it. Seemed disappointed. "Eh."

Queelic stood near him looking irresolute, breeches rolled to the knee. His father tried to catch the next wave. "Eh."

I said to Nall, "What will happen to Ab Harlan now?"

"Maybe his people will take him."

I did not think his people would want him. We had a glimpse of his round face, become what it had been all along: a sullen child's.

"I think he'll be a beachcomber," I said. "A crazy old beachcomber who lives on the shore, and we'll have to warn the kids away from him."

"Then one day he'll disappear, and we'll find him drowned, his bones washed by the tide."

On the beach above Ab Harlan and Queelic, Hsuu sat watching his children play. I looked from him to Nall and thought, Your father is as far beyond reach as mine is.

He caught my glance. "Maybe I like not knowing who he is. Kat, the world is bigger than the sea."

He gazed. I dropped my eyes, feeling my heart jump and flutter. His face wore a look I knew: dangerous, alive. I could see him asking himself, *What lies beneath the sea? Beyond the Gate? Could I go there and listen?*

Aieh had said, *That man will wreak upon you what he has upon me, just by being who he is.*

How could I bear it?

I took a breath. I thought, If I want a creature to drowse by the hearth, I had better get a cat.

We pulled each other into the waves with our rags on, took them off, scrubbed them, and threw them in lumps on the beach. I was shy of him and did not mind it. The very sand I stood on was new.

In wet clothes we went shivering to Mailin where she sat by the fire in front of the turquoise wagon, wrapped in a long cloak. Nondany held a mug of tea between his knees. Robin was there, and Suni and her children. Ab Hiun and his wife and child were gone, but sitting in the fragrant smoke was Ab Jerash. He seemed nervous, perhaps because Aieh was rubbing his back.

Queelic had left his father on the beach and stood talking with Jerash, weary and relentless. I heard him say, "—with the council, but don't expect it to be quick. If this world is to build lasting bonds, Jerash—"

"Cherish," said Aieh, rubbing. "Jerash," in a Rig accent, sounds like "Cherish."

The whole party saw us at once and came rushing and talking, all but Jerash, who blushed like a boy. Nondany smiled as though he knew the secret of joy itself. His laddie lay asleep on a blanket at the back of the lean-to—Nondany's for good, it seemed, for he had no family but a grandmother, who did not want him. "His name is Arem," said Nondany. "But not what you think. It's short for Aremyasnanatroy, some Waterfall dialect—it means 'Ploughs Forty Fields.' Poor piggie, someday we'll find out which fields are his."

Nall touched my hand. "Your sash, the one who made it—"

I nodded. "Nondany, I know a blind man who might teach him to weave."

"Is that so? We'll keep that in mind, you may be sure."

We embraced Queelic. To Jerash I said, "Good morning, Uncle. Is there any news of the delegation?"

For I felt a deep misgiving. The League, the Rig elders, Tansharians and Roadsouls and the Reirig's men—the world's thousand narrow-minded and frightened halves—would be together at that council. Whatever could they find in common?

"They have sent a rider," said Jerash. "They will be here tomorrow. And, Niece, I hope—The League would like—That is, Queelic and I and these good people"—he waved at the crowd around the fire, even Aieh—"would like you and Nall to join us in the council. To lead it, if you will."

"Lead it?" I said. "Us?"

"You seem to see both sides," he said. "The many sides. I had not known there were so many."

I did not look at Nondany. I knew he would look smug. I thought about how it might be for us to listen patiently while Roadsouls lied, Leaguemen plotted, Rigi dreamed, and Tansharians wandered off into beer recipes and love songs while their books sat unbalanced. To do our best not to choose one point of view over another; to know that none was absolute, yet make sure each was heard, so that—if it existed—we might find the place all patterns come from.

I looked at Nall. He nodded. "All right, Uncle," I said. "We'll lead it." And that was how I found the rest of my calling, the part that was not only songs.

Jerash nodded. Coughed. "Although, if you will pardon me—you may need more formal attire."

Mailin laughed. "We'll dress her."

Jerash thanked her and excused himself to other tasks. The instant he was gone, there was a scurrying under the cart, but I scarcely noticed it. I was thinking, first, that the Rigi's land was part of this land now; the way was open, we could go back and forth to Selí. To the Gate. Next I thought of those I wished could be here, around Mailin's breakfast fire.

My father was one. And Nall's ama. And Raím, and Jekka, and Bian, and Tadde, whom I had never met. And Jake the turkey man; I would go to Golden, and find out who in the world, besides me, had respected him.

I said, "Mailin, have you seen my aunt and the girls?"

"Around and about. Lali Nicane gave them a bed, but they were up at dawn. Your aunt is making the girls work at cleaning, nursing, whatever. She's a good woman—guilty and terrible. I wish I could get the girls away from her, but so far I've captured only one."

She pointed. In a tumble of children under the turquoise cart Missa groveled, her skirts hitched sideways.

"Oh, Mailin!"

"A deathly stomachache, skillfully feigned."

"If Auntie sees her like that, it'll be the end of *any* council!"

"I have placed my spies, and the sickbed is prepared."

So was breakfast. There was fish stew, hot corn bread with butter and honey, bacon and apricots and little withered figs. Dai appeared leading Moss, and we had milk from the pail; then Lilliena showed up with the ugly dog Sotis, half a cheese, and a bucket of eggs—oh, and a quart of raspberries. We fell to again, we ate everything but the dog and the dog ate anything we didn't. Where did that little being stow it all? A neighbor of Mailin's brought a lobster, very lively, but by then we were groaning so we put it in damp burlap to wait for dinner. An old man came lugging a tub of onions. Ab

Harlan had fallen asleep on the sand under a tattered blanket. The sun burned through the mist.

People came and went. It was Mailin's veranda without the veranda. They brought gifts of roses and pickled eggplant and clams and young basil and beer, and they asked for stories.

They wanted The Story. We began to tell it, in bits and pieces—I told some, and so did Queelic and Aieh. Hsuu came up from the beach, and Mailin asked him a question in Rig; he pursed his lips, grinned with his strong teeth, and never answered.

Nall listened. Sometimes he spoke, briefly, but after a spell of this friendly chaos he moved away a little and sat looking out to sea. Now and then a group of Rigi came looking for us, wanting to hear again about paddling to Stillness through the tide race or fighting the Reirig to the death—the exciting parts.

Mailin lured them off with food. "They want heroes," said Nondany. "I don't hold with heroes. This world, of which we are all a part, uses us to heal itself; willy-nilly, we are obedient to it, down to the last chimney sweep. Let us have fewer heroes and more songs! But no more songs for you, my love."

It was the broken dindarion he spoke to. He rubbed it with his sleeve. Sotis put both paws on his thigh, the way dogs do when they know you are grieving. "I never mourned my father so much," said Nondany.

I held out my hands. He gave it to me. It was so light—like nothing. I looked at Nall where he sat apart and quiet. Nondany followed my glance. "Yes," he said. "Oh, yes."

I took the dindarion to Nall. When he turned it in his hands it raised a whisper of its old deep hum.

I did not say anything but went to help Robin wash plates in a bucket. When they were clean, I went back to lean on Nall's shoulder.

"It's a boat," he said, working a loose strake. "A wooden drum. But I can't fix it, it's too hurt." He blew into the sound hole and listened as though at the mouth of a shell. "I could make a new one. Maybe."

As he tinkered, he hummed to himself, the Rigi's song. "New words?" I said, then wished I had not.

"It will not be I who hears them." He raised his head. That dangerous look. It said, *We are equals, we risk as we must.* "Maybe you will," he said.

Mailin chased the crowds away for a little. Queelic took a nap with his head in Aieh's lap. Under the cart Missa played hand slaps with three other little girls, and Nondany was eavesdropping. I bent to look in on them.

He said to the children, "Keep going, I almost know it." And to me, "This old brain! Apprentice, here's a task. Help me remember this."

I crawled in with them and sat down, saying, "Good day!" because two of the slappers were the little Rig twins in their beads. The third was a Roadsoul child, fair as a lily, and Missa was the fourth. Rosie was there too, in a red rage because they would not let her play.

"You're too little," said Missa. "This is a fancy one."

"*Pig babies!*" Rosie screeched, and stormed away.

The girls nudged their knees together, dusted their hands, slapped, and sang, "Beginning it—"

"Deeli!" cried a woman's voice. "Eresha!"

The twins stopped slapping with their mouths still open, rose, and were gone like juncos from a winter bush.

Missa was cross. "We can't do it, then. It takes four." Nondany knew better than to argue with the rules of childhood, but he looked downcast.

"I'll play," I said. "Nall! Come be fourth, Nondany can't slap."

He brought the dindarion and laid it in the sand against the cart wheel as if it were a violet, a skylark's egg. I took his hand and drew him down, and he snugged his knees in with ours.

"All right," said the Roadsoul child, raising her hands. "Here's how it goes."

> Beginning it,
> Nothing.
> Ending it,
> Nothing.
> In the middle, all of us
> Dancing in a ring-o—
> Fish, fiddle, grannie, griddle,
> Bird upon the wing-o,
> Cat, cow, piggie, plough,
> Every mortal thing-o,
> Out of nothing, into nothing.
> Take my hand and sing-o:
> Rise up!
> Sigh back!
> The sea is at the gate—
> *Dance!*

"Mister Nall," said Missa, "you have to slap." For he had stopped slapping, his hands in midair.

"Ah—"

"You have to rise up," she said, rising with her arms out,

sighing back like a cut flower. "You have to do that, or you can't play."

"Ah—," he said again. With a blind, listening face he rose as instructed, whacked his skull on the wagon bed where he had whacked it in the shelter on the Isle of Bones. He sat down clutching the back of his head, then slapped along a half beat behind the rest of us, saying, "Kat—Kat—"

"You're messing it up," said Missa.

He covered his face with his hands. "He banged his head," said the fair one.

"Twice in the same place," I said.

Weeping, he tried to slap and wipe his nose at the same time, but the Roadsoul girl said, "Don't get your snot on me," and he had to go off and blow his nose into the sand, because he had no handkerchief.

"He's no good at it," Missa told Nondany.

Nondany said, "Keep teaching him."

I scrambled after Nall. He reached his hand back upside down, as he had in the manat. I said, "Don't get your snot on me, either."

He took my hand anyway and wiped his eyes on his wrist. "Songs change nothing," he said.

This made me laugh. But he said, "I mean the kind of world this is. That those children may die next winter, some of them, and those who don't will have their hearts broken, see their life's work fail, go blind, grow old. Our children, too—and it means nothing. Which is the same as everything. And so we sing."

I took his hand and spoke into the palm of it. "Mystery."

Under the cart Nondany and the Roadsoul girl were teaching Missa a new song.

The sun is on the sea,
And the leaf is on the tree,
And the lark is on the thorn,
And the babe's born—
Once again!

Missa's voice was reedy and new. The lobster had gotten out of its burlap and came rowing over the sand, bent on escape. We watched it. As the crabs had eaten Tadde, we would eat the lobster and, in turn, someday, be eaten by worms, or else be ash to grow onions.

"That lobster doesn't know it's going to die. But we know we will," I said. For a moment I wanted my girlhood back, to sing my daydream out of the sea and be happy forever.

He put his arms around me. I felt the distance between us, always there. I thought, When death comes to him, he will go simply, like dissolving foam. But I shall go weeping, arguing, looking back.

He gave me a sweet, frustrated look that meant, *Can't you feel how easy it is?*

"It's not easy," I said. But as I spoke it got easier. I was looking at his mouth and thinking I would love him forever only for the way his lips tucked back at the corners, when those lips opened on a yell—the lobster had blundered into his toe and grabbed it. He danced about, cursing in Rig. I laughed so hard, I sat down with a bump and began to cry.

Nall held me tight, the lobster scrabbled toward freedom, Nondany's ugly dog caught it, and so it was eaten anyway, but not by us.

The Rigi's Song: Last Verses

Rake the ashes from the fire,
Cut the sash from off the loom,
Lock the gate and shut the byre,
Lay the body in the tomb.

Scarcely has the mourner's scream
Faded, and the drum is dumb,
When through the womb's gate to a new dream
The closed eyes of the infant come.

Year Altar Song. By Kat. Downshore.

From Nondany's New Papers:

Some Notes on the Rigi's Tongue

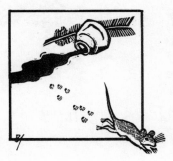

Some Notes on the Rigi's Tongue

Phrases

Aash ◆ Hush

Alele! Ai alele! ◆ Welcome! Be welcome!

Aremoi Lasai ◆ The Gate warrenhouses

Dua 'eam? ◆ Who are you?

Hom meshai ◆ My people

Huss ◆ Sleep

Ki nibo— ◆ But the dance—

Nibo kashoé ◆ The dance is ready

Shu-shu! ◆ Comfort sound, made when someone is grieving
or hurts her/himself; sometimes drawn out to *shuu*

ॐ

Word List

ama ◆ maternal great-grandmother

arem ◆ a warrenhouse; an underground Rig dwelling which houses a whole clan, many-roomed like a rabbit warren

hásjele ◆ rushing

heo ◆ too much

hsuu ◆ sea

im ◆ in

hun ◆ depth, deep

kas ◆ tidal wave

la ◆ a way through

las ◆ door or gate

Las ◆ the Gate

lassa ◆ threshold

manat ◆ small Rig boat made of whale, orca, or seal skin, with a closed deck like a kayak

mimo ◆ cousin

na' ◆ that

nall ◆ long wave

nani ◆ grandchild, great-grandchild

ne ◆ no

ni' ◆ this

ni'na' ◆ Rig slang for "changes"; literally, "this-that"

O he! ◆ Alas!

ovai ◆ or

rig (pl. *rigoi*) ◆ seal

sásjele ◆ splashing, bursting

uhui ◆ ghost

voi ◆ Rig boat made of orca skin, open like a dory

Old Town Names Chant

Many settlements in the coastal area were originally Rig and bore names in the Rigi's tongue. In time these were altered to fit the Plain tongue, but the old names are preserved in this children's rhyme.

> Tanshari, night starry
> Alore, surf roar
> Parvats, muddy flats
> Edraves, wet caves
> Shanever, little river
> Lelaido, otter slide-o
> Coraveech, whale beach

The towns in that rhyme are now known as:

Downshore
Lore
Beervats
Drays
Neverly
Lydo
Coretown

Roadsoul Rhyme for Counting Out

The Roadsouls are thought to be descended from the first Rig settlers. Among the many clues to this connection is their language, which is closely related to the Rigi's tongue. Here is a counting-out rhyme that preserves, as nonsense syllables, fragments of an ancient and famous Rig song:

> *Oisey hoikey,* out of the sea,
> *Neecy nosy,* shed your skin,
> *Jeecy leecy,* in again—
> *Nosh!*
> *Mosh!*
> Marry!

oisey hoikey; Old Rig *ose hokiel*: beautiful girl
neecy nosy; Old Rig *nacei noshai*: she emerges [from water]
    onto stone
jeecy leecy; Old Rig *chisi, lisi*: he steals, he grips
nosh; Old Rig *ne*: no
mosh; Old Rig baby talk for *mahosh*: mine

In some old stories the Roadsouls are called the Rigsouls and are described as Rigi who wander now on earth as seals do in the sea. One Roadsoul chief, asked whether his people were descended from the Rigi, nodded and said, "We left. Those people were too serious."

꙳

Acknowledgements

I would like to give special thanks to Lucia Monfried, my first midwife; Ginee Seo, who dared me to write "a big book"; and Susan Burke, who handled the results of that dare with clarity and grace. Also to Jan Priddy and Shannon Guinn-Collins, brilliant readers; Ken Hause, who can start a fire with a bow drill; and George Hersh, friend and visionary and wise heart.

And, of course, to Ursula K. Le Guin, whose maps continue to expand our known world.

꙳

Author's Notes

About Listening at the Gate

I began the stories that eventually became *Listening at the Gate* when I was a teenager. I hid them under the bed in a locked tin box, and eventually I tore them up. But I did not forget them, and years later, as a professional artist, I retold them in a long series of narrative watercolors. It is upon those stories and paintings that these books are based.

About the Roadsouls

Every society, it seems, needs to believe there can be humans who exist outside culture. Historically it is the Romani people—"Gypsies"—who have been unjustly described as glamorous, itinerant thieves who steal children, can foresee the future, and are unconstrained by the rules that limit the rest of us.

This need to believe—an "archetype"—must fulfill itself somewhere. But since it doesn't fit the Romani, I offer instead the Roadsouls: Roadsouls really *are* like that.